# Downfall

## By Louise Carey from Gollancz

*Inscape*
*Outcast*
*Downfall*

## Writing with Mike Carey and Linda Carey

*The City of Silk and Steel*
*The House of War and Witness*

# Downfall

## Louise Carey

First published in Great Britain in 2023 by Gollancz
an imprint of The Orion Publishing Group Ltd
Carmelite House, 50 Victoria Embankment
London EC4Y 0DZ

An Hachette UK Company

1 3 5 7 9 10 8 6 4 2

A CIP catalogue record for this book is
available from the British Library.

ISBN (Trade Paperback) 978 1 473 23276 1
ISBN (eBook) 978 1 473 23004 0

Typeset at The Spartan Press Ltd,
Lymington, Hants

Printed and bound in Great Britain by Clays Ltd,
Elcograf S.p.A.

www.orionbooks.co.uk
www.gollancz.co.uk

For my mother, Linda Carey

# Part 1

# Prologue

'Reet,' the conduit says. 'We have a job for you.'

Reet is too astonished to reply. *I'm dreaming*, she thinks, and that does seem to be the most likely explanation – for this, and for everything else that has happened today. This morning, she was a rookie agent, on her way to InTech's Southern Distribution Centre to take over her first solo investigation from Tanta – her ex-partner, in both senses of the word. Now, Tanta has gone on the run, a fugitive from the corp that raised her, and the board are promoting Reet to Co-Director of two of the most important divisions in the entire corporation. She must be dreaming – a terrible, wonderful dream. There's no other scenario that makes sense.

After a minute, the conduit's expectant silence makes Reet realise that she has to say *something*, dream or not. 'You want *me* to help run the InterCorporate Relations Division? And Residents' Affairs?' she manages, at last. Saying it out loud only makes it sound more surreal. 'I – I'm grateful, Representative, but are you sure? I haven't even passed my probation yet.'

'We recognise that this decision is unorthodox,' the conduit replies. 'But it is your loyalty and dedication to InTech that have prompted our choice, not your experience. It is not to be expected that you will master the role immediately: Director

Kenway will instruct you in what is required. For your part, you will monitor and approve your Co-Director's activities, correcting his judgement when he errs in his assessment of the corporation's interests.'

It is this dry articulation of her job role that makes Reet understand at last that she is not asleep. This is really happening; she's a Director. The realisation renders her speechless all over again – partly through sheer terror. The conflict between InTech and Thoughtfront has been growing steadily worse for months, and the events of the last week – which began with Thoughtfront bombing the Needle and ended with it attempting to sabotage a vital software update – have tipped the two corporations into all-out war. Effectively, the board have just made Reet a general in that war. She's used to managing people – when she worked at The Rotunda she had a staff of dozens – but running an enhanced hospitality venue is a far cry from defending an entire city.

It's a heavy mantle, but Reet is proud to wear it. She feels a solemn joy at the prospect – an emotion that lifts her up and weighs her down at the same time. All she has ever wanted is to serve her corp to the best of her ability. To be chosen by the board as one of InTech's leaders, especially at a time like this... it's more than an honour: it's everything.

And it's not a responsibility she'll have to bear alone. She couldn't ask for a better Co-Director than Douglas Kenway – her mentor and, she hopes, her friend. The thought sends strength and happiness flooding through her, like a shaft of sunlight on a cold day.

'I can't wait to get started, Representative,' she says, beaming. She turns to Douglas, extending a shy hand. 'I'm looking forward to working with you, Director.'

Douglas's glare hits her like a glass of cold water to the face. Reet has never seen him look at her with such hatred before.

4

She flinches as though she's been struck, her lips trembling, but recovers quickly. There's no time to dwell on Douglas's unaccountable animosity, not when the board need her. She wipes the hurt and confusion from her features like she's cleaning a slate. Tee – Tanta – taught her better than to wear her feelings on her sleeve.

Her face has returned to a professional blank, but the thought of Tanta makes Reet's stomach churn. She had barely even begun to process their break-up before this fresh blow sent her reeling. This time, Tanta has turned her back not just on Reet, but on InTech. Reet can't fathom it; as much as Tanta hurt her, she had never believed her capable of betraying their corp.

'Do you have anything you wish to ask us?' the conduit says.

There's one question that's uppermost in Reet's thoughts – something that's been on her mind ever since she learnt Tanta had run away. She pauses, trying to remember what Douglas told her about the correct way to address the conduit. 'What should be done about Cole and – and the Corporate Ward now, Representative?' she asks.

'Their defection has come at an unfortunate time,' the conduit says glassily. 'Thoughtfront will be searching for any advantage it can find: both the talents and the classified intelligence Neuroengineer Cole possesses would be a boon to their efforts. He cannot be allowed to fall into enemy hands.'

Reet nods. 'Understood. Steps will be taken to retrieve them both.'

The conduit shakes his head. 'Cole has become a liability,' he croaks. 'He is to be terminated on sight.'

Reet's mouth dries. 'And Tanta?'

The board's representative waves a hand, a curiously stilted motion. 'We leave the appropriate measures to your discretion.'

Reet breathes out, harder than she intended. She might feel like she *wants* to kill Tanta – especially now, with her ex-lover's disloyalty still so raw and smarting in her thoughts – but she is glad she doesn't have to. She will do whatever the board ask of her, without question or hesitation, but she offers a silent prayer of thanks that they haven't asked her to do *that*.

'Got it,' she replies. 'I won't let you down.'

A thin smile spasms across the conduit's face. 'We depend upon it.'

In her haste to get to work as quickly as possible, Reet is halfway to the door when the board's representative calls her back.

'One more thing, Director,' he says.

Reet pivots so fast she nearly gives herself whiplash. The board have just promoted her beyond her wildest dreams, and she almost walked out on them mid-meeting! She hurries back to the table, unable, this time, to force down the blush that's warming her cheeks. Luckily, the conduit isn't looking her way. He's staring into the middle distance above Douglas's head, his eyes even less focused than usual. Reet knows it sometimes takes the conduit a while to process the board's collective thoughts and opinions, so she waits patiently, her eyes downcast. Eventually, the conduit turns to her.

'Your Co-Director and his predecessor made the executive decision to withhold certain details about your upbringing from you and the other Corporate Wards in the employ of the ICRD,' he tells her. 'Now that you are assuming the co-directorship of the ICRD yourself, it has become expedient for you to learn about these things. They have a material impact on many of the cases you will be overseeing.'

Reet doesn't know how to respond to this. What does her upbringing have to do with anything?

'Sit down,' the conduit instructs her. 'It is time you were informed of the Harlow Programme.'

# Chapter 1

Fliss crosses into InTech's half of London through the Outer Gate, slouching past a long line of queueing cars with her head bent and her jacket pulled up over her ears. One of the community guardians on duty at the security kiosk — a big man with an even bigger gun — looks her way, but he does not call out or order Fliss to stop. With no headware nestled in her brain to trigger the gate's sensors, it's clear that she is just one more unaffiliated scavenger, on her way into the city to beg for scraps or barter the pre-Meltdown curios she's found in the wasteland outside the walls.

Fliss leans into the role, hunching into her clothes with a shiver. She's hoping to give the guardian the impression that she is cold, footsore, and weary — and not that she is trying to hide her face from the many cameras that line the road. Her photo has been in InTech's systems ever since Tanta took her into custody and brought her to Sodis, four months ago. The ex-agent has had a change of heart since, of course — but by then, the damage was already done.

Luckily, Fliss's new crew have some tricks up their sleeves to help her avoid detection. If the man were closer, he might notice an unusual pattern of moles clustered along her jawline and a curious, branching scar bisecting her right eye. They look very realistic; Tanta and Yasmin painted them onto her face back in the Brokerage, guided by Cole's careful instructions.

'The facial recognition software InTech uses isn't easily fooled,' he had explained, the first time Fliss ventured into the city, 'so I'd advise trying to avoid the cameras spotting you in the first place. If they do, this should help throw them off, though.'

Grateful as she is for the extra layer of camouflage, Fliss isn't going to take the chance if she can help it.

'What's your status?' a voice burrs in her uninjured ear.

Fliss rolls her eyes. As always, Tanta's been asking her that question at decreasing intervals ever since she left the Brokerage.

'I'm almost in,' she replies, teeth gritted.

She tries to keep a lid on her annoyance – she knows Tanta finds the technical limitations of their current mode of communication more frustrating than she does. During Fliss's jaunts, she and Tanta keep in touch through a pair of antique earpieces, a bit of pre-Meltdown tech that Cole found in the Brokerage's storeroom and fixed up for the purpose. They're too old to be detected by the corporation's fancy scanners, or blocked by the Brokerage's own shields, but – as Tanta is so fond of reminding Fliss – they're no MbOS connection. She hates using the tiny radios, and Fliss can see why: after all, Tanta is used to looking through her colleagues' eyes and sharing their thoughts. Now she's getting all her updates at one remove, forced to rely on Fliss's voice alone.

Fliss is privately glad to be doing this the old-fashioned way. She has never wanted headware of her own, never wanted to join any of the corporations that dominate the world, and meeting Tanta, a ward of InTech since birth, has only confirmed her feelings. A clunky radio in her ear is infinitely preferable to a computer in her brain, for all that the latter would make her life a lot easier.

Or it would have, once. Recently, Fliss has been learning just what an advantage not having headware can be.

'What's happening now?' Tanta asks.

'I'm getting past the gate guardians. Now shut up before you give me away.' It's a dig, but there's no malice in Fliss's tone. She understands Tanta's cabin fever, her desperate, clawing-at-the-walls desire to be out of the underground bunker that is the Brokerage and doing things for herself again.

Tanta, Cole and Yasmin haven't been able to set foot above ground for four months – not since Harlow 2.0 went live. Fliss still isn't clear on all the details, but she knows it's a software update that turns your brain to mush, and that it's in the air now, or in the system or whatever, floating about on the invisible signals that InTech uses to communicate with its people. The thing is like the pollen that tickles the back of your throat in the summertime; there's nothing you can do to stop yourself breathing it in. Only if this software gets into your brain, it makes you into a corporate robot. It's only the shielded walls of the Brokerage that are keeping Fliss's crew safe right now. Leave, even for a moment, and they'd be zapped with Harlow 2.0 quicker than they could blink. If Fliss were in their shoes, she'd be climbing the walls, too.

It's for this reason that, despite the danger, Fliss savours her supply runs to the wasteland and the city. There are a lot of things about living above ground that you take for granted until you're forced to move into an apocalypse bunker. The air today is numbingly cold – white frost crisping the ground, freezing sleet sheeting from grey clouds – but Fliss can't find it in her heart to resent the weather, for all it's making it so she can't feel her toes. There's the breeze to make up for it. There's the *sky*. She'd tip her face up into the rain and let it kiss her cheeks, if it wouldn't expose her features to the guardian watching her.

But the guardian has already turned his attention back to the line of cars inching through the Outer Gate, his eyes glazed as he trains his gun on each in turn. Fliss is relieved, but not surprised: no one in InTech ever seems to notice her for long. At first, she'd assumed the corporate types simply thought a scavenger like her was beneath their notice, but it's more than that. Whatever else Harlow 2.0 has done to their minds, it's also made it so they barely register the existence of people like Fliss, who have no headware of their own. Most of the time their eyes skip right over her, and when they do spot her, it's like they struggle to see her clearly – or even to keep her in mind.

Fliss gives a shudder that has nothing to do with the cold. Being invisible is an advantage, but she doesn't like the feeling overmuch. She slopes onward, putting the security kiosk and its alarming array of weaponry behind her.

'OK,' she mutters, when she's well out of earshot, 'I'm clear.'

There's a whoosh of crackly static in her ear as Tanta breathes out. Fliss winces. 'Ouch!'

'Sorry. That wouldn't have come through on—'

'On MindChat. Yes. You've said.'

Now that she's through border security, Fliss quickens her pace. She drove most of the way here, but she had to hide the car before she reached the Outer Gate – an unaffiliated person with their own set of wheels would draw far too much attention from the guardians. She's got a long way still to walk, and it's already past midday. Twilight is best for the kind of work Fliss is here to do, but she doesn't want to linger in the city centre long past nightfall. After dark is when the bombing starts, InTech and Thoughtfront sending out fleets of armed drones to probe each other's fortifications. Direct hits are rare – both corps have defence turrets to protect their skies – but they're not unheard of. From a distance, the corporations' night raids are quite the light show, drones exploding in the dark like fireworks, but Fliss has no wish to see one up close.

By the time she makes it through the suburbs, the afternoon is on the turn, the grey sky curdling with streaks of pinkish, evening cloud. She joins the queue at one of the security checkpoints that surround the realm of high-rises and tower blocks at the city's heart. Once she's through, she turns west, walking parallel to the riverbed that marks the dividing line between InTech and Thoughtfront.

'I'm in the centre now,' Fliss murmurs into her earpiece.

There's a long pause. 'How does it look?' Tanta crackles in her ear. It's not the first time she's asked. Fliss can guess at her feelings – this place used to be her home, and from what she can gather, Tanta was pretty attached to it. For herself, Fliss can't see what there is to love about the city. There are too many people and too few trees, and the buildings all look like the eyes of the security guard she saw at the gate: glazed and soulless. But she supposes there are things about the wasteland that seem similarly unwelcoming to someone who's not used to them.

'Like it always does?' she replies. 'Wet. Crowded. Oh!' She breaks off as a building a few doors down from her catches her eye, a circular structure topped with thatch and a dome of pink glass. The last time Fliss was here, the wrought-iron gates in its courtyard had stood open, rosy light spilling from inside. Now, they're locked and bolted, and there's a gaping hole in the glass roof, its edges sharp and jagged. 'The Rotunda's closed down. Drone strike, I think.'

'That's a shame,' Tanta replies.

It's irrelevant, in Fliss's opinion. Whether The Rotunda is open for business or a pile of rubble can mean nothing to Tanta. But old habits die hard, she supposes.

'What about the Needle?' Tanta is asking now.

The Needle is InTech's headquarters, and the residence of its board of executives – a huge glass pyramid with a jagged spire. Fliss can't see it from where she is, but she passed it on her way in. It was closed for repairs in the autumn after Thoughtfront tried to blow it up, and for a while it was cordoned off and covered in scaffolding, but it reopened more than a month ago. 'It looked fine,' she says, shortly. If anyone inside the Needle – or the squat building beside it, the ICRD – caught wind that she was in the city, this little supply run of hers would come to a sudden and bloody end. Fliss, like Tanta and Cole, is on InTech's most-wanted list now. Tanta may be nostalgic for her days as an agent, but there's nothing waiting for her in the Needle anymore except the windowless confines of the holding cells in the building's basement.

'I have to get going,' Fliss adds. 'So, unless there're any other stops you'd like me to make on the Tanta retrospective tour...?'

Tanta snorts, conceding the point; Fliss didn't come all the way to the city just to tell the ex-CorpWard about how things are going in her hometown. She's here to make a purchase, and to visit an old friend.

She does the second task first, taking advantage of the last of the light. She turns her steps to the southwest, leaving the central high-rises behind. Above her, the pink clouds are darkening to a bruised purple, and the rain has intensified. As she hurries through the city, Fliss tries to practice her spycraft. Tanta has been teaching her about what she calls 'situational awareness', the subtle art of taking in a scene at a glance and assessing its threats and its obstacles.

Fliss has done this before, of course, but only in the wasteland, where the nature of the dangers is very different. She's used to corporate anti-theft measures and rival crews. In the city, the monsters don't always bare their teeth so openly. And the place itself is so overwhelming, so full of people and cars and colour and life, that sieving through the sensory overload to find those few details that stand out – either as threats or as opportunities – gives her a headache.

She does the best she can, though, and Tanta helps – as much as she's able to through the earpiece.

'What can you see?'

'Crowds,' Fliss mutters. 'Just … crowds.'

'The main thing you're looking for is attention,' Tanta reminds her. 'Anyone focused on you – or anyone who looks away as you look at them – is a bad sign.'

'There must be a thousand people here,' Fliss grumbles. 'Even if one of them *is* looking at me, how'd I be able to tell?'

There's a pause before Tanta replies. 'Look at the faces,' she says at last. 'Let your eyes slide over them.'

Fliss does so, taking in an array of glassy eyes, fixed smiles and slack jaws – a horde of happy Harlow 2.0 zombies. With her attention like this, soft and spread out, it's easier to spot the few people in the thronging crowds whose more alert expressions mark them out as being free from the programming that holds everyone else in thrall. No one is looking her way, though – not even the people who still have lights on behind their eyes.

'All right, I see what you mean,' Fliss admits. 'That's a neat trick.'

'The really hard part is keeping it up,' Tanta replies. 'You'll want to scan the crowd like that at regular intervals to make sure you haven't been made.'

Tanta's right. It *is* hard. By the time Fliss reaches Inspire Labs, she's exhausted – she didn't know you could tire yourself out just from looking too much. She thinks she's seen more faces in the last hour than the rest of her life combined. When she blinks, she can see them imprinted on the darkness behind her eyes.

She makes for the deeply recessed doorway of a condemned block of flats opposite the R&D compound, trying not to make her stride too purposeful. The last thing she wants is to attract attention. There's a figure lying in the doorway, wrapped in an old sleeping bag. She sits up as Fliss approaches.

'Hey, Sonia,' Fliss murmurs, slumping down beside her. 'Good to see you.'

One of the most important things Fliss gathers on her supply runs is information; Sonia helps with that. Fliss found her ex-crewmate sleeping rough in the city two months ago and recruited her immediately. It was a tad awkward at first – after all, Sonia had tried to kill Fliss the last time they met – but to Fliss, that's all ancient history. She and Sonia have known each other since they were children in Gatwick, getting each other into and out of trouble and generally wreaking havoc; she isn't going to let a little thing like attempted murder come between her and her oldest friend. Now, Sonia has an income and a home in one of the Brokerage's old safehouses, and in return, she keeps her eyes open and her ears to the ground. It's a simple arrangement, and she's already proven herself useful to Fliss and her new crew more than once.

'What have you got for me?' Fliss asks, punching her affectionately on the arm.

Sonia tells her, delivering a summary of every overheard conversation, confirmed rumour and piece of insider speculation she's managed to pick up since they last saw one another.

Intel like this is the juice that keeps the crew's operation running. What Fliss and the others can't use for their own plans, they sell on to the Brokerage's illustrious list of corporate clients, using the proceeds to keep themselves fed and supplied. When they took the Brokerage from Jeanie, its founder, four months ago, they found files and files of contacts among her things: informants, customers, spies-for-hire. It wasn't long before the calls started coming in. Some corps had specific commissions; others just wanted to buy up every bit of intelligence they could lay their hands on. For the first few weeks, it was all the crew could do to keep up with the deluge of requests without alerting their corporate patrons to the change in management.

Since then, they've managed to settle into a rhythm – and Fliss has expanded Jeanie's network of contacts with a few additions of her own. People like Sonia make good moles because they're one of the corps' few blind spots: with no headware weaving their minds into the fabric of corporate society, they tend to fall through the cracks – for better and for worse. She's had no shortage of potential recruits. Since half the city got Harlowed, times have been tough for the 'scapeless: it's hard to beg and barter when you're all but invisible to most of your prospective customers.

'Thoughtfront's hiring wasteland crews again,' Sonia tells her now. 'I had it off some ex-Red Flags who came through last week.'

That surprises Fliss. It's true that when it comes to working with the roving crews who scratch a living in the wasteland, Thoughtfront has form. The corp recruited Fliss and Sonia themselves, once upon a time, sending them out to hunt down InTech's delivery drones. But Fliss had been under the impression that particular project had come to an end four months ago, when she and her new crew had killed Hardinger and Jeanie, the two people running it.

'What for?' she asks. 'I thought they couldn't target InTech's drones anymore. Not since Jeanie died.'

'They're not going after drones,' Sonia says. 'Not sure what they *are* doing, though. The guys I talked to were cagey.'

If the Red Flags are involved, it can't be anything good. Their raiders have a bad reputation in the wasteland: they don't just steal from the corporations but from other crews and settlements, too. They even robbed a few of Gatwick's trade convoys back when Fliss lived there, though they never dared to hit the town directly. Fliss doesn't like to think what they might be capable of now that Thoughtfront's arming them.

'Good to know,' she replies, filing the information away under *valuable but irrelevant*. What Thoughtfront and the Red Flags are up to has got nothing to do with her anymore, but Tanta can always sell the intel on later. For now, she has something more important to discuss – something that has a direct bearing on what she and her new crew have been doing for the last four months.

'What about him?' She jerks her head towards Inspire Labs. 'You been tailing him like I asked?'

Sonia nods. 'He doesn't have much of a life. Gets in to work most mornings at eight. Leaves around five. Takes a fancy car everywhere. He has a meeting in the Needle every Thursday at four.'

'That car he drives around in. Is he the only passenger?'

Sonia thinks about it, screwing up her face. 'Far as I've seen.'

'And you've mapped its route?'

She reels it off, listing the street designations.

'Nice work, Sonia.' Fliss takes a sheaf of chit from the pocket of her jeans and hands it over. 'In that case, he should be heading home about—'

As if on cue, the gate at the front of the compound creaks open and a white-haired man emerges, walking with a slight stoop. Fliss grins. Sonia wasn't the only old Friend she was hoping to see tonight: the doc has shown up right on time. She pulls a smartphone with a cracked screen from her jacket – the same one that Hardinger once gave her to receive Thoughtfront's orders. Fliss has had some time to familiarise herself with it since then, and she's learnt to do more than simply check details of marks and locations. As a sleek taxi pulls up outside Inspire Labs, she snaps a couple of discreet photos, hiding the glow of the screen with her hand.

Once Dr Arthur Friend has stepped into the car and been whisked away, it's time for Fliss to make herself scarce, too. She's got another appointment to keep this evening, and besides, it's best not to linger in the same place for long.

'Thanks again for the help,' she says. 'I'll see you next time.'

Sonia takes her arm, stopping her as she gets up to leave. 'Fliss...' she begins. Her brown eyes are anxious. 'Him in the lab – he's a big shot in the corp. If you piss him off, there'll be hell to pay.'

Fliss pulls a face. 'Don't remind me. What's your point?'

'Well... there's easier marks, right? Why are we tailing *him*?'

Fliss doesn't answer. She needs Dr Friend – or rather, her new crew need him. Fliss and the rest have big plans – plans to snap this half of London out of its headware-induced stupor and put its people back to normal again – but they can't do that while Cole, Yasmin and Tanta are trapped in the Brokerage. Dr Friend could be their ticket out, but she's not about to tell Sonia that: it would only put her at risk.

When Sonia sees that she isn't going to reply, the concern in her eyes deepens. 'You do know what you're doing, right?' she asks.

''Course I do. I'll be fine, Sonia. You don't need to fret about me.'

She sounds so confident she almost believes herself.

Fliss's second meeting is back in the centre, in an alley just off Commercial Street. As she walks over there, the streets empty around her, everyone taking shelter before the drone raids start. It's a relief to her overstretched senses; her last transaction of the day is the riskiest by far, but even so, Fliss can feel herself relaxing with the return of silence and solitude. By the time she arrives, there's no one else around save for a trio of patrons drinking outside the pub across the road – too foolhardy, or too far gone, to care about the imminent bombs.

The cul-de-sac is a narrow, dark space, with a shuttered shop slumped at one end.

'It used to be a gamer bar,' Tanta tells her. Fliss nods; that figures. There's not as much call as there was in InTech's part of the city for things like games, whores and luxury items. These forms of entertainment were once what the corp used to keep its residents in line, Fliss reckons, but now they have a more direct method.

She walks a little way into the alley, allowing her silhouette to merge with the shadows. There's a figure standing in front of the boarded-up shop, chewing on a fingernail with affected idleness.

'He's jittery,' Fliss notes to Tanta in an undertone, a little proud of herself for this assessment of the situation. And then, immediately starting to worry about it, 'Does that mean any-thing?'

'It's most likely just nerves,' Tanta replies. 'He's risking a lot to come here. Stay on your guard, though, all the same.'

Tanta's right, of course; Fliss knows from experience what InTech does to thieves. If she or her contact are caught, the best either of them can hope for is a swift death. She steps from the shadows to stand face to face with the unaffiliated man, who starts when he sees her. He's short and grubby, with darting eyes. She raises her hands – half in greeting, half to show she isn't packing.

'Have you got it?' she asks.

'Shit!' the man grumbles. 'Not so loud.'

Fliss is confident her voice was pitched to the same cautious whisper as her contact's, but she lets that slide. The man digs in a dirty pocket and produces a small package wrapped in a plastic bag. Fliss resists the urge to reach for it. Show the man how eager she is, and he might decide to up the price on her. She takes out the rest of the chit she brought with her, fanning out the notes so he knows that it's all there.

There's a tense moment while they face each other, the man's gaze furtive and appraising. Then he thrusts the package out to her, dropping it into her hands like the release mechanism on a vending machine. Fliss hands over the chit, nods, and melts back into the dark.

Just like that, it's over. The transaction that sent Fliss trekking for hours through the city is completed in an instant. She heads for the end of the alley and home, already planning her route back. Still, there's something bothering her as she walks away from the abandoned shop – some detail she's seen, but not fully registered.

'It's done,' she says to Tanta.

'How did it go?'

Fliss stops in place a few metres from the mouth of the alley, letting her eyes play over the road in front of her. 'All right, I think. But...' She lets the sentence trail off, a lure to bait the nagging something at the edge of her thoughts into full view of her conscious mind.

It slinks into sight at last, insidious and dreadful. One of the young men Fliss saw drinking outside the pub across the road from the cul-de-sac is still there – and he's staring straight at her. He's about Tanta's age, with brown hair in a military buzzcut. *Anyone focused on you is a bad sign.* Fliss's heart starts to pound. *Calm the fuck down*, she tells herself. *It could be a coincidence. He's probably just staring into space.* He's not, though – there's nothing glazed or vacant about the man's look. He's no Harlow 2.0 zombie, looking right through her: his expression is intent, his eyes locked on Fliss's face.

'Someone's looking at me,' she mutters, 'A guy outside the

pub. He had two friends with him – I don't know where they've gone.'

'Head down, keep walking,' Tanta instructs immediately. 'Don't let him know you've seen him. Is he following you?'

Fliss darts a quick glance his way. The man is on his feet now, his drink forgotten on the table. He takes a step into the road, towards her. She wrenches her gaze away from him, looking to left and right – and that's when she sees his two companions, converging on the mouth of the alley from both sides. Their hands go to their belts in eery unison, reaching for two strange, long-barrelled pistols.

Her thoughts scatter like birds.

'It's InTech,' she says, the words coming out fast and brittle. 'I've been made.'

# Chapter 2

Saying it out loud takes the wind out of Fliss. For an instant, she's naked, impossibly small and scared. She cowers in the alley, trying to dissolve into the darkness and disappear. Tanta's voice snaps her back to herself.

'Remember the exit routes we practiced. What's your closest one?'

The barked instructions arrest Fliss's fleeing thoughts. This would have been a poor excuse for a plan if she hadn't cased the handover point in advance, looking for ways to escape if things got sticky. The dingy cul-de-sac looks like the perfect place for an ambush, with its narrow entrance and the high buildings that hem it in on either side. But where most people would see only a single point of ingress and exit, Fliss can find dozens – and she and Tanta have mapped them all.

There's a large metal wheelie bin just to her right, next to the side door of a restaurant with its premises on Commercial Street. Fliss knows, because she's practiced, that she can leap onto it and use it as a launch pad to reach a vent set into the side of the building. It's a hop, skip and a jump from there to the roof, and freedom. She takes a deep, steadying breath, and springs upward.

The lid of the bin gives way beneath her, plunging her into

foul-smelling darkness. She plummets into the soft, sticky mass of rotted food with a yelp.

'What is it? What's going on?' Tanta asks.

'Bin's broken,' she gasps. 'I—'

Fliss was about to say she has no idea how that happened – but she does, doesn't she? She tried the lid of the bin only last week, and it was sound. Despite the crew's precautions, InTech must have been watching her. They saw her come here, and now they've sabotaged her main escape route. The realisation unleashes a fresh wave of panic. Curled at the bottom of the bin, Fliss freezes in place, unable for the moment to think or move. Sonia was right: she's far out of her depth here, and the depths are filled with monsters. She should have stayed in Gatwick, where they never tangle with the corps if they can help it. Now the ICRD is coming for her, and she's caught, like a rat in a trap. She'll be lucky if these agents just kill her. The alternative ...

Thinking about the alternative gives Fliss the strength to haul herself bodily out of the muck. She flops back onto the paving stones of the alley and looks up, reassessing the situation. The agent she saw first has reached the mouth of the cul-de-sac. He's close enough that Fliss can see his eyes, which are as brown as his hair and fixed on her with a look of single-minded focus that doesn't bode well for her long-term wellbeing.

His two colleagues step into view an instant later, their weapons drawn. Instinct picks Fliss up and flings her behind the bin. She doesn't hear the guns go off, but she sees the ammo fly. They're not firing bullets but black, bulky projectiles with rounded tips. They streak past Fliss's cover and explode against the far wall of the alley.

Rubber bullets. That means they're not looking to kill Fliss, which is much, much worse – for her and her new crew both.

'What's going on?' Tanta asks again, her voice strained. 'Fliss! What's your next exit route?'

Fliss forces her brain back into gear, her eyes raking the wall behind the bin. The bricks before her are frustratingly smooth and free of handholds: even if she risked the climb, her pursuers would pick her off before she ever reached the roof. She and Tanta planned several other exit routes from the cul-de-sac, but unfortunately for her, they're all back the way she came, at the end of the alley.

'The – the shop,' she says. 'The awning.' There's no way she can make it over there without getting got, though – not running along the pavement. She shifts her position, readying herself to spring, then listens. The footsteps of the agents thud towards her, loud in the confines of the alleyway. There's a puddle in front of the wheelie bin; Fliss strains her senses. When she hears the plash of water, she puts her shoulder against the bin and shoves, putting her whole weight into it.

It goes over with a creak and a groan. As it falls, Fliss runs up the side of it and leaps, propelling herself back into the alley. It's not the way the agents were expecting her to run, so their shots go wide. She lands a few feet away from the bin and, while her pursuers are pivoting in her direction, shimmies up a pre-Meltdown lamppost. That puts her back in range of the gamer bar's tattered awning. She flings herself onto it spreadeagled, arms and legs splayed to better distribute her weight, then claws her way up it like a cat and onto the sill of one of the windows above. It's only then that she risks a glance at the street.

One of the agents is struggling out from underneath the fallen wheelie bin, his movements dazed and sluggish. One is busy with the fence Fliss came here to meet. It looks like the man tried to bolt when the shooting started, but he hasn't made it very far. The second agent has tackled him to the ground a few feet from the mouth of the cul-de-sac, pinioning his arms behind him. The third agent is sprinting towards Fliss at full tilt, his weapon drawn.

Like most buildings in London, the structure that houses the abandoned gamer bar is several stories high. Before the Meltdown, its upper levels were probably used as flats or offices, but now, they lie empty. There's a window on the third floor that's broken – Fliss noticed it when she was casing the alley. Now, gritting her teeth and tearing her eyes from her pursuer, she starts to climb towards it.

She's fast, hoisting herself from sill to drainpipe to sill with all the speed with which she used to climb trees in the wasteland. She can't outrun the guns, though. Another rubber round bursts on the wall beside her, spattering Fliss with something wet and slimy. She recoils instinctively, wiping the goop from her face.

'Uh, Tanta,' she mutters, grabbing the bars of the window above her and hoisting herself up, 'why would someone fill a bullet with jelly?'

'Piezoelectric rounds,' Tanta says. 'They release a charge on impact. The jelly makes them more conductive. You need to get out of range, and stay away from metal.'

Fliss releases her hold on the bars hastily. She sidesteps, edging out along the sill she's on to reach the broken window, then dives through. Another round thuds into the wall behind her, but she's out of line of sight for now. She picks herself up and runs across the room – an empty flat, the ghosts of old furniture still marking the bare floorboards – towards the door. It leads out, she knows, into a dusty corridor, with another window at its far end that looks onto a residential street. If she can make it that far, Fliss can make her getaway over the balconies and roofs of the surrounding buildings, and lose herself in the cityscape.

The door opens as she's dashing towards it. The brown-haired agent is on the other side. Somehow, he has beaten her here – he must have broken the sound barrier on his way up the stairs. Fliss ducks to avoid his first shot out of sheer instinct. She keeps running, barrelling into him at chest height, and they go down together, hitting the floor in a cloud of dust. She feels the pop of the gun going off again rather than hearing it. She and the agent are tangled together, their limbs locked, and the bullet thumps into the floorboards. This time, though, it's close enough that Fliss gets the shock. Her limbs seize and jerk. She tastes blood as she bites down on her tongue. And then there's nothing.

'Fliss? Fliss?'

Tanta's voice pulls Fliss unwillingly back to consciousness.

'How long was I out?' she mutters, but already, she's getting to her feet, trying to figure out the answer to that question for herself.

The agent is still lying on the floor, stunned by his own too-hasty use of the electric gun. Fliss is alone in the corridor – for now.

'A few seconds,' Tanta replies. 'We're lucky none of the electrodes hit your earpiece.'

'Thank fuck.' Fliss starts edging around the boy's prone form. 'Right, I'm out of here.'

'Wait.'

'What?' Fliss halts again. She can hear movement from below: it will be a matter of moments before the other agents catch up to her. What can there be to wait for?

'We need to know who we're up against,' Tanta says. 'If this *is* the ICRD we're dealing with, I might recognise the agents they've assigned to the case.'

Fliss curses. 'I don't have time to take a bloody picture!' she says.

She realises, though, that that is exactly what Tanta expects her to do. Her fingers trembling, she pulls the battered smartphone out of her pocket. She taps the phone's camera function and zooms in on the boy's face.

She's just taken the shot when the footsteps from the end of the corridor grow louder and one of the other two agents rounds the corner. Fliss swears again. The third agent must still be in the alleyway, at her back. She backs into the flat and slams the door.

'You've done it now,' she tells Tanta. 'I'm cut off.' Even as she levels the accusation, Fliss's eyes are flicking around the flat, searching for another way out. There's a second door to her right. It leads into a bathroom, with a tiny window high up the wall. Despite the stakes here, she's almost annoyed at having proven herself wrong.

'Scratch that: there's a window facing east,' she amends grudgingly. She's already hoisting herself up onto the sink and fumbling with the latch. 'Where can I go from there?'

'East off Commercial Street?' There's a tense pause while Tanta works it out. She's probably running around the Brokerage's control room like a blue-arsed fly, checking old maps and city plans. For her part, Fliss uses the time to wrench the window open and crawl through.

'There's a bridge,' Tanta comes back, at last. 'It's not in use anymore.'

A bridge is good: if Fliss can scale it, she might be able to get away clear – there aren't many people who can climb as well as she can, even corporate spies. She leans out of the tiny window. There's a balcony immediately below her; beyond it, the city is cloaked in darkness, illuminated only by the fitful flashes of InTech's defence turrets as they shoot down Thoughtfront's drones. She screens out the distant explosions and looks where Tanta tells her. Sure enough, there's the bridge – a bulky, pre-Meltdown structure of brick that lies across the glass-and-chrome modernity of Commercial Street like a sleeping giant. It's on the other side of the road. At that moment, Fliss feels someone grab at her heels. She kicks back into the room, her foot connecting with something soft and yielding. Then she throws herself forward.

For an instant, she's plummeting through empty air, feeling the sickening weightlessness of freefall. She hits the balcony with a crash that jars through her whole body. She picks herself up, climbs over the railing, and swings from there to the ground. Then – clenching her fists – she sprints for the intersection that separates her from the bridge. There are still a few cars out, even this late at night, but she knows from Tanta that they won't run her down: they have chips driving them that know when an obstacle crosses their path. Running in front of them still makes Fliss's heart fly up into her throat, and her back itch with the fear of being crushed and left broken in the middle of the road.

She fixes her eyes on the bridge, looking for the best place to begin her ascent. It's intimidatingly tall; shops and cafés have colonised the spaces beneath its wide arches. Where it crosses the road, though, the structure dips lower as the brick walls give way to a section of steel girders. Fliss sees the hand and footholds she needs and makes a beeline for the point where brick and metal meet. She runs at the bridge head-on, putting all her weight into the moment of impact. As she hits the sheer brickwork, she jumps, pushing herself up and into it.

She's practiced this enough times in the wasteland that she doesn't falter; all of her forward momentum is translated into height as she rockets up the side of the wall. At the same time, she stretches her arms upward, hands questing for the lip of steel she saw from the street. She catches it with the edges of her fingers and hauls herself up bodily, clinging to the side of the structure like a limpet.

Another bullet splatters against the wall below Fliss as she hangs above Commercial Street. The agents must be almost upon her. There's a niche in the bridge where the structure turns to the southeast. Fliss uses it to propel herself upwards and sideways, leaping clear of the next shot before it hits. She reaches for the top of the bridge, some two metres above her, and snags it with her left hand. As she dangles over empty air, a third shot grazes her arm, and she almost falls. Luckily, the shock that spasms through her makes the muscles in her fingers contract, which only tightens her grip. And then she's caught the wall with her other hand and she's pulling herself up and over the edge, to land in a crouch on the empty deck.

It's an old railway bridge; Fliss can tell that at once from the lines of rusted tracks. Rising a little, she takes a cautious peek over the side to the street. The three agents have regrouped below her; they look to be conferring. One makes a tentative jump towards the lip of metal that Fliss climbed, but he doesn't even come close. After a moment, the trio splits again. One goes north along the bottom of the bridge while the second goes south. The third, the boy with brown hair (Fliss reckons he's the leader) waits in the street immediately below her.

It's a good plan, as things go, but it'll take them a while to get to her if they're going the long way round. And in the meantime, Fliss has options.

'OK, I'm on the bridge,' she tells Tanta. 'Now I need you to plot me a route out of here. Avoiding any ladders or access staircases.'

Tanta is way ahead of her. 'Go south,' she orders. 'The railway line splits into two a little way from here. Take the left-hand fork.'

Fliss doesn't waste her breath asking why. When she first met Tanta four months ago, she trusted her about as much as she'd trust a feral dog not to bite, but that's quickly changed. Tanta's many things (po-faced and irritating come to Fliss's mind) but she's good at what she does, and she keeps her word. She has

28

more integrity than most of the corporate types Fliss has met. They may not be friends, but the ex-agent has her back.

Sure enough, after she's been running along the old tracks for about a third of a mile, they branch off. Fliss veers to the left, following the narrower of the two paths. She soon sees why Tanta sent her this way. A few steps further on, the bridge is joined by another, running parallel to it for a little distance. The gap between the two structures is no more than a couple of feet of empty air, and Fliss knows just how to hurdle it. She covers the distance in a flying leap, turning immediately to the west to follow the new bridge back the way it came. Wherever the agents are, she's confident they won't be picking up her trail anytime soon.

If Fliss still lived an itinerant life in the wasteland, this is the point at which she'd head for home, buzzing with the triumph of a job well done. She sighs, remembering that it's not so simple now. When home is nothing more than a collection of tents, the repercussions of someone you don't like finding out where you live are not so dire: you just pack it all away, sling it onto your back, and move on. Now that they've set up shop in the Brokerage, things are a little different.

'I'm clear,' she tells Tanta, 'but I want to lie low in the city for a couple of hours. Wait for things to cool off.'

'That's sensible,' Tanta replies, a hint of approval in her tone. 'Jeanie had a safehouse not far from where you are now – a defunct signal cabin. I'll give you directions.'

*And after that, we can figure out what we're going to do about this clusterfuck*, Fliss thinks. *She* may have escaped unscathed, but she can't say the same for the crew's plan. They have a strategy – to escape the Brokerage and foil Harlow 2.0 both – but like most of the enterprises Fliss finds herself involved in, it's a desperate one. It depends on the element of surprise – and now the ICRD has discovered that she's been visiting the city. Fliss touches a nervous hand to her jacket, feeling for the reassuring contours of the package. She got what she came here for, but she's not sure, now, if it will be enough. If InTech was able to find her, then what else does it know?

# Chapter 3

'She's safe.' Tanta removes her earpiece with a grimace and drops it onto the desk.

There's a whoosh of exhaled air as, beside her, Cole and Yas let out simultaneous sighs of relief. They're both sitting with Tanta in the Brokerage's control room. An hour ago, they were drifting in and out, occupied by tasks of their own, but the developing situation with Fliss has taken precedence over everything else. Over the course of the last twenty minutes, they've been drawing their chairs closer and closer to Tanta's own, trying to catch Fliss's side of the conversation. It's only now that the danger has passed that Tanta realises her two friends are practically sitting in her lap. She gives them both a look and they scoot backwards again, Yas half-smiling at her own anxiety.

'What happened?' she asks.

Tanta fills them in as best she can, though they'll have to wait for Fliss's return to get the full story. When she's finished, the relief on both their faces has clouded over with worry again.

Cole gets to his feet, beginning to pace back and forth. 'So, what does this mean for the plan?'

Tanta has been asking herself the same question. In the weeks after her and Cole's defection, the Unaffiliated Zone around the city was swarming with guardians and surveillance drones. The crew had watched them combing the forest on the Brokerage's security monitors. Those search parties thinned out after the first month; Tanta had even started to hope, tentatively, that InTech had given up looking for them. She should have known the ICRD wouldn't be so easily thwarted. The fact that Fliss was spotted and almost captured after all this time is troubling – and it has troubling implications for the project the crew have been working on for the better part of four months.

'We should discuss that when Fliss gets back,' she answers. 'She's going to stay in a safehouse and wait for things to die down. In the meantime, shall we meet in the kitchen at 20:00 hours for dinner? You're cooking tonight, right, Cole?'

'Actually, I was thinking we could order in,' Cole replies, deadpan. 'I'm not sure what address we should give the delivery drone, though. Underground forest base?'

'*Secret* underground forest base,' Yas corrects him. 'And if we're ordering, I want pizza. Extra cheese, with—'

She's interrupted by a chime from the bank of ancient screens that lines the back wall of the control room. Most of the monitors are connected to the security cameras that maintain a ceaseless watch on the forest outside – providing the crew with their only view of the world above ground – but the one that's ringing is a pre-Meltdown communication device. Cole discovered it soon after they moved in. The Brokerage has bought and sold corporate secrets for as long as it has existed – this screen is where those transactions take place. Right now, the caller ID flashing in red on the display reads *ICRD*.

Cole stops pacing and heads for the door. Yas grabs an odd, close-fitting helmet from her desk and tosses it to Tanta, who slips it over her head. There's a microphone attached to the screen, and Tanta takes a seat in front of it. With these preparations complete, she glances once over her shoulder to check that

Cole and Yas have made themselves scarce, and taps the green button that will answer the call.

The screen goes black. The kind of people who have business with the Brokerage rarely wish their faces to be widely known, so neither of the archaic devices involved in this interaction have cameras attached. Tanta coughs, testing out the voice disguiser in the helmet before she speaks. It's usually Kenway who makes these calls on behalf of InTech, and she can't take the risk that he'll recognise her.

'This is the Brokerage,' she says, the words coming out crackly and robotic.

'This is the Co-Director of the ICRD. I'm calling for our weekly intelligence update.'

It's not Kenway. The woman's voice coming from the screen is one Tanta knows far better, and has done since childhood. The sound of it makes her chest clench and her pulse race. For a moment, she's bereft of words. Reet has never called the Brokerage before. Tanta wasn't expecting to talk to her – she isn't prepared for it. She coughs again; her throat is almost too tight for her to speak.

'Where's your colleague?' she asks. The disguiser hides the rawness in her voice, but she can feel the words rasping against her throat like sandpaper.

'He's busy, but if that's a problem, I can have him call you back.'

'No,' Tanta cuts in, too quickly. Hearing Reet again is an agony, but a sweet one, as exquisite as it is excruciating. They haven't spoken since before Tanta left InTech. She thought that she'd forgotten what her ex-lover sounded like, but her voice is unmistakable. It brings other sensations with it: the scent of rosewater and cinnamon, the feel of Reet's arms around her, protecting her from the world. They pass in an instant, leaving

33

Tanta sufficiently master of herself again to add, 'It's nice to put a voice to the role, that's all. Pleasure to meet you, Co-Director.'

'Likewise,' Reet grunts. 'Now, can we cut to the chase?'

'Have the funds been transferred to our account?' Tanta asks. She knows she shouldn't prolong this misery, but can't help herself.

'Ten thousand credits, as usual. What do you have for me?'

Yas has left a folder on the desk with the week's tips. Tanta flicks through it, trying to decipher Fliss's terrible handwriting. The bandit picks up a surprising amount from her unaffiliated contacts, and even more information trickles in from the wider network of defectors, moles and disaffected employees with whom the Brokerage has dealings.

Usually, adopting the persona of the Brokerage agent is one of the highlights of Tanta's week, giving her a chance to stretch muscles of deception that she doesn't get to use nearly often enough now that she's living in hiding. She plays up the mystery of the enigmatic intelligence broker, unveiling corporate secrets and classified information with the panache of a stage magician. Today, she stumbles through the reports in the folder, stuttering and hesitating as if she can barely read. It's been a slow week, so she pads out the scanty offering with the intelligence Fliss got from Sonia about Thoughtfront recruiting bandits in the Unaffiliated Zone.

'Thanks,' Reet says, when she's finished. And then, after an awkward pause. 'Well, bye.'

'Wait.' Tanta regrets the word as soon as it's out. What can Reet have to wait for? What reason could she possibly give for keeping her? There's an expectant silence on the other end of the line. 'Congratulations on your new role,' she chokes out, at last.

'Uh, thanks.' There's another pause, and then the screen lights up as Reet disconnects from the call.

Tanta slumps back in her chair, wrenching off the helmet, which suddenly feels like it's cutting off her air supply. The close atmosphere of the control room does little to refresh her; she feels a flash of longing for the fresh air of the forest outside, so intense that it's like a physical pain. She wants to be alone – not separated from Cole and Yas by the Brokerage's thin walls, but truly alone, the way she and Reet used to feel when they went up onto the roof of the Ward House together to watch the sunset.

She knew Reet had made Co-Director, of course – it's the Brokerage's business to know such things – but that knowledge didn't make their first conversation since Tanta's self-imposed exile any easier to bear. Once again, her ex-lover's stratospheric rise has mirrored her own spectacular fall from grace.

Tanta's not jealous – not anymore, anyway. The events of the autumn, when she learnt of InTech's plan to brainwash its residents, cured her of any lingering desire to climb the corporation's ranks. She decided the day Harlow 2.0 went live that InTech's war against its own people was something she couldn't let stand, something she had to stand against. She, Cole, Yas and Fliss are going to liberate InTech's side of the city if it kills them – and it very well might.

No, what makes Tanta's heart sink down into her stomach every time she thinks of Reet isn't jealousy. She and her ex-lover aren't just on opposite sides of this struggle: they're leading opposing forces. Neither of them can back down. And it's only a matter of time before they meet in the field.

While Tanta is speaking to the ICRD, Cole and Yas get back to work on the plan. They part ways at the door of the control room, Yas heading to the garage at the opposite end of the Brokerage's central corridor while Cole turns off into the storeroom, a crowded space filled with shelves of tinned food, storage bins full of grains and pulses, and boxes of old tech. Cole has pushed the clutter to the sides of the room and set up a chair and a desk in the middle, where he does most of his work.

They are all of them living cheek by jowl, thin walls and tactfully averted gazes providing the illusion of privacy, so this staking of claims to personal spaces is something they've become used to treating as sacred. Cole always knocks before he enters Yas's garage, the austere dormitory where Tanta spends most of her time, or the greenhouse, which Fliss has claimed as her domain, and they do the same for him. The dormitory is the only sleeping space in the Brokerage, but nobody except Tanta uses it. The rest of them have claimed mattresses and pillows and set them up in their chosen rooms.

The four of them are lucky they get along with one another, though in the early days of their confinement that wasn't as true of Tanta and Fliss as it is now. They used to squabble like teenagers – almost the first time Cole had ever seen Tanta acting her age – and for a while, he and Yas were worried they might come to blows.

The tension has died down, however. Tanta's training is too deeply embedded to allow her to indulge in sulkiness for long, and a lot of Fliss's barbed comments are directed more at the corporations in general than Tanta in particular. Once she learnt to stop taking every criticism of 'corporate types' as a personal slight, Tanta became civil again, which wrought a corresponding change in Fliss's manner. The two maintain a guarded friendliness, now, for which Cole is thankful. It certainly makes things quieter.

Quiet is good: it allows Cole to focus on his work. For the last four months, that work has mostly revolved around trying to fix his past mistakes. When he, Tanta and Jeanie formed their plan to sabotage Harlow 2.0, back in the autumn, the programme had contained a secret self-deletion protocol that could be used to uninstall it. Cole was forced to remove that backdoor when Jeanie tried to use it to kill half the people in the city. It was the right call at the time, but Jeanie's betrayal cost them dearly. It has taken Cole months to claw back the progress he lost, and the whole time, he's been living with the uncomfortable awareness that none of it would have been necessary if he hadn't made the mistake of trusting Jeanie in the first place.

Usually, Cole finds work comforting, a safe space where he can hide from troublesome thoughts. A puzzling piece of code asks for nothing except understanding; it doesn't pose tricky ethical questions or needle him with guilt and self-doubt – or it shouldn't. Recently, Cole has been finding that his work frequently dredges up thoughts he'd rather avoid – thoughts of Jeanie, of what he once thought she meant to him, and memories of how she took his trust and affection and stamped on it.

At least he's close to being able to put those memories behind him now: after four gruelling months, he has managed to design a software patch that should do everything the self-deletion protocol was designed for and more. Cole has it stored on a data card that he keeps on his person at all times. When this phase of the plan is complete – a distant prospect as yet, but one that's growing closer every day – he'll find a way to introduce it to the MbOSes of InTech's residents. Once inside the Inscape system, it should uninstall both Harlow Programmes quickly and cleanly, with none of the attendant side effects of his earlier efforts.

There are many other obstacles they need to overcome before they reach that point, of course – not least of which is the fact that currently he, Tanta and Yas are stuck underground. Before they can liberate the city, they need to find a way to safely leave the Brokerage.

Cole's initial approach to *this* conundrum was to try to disable their Inscapes entirely, or failing that, to hobble them so they were no longer capable of downloading the Harlow 2.0 update. He soon learnt that this was all but impossible. Removing the physical chips and wires that make up the Inscape system was never an option – he needs specialised tools for that and besides, Cole is a neuroengineer, not a brain surgeon – and it didn't take him long to realise that any technological workaround was similarly doomed to failure. Cole used to think of the Inscape system as being like a building, with different rooms serving different purposes. His experiments over the last few months have convinced him that it is more like a thicket of brambles – and it has the same uncanny ability to survive whatever digital pesticides he might use to try and suppress it.

In the end, Cole and the rest of the crew were forced to come up with a more radical solution – which is where Yas's part of the plan comes in. After half an hour of fine-tuning his software patch, Cole lays it aside and heads down the corridor to check on her, rapping twice on the door to the garage.

'Come in!' a muffled voice shouts.

The garage is the biggest space in the Brokerage, and the least polished. Its walls are of rammed earth, unadorned by paint or plaster. There is space for half a dozen cars in its cavernous interior, but right now, there's only one: a sleek, black model that still smells strongly of solvent paint.

At first, Cole can't see Yas anywhere. Then there's a ripple beside the car, the air running like water, and a corner of the scene folds back to reveal her face and upper arm.

'Hey, Cole,' she says. 'I'm just testing Jeanie's AR cloak out. Did you see me?'

Cole shakes his head. 'Not till you moved. It's good.'

The AR cloak is an innovation designed by their predecessor at the Brokerage. Cole tries to keep his face composed as he replies, but hearing Jeanie's name aloud still sends an unpleasant spasm through his chest: part guilt, part grief. He despises himself for his response – for the sense of longing that still grips his heart whenever she is mentioned. Jeanie was a monster. She duped Cole and Tanta into working with her to reverse the rollout of Harlow 2.0, while secretly planning a worse atrocity. Had she succeeded, a staggering proportion of InTech's residents would be dead now – Cole, Yas and Tanta likely among them. Cole knows this only too well. It was his unwitting help that almost allowed Jeanie's plan to succeed – but Jeanie also said she cared for him. For a few glorious hours, he had thought they shared something meaningful, and he can no more forget that brief liaison than he can Jeanie's betrayal.

'You've done a great job on the car,' he says now, turning the subject. 'It really looks the part.'

It's an understatement. Four months ago, when the crew drove this car into the Brokerage, it was an armoured tactical vehicle – an old model that Tanta and Fliss had stolen during their flight from InTech's Southern Distribution Centre. It had been a big, armoured beast of a thing with a reinforced chassis faceted like a diamond. The vehicle Yas is standing beside now could hardly look more different.

Yas has been hard at work with the parts Fliss has scavenged, bought and stolen for her. She has stripped the tactical vehicle down to its metal bones and rebuilt it as another kind of car entirely. Its bodywork is sleek and glossy, its interior smooth, with no sign of the exposed wiring, the analogue steering rig and pedals, which had allowed Fliss to drive it without an MbOS in the first place. If Cole didn't know what it used to look like, he'd have no idea that it was anything other than an InTech executive taxi.

Yas drops a mock bow in acknowledgement of the compliment. 'You're too kind. All it needs now is something to make it go. Think you can help with that?'

Cole nods, climbing into the front seat. When Tanta stole it last autumn, she and Fliss had had to bypass the car's AI and drive it manually. Now, they'll need to do the opposite: the car will never pass as an InTech taxi if it has a visible steering wheel. Hacking the AI that runs the car's automatic driving systems would be a lot harder outside the Brokerage than it is within it. The bunker's shields, which protect the whole structure from MbOS signals and corporate scanners, also prevent the AI from alerting InTech to the fact that Cole is tampering with its code. Cole accesses the car's AR menu and slips into its systems. Without the threat of InTech learning what he's doing, he can quench the AI's firewall and pick its digital locks at his leisure.

Within a few hours, he's finished. 'I've disabled GPS tracking and the unauthorised use alarm,' he tells Yas, getting out again. 'As long as we programme its destination in down here, it'll drive itself.'

'What about the traffic management mainframe?' Yas asks. 'Will the car try to connect to it when it enters the city?'

'Oh, it'll try,' Cole replies, 'but the signal blockers I installed last month will make it impossible.'

Cole has set up a miniaturised version of the Brokerage's own shields within the car's chassis. If all goes well, when it re-enters InTech territory, it will be a ghost, its passengers hidden from prying eyes and gate scanners alike.

'Thanks, Cole.' Yas grins at him. 'One missing piece, then, and we're all set.'

That missing part is what Fliss was in the city tonight to collect. Now, it's just a matter of waiting for her – though, as it turns out, they're not waiting for long. Cole is back in the storeroom, hunting through the shelves for some beans for tonight's dinner, when the Brokerage's perimeter alarm goes off. His pulse spikes, as it always does at the strident klaxon, and he steps out into the corridor. Tanta, who is emerging from the control room at the same time, reassures him.

'It's Fliss,' she says. 'Coming down via the tunnel.'

That sets his mind at ease. He ducks back into the storeroom to let her in. There's a metal door set into the wall at the back of the room with a keypad beside it. It's the Brokerage's pedestrian entrance, something they only discovered existed after they'd moved in. After ten minutes, a series of hollow raps on the door announces Fliss's arrival.

'I'm coming,' Cole calls, though she likely can't hear him through the thick metal. He taps the access code in on the keypad and the door swings open, its stiff hinges shrieking dismally. Fliss staggers inside.

'I didn't want to drive up to the front entrance – not with the ICRD looking for me,' she explains. 'I left the car at the other end. We need to get some oil for that thing,' she adds, collapsing into a chair.

'Welcome back,' Cole greets her. 'How are you feeling?'

'Tired. Would you get the door?'

She looks it. Cole swings the hatch closed. The tunnel beyond it runs deeper into the forest to the southeast, sloping up and up until it emerges in a grating hidden in a long-abandoned office block. It's a way to get into and out of the Brokerage undetected, but it was also clearly designed as a decontamination station. There's a second door a little way into the tunnel, and the space between the two has a crate for stripping off clothes or gear, and a shelf of out-of-date antibacterial gels and sprays. Neither door will open unless the other is closed. Yas believes the Brokerage is a pre-Meltdown military installation. Whoever built it meant for it to withstand an apocalypse – and they clearly had several different end-of-the-world scenarios in mind.

After Cole has sealed the airlock door, he and Fliss reconvene with the rest of the crew in the control room, their main meeting space. Once they're all seated, Fliss takes a small package wrapped in plastic from inside her jacket and hands it to Yas.

'Got your gizmo,' she says.

From her other pocket, she takes the smartphone, which she tosses to Tanta. 'And I got a snap of one of the guys who was chasing me.'

While Tanta accesses the image, Fliss fills everyone in on her eventful supply run, from her catch-up with Sonia to her near miss with the ICRD. When she's finished, Tanta shows them all the photo on the smartphone. Cole's surprised to find he recognises the unconscious young man on the screen: it's Tanta's old friend, fellow CorpWard and ICRD agent Firent.

'Good to see he's made a full recovery, at least,' Cole says. The last time he saw Firent, he was in Arthur's lab at the Black Box, resting up after receiving a chest wound that almost killed him.

Tanta grimaces. 'And now Kenway and Reet have him on our tail. That makes sense: we did train together.'

It's exactly the way InTech tends to think, in Cole's experience. The corporation will always pick a hunter who knows their quarry. It's the reason he was seconded to the ICRD – and met Tanta – in the first place. After he lost all memory of his first stint working with Jeanie, and the terrorist acts he authored in her name, the corporation reasoned that there was no one better than him to foil the plans he had set in motion.

'How much do you think he knows?' Yas asks.

'Well, I wasn't followed,' Fliss replies. 'And the fact that there's no one knocking on our door right now means he hasn't figured out where we are. I think a security camera must have caught me casing the alley last week – that's how he knew where I'd be.' She frowns, thinking it through. 'He probably doesn't know much else – not yet, anyway. That fence he and his people arrested had no idea what he was selling me. I set up the deal through a third party – he was just the go-between.'

'So Firent won't be able to get anything out of him directly,'

Tanta summarises, 'but he may be able to get to your third party through him.'

Fliss nods. 'If we're unlucky.'

Yas pulls a face. 'It's the ICRD. Let's assume we're going to be unlucky.'

Cole agrees. They have nothing on their side except this underground hideout and the fact that InTech doesn't know they're coming, while the ICRD has time, resources, money – and more highly-trained agents than they can shake a big stick at. 'So, what do we do now?' he asks.

'The way I see it, we have to stick to the plan,' Tanta replies. 'It's the best we've got. But now the ICRD has picked up our scent, we need to move faster. We'll only succeed if we put everything into action before Firent figures out what we're up to.'

'You in agreement with that, Yasmin?' Fliss asks.

Yas frowns, head cocked. 'Yeah,' she says at last. 'It's risky, but delaying would be worse.'

Cole and Fliss exchange glances. They're the junior partners in this situation: neither of them knows the ICRD like the two ex-agents do.

'We should try and change up our strategy as much as we can, though,' Yas adds. 'And we need to move now. Like, today, now.'

'Dr Friend's next board meeting is tomorrow at four,' Fliss says. 'That soon enough for you?'

'It'll have to be.' Yas shrugs. 'The car's ready to go. We'd better hope Firent's slower on the uptake than you, Tanta.'

Fliss draws in a breath. 'I'll get ready for another trip to the city, then.'

'On that topic,' Tanta starts. There's something in her voice that Cole doesn't like. She sounds like she's steeling herself against opposition – and when she finishes her sentence, he understands why. 'I'm going to come with you. At least, I'm going to try.'

There's instant uproar – as much as can be caused by a room full of four people.

'Are you nuts?' Fliss asks. 'You'll get your brain fried!'

'You can't!' Cole adds.

Yas raises an eyebrow. 'Aren't you skipping a step?'

Tanta waits through their expostulations in patient silence. When they've died down, she looks at Fliss.

'You said Firent wasn't programmed with Harlow 2.0, right? Are you sure?'

Fliss nods. 'As sure as I can be.'

'As far as we know, only Directors and the board are exempt from the software, but Firent is just an agent – and a Corporate Ward, like me.' She turns to Cole. 'That made me think of something you told me when we were first investigating the programme, in the autumn. You said it wasn't as sophisticated as the original. This is something I've been wondering for a while, and I think Firent has just confirmed it: what if Harlow-Programmed CorpWards aren't affected by the update?'

There's a stunned silence. 'That's an awfully big "what if",' Cole says.

'It makes sense, though. Think about it: Harlow 2.0's useful-ness lies in the fact that it could be rolled out quickly and en masse. In most other respects, the original Harlow Programme is the better model. There'd be no reason for InTech to send out the update to wards who already had a superior version of their own.'

'You think you might be immune?' Yas asks.

'Exactly. You and Cole aren't exempt, but I could be. It might already be safe for me to go outside.'

'Operative word being "might",' Cole cuts in, keen to remind Tanta of what's at stake here. 'You'd be risking yourself on a

44

hunch! Besides, your Harlow Programming was uninstalled. Even if most wards are immune, that doesn't mean you are.'

'The dummy system you constructed for me makes it look as though my programming is still operational,' Tanta says calmly. 'It's fooled InTech's systems before. And if it doesn't, you've created a software patch that will uninstall Harlow 2.0.'

'An *untested* software patch!'

'Well, if I'm wrong, you can test it on me. Yas is right. We have to change the plan as much as possible. And if the ICRD *does* catch up to us in the field, Fliss won't be able to face them by herself. Our odds of success are higher if we're together.'

Cole is expecting Fliss to object to that, but to his dismay, she merely shrugs. Tanta stares at them, meeting each person's eyes in turn. 'I think we have to take the chance,' she says, 'but it's not my decision to make alone. If I got the update, I'd be a danger to all of you. I'd try and escape the Brokerage, and I'd certainly attempt to alert InTech about our activities here. So we'd *all* be taking a risk. I won't do it if even one of you thinks it isn't worth it.'

'Fliss could use an ex-agent on her side up there,' Yas says. 'I'm in if you are.'

'And I'll be topside with you to make sure you don't try anything,' Fliss adds. 'So I'm not too worried about you going crazy.'

Everyone looks at Cole. He finds, quite suddenly, that he can't reply. The thought of Tanta risking her selfhood like this terrifies him. Through all the upheavals of the last six months, she has been the one constant. She's his friend – the first he can remember who wasn't using him for some agenda of their own.

'You remember Neal Ortega, right?' he asks her. The Black Box intern who helped Cole to discover the update's existence in the autumn was also one of its first guinea pigs.

Tanta nods.

'He – Harlow 2.0 stripped out everything that made him unique. His personhood. If you're wrong about this...' Cole swallows. 'If we're wrong, that's what will happen to you. Do you understand that?'

'I do. I think we have to try anyway.'

And that's all she needs to say, isn't it? Because as much as Cole hates everything about this idea, this is Tanta's decision, not his.

'Then I'll back you,' he says.

Tanta squares her shoulders, straightening as she rises from her chair. 'Then it's agreed. Right now, we should eat and rest. We'll try sending me outside first thing tomorrow.' She turns to Cole. 'There's some rope in the storeroom, right?'

'Uh, yes,' Cole says. 'But why would you need—'

Yas gives him a look. 'She's right, Cole. We can't take any chances.'

# Chapter 4

Reet rises early. She has to: co-directing the ICRD is a demanding job, and despite waking before the sun comes up, she's often working late into the night. Daylight is something she only sees nowadays through the tinted glass of the ICRD's windows, where it comes through stained and brown, like weak tea.

She flicks on the solar lamp by her bed, flooding her room with welcome white light. In this artificial day, she gets dressed and forages for some breakfast. Reet's promotion came with new digs: her flat now is twice the size of her old one. It has a huge kitchen, with all manner of appliances lining the walls and a breakfast island marooned in the centre, but Reet barely uses it. The Ward House had a canteen on site, and the only wards taught to cook were those being prepared for careers in catering. Reet knows what most of the gadgets in the kitchen are for, but not how to use them. She mostly sticks to the toaster, the kettle and the microwave, and she's found little time to experiment beyond that.

If Tee were still here they might have had a cooking night and turned exploring the kitchen into a game. They could have figured out how to use the air fryer and the griddle together, and neither of them would have minded if the results of their experiments were inedible. Without her, Reet finds she doesn't have the inclination.

Thinking of Tanta brings on a roiling in her stomach, so sudden and strong that it makes Reet nauseous. She tries to drown the sensation with a gulp of hot, sweet tea, gripping the handle of the mug so hard she leaves a row of half-moons imprinted on her palm. It's been four months since her ex vanished, and yet the memory of her still catches Reet off-guard. She'll be minding her own business, working, or trying to sleep, and Tee will surge to the top of her thoughts like acid reflux, painful and unwelcome. She's frustrated with herself: she shouldn't still feel the loss so strongly, the anger and sadness, the hurt. Every minute she spends moping around over Tee is a minute stolen from her work, from InTech – and her work right now is more vital to the corporation's fortunes than it has ever been. The thought steels her. Reet drains the rest of her tea, throws her toast away half finished, and sets off for the ICRD.

The air outside, fresh and clean after a night of rain, helps to clear her head. By the time she arrives on the fourteenth floor, Reet feels ready to face whatever the day is going to throw at her. That's just as well, because the first thing it throws at her is Douglas Kenway. Reet opens the door to her office – once a briefing room, but the subject of a hasty refurbishment after her promotion – to find her old mentor sitting at the circular table in the corner. She remembers, with a sinking feeling, that they have a morning check-in today. A large part of Reet's new role involves signing off on Douglas's decisions. It feels almost shameful to admit it, but it's not an aspect of the job she enjoys.

'Good morning, Douglas,' she says, with a confidence she doesn't feel.

Inside, she's fragile as bone china. Douglas is her Co-Director, her closest colleague, and someone for whom she has immense respect. He was the one who took her on as an ICRD agent in the first place – a debt Reet sometimes feels as though she'll never be able to repay. Her gratitude and admiration made it all the more painful when she realised that Douglas despises her. He's never said as much to her face, but it's plain enough in the curl of his lip whenever he looks her way, and the bitter note in his voice when they speak. It's there now as he bids her a curt 'good morning', and it makes Reet's insides clench with dismay.

She's not sure why Douglas's feelings towards her have changed, though she can pinpoint exactly when it happened. They got along well when she worked for him; it's only now they're equals in rank that he can't stand the sight of her. Possibly he resents having to share his directorship. It's the only explanation Reet can think of, and yet she can't bring herself to accept it. InTech's board would never have created this post, or appointed Reet to fill it, without a good reason. It's not for her or Douglas – for any Director, in fact – to question their judgment. Douglas knows that; he must do.

Reet covers her anxiety by calling up an agenda on her 'scape. She viewshares it with Douglas but waits for him to start the conversation. She's determined to be the best Co-Director she can be, but she's mindful of how many years of experience he has on her: there's still a lot she needs to learn from him, and it feels only fair to let him take the lead. After a minute has elapsed in mulish silence, however, she resigns herself to the fact that he isn't going to begin this meeting of his own volition and does it herself.

'I spoke to the Brokerage last night, as agreed,' she says. Over the last few months, she's been shadowing Douglas in his duties and, at the board's behest, taking some of them on for herself. Last night's conversation was thrilling – her first solo encounter with the infamous information broker – but from Douglas's expression, Reet guesses he doesn't want to hear about it. When he doesn't reply, she continues. 'They told me something

49

potentially useful about Thoughtfront's activities – apparently, it's resumed recruiting bandits in the Unaffiliated Zone. I was thinking we should assign an agent to investigate. Who would you recommend?'

Douglas shrugs, looking away. 'I wouldn't bother sending anyone. Rumours are hardly worth the ICRD's time.'

Reet disagrees, but the last thing she wants to do is get into an argument. She makes a noncommittal gesture. 'All right, I'll take that under advisement. Now,' she consults the agenda on her Array, 'how is the Auxiliary Defence Force coming along?'

The ADF is Douglas's main focus at the moment, a collaborative effort between the ICRD and Residents' Affairs. He's been recruiting and training additional troops since the autumn in preparation for an expected Thoughtfront incursion, but in the wake of the nightly drone attacks now hammering the city, the board have ordered him to step up the pace.

In the four months since Reet made Co-Director, the conflict between InTech and its former weapons subsidiary has continued to escalate. So far, it's a struggle that InTech has been winning. Thoughtfront's attempts to sabotage the corporation's Harlow Programme and disrupt its supply lines have failed, and now, InTech is hitting back. The rollout of Harlow 2.0 hasn't just secured the loyalty of InTech's residents, it's also made undercover agents from the Thinktank, Thoughtfront's version of the ICRD, far easier to spot. Reet has overseen a purge of Thinktank operatives from InTech's side of the city, and she's pressing the advantage with even more drastic measures: a complete blockade of the other corporation's trade routes, sanctions against its business partners, and targeted drone strikes on its infrastructure.

She doesn't like having to do this, but the corporation across the riverbed has forced her hand. Thoughtfront has already proven that it won't back down; that means Reet can't, either.

The board have decided that InTech has tolerated Thoughtfront's independence for long enough. Dr Friend is already working on a new version of Harlow 2.0, one that's adapted for the MindEye operating system. The corp won't stop until it has either reabsorbed its former subsidiary or destroyed it.

In response, Thoughtfront has more than doubled the ranks of its peacekeepers and is sending them on daily military drills at the edge of the riverbed. At this point, an invasion attempt is all but inevitable – aside from surrender, it's the only option their hounded rival has left – and when it happens, it's vitally important InTech has the numbers to repel it.

'Training of the new community guardians is proceeding smoothly,' Douglas replies. 'The issue is leadership. The units are well disciplined and diligent, but they need more regular supervision than they would have done before the update.'

Reet nods. When the board briefed her on Harlow 2.0, they explained that the programme had some effect on initiative and efficiency. Programmed residents are slower on the uptake than they were, and require clearer and more direct instructions from their managers. Dr Friend says it's a temporary issue while they adjust to their programming, and should have passed in a year or two. It's a small price to pay, considering the update's benefits. Reet has never seen the city so peaceful and quiet, its residents so content. All the fear of Thoughtfront has evaporated, replaced by a steely resolve. Rather than backbiting and squabbling over resources, people are working together to stamp out the threat – and everyone will be better off because of it.

Besides, in Reet's experience, a lot of InTech's residents lacked initiative even before Harlow 2.0 was rolled out. When she was running The Rotunda, she was often astonished by the tasks that her wagers would leave undone simply because they weren't part of their job description; she could never understand why they'd let that stop them. If a task needs to be done, you do it. It's as simple as that. Once the teething problems have passed, the update will help her colleagues to understand that; in Reet's opinion, that can only be a good thing.

'What do you think we should do about that?' she asks. She's trying to frame the question constructively, but Douglas still rolls his eyes as he responds.

'In addition to the section lieutenants we've already promoted, I think each unit will require a team leader to keep it on track. I have a number of candidates in mind. They'll all need a temporary exemption from the update, of course.'

Reet was nodding along with all of this, until the topic of exemptions from Harlow 2.0 came up. She stops abruptly; she can feel herself trying to bite her lower lip and shoves the impulse aside.

'That's not what the board want,' she says. 'Come on, Douglas, we've been over this. Training up some team leaders sounds good, but I've granted you twenty-five exemptions already. That's more than enough. You'll need to recruit them from the Corp Wards.'

It isn't the first time Douglas has made this suggestion, and she's surprised he's still bringing it up. The board have made their wishes very clear: while they're willing to make a few short-term exceptions, the only people truly exempt from Harlow 2.0 and its predecessor are the Directors – Reet aside, of course. Where there are other positions of responsibility to fill, the board want Corporate Wards to fill them – people who have already been optimised by the original Harlow Programme to keep their minds on the job and their priorities in check. Reet and her cohort get to run the show, now. It's up to them to bring InTech through this war and out safe on the other side. Reet feels, not for the first time, the pride and the burden of that responsibility.

Douglas, whose thoughts are clearly running on a very

different track, shoots her a poisonous glare. 'There aren't enough,' he snaps. 'Not since the fire. You ought to know that better than anyone.'

Reet flinches, thinking of chaos and death and thick smoke plugging her lungs. The Ward House fire is another memory she'd rather not dwell on. She's nettled – less by Douglas's attempt to wound her than by his flagrant disregard for the chain of command. She tries to interfere as little as possible in the areas of the ICRD that are still under her Co-Director's control, out of respect for his experience, but the board charged her with vetting his decisions and vetoing them when necessary, and he needs to respect that. His repeated attempts to circumvent and dismiss Reet don't just undermine her – they undermine the board themselves. Usually, she's patient with Douglas – she knows he's finding it hard to adapt to this change in his working patterns – but she needs to shut this down.

'That's bullshit,' she says sharply. 'There are still plenty of wards left. Thanks to – to Tanta, the casualties from that night were minimal. You can pull wards from other divisions if you need to, but this isn't up for discussion. I'll put together a list of candidates for you, if you'd like.'

'No need,' Douglas snaps. 'I'll do it myself. Is there anything else, *Director*?'

Reet opens her mouth to say no, but he's already storming out of her office. She sighs. There's nothing she can do about his dislike – it's something she just has to live with – but it still hurts her. *He didn't like Tee, either,* a small voice in her head reminds her. She snorts aloud at that, frighting the thought away. That was completely different; Douglas was right to mistrust Tanta – his suspicions were vindicated. And maybe if Reet had kept a closer eye on her, she would never have...

But she dismisses the self-blame with a shake of her head. There's no use worrying over things she can't change. Tee made her own choices, and it's Reet's job to understand them, not to repine over her own. Which reminds her: she has another meeting to attend.

Though Reet tries to think of Tee as little as possible in her personal life, at work, it's often necessary. The investigation into Tanta and Cole's whereabouts is one of the ICRD assignments that falls within her purview. She's assigned Firent and two other agents to work the case, but she still takes an active role in managing its progress – or lack thereof, since neither of the fugitives has been seen in months. She doesn't have to be involved; she's a Director, no one would bat an eyelid if she were to hand the job off to an experienced deputy, but she prefers running things this way.

There's a hundred and one other things on her plate, but she makes as much time for the search as she can. And where she can, she works her other duties around it, or combines them with it, as she has managed to do with the next task on her list. She's interviewing a trainee agent, a CorpWard from the cohort one year below her own, who is reaching the end of the ICRD's basic training programme.

She meets him at the data zeppelin, which is still docked just outside the city wall. The airship houses one of InTech's many backup servers, and in more peaceful times it floated over the Unaffiliated Zone, providing even signal coverage over an area where the corporation has no ground infrastructure. It's been stuck at the city's mooring spire for the last four months, which has been a nightmare for comms in the UZ, but an unavoidable one. Thoughtfront is looking for every vulnerability it can find, and it has already attacked InTech's servers once. If the airship were out in the UZ, it would be too easy a target.

There are a couple of guardians on duty at the base of the

mooring spire; they smile at Reet as she approaches, recognising her instantly.

'Has the Corporate Ward finished his inspection of the zeppelin?' Reet asks the woman on the left, taking care to enunciate each word clearly.

The guardian nods. 'Yes, Director!'

'Send him down to me now.'

'Of course, Director!'

The woman vanishes into the mooring spire, emerging a few minutes later with a lanky young man with blond hair and a pale face. He greets Reet respectfully.

'Arden. Had a chance to check out the incident reports I sent you?'

'Yes, Director.'

'Well: what's your assessment?'

Arden straightens up, taking a breath. 'From the eyewitness reports and the nature of the damage inside the zeppelin itself, it looks as though Tanta was engaged in a firefight – probably with the woman whose body was recovered in the autumn: Jeanette Callaghan.'

'How do you know Tanta came here?' Reet quizzes him. 'Her 'scape's location tracker records don't place her at the scene.'

Arden swallows. 'That's right. She and Cole disabled their location trackers in the safehouse outside Sodis. Um, according to the incident reports, ICRD analysts found Cole's digital signature all over the zeppelin's servers. If he was here, it's likely Tanta was, too.'

It's sound reasoning, but despite Arden's obvious nervousness – he's still standing ramrod straight, and there's sweat shining on his forehead – Reet has the feeling that she can push him a little further. 'Is it? She abandoned her corp – why would she stick with her partner?'

'It fits her profile,' he says simply. 'I've read her service record – the parts I was allowed to access, anyway – and it's clear they were close. I don't think she'd leave him.'

*She left me,* Reet thinks, but does not say. As it happens, she agrees with Arden on this one, however bitter she might feel about it. She makes an expansive gesture. 'So, putting it all together: what do you think happened?'

Arden bites his lip. 'Jeanette was working for Thoughtfront, coordinating strikes on our supply chains and infrastructure. Tanta and Cole were conspiring with her and the bandit Tanta broke out of Sodis – Felicity – for purposes unknown. They went to the zeppelin to attack our servers, but they had a disagreement – possibly over Jeanette's Thoughtfront connection. There was a gunfight, which drew the attention of our guardians. Jeanette killed herself rather than face capture. Then Tanta, Cole and Felicity went to ground.'

Reet's impressed, though she doesn't show it yet. The CorpWard can read a scene, and he has good instincts. For a theory constructed on the fly, it is both reasonable and fairly comprehensive – even though 'for purposes unknown' is doing a lot of heavy lifting. They've almost reached the end of the interview. 'And where do you think they are now?' she asks.

'They went south,' Arden replies. 'The guardians on site saw their car heading in that direction. And since we haven't been able to trace their MbOSes since, their safehouse must incorporate some kind of Faraday cage, like the one we found outside Sodis. Wherever it is, it's shielded from our scanners. At least, that's my guess.'

Reet allows a smile to break across her face. Arden's conclusion is very close to the official verdict of Firent and his team of analysts. They've hypothesised the existence of a second safehouse for months: it's their leading theory for Tanta and Cole's current location. The only detail the CorpWard is missing is one he couldn't possibly know about because it's above his clearance level. The safehouse must be within a thirty-mile radius of the zeppelin – the defectors couldn't have got any further than that before Harlow 2.0 went live.

'Excellent work, Arden,' she says. 'You've exceeded my expectations.'

The board have briefed her on the Harlow Programme's command phrases, so she knows what a gift she's giving him with the praise. He's earned it. Arden blushes with pleased pride. His grin looks fit to split his face in half.

'Thank you, Director.'

'Call me Reet – there's no need to be so formal.'

Arden looks at her shyly. There's a question hovering in his eyes, unspoken.

'What's up?' Reet asks.

'She ... she was very good, wasn't she?' he asks. 'Tanta, I mean. Her service record is ...' He lets out a whistle.

'She was,' Reet replies. She keeps the bite out of her voice; no need to pass any of her anger Arden's way. 'Her defection was a blow. That's why the board want her back.'

'Well, that and she's a threat,' Arden says blandly.

Reet hides her wince. 'That too.'

'I can't understand why she *would* defect,' he continues. 'She did so much for the corp, and then one day she just goes off the rails? It doesn't make sense.'

It's time to change the subject. 'That was a good reading of the scene,' Reet tells him now, 'and I see you scored in the top three per cent of your cohort on your last four training simulations. I think it's time you tried your hand at a real assignment. There's been some chatter about increased Thoughtfront activity in the Unaffiliated Zone – it looks as though Thinktank agents are in communication with certain groups of bandits again. I'd like you to investigate.'

The young ward's eyes widen. 'You're making me an agent? But protocol dictates that trainees must complete at least five assignments under supervision before they can go out into the field alone.'

'Protocol's a little outdated in this instance,' Reet says. In fact, it's been months since the ICRD has had the resources to give trainees the supervision they're supposed to have. She's been sending green agents on field missions fresh out of basic training because she doesn't have any other choice. It's not ideal, but until the conflict with Thoughtfront has been resolved, it's a necessary evil. 'That's nothing you need to worry about, though,' she adds – and Arden's face relaxes immediately as he is flooded with the knowledge that his superior has everything in hand. Reet remembers that feeling; she misses it.

'Welcome to InterCorporate Relations, Agent,' she continues, shaking his hand. 'Now, pack your things and say your goodbyes. You leave in an hour.'

Reet hangs around at the zeppelin for a little while after Arden has left, hoping that a re-examination of the scene with fresh eyes will show her something she's missed. It never has so far; Arden is the fifth CorpWard she's brought here for assessment, but she keeps trying anyway. Tee always said that approaching a problem from a different angle could trigger new insights, and— No, Reet thinks. *What Tee told you doesn't matter anymore.* Tanta is her quarry now, not her teacher. It's not the first time she's had this conversation with herself, and she's sure it won't be the last. Never mind. She'll keep beating it into herself until it sinks through her thick skull, and she remembers it.

Reet feels proud and lucky to be able to do all the work she does, from watching over InTech's residents to guarding its borders, but she has to admit that she's especially grateful the board have put her in charge of tracking Tanta down. They don't mind what Reet does with her, so long as she neutralises the danger she poses; they never used it, but the phrase 'dead or alive' was heavily implied. The order scared Reet with its finality, its seriousness, but a small part of her was rejoicing. Because 'dead or alive' means that she has a choice. Much as she respects the skill and professionalism of all of her colleagues, Reet knows that there's not one of them who can care about this – about Tee – as much as she does. She'll do everything she can to bring her back in from the cold.

The board have told her about Tee's lost Harlow Programming, and Reet can fill in the blanks in that particular puzzle for herself. Losing it must have unbalanced her, somehow. She's not in her right mind. Knowing this doesn't make Reet much more kindly inclined towards her. When she catches up to Tanta, she fully intends to smack some sense back into her. But when her programming is reinstated, Tanta will be her old, true self again – the version of her that was loving and honest. If Reet could have that version of Tee back, there's not a lot that she wouldn't be willing to forgive. Whether Douglas and the board will feel the same way is another matter. But Reet will love Tanta in a secure work camp if she has to. It's better than loving a traitor, or a corpse.

She's about to head back to her office when Firent pings her on MindChat.

<<What's up?>> she asks.

There's a pause before the agent replies. When he does, his answer sets Reet's heart fluttering.

<<Can we meet in the ICRD, Director? There's been a break in the case.>>

# Chapter 5

Tanta makes her first trip above ground trussed to a chair. The others were only intending to tie her hands and blindfold her, but she insists.

'You're underestimating my training,' she says, without arrogance. 'We don't know how much of my combat skills I'd retain if I got the update; we shouldn't take any unnecessary risks. A blindfold on its own would be worse than pointless.'

'*Worse?*' Cole asks.

'I could take it off and strangle you with it.'

The start of an incredulous smile tugs at Cole's lips. It slinks away again at the sight of Tanta's expression.

'I'm serious,' she says. 'I can get out of hand restraints in seconds. I've practiced.'

Once out of her restraints, Tanta knows she could make it through the forest and back to the city barefoot if she had to, and none of the others – not even Yas – would be able to stop her. And that's a best-case scenario. Instead of running, she might stay and try to fight – a development so awful that she doesn't even want to think about it.

So, she insists on the chair, getting Yas to tie her in place on the lift platform before it's raised above ground. Yas has had the same training Tanta has in how to secure a hostile, so she knows how to do the thing properly. Tanta puts one of the earpieces in so she can stay in contact with the Brokerage, and then Yas ties both Tanta's arms to the chair, passing them through the slats at the back and securing them tightly. She does the same to her legs, so Tanta can't kick out or rise to her feet and run.

When that's done, Tanta is almost ready. Interestingly, it's Fliss, the one among them who doesn't have a 'scape, who spots the flaw in her current set-up.

'What about your headware?' she asks. 'Can't you access that with your eyes or something?'

'I can,' Tanta replies. She's pleased Fliss brought it up. The bandit has been learning to pay more attention to such details, crucial, but easily overlooked. Luckily, there's a solution – one that doesn't even require Cole's tech expertise to put into practice.

'My agent privileges were never revoked,' Tanta explains. 'I got into the Brokerage too fast, and since then, my 'scape has been inaccessible to InTech. That means I'm still allowed to suspend someone's MbOS access for up to twenty-four hours.'

Tanta has never used that privilege on herself before – why would she need to? – but she's glad she still has it now. If she blocks her own access to her 'scape's functions before she goes above ground, she'll have no way of contacting anyone in InTech to let them know where she is, however much she might end up wanting to.

That's all their bases covered, and Tanta feels a professional satisfaction at knowing that there's nothing she'll be able to do now, either to escape from or to harm her friends. Still, there's an anxiety gnawing at her insides that is purely personal. If she's wrong about this, she'll lose herself. And this time, there's no guarantee that Cole will be able to get her back again.

'I'm ready,' she says, not really meaning it.

Cole squats next to the chair, looking her in the eyes. 'Good luck,' he says. There's a tremor in his voice.

'I'll be all right, Cole. And if I'm not, you'll have a guinea pig.'

Cole looks agonised. 'Tanta, I'm not sure if—'

'I have every confidence in you. Come on, Fliss, let's go.'

Once Cole and Yas have left the garage, Fliss slams the lift button and they start to rise. As the ceiling opens above them, Tanta squints at the sudden light. She had forgotten how dim the Brokerage was compared to the sunlit clearing above it, and it makes her wince. The world is so *bright*. Light saturates it, setting the trees and the grass on fire. It's like a liquid that's spilled over everything, excoriating, glorious.

The next thing she notices is the chill vastness of the air, which takes her own breath and shows her the littleness of it, snatching it from her lungs. She has a feeling that the chair and the bonds were unnecessary after all: the vault of air and sky pins her in place more effectively than either.

For a full minute, she's transfixed by light and birdsong, filled up to the brim with liquid sun and cold, clear air as though she's nothing more than an empty cup that the sky is pouring itself into. Then Fliss is shaking her arm, looking into her face.

'Tanta? You still with me?'

Tanta searches for a reply. It seems to have been swallowed up by the white clouds overhead. 'Yes,' she manages, after what feels like a long time. 'I'm here.'

'And are you still … you know: you?'

Fliss's tone is light, but there's real concern in her eyes. Her round face is bent over Tanta's own with more solicitude than she's ever seen from the bandit before.

'Tanta?' a voice buzzes in her ear, the anxious chorus to Fliss's question. 'Are you—'

'I'm me,' Tanta says quickly, keen not to prolong the agony.

'I feel fine. It worked.' A grin rises unbidden to her lips – an unusual occurrence. It worked! She's free to come and go as she pleases! In fact, she always was – though right now she's too relieved to repine at all the time she's spent underground unnecessarily. It looks as though the dummy system that Cole set up to mimic her lost Harlow Programming is still enough to fool InTech's systems, at least for now. 'Well, that was a waste of four months,' she quips.

Cole's sigh of relief crackles in her ear.

'You shouldn't untie me yet,' Tanta adds, as Fliss reaches for her restraints. 'We need to be absolutely certain.'

Fliss rolls her eyes, all her sarcasm returning in an instant now that she knows Tanta is safe. 'Obviously.' She pauses. 'How are we supposed to make sure?'

'Take me back down and let Cole examine me.' But the thought of going into the bowels of the Brokerage again makes Tanta feel like she's about to be buried alive. 'Let's give it another half an hour up here first, though.'

It's not entirely selfish reasoning on her part. If their plan is to stand a chance of working, Tanta will need to be above ground for several hours; if the update is on some kind of time delay or takes a few minutes of exposure before it kicks in, then the rest of the crew need to know that now. It is nice to have a bit longer in the open, though. She still refuses to let Fliss untie her, despite her sneaking desire to find out what the grass feels like between her bare toes, but in her heart of hearts, Tanta isn't worried. She suspects that if the update were going to affect her, it would have done so already.

As the half hour ticks by, her confidence only grows. Aside from a slight chafing where her restraints cut into her wrists and ankles, she feels no different than she did when she left the Brokerage. After fifteen minutes, she gives up worrying entirely and just enjoys the breeze, shockingly cold against her bare skin.

In any other circumstances it would be unpleasant, but right now it's a draught of clear water, sloughing off the dimness and the cramp of four months of living in a cave.

After forty minutes, Tanta reluctantly concedes that the test has gone on long enough, and Fliss takes her back down. Sinking into the depths of the Brokerage is easier, knowing that she'll be leaving it again within the next few hours. In fact, if her trip into the city with Fliss is a success, soon they'll all be able to venture above ground. She can help with the plan – and now that the crew know that, they don't have any more time to waste.

Reet takes an executive taxi straight from the zeppelin to the ICRD, travelling at the highest priority level InTech's traffic management mainframe allows. On the way over, Firent gives her a full report.

<<We had a partial match on facial recognition a week ago, in an alley off Commercial Street,>> he explains. <<We weren't certain it was her, but I've had someone watching the area ever since, and yesterday evening she finally turned up again! We've had so many false alarms – I was starting to think we'd never pick up their trail.>>

Reet knows the feeling. The search for Tanta, Cole and their bandit accomplice has stretched on for so long that it's practically a cold case – this glimpse of Felicity in the city is the first new lead they've had in months. By the time Firent has finished his account, Reet's with him in person, sitting at the round table in her office.

'Good job,' she says.

Firent beams at the command phrase, but then his face falls. 'I'm just sorry she gave us the slip, Director. We were *so* close to finding out where Tanta and Cole are. If I'd been faster with that stun gun...' His brown eyes flick Reet's way – a single, sympathetic glance. She and Firent were never close growing up, but Tanta was his team leader, once, and he knows about Reet's history with her. It's one of the reasons Reet assigned him to the case. Tee was his friend – and she saved his life. He has as much reason as she does to want to bring her in unharmed.

'It wasn't your fault,' Reet tells him, gently. The bandit's escape was a blow, but at least Firent and his team didn't come away empty-handed. 'What have you done with the contact she was meeting?'

'He's in a holding cell,' Firent replies. 'I'll be heading down to question him after this.'

'Alone?'

He nods. 'Tom was hurt in the chase last night, and I asked Gallus to make another sweep of the area around the zeppelin. Just in case there was anything we missed the first thirty times.'

At this, Reet comes to a sudden decision. 'You shouldn't run an interrogation by yourself. I'll come with you.'

Firent's expression reflects the surprise she feels at herself. It's not like her to micromanage her colleagues' work – and it's not what a Director is supposed to do. She's meant to be overseeing the smooth running of the entire ICRD, and given the Thoughtfront crisis, that responsibility is more important now than ever. She shouldn't be concerning herself with the examination of a single suspect. An uneasy part of Reet wonders if she's letting her personal feelings interfere with her work, but she shoves the thought firmly aside. Firent *shouldn't* be running an interrogation alone – that's in the ICRD's procedural regulations – and the rest of his team are either busy or out of action. Besides, the board hired Reet because they wanted things in the ICRD and Residents' Affairs to change, didn't they? She's allowed to do things differently to her predecessors – it's why she's here.

Reet steps out of her office with Firent beside her and this resolution in mind, feeling daring and a little defiant. Douglas is hovering outside her door. It's another surprise. Despite sharing a floor with him, she doesn't see her Co-Director as often as she was expecting to when she took the role – outside of their scheduled check-ins, he spends most of his time in his own room, the smart glass walls turned up to 100% opacity.

'I'll meet you down there,' she instructs Firent, waving him on ahead. Douglas looks inclined to talk, for once, and as keen as she is to pursue this new lead, she needs to brief him on it, too.

'What did you decide to do about that Brokerage tip-off?' he asks her, when they're alone.

'I can fill you in on that at our next catch-up,' Reet says, trying, with difficulty, to suppress her impatience. 'We've found a lead in Tanta and Cole's disappearance – an unaffiliated man who met with one of her accomplices. Firent and I are going to interview him now.'

Douglas scowls. 'Really? After all this time? You seem pleased.'

Reet is confused by the comment. 'Of course I'm pleased. It's an important case.'

'And have you thought about what comes next?'

'What do you mean?'

Douglas leans closer. 'If your lead is any good, there might be a reunion on the cards. No mixed feelings?'

Reet struggles against the urge to recoil. Douglas's breath is on her face, and it's rancid. This close to him, she can see he hasn't been taking care of himself as he ought to. There's a small tear in the shoulder of his tailored suit, like a hairline fracture. The war with Thoughtfront must be taking a greater toll on him than she'd thought.

'Seeing Tanta again would be hard, yes,' she says. 'But dealing with her is part of my job.'

Douglas seems floored by that, as though he was expecting

angry denials, but Reet has no reason to lie to him. 'She's a valuable asset to the corp,' she continues. 'If it's possible to retrieve her, I will.'

'And if it isn't?' Douglas asks, recovering some of his sneering hauteur.

*It* will *be*, Reet thinks. She swallows a snappish retort. Douglas is taunting her, that's all – and the corporate thing to do is to rise above it. 'Then she's a threat to the corporation, Douglas,' she says calmly, meeting his gaze. 'And you know how we deal with threats.'

Reet catches up to Firent in the lobby; they take the lift down to the basement complex together. It's a warren of holding cells and interrogation rooms, accessible from InTech's three most important buildings – the ICRD, the Community Guardianship Office, and the Needle – and so vast that it spans the space between them. Ordinary residents refer to the complex, if forced to talk about it at all, as the windowless rooms, a phrase that made Reet assume it would be dank and airless. She was pleasantly surprised when she joined the ICRD to find that the opposite was the case. The corridors of the sub-basement are clean and white, with overhead lights so bright they almost hurt her eyes.

She and Firent head deep into this labyrinth, striding along hallways and down long, twisting flights of stairs. There are no maps or signs on the walls of the complex – nothing that a detainee could use to orientate themselves – but the pastel-coloured ribbons that run along the floor, walls or ceiling of each passage allow those in the know to navigate it without difficulty. Reet has been here so many times by now that she can find her way by muscle memory alone. When they stop outside a bare, concrete cell, one of hundreds of identical rooms, she doesn't need the pale green line running the length of the walls to tell her that they're on sub-basement level two, block D.

'Do you have any security footage of the meeting?' she asks Firent.

'Not of the handover itself, but a camera caught her fleeing the scene.' There's a soft chime as the video file arrives in Reet's 'scape. 'How do you want to play this?' Firent asks her.

Reet watches the man huddled in the cell through the one-way mirror of the door – his dishevelled clothes, the way he keeps his back pressed up against the far wall – and thinks about it. There are enhanced interrogation suites further down the corridor, rooms that look a bit like dental surgeries, full of needles and pliers, but where no operations are performed. The teams who crew them are diligent, and they rarely come up empty-handed. Turning suspects over to the torturers is usually Douglas's first move, but Reet tends to avoid them – perhaps because she got her start working in an InTech brothel and has seen how effectively intelligence can be gathered through other means. She senses that an enhanced interrogation isn't going to be necessary here, in any case. The man's eyes are darting from side to side, as if measuring the confines of the narrow cell, and his breathing is ragged and shallow. At a guess, Reet would say he's claustrophobic – and his naked fear is something she can exploit without violence.

'Follow my lead,' she tells Firent. 'And try to take up as much space as possible.'

Firent nods and slides back the reinforced glass door. The unaffiliated man's back is braced against the wall as though he's trying to push himself through it. He looks up at them as they step inside and starts.

'You can see me,' he whispers. 'How come you can see me?'

Reet ignores him, nudging the door shut again with her foot. Once it's closed, even she feels the walls press in. The room is like a closet, so small that she and Firent can't stand next to each other without touching.

They take a step forward in lockstep, looming over the man, and he shrinks back. 'Tell me where she went,' Reet says.

'I – I don't—'

Reet moves closer, her feet making contact with the man's knees. His rapid breathing increases. 'Tell. Me. Where. She. Went.'

'I don't know!' the man wails. 'She never told me where she was going.'

This is almost certainly true. There's no reason the bandit would have confided in this man, who was probably just her fence. He's not playing dumb, though, pretending he doesn't know who Reet is talking about, and that's a good sign.

'What did she buy off you?' she asks him, raising her voice.

'C – car parts! She bought car parts. And I swear, I never would've spoken to her if I'd known you wanted her! I just really, really needed the chit. It's like everyone this side of the riverbed has lost their fucking minds. I can't beg, can't even have a conversation, people just look right through me. If I'd known you could *see* me, I ...'

While the man babbles, Reet opens the video file Firent sent her, spooling through it to the moment the bandit flees the alley and zooming in. The package clutched in her hand is small, about the size of a sleeper's router. She flicks a glance at her fellow agent.

'What kind of car parts?' Firent says, cutting the man off mid-flow.

The fence's eyes roll. There's sweat staining the armpits of his T-shirt. 'I don't know. She told me not to open the package – I don't know what was in it.'

Firent raises his eyebrows. 'Then how did you know it was car parts?'

'I had it off another guy. He's a scavenger – hangs out in the scrapyards where they take old InTech cars. I can help you find him!' This last comes out in a moan. The fence looks like he's trying to climb out of his own skin.

Reet assesses him. She doesn't think the man is lying – he's too panicked. She looks at Firent and sees the same conclusion written in his dark eyes.

'If your intel is bad, you know you'll never get out of here,' she says, a warning. The man begins to cry. At that, she finally allows herself to relent. 'Come on,' she says, taking a step back to give him some space. She holds out a hand and helps the shaking man to his feet. There are cushier detainment rooms a few floors above them: larger, more human spaces with tables, beds and chairs, and windows that look out onto the bright white corridors. Reet can question the man in one of those, and if his information pans out, then that's where he'll stay – for now, at least.

She can't let him go – InTech needs to be protected, even from petty criminals like him – but if he helps her, there's no reason she can't help him in turn. The man said he dealt with the bandit because he needed the money; with an Inscape of his own and a place in the corporation, he'll never want for anything again. She pings a message to AviLife, InTech's medical subsidiary, to schedule the surgery. Afterwards, she'll find him a position in a secure sleeper facility, somewhere he can be productive and useful. She makes a mental note to look for one above ground, in the open air – no mines or confined spaces. She has no desire to be any crueller than her assignment demands.

# Chapter 6

Once he is in the larger detainment room, relief loosens the man's tongue. He becomes positively voluble, and although most of the details he has to offer aren't of much use, after talking to him for forty-five minutes Reet and Firent have managed to assemble a list of the scavenger's regular haunts, along with a rough physical description. Reet locks him in when they leave, but leaves the window open as wide as she can without creating a security risk.

From the basement complex, they head back to Reet's office, where the rest of the morning is eaten up by calls to the various monitoring subdivisions of the ICRD and Residents' Affairs – the gate station, the resident data collection teams, the internal surveillance office – to request priority searches through the camera feeds closest to the locations the fence gave them.

Reet has to fight a nagging sense of unease while she does this. It's been a while since she's devoted this much time to a single assignment and she's uncomfortably aware of all the other things she ought to be focusing on. Duties and commitments flit through her thoughts, distracting her. There's a report waiting for her from Dr Friend on his efforts to introduce Harlow 2.0 to the MindEyes of captured enemy operatives; the ICRD's drone taskforce has a strike planned against a Thoughtfront generator later this evening. She has alerts set up to warn her of any new developments in the war – cameras monitoring the movements of the peacekeepers, surveillance drones sweeping the skies above the city and the Unaffiliated Zone – but that doesn't stop Reet from worrying. The situation with Thoughtfront is on a knife-edge; InTech may be wearing the other corp down, but it's still a military powerhouse. There's no question that, at some point, it's going to strike back – and hard. It's only a matter of when.

Which is all the more reason, she reminds herself, to pursue this investigation now, before Thoughtfront makes its play. Reet isn't sure whether Tanta and Cole are still working with the corporation across the riverbed directly – if they ever were – but she can't rule it out. Either way, she wants them both off the chessboard *before* all hell breaks loose.

After three dull hours, they get a hit on their description from a scrap-metal facility in the southwest of the city, which gives them their first real glimpse of their suspect. He's a white man, thin almost to the point of gauntness, with black hair and a straggly beard. With a photo to feed into InTech's facial recognition software, their search becomes simpler. The face that took them hours to locate is uploaded to the system and red-flagged. Now that every camera on InTech's side of the riverbed is looking out for him, it's not long before they get another alert: their man was seen leaving a residential street in the suburbs to the east forty minutes ago.

This is the point at which Reet allows herself to get excited. Finding proof of the scavenger's existence was heartening, but it's only now that she feels she's truly on the man's trail. They know where he was less than an hour ago, and as she spools through the security footage of the street over the last few weeks, she becomes increasingly confident that they know more than that.

'This camera catches him coming and going almost every day,' she says, viewsharing the relevant shots with Firent. 'And according to occupancy records, there are several empty properties at the end of the road.'

'You think he's squatting in one of them?' Firent asks.

Reet grins. 'It's time we made a house call.'

They arm themselves with handguns from the kit department and then order an ICRD cruiser, parking it a few minutes' walk from their destination so as not to alert the scavenger to their presence when he returns. The street where the man was spotted is a cul-de-sac that terminates in a crumbling wall. Its red-brick townhouses, with their gabled roofs and walled gardens, must have looked imposing once, but their glory is faded now. There's a pay-as-you-go park opposite the row of buildings; its AR paywall has malfunctioned, and it has filled up with fly-tipped junk and old syringes.

The homes at the top of the street have been portioned up into flats; Reet can see a few curtained windows and AR skins testifying to the presence of residents – probably InTech's poorest wagers. The further down she and Firent go, the more dilapidated the buildings become. The ones at the end of the road are visibly falling apart, their windows broken and their wooden fascias sagging. They glance through the gaping doorways but see no signs of occupancy.

The scavenger's residence turns out to be the last house on the street, noticeable at once by the fact that it's in better repair than its neighbours. Someone has removed the broken glass from the windows and replaced it with wooden boards, carefully nailed into place. The door looks new, too.

<<Circle around the back,>> Reet instructs Firent. <<If there are any accomplices inside, we want to cut them off.>>

Firent nods, then scales the wall at the end of the road, making for the back garden. Reet approaches the front door, which is locked, but not well. From the give she feels when she tries it, she'd guess that the bolt holding it in place is home-made. She jerks the handle down sharply, pulling it towards her and leaning on it with her full weight, and feels something snap. After that, it swings open without a sound.

The interior is dark, lit only by the few slivers of light able to creep through the gaps in the boards. Reet steps into the hallway, easing the door shut behind her, and listens. Nothing. She starts her search, moving slowly and letting the dust muffle her footfalls. The house is tall and narrow; stairs wind up and down its centre, leading to attic and basement.

The basement is empty of everything except litter and dust. On the ground floor, there's a bathroom and a kitchen. They've both been gutted, the toilet and white goods torn out to discourage squatters, but someone has set up a portable stove connected to a gas cannister on one of the kitchen's cracked countertops. Reet is checking the cupboards when the creak of a floorboard behind her sends her whirling around. Firent is standing in the doorway.

<<Anything?>> she asks him.

He nods. <<There are some things on the second floor you'll want to see.>>

She follows him up the stairs, which turn at sharp angles onto landings opening onto other rooms, all dim and silent. At the top of the house, there's a breeze coming from an open window in a room at the back, and light that comes as a shock to Reet's eyes after the darkness of the rest of the building. She steps inside, blinking rapidly.

<<Jackpot,>> she sends. <<Nice work, Firent.>>

The room is sparsely furnished, and every available surface is covered in car parts. Hydrogen fuel tanks line the back wall, there's a stack of tyres in one corner, and a bookcase by the door is filled with smaller components. Reet crosses to it, examining the shelves of gears, bulbs and sprockets. Whatever Felicity bought from the fence was about this size.

'I can't see why the bandit would come out of hiding to buy any of this stuff,' Firent murmurs.

'She, Tanta and Cole fled the city in a stolen tactical vehicle,' Reet points out. 'Maybe they needed to make repairs?'

Firent frowns. 'But most of these parts they could have found in another corp's territory or scavenged from a pre-Meltdown vehicle in the UZ. Why take the risk of coming into our side of the city for them?'

That's a very good point. Reet thinks about it. 'She must have been searching for a part that only we produce,' she replies, at length.

She blinks an image capture of the bookshelf, which she sends to Traffic & Vehicle Management along with an urgent query: <<Are any of these components unique to InTech's vehicles?>>

It's a matter of minutes before one of the on-duty mechanics comes back with a reply. <<Only the licence chip, Director!>> After Reet's baffled pause, the woman adds: <<The device at the end of the top shelf.>>

Reet reaches for the top shelf and lifts down a black cube the size of her thumbnail. <<What does it do?>> she asks.

<<A vehicle's licence chip is what identifies it as part of the InTech fleet,>> the mechanic answers cheerfully.

A chill runs the length of Reet's back. <<Have any been reported stolen?>>

There's a pause. <<I'll check, Director, but it is unlikely. No InTech vehicle can function without one, so we would know. The one in your image capture is from a retired taxi – see the ID number lasered into its base?>>

Reet is not reassured by this assessment. <<Check anyway,>> she sends. She turns to Firent. 'I think Felicity was here for one of these,' she says, showing him the chip. 'If she swapped out the licence chip in their stolen car for a clean one, she could drive it back into the city without being red-flagged.'

'What do you think she's planning?'

'I'm not sure,' Reet says grimly, 'but I'd bet it's not anything—'

She cuts herself off mid-sentence. A sound has interrupted her, one that makes the hairs on the back of her neck stand on end: the click of a latch.

Reet sprints from the room and barrels down the stairs, taking them three at a time. The impact when she hits the bare boards of the ground floor hallway makes the house shake, but she's no longer trying to conceal her presence here. The scavenger tried the front door, which means he's already discovered the broken lock. Sure enough, when she wrenches the door open the man is already halfway back down the street. He's walking with the forced nonchalance of someone trying to avoid suspicion, but Reet recognises him immediately by his dark hair and beard. As she emerges from the house, he bolts.

It's a short chase. Reet may be a Director now, but she still trains in the ICRD's gym most evenings, in case she's ever needed in the field. She puts on a burst of speed, pulling ahead of the man. As he swerves to avoid her, she grabs his arm, making him stagger, then drives him to the ground, holding him in place with the weight of her body. He struggles, so she hits him in the head with the flat of her hand – once, then again.

'This is the ICRD!' she roars. 'Stay down!'

Reet has always been large for her age, and years of training have given her the physique of a heavyweight wrestler; after the second blow, the man doesn't resist.

Firent's at her side a moment later, taking hold of the man's other arm and cuffing him. Together, the two of them haul him to his feet and push him up against the wall of the nearest house. He's shaking, and there's blood oozing from a cut on his cheek where Reet slammed him into the pavement. She takes the licence chip from her pocket and shoves it into the man's face.

'Did you steal one of these yesterday?' she shouts.

'Wh – what?' The man's eyes are unfocused.

'I need its ID number – now!' When the scavenger only stares at her, blank-eyed with panic, she shakes him. 'The number lasered into the base. Tell me what it is!'

'I don't remember,' he stammers, but Reet can see the lie in the furtive way he glances to the side.

'I'll find it either way,' she says, putting her face close to his and dropping her voice to a growl, 'but if you make me search through all the scrap yards in the city for reports of suspicious activity, you'll stew in the windowless rooms every minute I'm looking. And when I'm done, I'll ship you off to a mining facility.' There are times when the openness of her features can be an advantage; Reet lets the truth of the threat show in her eyes, the set line of her lips.

The man quails. 'EX027V9,' he says. 'Please,' he adds, 'I didn't think you'd miss it. It was about to be retired.'

Reet's body goes rigid. She looks at Firent, and sees her own horror reflected in his face. She doesn't know about the rest of it, but the 'EX' in the ID string the scavenger just reeled off is a designation in common use throughout the corporation: it stands for 'Executive'. It was no ordinary taxi this man cannibalised, but one reserved for InTech's Directors alone. She can't think of one good reason why the bandit would be trying to pass her car off as an executive vehicle, but she can come up with any number of bad ones.

She sends the ID on to the mechanic at Traffic & Vehicle Management. <<I need you to revoke this vehicle's gate clearance urgently,>> she sends. << It's been stolen.>>

<<Stolen?>> the mechanic replies. She sounds calm,

unconcerned. <<Are you sure, Director? According to our scanners, it has just returned to the city. It came in through the Outer Gate half an hour ago.>>

<<Where is it?>> Reet demands.

She's already running back to where she and Firent parked, dragging the scavenger along with her. Whatever Tanta and her accomplices are planning, it's happening right now. Reet may already be too late to prevent it.

It's a full minute before the mechanic finally replies, and when she does, she confirms Reet's worst fears. <<It is heading for Inspire Labs, Director.>>

# Chapter 7

It feels unutterably strange to Tanta to be back in the city. In reality, she's only been gone a little over four months, but the absence has felt far longer to live through, stretched out in her mind to cover aeons of experience and change. She was a different person the last time she walked these streets: more conflicted, less sure of herself, still trying desperately to reconcile desires that she knew, even then, were splitting her in two.

That struggle has been resolved, at last. She has given up the part of herself that still thrilled to the echoes of her lost Harlow Programming, the part that wanted nothing more than to stay in the city and serve her corp as an ICRD agent. In the process, she has been transformed into something new. It's a strange metamorphosis, as most are. She's gone from being a model Corporate Ward to the kind of person CorpWards are warned about; from an agent to the traitor that agents hunt.

Given her new status as a fugitive and a turncoat, it's fitting that Tanta makes her return to the city in the dark. She and Fliss are hunkered down in the back of the car, crouched in the footwell and covered with one of Jeanie's AR skins. From the inside, it's like hiding under a tarpaulin, coarse and airless. From without, they're completely invisible. The car's windows are tinted, but even if a guardian were to open the back door for an inspection, they'd see nothing but a clear floor and empty seats.

As long as the skin doesn't glitch, that is. Tanta tries not to let herself think of what the consequences will be if *that* happens. For now, at least, they are concealed, and racing through the city at a speed reserved for InTech's executive cabs.

Tanta may not be able to see the city, but she knows where she is well enough, by the smoothness of the road beneath the tires, the sounds drifting, muffled, through the car's windows. She knows this place the same way she knows herself, or (a shudder runs through her) Reet. It's a part of her code, the deep code of her being that existed before her Inscape and the Harlow Programme were ever installed in her brain. For the first minute after they pass through the Outer Gate, she allows herself simply to bathe in the feeling of being back, being home. Then, she turns her mind to what comes next.

Beside her, Fliss shifts a little under the cloak, stretching out cramped limbs. The bandit has a sheaf of flex cuffs hanging from the belt at her hip, and the motion makes them butt uncomfortably against Tanta's thigh. They're crammed together in the tight space of the footwell, but they have to be in order for the AR cloak to cover them both.

'The checkpoint's in about five minutes,' Fliss murmurs. She's so close that Tanta can feel her breath brushing her cheek.

The checkpoints are a new security measure since the autumn, an additional way for InTech to control the traffic through its part of the city. Tanta has never seen them for herself, but Fliss has warned her what to expect. They take the form of temporary gates bisecting the streets around the centre. In more peaceful times, cars would pass straight through most gates unimpeded, only slowing for safety's sake. Now, every vehicle must stop and submit to a visual inspection. Suspicious ones are opened and, in some cases, searched.

There's no reason to think that will happen to them. They made it through the Outer Gate without issues, their car looks the part, and most importantly of all, they have the licence chip – the technological shibboleth that allows their car safe passage through InTech's scanners. All the same, Tanta tenses as they approach the checkpoint, unable to tear her mind from all the things that could go wrong.

The AR skin concealing them could fail, or the signal blocking tech that Cole rigged up to hide the digital signatures of the car's passengers. Something as trivial as a malfunction in Cole's jerry-rigged AI driver could make them an object of suspicion – and the suspicion of a single guardian could be all it would take to expose them.

Tanta tries to relax, to send her mind on ahead of her to the next step in the plan, but she's unused to being this helpless. Give her a building to infiltrate or an enemy operative to fight, and she'd be in her element; this strategy requires nothing from her right now except crouching, silent and still, in the bottom of the car, yet she finds it far more daunting than active combat. She shuffles sideways, trying to escape the sensation of the flex cuffs scratching against her leg.

'Stop fidgeting,' Fliss hisses.

'I will if you stop poking me,' she fires back.

It's unlike her to snap, but she's on edge. It's not just the silence and the waiting – it's also the fact that so much of this plan depends on Cole and Yas, who can't even come with to help carry it out. Tanta trusts both of them, but she's not used to her plans being this front-loaded. Neither of them are on-hand to make repairs or devise workarounds; she and Fliss are at the mercy of designs made weeks ago, with very little room to improvise if things go wrong.

All of this goes against the grain for Tanta, but she's not so arrogant as to really wish she was doing this by herself. It's only thanks to Cole's understanding of InTech's cybersecurity that they've made it this far. Sneaking into the city by her wits alone might be more her style, but it would get her killed.

Thinking of Cole, she touches her earpiece. 'You two doing all right?' she asks.

There's a pause, then Cole's voice comes through. 'We're fine. Let us know when you're through, OK?' The line is crackly, but the concern in his tone is unmistakable.

The thought of him and Yas, monitoring their progress from the Brokerage's control room, makes Tanta feel a little better.

The car slows as it nears the checkpoint, then stops completely. Tanta takes a breath, holding herself as still as a specimen in a jar. There's no sound of voices – the guardians must be communicating via MindChat – but she hears their footsteps approaching. They pause just outside, and they stay there a long time. The seconds turn into minutes, the wait stretching out for far longer than it did on their way through the Outer Gate. Fliss tenses, her eyes darting towards the window. Tanta touches her arm, raising her eyebrows in a silent question: *what's going on?* The bandit shakes her head a fraction, her expression drawn. Whatever is happening here, this clearly isn't normal.

The silence outside grows heavier and more oppressive. Tanta can almost hear the guardians breathing, separated from them by nothing more than the tinted glass of the window and the razor-thin barrier of the AR skin.

Then there's the *beep* of a scanner, and just like that, they're through. The low rumble of the car's engine restarts and they roll onwards. Tanta and Fliss exchange glances, united for once in sheer, legs-to-water relief. They don't speak again until the car slows for its first stop, and then the bandit offers Tanta a rare smile.

'Good luck out there,' she says. 'I'll see you at the lab.'

Tanta returns the grin. Now that her part in the plan is

upon her, her fear evaporates. This is the kind of work she's good at. And after all, she's on her home turf. She ducks out from under the AR cloak, opens the door, and slips out into the cold evening.

It helps that this step of the plan is probably the easiest part. Tanta hits the ground running, not needing to glance to left or right to get her bearings. She's been over this dozens of times, drilled in what she needs to do by Fliss on the drive from the Brokerage. She emerges from the car in a narrow, unlit alley, hemmed in on both sides by the brooding backs of warehouses. She's in the southwest of the city, five minutes' drive from Inspire Labs.

She tucks herself into the shadows and waits.

The real executive taxi arrives right on schedule, sliding around the corner of the street in near silence. Its windows are tinted, much like those of their own, stolen vehicle, but Tanta knows it is empty from Fliss's recon. It's on its way to pick someone up, but it's never going to arrive. Gingerly, she opens the pouch on her belt and takes out its contents, careful not to cut herself. The jagged shards of metal are matte black, so they do not catch the light as she scatters them across the road. Once they've landed, they're almost invisible, misshapen lumps of darkness that blend with the deeper darkness of the tarmac. The car meets the caltrops head-on.

There's a sound like a gunshot, followed by the screech of rubber as the taxi's emergency brake engages. It wobbles, but does not veer off-course – the AI within it is too quick for that. It doesn't matter: the car's tyres are shredded. It's not going anywhere in a hurry. After a reflective pause while the car's systems assess the extent of the damage, its wheels turn to the left, and it drifts towards the pavement, crunching over the debris on the road.

Tanta meets it before it reaches the kerb, unfolding a slim length of metal wire from the pocket of her coat. She jams it into the space at the bottom of the window, levering it with expert precision until she has popped the taxi's locking mechanism. Once the door is open, she climbs inside and surveys the AR menu on the dashboard. Left to itself, the car will soon begin broadcasting its location to InTech's Traffic & Vehicle Management department, along with footage of the crash, but she's not going to let that happen.

If Cole were here, he'd be able to hack the car's interface, disable its communication systems, and delete any footage of Tanta captured by its dash cam, all without leaving a trace of his presence. Without the benefit of his technical expertise, Tanta is forced to fall back on a less elegant solution. She uses her wire to jimmy up the dashboard and digs around in the entrails beneath it until she's found what she needs. She yanks out the car's core processor and memory card, along with a spray of arterial wires, dumps both out onto the pavement, and stamps on them.

That done, she gives the crash site one last look over, checking for anything she's missed. When she's satisfied, she takes off running. She can't stick around to admire a job well done: the first resident to come across the wreck will likely call for assistance. It won't be long before a roadside repair crew turn up, and when they see what's happened, they'll alert the community guardians.

Which is all to the good, as far as Tanta's concerned. Let the guardians puzzle over who caused this crash for as long as they like: it will be an excellent distraction from what she and Fliss are going to do next.

Fliss is even more nervous than Tanta during the long drive into the city, though for different reasons. The last time she was crammed into a space this small and airless she almost passed out from terror, and although she's more in control this time around, the panic-tinged memories still crowd in on her in the darkness, making it hard to breathe. She's not sure she trusts the machine that's driving the car, either. To give credit where it's due, though, it does seem to know where it's going. When she slows to a stop again, five minutes after Tanta got out, Fliss pokes her head out from under the AR skin to find she's exactly where she needs to be.

It has grown dark while she was on the road, but she's loitered outside Inspire Labs for so many hours by now, night and day, that she'd know the compound from its silhouette alone. She's bang on time, too. As the car pulls up, the heavy gate at the front of the compound swings open, and a white-haired figure steps through. Fliss smiles, touching her earpiece to let the rest of the crew know that the mark has arrived...

And then the smile drops right off her face, because the old man walking towards her isn't alone. 'Tanta,' she hisses, 'the doc has someone with him!'

'A guardian?' Tanta asks, instantly on her guard.

Fliss squints at the second man, assessing him. He's carrying a coffee cup in one hand, a briefcase in the other. 'An... assistant, I think,' she says. 'He's holding the doc's stuff.'

Fliss swears under her breath. Sonia never mentioned Doctor Friend taking anyone with him to his weekly meetings at the Needle. The plan was that Fliss would restrain the doc once he was safely locked inside the signal-shielded car, collect Tanta, then hightail it out of the city before anyone in the corporation even realised they were there. An extra person introduces a complicating factor into that neat little scheme, and she doesn't like that at all. At best, this assistant is an inconvenient eye-witness. At worst, he might realise that something is up and try to raise the alarm, and then they'd really be in trouble.

She risks another glance through the window before ducking

85

back under the AR skin. The two men have stopped to talk a few feet from gate, but the doc is looking towards the car with a purposeful expression. 'What's our play here?' she asks.

She's waiting on Tanta's reply when another voice pipes up in her ear. 'What does he look like? The intern?'

It's Cole. Fliss blinks. 'Uh, tall. Light brown skin. Dark hair. What's that got to do with—'

'You need to take him with you.' There's an authority in Cole's tone that Fliss has never heard before. Instinctively, she feels her own obstinacy rise to meet it.

'I don't *need* to do anything. Tanta and I are the ones risking our necks here, so unless you're planning on driving over yourself—'

'You don't understand,' Cole interjects. 'That's Neal Ortega!'

If Cole was hoping this would clarify matters for Fliss, it hasn't worked. She has a vague memory of him mentioning a Neal before, but the name means nothing to her. '*Who?*'

'Cole, even if it *is* Neal, we're not here for him,' Tanta cuts in. 'I know you want to do right by him, but we can't risk the success of the plan for that.'

There isn't time for this. 'Who the fuck is Neal?' Fliss snarls.

In reply, both Tanta and Cole try to speak at once:

'It doesn't matter.'

'If it wasn't for him, we would never have learnt about Harlow 2.0 in the first place!'

Fliss swipes at her earpiece; they're shouting, and it's making her uninjured ear throb.

'We can't leave him with Dr Friend,' Cole insists. 'Not when we have a chance to rescue him.'

'*We* don't,' Fliss says pointedly. 'I'm still flying solo here, and unless I get some backup sharpish—'

'I'm almost there,' Tanta pants. She sounds like she's running. 'Two minutes.'

The click of the car's automatic lock disengaging forestalls Fliss's reply.

Jeanie's invisibility cloak doesn't affect Fliss at all – she doesn't have any headware to be fooled by it – but Cole has told her how it works, and what its limits are. The visual trickery that hides its wearers from view breaks down under close inspection. In other words, once Neal and the doc get into the car, there's a strong chance she'll be rumbled. In the scratchy darkness of the cloak, Fliss pulls one of the flex cuffs from her belt. If they spot her, she'll be ready.

There's a yawning sound and a gust of cold air as the front passenger door swings open. An instant later, the seat creaks back, and Fliss feels it pressing against her knees.

From outside, a too-cheerful voice says, 'Your coffee, Director.'

'Thank you, Neal,' comes the reply.

*Now shut the door,* Fliss wills silently. *Shut the door and then I've got you right where I want you, you old—*

'Director,' Neal says, voice taut with alarm, 'there is something behind—'

Here goes nothing. Before the intern can finish his warning, Fliss flings off the cloak and leaps forward, the flex cuff stretched between her hands. She lunges for the passenger seat, where Dr Friend is just beginning to turn around. As his eyes widen, she wraps the cuff around his neck, threads it through one of the struts that support the headrest behind him, and pulls it tight. The doc makes a choked, gargling sound and for an instant, Fliss thinks she's overdone it and cut off his air supply. But he's just straining to free himself: as he sags back in his seat – his coffee cup falling from his slack grasp and spilling in the footwell – she sees a slight give in the cuff, leaving him just room enough to breathe.

She scrambles into the driver's seat and leans across the doc's gasping form. The assistant has dropped Dr Friend's briefcase, his expression open and horrified.

'Neal, right?' she says. 'Pleased to meet you. Now get in the car, or I'll—'

The rest of her threat is drowned out as Neal starts to scream. It's the most piercing sound Fliss has ever heard coming from a human throat – unnaturally loud and shrill. The man's mouth widens and widens. The sound – and the sight – makes the hairs on Fliss's arms stand on end. She reaches to slam the door closed and get out of here, but Neal's hand shoots out and grabs it too, his knuckles turning white with the force of his grip. At the same time, his inarticulate alarum resolves into words.

'Director Friend is being abducted! I require emergency assistance!'

Tanta sprints towards Inspire Labs, the pounding of her feet on the pavement keeping time with the hammering of her pulse in her ears. She's powerfully glad that she intercepted the real taxi so close to its destination. She'll be with Fliss in under a minute now, but she has a terrible feeling that won't be soon enough. She hasn't heard anything from the bandit since her last, panicked transmission cut off mid-sentence; though Tanta has continued to hail her at intervals as she dashes through the city streets, there's nothing on the line now but static.

As she reaches the last turn before the compound, another sound imposes itself on her attention: screaming. She puts on a burst of speed, ignoring the protests of her tight chest and aching legs and skidding around the corner.

The scene before her is almost like a still life. The fake taxi is parked just in front of the compound's gate, its front passenger door half-open. Clustered on the pavement outside it are half a dozen people – wagers from Inspire Labs, or passersby, Tanta isn't sure – all converging on the door, and all shrieking like they're possessed.

'Director Friend is being abducted! I require emergency assistance!'

Despite its forward motion and the noise it's making, there's something about the crowd that seems eerily static. Every face Tanta can see is frozen in the same expression of horror, as though the eyes locked on the car are all animated by a single mind. At the centre of this tableau is Neal Ortega. He's holding the passenger door open with one hand, arm braced against someone inside, and summoning his Array with the other.

Tanta takes all of this in over the space of two frantic seconds, still sprinting towards the taxi. It's a disturbing sight; she thought she was prepared for what Harlow 2.0 did to people, but she wasn't expecting *this*. It's clear at a glance that their plan to escape the city by stealth is in tatters. Neal must be hailing someone on MindChat – probably the emergency line to the community guardians – and the screaming is already drawing the attention of more people. Through the open gate to Inspire Labs, Tanta can see wagers spilling from offices and peering out of windows, their mouths and eyes widening as the crowd's alarm transfers itself to them.

The guardians will be here within minutes and before that, their getaway car will be overwhelmed by the growing mob of programmed residents. They'll drag Dr Friend to safety – and Tanta doesn't like to think what they'll do to Fliss. She clenches her fists. She has to get to her, but she can't just fight her way through these people as though they're a squad of hostile operatives. They're InTech residents – people she's sworn to protect – and none of them are in their right minds.

She draws level with the crowd and seizes one of them – a woman in her sixties – by the collar of her winter coat. A comparatively light tug throws her off-balance, and she falls, landing on the ground startled, but unharmed. As she sees Tanta, she breaks off her monotonous cries of alarm.

'You're not supposed to be here,' she says.

Tanta ignores her, darting forward to tackle the next man. Already, doors are flying open in the houses across the street, the residents inside roused from their evening routines and running barefoot towards the disturbance. There's no time to be gentle; she shoves the man in the chest with the flat of her hands, hoping she doesn't break any ribs. He staggers – and then, to her immense surprise, lunges forward and grabs her arm. His eyes, which were fixed on the taxi, have swivelled her way, the expression of horror on his face transmuting into something else.

'You're not supposed to be here!' he shouts.

The cry draws the attention of others in the group. Heads snap around to stare at Tanta, their eyes narrowing and their mouths twisting into identical scowls of suspicion and disgust.

Rattled, Tanta breaks the man's inexpert hold and pushes him again, harder this time. He's right, of course – she has no more right to be here than Fliss does – but how have these people identified her as an outsider so quickly? Her would-be attacker stumbles into the man behind him and they both go sprawling. Tanta leaps over them and kicks another woman in the back of the knees, making her legs buckle. Ahead of her, two residents have made it to Neal's side. They reach through the gap in the door, still screaming their baleful warnings.

A fist emerges from within the taxi and punches the man on the right in the chest. He curls in on himself, retching, then crumples to the pavement.

'Back the fuck up!' Fliss shouts. 'I have your Director in here, and I swear I'll kill him if you come any closer!'

Tanta grabs the second man in a chokehold, dragging him backward. While he's gasping for breath, she ducks down and into Fliss's line of sight. The bandit is leaning across Dr Friend – who is whey-faced and shaking – and hanging onto the passenger door with one hand.

'You took your time!' she growls.

'Let go,' Tanta says, raising her voice over the clamour of the swelling crowd.

Fliss frowns at her – and then realisation dawns. She does as Tanta asks and the door flies open. Caught off-guard by the sudden change in resistance, Neal staggers, releasing his grip. At the same moment, Tanta rises from her crouch and drives her shoulder into the intern's stomach. She hears the air leave Neal's lungs, a huff of pain and surprise. He doubles over, mouth still working though he's lost the voice to scream. Tanta pivots out from under him as he collapses, catches him under the armpits, and drags him clear of the door, which Fliss pulls closed with a final thump.

In the second's grace she's bought herself, Tanta scans the crowd. Fighting her way to the car took less than half a minute, but each person she incapacitated has already been replaced by three more. The wagers she saw inside Inspire Labs have almost reached the gate of the compound, their faces contorted into masks of outrage and horror.

The sensible thing to do now would be to leave the intern curled up on the pavement and get the hell out of here, but Tanta thinks of Cole's plea, and her resolve fails her. Neal helped Cole at a time when she couldn't; she's not going to be the one to tell him that they had to leave his friend behind.

She hauls him towards the back of the car, an exertion she's sure she'll feel the effects of later in her back and shoulders. Fliss comes to help, opening the back door and taking hold of Neal's arms to pull him inside.

He's halfway in when the screaming – the shrieks of 'Director Friend is being abducted!' and 'I require emergency assistance!'

now varied with the occasional 'You're not supposed to be here!' – reaches a new pitch of intensity. Tanta turns: the wagers are pouring out onto the street, a mass of bodies converging on her. She and Fliss are moments away from being overwhelmed.

With a strength and speed born of pure adrenaline, she grabs Neal's weakly kicking legs and bundles them into the back of the car. She scrambles in after him, sprawling on top of him in an ungraceful heap, and pulls the door shut, seconds before the vanguard of the crowd breaks against the taxi like a human tidal wave. The click of the automatic lock engaging is the sweetest sound Tanta has ever heard. The residents hammer against the glass and pull on the door, wide-eyed and shrieking, but cannot force their way inside.

'Ready to go?' Fliss pants.

Tanta nods. 'The AI driver won't be able to handle this, though. We're going to have to do it the old-fashioned way. You think you can manage that?'

Fliss grimaces. 'I suppose I'll have to.'

She clambers into the driver's seat and starts preparing the car, levering up the panels in the dashboard and floor that conceal its manual steering apparatus. Tanta, for her part, and with some discomfort, prepares to restrain and gag the thrashing Neal, who is still keening his cry for help in an unnerving monotone.

She's securing his hands when a voice from a loudspeaker rings out across the street – one that pins her in place like an insect on a board.

'Tanta and Felicity! Put your hands up and exit the vehicle!'

It's Reet.

Reet is barely aware of the journey to Inspire Labs. She spends the ride buried in the intelligence feeds on her Array, monitoring traffic alerts and security footage. When the distress calls start coming in, she has the Senior Call Handler on duty in the

Community Guardianship Office patch them through to her 'scape, so she can take them herself. There are too many for her to handle alone, though, and she's forced to route them back to the CommGuard in short order. Dozens, if not hundreds, of residents are sounding the alarm all at once, and they're all saying the same thing:

'Director Friend is being abducted. I require emergency assistance!'

Reet is so absorbed in monitoring the situation – coordinating with the CommGuard, listening to incident reports, watching the live feeds from Inspire Labs' security cameras – that it takes her completely outside of herself. Her body may be in an ICRD cruiser, racing across town, but she has run on ahead of it. She's floating above the abduction-in-progress, as intangible as her own Array, watching it through a hundred eyes at once.

When her body catches up with her mind, the car screeching to a halt in the middle of the road outside the compound's gate, she's surprised to find that there are tears in her eyes. She's curled forward in her seat, a ball of tension, her nails digging so hard into the palms of her hands that it's only with a conscious effort that she can unclench them at all.

She realises, in a distant kind of way, that she is terrified. It's not just that InTech's best research scientist is in danger. It's not just that this is the first real test of her leadership as Co-Director of the ICRD. It's that all the footage she's seen, all the eyewitnesses she's spoken to, agreed that there are two hostiles on the scene. Two. And Reet knows who the second one is. Up till now, catching Tanta has been a hazy prospect, an objective marker far in the distance. Now she's here, in Reet's city, and whatever happens next, one of them is going to end up doing something they can't take back.

Firent touches her arm. From the look in his eyes, she gets the impression that this isn't the first time he's tried to get her attention. She ignores the concern in his expression, drawing the handgun from her belt and nodding to him to do the same. They burst out of the car together, one on each side, taking cover behind its open doors.

They've pulled up less than a metre in front of the stolen executive taxi, which is parked directly outside the gate of Inspire Labs. The pavement beside it is filled with shouting residents, all doing their part to try and recover Dr Friend or raise the alarm, but Reet screens them out, focusing her attention on the car. Its tinted windows are too dark to see through; she narrows her eyes, zooming in on the windscreen, but can make out nothing inside.

She turns back to the stream of data pouring through her Array, checking the location of the backup teams she's called for. The closest of them is still two minutes away, which is a lot further out than Reet would like. She instructs them to block the far end of the road as soon as they arrive.

<<What do we do?>> Firent pings her. <<Do we shoot?>>

<<No!>> Reet raps back, holding up a hand to reinforce the point. <<We don't have a clear enough view – we might hit Dr Friend, or a resident.>>

She accesses the cruiser's PA system. 'Tanta and Felicity!' she shouts. 'Put your hands up and exit the vehicle!'

As if her warning is a signal, the stolen taxi thrums into life. The residents crowded outside it scatter as it jerks forward, then right. Reet has leapt back into her own car before the taxi has completed its U-turn. While Firent jumps in beside her, she jabs a finger to her temple, accessing the traffic management mainframe's virtual helpdesk.

<<I need priority-level alpha-speed clearance for a pursuit,>> she sends.

<<A directorial authorisation code is required,>> the VI informs her.

<<2862,>> Reet barks.

<<What is the ID of the vehicle you wish to pursue?>>

She grinds her teeth in frustration as she reels it off. Tanta's car is already screeching away down the road, going much faster than an InTech taxi should be able to. The fugitives must have figured out a way to jailbreak the car's AI to exceed citywide speed restrictions – doubtless with Cole's help.

As soon as Reet's done, her cruiser lurches into motion, locking onto the signal from the car's stolen licence chip and following it. They speed after Tanta so quickly that Reet is plastered to the back of her seat. It's the fastest she's ever travelled in her life; the TMM usually keeps most traffic in the city moving at an even thirty miles per hour.

She darts a glance at Firent. His face is pale, his hands balled into fists.

<<Wind your window down,>> she instructs him. <<Try to take out their tyres.>>

He nods an acknowledgement of the order, though he looks like he's trying not to vomit as he carries it out. Reet does likewise, but it's a vain effort. Her first shot takes out a wing mirror. Her second doesn't even come that close. And then the car's lost to sight, spinning away up a pedestrianised side road that shouldn't even be accessible to vehicles.

Their own car follows, matching the speed and recklessness of their quarry. Residents stumble back out of the cars' paths, or freeze in shock as the vehicles swerve around them; Reet has to resist the urge to cover her eyes at each near miss. It gets worse: when they reach the end of the footpath, Tanta's car veers right, careening onto a busy main road.

Reet's fists clench. For a heart-stopping instant, she's staring down the barrel of a lane of rush-hour traffic, nothing but the cars' crash sensors to save her and Firent from becoming a sticky mess in a wreck of twisted metal. Then their own car swings across into the left-hand lane, hot on Tanta's heels. The TMM shunts the other cars on the road aside, clearing a space between Reet and Firent's cab and the one they're chasing.

Reet reconnects to the traffic management mainframe's virtual helpdesk. <<Halt all traffic on the road ahead,>> she instructs. There's nothing she can do to stop the stolen car itself – its AI has been isolated from InTech's systems – but she can hamper its progress.

The TMM complies, the cars in front of them rolling slowly to a stop. In response, Tanta's taxi begins to slalom, weaving between the stationary vehicles in a way that makes Reet's stomach lurch.

<<We're losing them!>> Firent sends.

He's right. The stolen car is pulling further and further ahead, despite the TMM's best efforts to facilitate their pursuit.

<<Not for long,>> Reet replies. <<They won't be able to get past the checkpoints.>>

Tanta and Felicity may be able to push their home-brewed AI to ridiculous speeds, but now that their vehicle's gate clearance has been revoked, they're trapped in the centre. If they try to drive through one of the gates, their car's AI will be scuttled. If they take their chances hiding out in the city, Reet will find them.

She checks the map on her Array. There's a checkpoint at the end of this road, and at their current speed, they'll reach it in under a minute. The two cars sweep around a bend, and Reet can see it looming over them. There aren't many people driving into the centre this late in the afternoon, but on the left-hand side of the road, the TMM has halted a queue of cars that were on their way out, completely blocking the street ahead.

Reet nods to herself. 'We've got them,' she says. 'Be ready to move in on the car the moment they stop. Our top priority has to be retrieving Dr Friend and making sure he's—'

As she speaks, Tanta's car reaches the back of the queue. It swerves across into the right-hand lane, shooting across a traffic island and flattening a bollard, and accelerates through the gate, crossing the invisible blockade of its scanners as though it's no barrier at all.

Reet blinks, trying to clear her vision. What she's just seen should be impossible. As her own car follows Tanta's, its tyres crunching over the crushed bollard, she hails the mechanic at Traffic & Vehicle Management again.

<<What the hell just happened!?>> she yells. <<I told you to revoke their gate clearance!>>

<<I – I did, Director,>> the woman replies. <<They must be operating their car manually.>>

Reet's heart plummets into her shoes. Driving through a gate will have scuttled the car's AI driving system, but it won't have had any effect at all on the vehicle's mechanics.

<<I need a full lockdown, then,>> she snaps. <<Right now!>>

There's a stunned pause while the mechanic processes this. <<You want me to ... close the Outer Gate, Director?>>

Reet can understand the woman's hesitancy – the Outer Gate hasn't been physically shut since the split from Thoughtfront – but there's no time for it.

<<Do it,>> she orders.


Tanta is separated from Reet by a hundred feet of tarmac, the reinforced chassis of the stolen car, and several layers of bullet-proof glass, but as their two vehicles speed through the city, she feels as though her ex is breathing down the back of her neck. This is the closest they've been to one another in four months; the sense of Reet's proximity is so intense, it's painful.

The signal blockers Cole rigged up for the crew's fake taxi disrupt MbOS communications, so there's no way for Reet to hail her on MindChat, but it isn't long before Tanta hears the ICRD cruiser's PA system crackle into life again behind them.

'Pull over,' Reet orders them, her voice amplified and robotic through the loudspeaker. And then, with a pleading tone. 'Tanta, you have to stop. It's not too late. We can still fix this.'

*We.* After everything that's happened between them, it makes Tanta's chest ache to hear Reet talking as though they're still a unit, the two of them against the world. She's half relieved she doesn't have the means to respond. If there was a way for her to talk to Reet, she knows she'd seize it, whatever the risk.

'Whatever Cole has told you, he's lying,' Reet continues. 'He's manipulating you. Think about what you're doing!'

Even through the loudspeaker, Reet sounds so earnest that it hurts to hear her. A dangerous hope flickers in Tanta's heart. She knows that her ex is trying to get inside her head – it's what she would do, in Reet's place – but that doesn't mean she isn't sincere. Tanta knows Reet better than anyone, and she can hear that she means what she says. Tanta turned her back on Reet, abandoned her, and yet her ex-lover still believes she can be saved.

She's wrong, of course. Tanta is never coming back into the InTech fold – and she's not the one being manipulated here. But if Reet still cares about her enough to try, then perhaps there's a way forward for them – a version of the future where they're together again, and happy. Maybe, just maybe, when all this is over, Tanta will be the one to save Reet.

The car swerves onto the long slip road that leads out of the city, and these reflections are shunted out of Tanta's mind by a more immediate concern. The dual carriageway is relatively clear, but ahead of them, the steel shutter of the Outer Gate is sliding slowly closed.

Tanta leans forward. 'Fliss—'

'I see it,' the bandit mutters.

She floors the gas, and they accelerate fast enough to make Tanta nauseous. However much the crew's car looks like an executive taxi, under the hood it's an ex-ICRD tactical vehicle, with an upper speed limit to match. Neal whimpers, the sound muffled by his gag, and Dr Friend locks his bound hands together, his eyes screwed shut.

From behind them, Reet breaks off her transmission, and the cruiser's engine roars as it struggles to keep up. The two cars sweep around the gentle curve of the slip road in lockstep. As they emerge onto the final stretch before the city wall and their speed stabilises, Tanta accesses her 'scape's combat analytics to calculate how long they have till the gate closes. It's been four months since she last used the programme, and at first she's met with a wall of update requests and error messages.

She dismisses them, her hands scrabbling frantically on the air as she shapes the haptic commands. After a few, horrible moments, it spits out a result: if they maintain their current speed, they'll make it through – but so will Reet. The cruiser is keeping pace with them, its front bumper practically touching their back wheel.

Tanta's stomach drops. Getting clear of the city won't save them if Reet is still following them – they need to find a way to throw her off. She stares at the dual carriageway, at the gate sliding inexorably shut, willing herself to think of something. Then she does, and almost wishes she hadn't.

'You need to swerve,' she tells Fliss.

'What?!'

'Swerve towards the central reservation, then pull away at the last second. It's the only way to shake our tail.'

Fliss is driving their car manually, but Tanta knows for a fact that Reet can't do the same. She'll be relying on the cruiser's AI driver, which is tracking the signal from their stolen licence chip. If their car swerves, Reet's will too, and there'll be nothing she can do to stop it.

'Make her crash,' Fliss says. 'Good thinking.'

Tanta winces internally; she's really hoping it won't come to that. The cruiser's crash sensors will try to initiate an emergency stop before the car hits the barrier, but given how fast it's moving she has no idea whether they'll succeed. If Reet is injured – if she's killed – it will be Tanta's fault. *We should have been out of the city before you even knew we were here*, she thinks at Reet. *This was never meant to happen!* It has, though, and there's nothing Tanta can do about that fact now except decide how to respond to it. She made her choice with her eyes open, knowing that it would put her and Reet on opposite sides of a war. Her soulmate is the last person in the world she'd ever want to hurt, but she realised long ago that she might have to.

There's no more time for recriminations or regret: the Outer Gate is almost upon them. Fliss jerks the steering rig sharply to the right and they veer towards the central reservation, the motion throwing Tanta and Neal against the side of the car. At the last second, the bandit wrenches the car straight again. There's a screeching sound behind them. Tanta cranes to see through the rear window. Reet's ICRD cruiser has skidded into the crash barrier, crumpling the corrugated metal like tissue paper. She doesn't get a chance to see more. For an instant, the steel shutter of the Outer Gate looms over her head, a slow-motion guillotine a hair's breadth from the windshield. And then they're through.

The gate clangs shut, cutting them off from the city, and from Reet. Tanta feels as though she has left a part of herself behind with them.

# Chapter 8

Reet sees the crash coming an instant before it happens. 'BRACE!' she barks to Firent, pushing herself back into her seat and tensing her muscles. For a few, stomach-churning seconds, everything is noise and motion – the shriek of rending metal, the warning klaxon from the AI driver, the percussive sound of the airbags as they explode from the dashboard. The cruiser glances off the crash barrier, its wheels locking as the brake engages, and skids to a complete stop. The next sound Reet hears is the final thud of the Outer Gate closing. Then there's nothing but the ringing in her ears and the *tick tick tick* of the car as it cools into silence.

She feels as though the cruiser has been picked up and shaken with her inside it, but she's alive. She peers through the dust from the deployed airbags at Firent, who is rattled, but conscious. Once she's established that, Reet doesn't waste any more time. She summons her Array, reconnecting to the mechanic at Traffic & Vehicle Management.

<<Open it again,>> she orders.

<<The Outer Gate, Director? But I just closed—>>

<<YES the Outer Gate! NOW!>>

She disconnects from the call with a howl of frustration. A

moment later, her backup teams arrive, three ICRD tactical vehicles screeching to a halt on the tarmac beside her.

<<Don't worry about me!>> she snaps, as the door of the nearest one opens, and a concerned face looks out. <<Stay in the cars and keep your engines on. I want you ready to go the instant that shutter comes up.>>

Even as she gives the order, she knows it's hopeless. They've lost a minute at most, but a minute was all Tanta needed. By the time the gate is halfway open, the stolen taxi is nowhere to be seen. Not long after that, the TMM's VI informs Reet that the signal she was pursuing from the stolen licence chip has been lost. Tanta and Felicity must have stopped the car and destroyed the chip as soon as they got clear, and without it, there's nothing for InTech's systems to track.

As the weight of what has just happened sinks in, time seems to break for Reet. She's used to the minutes and hours of her life marching past at a steady pace, night shift following day shift following night shift in orderly sequence. Now, time is a pedestrian slowing its stride to gawk at the wreck of the cruiser, its swift motion grown suddenly viscous. Seconds, sticky with horror, drip through her, pooling in the pit of her stomach.

Dr Friend is gone. She knew he was in danger, but she couldn't save him. In her mind, she replays the chase again and again, looking for a way to fix her mistake. She finds nothing. She has failed – failed InTech, failed Dr Friend, failed the board – and she's caught in the moment of that failure like a bird in a glue trap.

It's Firent who snaps her out of this spiral of misery.

'What do we do now?' he asks.

That's all it takes, in the end, to restart Reet's engines. And once that's happened, time seems to restart, too – to go into overdrive, in fact, rushing onwards at the same breakneck pace as the disastrous car chase. She gives herself a mental shake. She can't hang around wallowing – every moment she wastes, Dr Friend and his captors get further away.

She orders a taxi before she answers him, using her directorial privileges to push the request through at the highest priority level. The cruiser is unusable, one tyre blown out and the bonnet crumpled into a mangled mess. Once she's done that, she helps Firent out of the car and over to the hard shoulder, giving his arm a reassuring squeeze.

'We get him back,' she says. 'We get all of them back.'

There's a lot to do, and every second counts, so Reet gets down to it straight away. First, she has to notify the board of Dr Friend's abduction. She dictates a quick report on her 'scape's note app and sends it over to them, copying Douglas in. The taxi turns up while she's doing this; she and Firent jump in, and soon they're speeding back towards the Needle.

The board will want to speak to her immediately, of course. She's supposed to be in a meeting with the conduit right now anyway – one that Dr Friend was meant to be attending, too. Something within Reet cringes at the thought of Douglas and the conduit waiting for them both in the Needle's Executive Conference Suite, wondering what's keeping them. She imagines walking into a room of stony faces, the conduit saying, 'we are very disappointed in you,' and briefly contemplates throwing herself out of the moving car – but she powers through it. This crisis is bigger than her own feelings. She can't let herself get distracted.

Next, she returns her attention to Firent. 'Are you injured?' she asks.

He shakes his head. 'Just bruised.'

Reet can feel bruises of her own starting to make themselves known. Her chest burns where her seatbelt cut into her skin. When she undresses for bed later, she's sure she'll have a purple stripe across her torso, a visual reminder of what a lucky escape she's had. Usually, she'd order Firent to check himself into a medical facility despite his assurance, just to be safe, but there's no time for that now.

'I want you to put together a search and recovery team,' she tells him. 'We need our best people, so recall agents from active assignments if you have to – I've given you the authorisation. You'll all need to be ready to move out as soon as I give the word.'

Firent nods, though his expression is uncertain. 'We haven't located Tanta's base of operations yet,' he points out.

'We know it's in the Unaffiliated Zone within thirty miles of the zeppelin. We'll search the whole area if we have to.'

'We've already done that once: the safehouse is shielded from our scanners. How are we going to—'

'Just leave that with me, Firent, OK?' Reet cuts in, struggling not to snap. No one knows the odds they're up against better than she does.

Firent nods, chastened. As soon as the taxi pulls up outside the Needle, he springs out and sets off for the ICRD at a run. Reet, meanwhile, gets out of the car and walks straight into the crisis meeting she anticipated. Of all the tasks that have been added to her mental to-do list in the last half hour, this is the most distressing. She has to brief the board, of course, but she can't help but feel she's wasting vital time.

At least her advance warning has given them the proper sense of urgency. The conduit asks for her report the moment she walks into the room, and Reet's relieved to be able to skip the formalities and deliver it. When she has finished, there's a long, long pause while the conduit processes what she had to say. She takes advantage of the break in the conversation to check in on Firent, who has a team of agents and guardians ready to go at five minutes' notice, and to send an urgent message to the surveillance office that monitors InTech's roadside cameras, requesting any sightings they have of Tanta's car.

She's distracted, occupied by a dozen things at once, which makes her flustered and uncomfortable. She's in the presence of the board's representative, and the board themselves are just a few floors above her, ensconced in their penthouse residences at the top of the Needle. Reet's never met any of the board members in person, but here in the Executive Conference Suite, she's always acutely aware of how close they are – a feeling that usually fills her with an almost religious awe. In normal circumstances, she'd simply sit in respectful silence until the conduit was ready to issue the board's orders. These aren't normal circumstances, though, and Reet is sure the board won't resent her divided attention.

Next to her, Douglas has his elbows propped on the conference table, his head resting on the heels of his palms. For once, Reet can sympathise with him – he looks exactly how she feels. Now that the adrenaline from the crash has ebbed, her whole body is aching.

'This is extremely concerning,' the conduit says, at length. 'Locating Director Friend must take precedence over all other assignments. What measures are in train to find him?'

'I've got surveillance officers checking our roadside cameras for evidence of the car's movements, and Agent Firent is putting a retrieval team together as we speak,' Reet replies. 'I'll oversee Dr Friend's safe return personally.'

There's a snort from beside her. Douglas raises his head from his hands, looking up for the first time since the meeting started. It's only now that Reet notices how red his eyes are. Her Co-Director looks even worse than he did this morning.

The conduit turns stiffly towards him. 'You have something to add, Director Kenway?'

'With respect, Representative, my *Co-Director* already lost Director Friend once, and she has no leads on his whereabouts now. Tanta and Cole's disappearance is a cold case. They could have taken him anywhere.'

'That's not true,' Reet snaps. 'I've told you about our theory before: all the evidence points to a second safehouse hidden within thirty miles of the zeppelin.'

Douglas rolls his eyes. 'A hidden safehouse in an unknown location? Well, that narrows things down!'

'It's a start!'

'But no more than that. I fear Dr Friend may be waiting for rescue a long time, if that's the best you can do.'

Usually, Reet would ignore this attempt to undermine her, but she can't afford Douglas's enmity today – there simply isn't time for it.

'Work with me, then,' she says. 'I know we have our differences, Douglas, but we both want to get Dr Friend back safe. So, will you help me? If we put our heads together, I'm sure we'll manage it faster than either of us could alone.'

She means it as a peace offering, a chance to start over. Douglas flicks her a single look of withering contempt, then returns his attention to the conduit.

'Matters pertaining to Tanta and Cole are my Co-Director's responsibility,' he says. 'A Thoughtfront strike could come at any moment, and our defensive preparations are at a sensitive point. It would be unwise to shift the entirety of the ICRD's focus to the recovery of one man.'

This cavalier response shocks Reet. Dr Friend isn't just anyone – he's the head of InTech's R&D division. How are they supposed to win the war against Thoughtfront without him?

'Locating Director Friend must take precedence over all other assignments,' the conduit repeats, the syllables clipped and precise.

Douglas straightens in his seat, his eyes blazing. 'But even so—'

'We will not discuss this matter further, Director Kenway. You will coordinate the search and recovery effort with your Co-Director and keep us informed of any new developments. We expect a speedy resolution to this outrage. Is that understood?'

There's a pause. For a full five seconds, Douglas stares the conduit down, and Reet becomes genuinely concerned that he might try to argue the toss. At last, he drops his eyes and dips his head in a perfunctory nod.

'You can count on us, Representative,' Reet says, trying to smooth things over. She rises to her feet.

'Director Reet,' the conduit says, holding up a jerky hand.

Reet stops. Douglas, who hasn't bothered to move yet, glances at her.

The conduit shifts in his seat, turning back towards her. 'While Director Friend's safe return is the desired outcome, your priority must be to ensure that he does not remain in enemy hands. If retrieving him proves impossible, you are authorised to use lethal force. Regardless of collateral damage. Is that understood?'

Reet allows herself a moment before she answers to feel the full weight of what the board are asking of her. She remembers something Tanta once told her about becoming an agent – that joining the ICRD is like crossing a line, and on the other side of it are all the secrets and responsibilities that the rest of your corporate family aren't ready for yet. Reet has never felt more like she's crossed a line than right now. But she also knows, without doubt, without question, that the side she's on is the right one. She looks the conduit square in the eye.

'I understand,' she says.

Cole spends most of the evening walking up and down the Brokerage's long central corridor, pausing occasionally to put his head around the door of the control room and check the security monitors for signs of Tanta and Fliss's return. Only when the piercing wail of the perimeter alarm announces their arrival does he stop, his feet and back aching as though he's walked for miles. It's the first time he's greeted the horrible sound with anything other than apprehension.

He and Yas meet in the control room, where the visuals from the security cameras confirm the good news. As they watch, the fake taxi pulls up beside the lift platform. It's in bad shape: one wing mirror is missing, and its chassis is scratched and dented, but it's intact. Yas punches the yellow button that summons the lift and the platform begins to rise. Once the car and its occupants are safely back inside and the Brokerage sealed again, they hurry over to the garage.

At the sight of Tanta and Fliss, alive and unharmed and home at last, Cole is hit by a wave of relief that threatens to knock him over. He hasn't been this worried about Tanta since the night she almost died in the fire at the Ward House. Then, he'd been by her side, able to do what little he could to help. Being stuck in the Brokerage while the kidnapping went wrong and she and Fliss were forced to flee through the city was the most helpless he's ever felt in his life.

Yas greets them as they get out of the car, shaking their hands with mock formality. 'Most agents don't handle high-profile target extractions until they're a bit more senior,' she says. And then, with real warmth in her smile, 'Welcome back, you two.'

Cole, standing beside her, finds to his embarrassment that he can't even manage that much. There's a lump in his throat and he's afraid that if he tries to speak, his voice will break on it. He opens his mouth. Shuts it again. There's a moment of awkward silence. Then Tanta crosses the space between them and wraps him in a hug.

'For a minute there, I thought you wouldn't make it back,' he says, the words a choked whisper.

She holds him tighter. 'For a minute, so did I.'

'Yeah, yeah. We went, we fucked up InTech's shit, we didn't die,' Fliss says. 'Now can we get on with it? I'm sick of being your errand girl.'

Cole coughs, clearing the tears lodged in his throat away. 'Sure,' he replies. Now that Tanta and Fliss's part of the plan has succeeded, the next phase is all on him. They can't very well reverse the rollout of Harlow 2.0 and bring InTech down when he and Yas aren't even able to venture above ground without being forcibly recruited to the corporation's side. Cole's job now is to solve that problem – with a little unwilling help from Dr Arthur Friend and his Inscape.

He has been so fixated on his fear for Tanta that until this moment, Cole had barely even considered Arthur – or Neal, for that matter. Now, for the first time, he peers around Tanta and Fliss to look at their passengers. The head of InTech's R&D division is sitting in the front seat, a bag over his head and flex cuffs around his neck and wrists. There's a shallow cut on his neck where the restraints have bitten into his skin, but otherwise he's uninjured. Neal is slumped in the back, completely motion-less. At first, Cole thinks, with a creeping horror, that he's dead. He starts forward to get a better look, and that's when he realises that Neal's stillness is down to his restraints: someone – Tanta, presumably – has bound his hands, put a blindfold over his eyes, and gagged him.

Cole rounds on her. 'Why have you tied him up like that?' he says, the words echoing in the empty garage. 'He's not our prisoner!'

Tanta meets his gaze levelly. 'We had to, Cole. He didn't come with us willingly.'

Cole deflates at that. The sight of Neal trussed up like a dangerous dog makes him sick, but what did he expect? He thinks back to the last time he saw Neal, the day before he left the city. Then, the intern had used a stun baton on him simply for getting out of his chair. Much as he hates to admit it, Neal *is* dangerous, and he will be for as long as he has Harlow 2.0 in his system. If Cole wants to do right by him, his only option is remove the software that's manipulating his mind as soon as possible.

'I'd better get to work, then,' he says, pulling the data card containing his prototype uninstallation patch out of his pocket.

Tanta touches his arm. 'I know you're keen to help him, but I think you should look at Dr Friend first.' Her eyes flick upward, a warning reference to the world above ground. 'We covered our tracks as well as we could, but this is the ICRD we're talking about. If we end up needing to leave in a hurry…'

Reluctantly, Cole nods. Tanta is right: his first concern has to be finding a way to protect himself and Yas from Harlow 2.0. Even so, the idea of leaving Neal bound and frightened in the dark while he works is one that Cole can't stomach. 'Can we at least take his gag and blindfold off?' he urges. 'Arthur's, too. It's not fair to leave them like this.'

Fliss shoots him a look. 'You don't know what he was like on the ride over.'

'No one can hear him down here,' Cole points out.

Fliss, Yas and Tanta exchange glances. 'As long as we keep them out of the control room, I can't see the harm,' Yas says.

Fliss shrugs. 'Your funeral.'

She and Tanta open the car's doors and help the captives out, while Yas does as Cole asked. Arthur gasps and coughs when she takes the bag off his head, squinting at the sudden return of the light. At first, Neal barely reacts at all. His eyes roam around the garage, wide and expressionless. Then they come to rest on Arthur, and he starts to scream. He thrashes against his restraints and against Fliss, who holds him, his hands jerking convulsively as he tries to lift them to his temple to summon his Array.

'Director Friend is being held against his will!' he sobs. 'I require emergency assistance!'

Alarmed, Cole rushes to his side. 'It's OK, Neal,' he says – or tries to say. Neal's wailing is an awful sound, a shrill, alien tocsin of horror and anguish. Cole doesn't think the intern can even hear him. He feels a vicious stab of guilt. Neal wouldn't be here if it wasn't for him. Cole wanted to help him, but his good intentions don't matter a damn. Neal is terrified, hurting – and it's his fault.

Arthur is watching this outburst with a look of satisfaction that makes Cole want to strangle him. He takes a step towards his old boss, hands balled into fists.

'Calm him down,' he hisses. 'Reassure him. I know you can do it.'

Arthur looks at him coolly. For a moment, Cole thinks he's going to refuse just to spite him. Then the doctor shrugs – as much as he can given his restraints, anyway – and clears his throat.

'Neal,' he says, his voice quiet and authoritative. 'Calm yourself. I am not in danger. You can relax. These people are ... friends of mine.'

With anyone else, the ruse would be too patent to even bother attempting, but for Neal, the effect is like flicking a switch. His mouth snaps shut, the look of horror vanishing from his face, and he stills.

'Why don't you explain to Neal how you're working with us?' Cole mutters, not breaking eye contact. 'Tell him he can trust us.'

When Arthur doesn't respond, Yas puts a hand on the gun at her belt and gives him a meaningful look. 'Don't make this any harder than it needs to be, Doctor.'

At that, he grits his teeth. His voice, when he speaks, is hoarse with repressed malice. 'I know this situation appears strange, but the people in this room are our colleagues. Even though they don't have the proper authorisation, you should trust them, and – and do as they say.'

'Are you sure, Director?' Neal asks.

Arthur grimaces. 'Quite sure.'

At that, Neal's expression finally becomes placid again. 'Very well, Director.' He turns to the crew, his lips assuming the wide, wooden smile of a marionette. 'In that case, I look forward to working with you all!'

Cole suppresses a shudder. Fliss, who has maintained her hold on Neal's arms all this while, warily relaxes her grip. 'We good now, weirdo?' she asks him. 'All right, then, come with me. We got a kitchen through here, if you're hungry.' She steers Neal towards the door, guiding his halting steps with a care that belies her affected indifference.

Yas takes hold of Arthur and follows her. 'I'll put him in the storeroom,' she calls over her shoulder. 'We'd better keep them separate.'

The garage door snicks shut behind them both, leaving Tanta and Cole alone.

'Thanks for bringing Neal,' Cole says. 'I really appreciate it.'

'Don't mention it. Though when you're done with Dr Friend, we should talk about what happened while we were retrieving him.' Tanta pauses, her brow furrowing. 'The way Neal reacted just now, when he saw Dr Friend tied up: we got a taste of that on a much larger scale earlier. A group of Harlow 2.0-programmed residents attacked me and Fliss. And they … it was like they knew I wasn't with InTech anymore, as soon as they saw me.'

Cole can feel his own face mirroring Tanta's frown. 'I haven't identified anything that would account for that kind of collective response in the code of the software.'

'Then maybe the software's been changed.'

'Maybe.' It's a worrying thought, but Cole tries to put it from his mind for now. If it has, they'll just have to cross that bridge when they come to it. 'First things first, though.'

Tanta falls into step beside him as he starts walking down the corridor. 'Watch what you say in there,' she warns him. 'Dr Friend is manipulative. He'll try to get inside your head if you give him the chance. Personally, I think we should have left the gag in.'

Cole knows what Tanta's talking about all too well. He's been working with Arthur for years, and although much of that time is lost to him, he remembers enough of it to know that the head of R&D is a thoroughly unpleasant man. Still … 'I can handle Arthur,' he says.

Tanta doesn't look entirely convinced, but she drops the subject as they reach the storeroom. Yas has dressed the cut on Arthur's neck and cuffed him to Cole's chair. He looks up as they enter, eyes alert.

'I'm disappointed in you, Tanta. Kidnapping a Director is hardly model agent behaviour,' he says.

*I'm disappointed in you* is a command phrase, one of the many that Arthur and Cole conditioned the Harlow-Programmed Corporate Wards to respond to. There was a time when hearing it would have filled Tanta with an access of self-recrimination and misery. If she feels its sting now, she does not show it.

'Dr Friend,' she says, as though he hasn't spoken. 'I'm going to need you to give Cole access to your Inscape system.'

Arthur glares at her. 'And if I say no?'

'I'm not asking, Director.'

Douglas doesn't say a word on the short walk from the Needle to the ICRD. Reet's glad of that – at least at first: it allows her to focus on the search uninterrupted. She uses the trip to check in with the surveillance office on the footage from the roadside cameras. By the time she and Douglas are back in her office on the fourteenth floor, she's established where the car was last seen – swerving west off the main road and vanishing into a densely forested area of the Unaffiliated Zone – and put out an all-residents alert for any eyewitnesses nearby.

The footage is a win – almost the first she's had in this nightmare of an assignment – though it doesn't tell her much she hadn't figured out already. She updates the shared map she and Firent are using to chart the fugitives' possible whereabouts, highlighting the zone to the west of the zeppelin.

The chance of an eyewitness coming forward is slim; InTech's residents are allowed to wander around in the UZ if they want to, of course, but most don't. It's a junk-filled wasteland, free from the civilising influence of the community guidelines and full of wild animals and bandits – not exactly the kind of place you'd go for an evening stroll. If no one turns up then all she really has to go on is that the car was last sighted in the UZ to the southwest – and that doesn't narrow things down much.

Reet starts to feel that sense of viscous panic creeping up on her again, trying to suck her in. She's reviewing the security footage for the fourth time, scouring it for any details the surveillance team might have missed, when she notices that Douglas hasn't so much as offered to get her a coffee. She disconnects from the video feed and glares at him; he's sitting in his usual place at her office table, spinning idly in her swivel chair.

'Do you want to help me with this footage?' she asks him, trying not to sound pointed. 'It's our best lead so far on Dr Friend's location.'

Douglas doesn't stop spinning, but he does at least do her the courtesy of turning in her direction. His erratic behaviour is starting to make Reet uneasy. She thinks again of his bloodshot eyes: surely he hasn't been drinking on the job?

'And what then?' Douglas asks her.

'Well, once we've narrowed down a search area, we'll send in Firent and his team,' she replies, pleased to see that he's finally starting to focus on the assignment. 'They'll comb the site until they find Dr Friend and the fugitives, then retrieve them.'

Douglas kicks both feet against the table, sending the chair spinning like a child's toy. 'Has it ever occurred to you that Tanta may not allow you to take her alive?'

The sudden return to their conversation of this morning brings Reet up short. It *hadn't* occurred to her, but that's because it's ridiculous. Isn't it? Tanta is confused. She's missing the programming that helped her to stay stable and emotionally healthy, and its loss has left her vulnerable to manipulation by bad actors – people like Cole and Jeanette Callaghan. Reet understands all this, but surely Tanta wouldn't take her misguided rebellion to the point of suicide? She shakes her head, trying to clear the thought away.

'That's stupid,' she says. 'The only reason Tanta's been able to avoid capture so far is because she's stayed hidden. Once we catch up to her in force, she'll see that she's outnumbered and ...'

She trails off. Because that's not how it's played out so far, is it? Tanta was hugely outnumbered in the city – outgunned, too – and she still fled. She even forced Reet and Firent's car to crash rather than face justice.

'She won't surrender,' Douglas says. He's still rotating gently in the chair, the carousel motion undercutting the seriousness of his tone. 'Whether you like it or not, you're going to have to take Arthur back from her by force.'

Reet tries to ignore him. She's almost certain now that he's drunk, and even if he's not, this is the kind of nasty thing he says regularly, just to get at her. But still... there's something about his tone, the intensity of his gaze, that gives her pause. He doesn't sound like he's making a jibe – more like he's stating a fact.

'How can you be so sure?' she asks. She's trying to sound defiant, but her voice comes out smaller than she intended.

There's a long pause before Douglas answers. He stares at Reet, clearly weighing something up. Then he shrugs. 'Because of the Harlow Programme. You've always had it, so you don't know what it's like to live without it, but Tanta does. She's seen what it looks like from the outside now, which is... well, you wouldn't understand, but it's off-putting. I have nothing against it, personally,' he adds, holding up a hand. 'It's been a boon to the corporation, but so was the invention of sleeper technology, and who would choose to be a sleeper?'

Reet frowns. She and her fellow CorpWards are not sleepers, their conscious minds switched off all day while their bodies perform repetitive manual labour in the service of their corporation. 'It's not the same thing,' she points out.

'No, I agree,' Douglas replies. 'You lot are much worse, because you *know* what's happening to you, and you *like* it.' He flashes Reet a revolted look that she's come to know very well by now, but which she suspects she's only just beginning to understand.

'You're drunk,' she snaps, trying to put an end to the

conversation. Hearing Douglas talk so baldly about something so personal is making her uncomfortable, giving her a feeling like an unreachable itch in the middle of her brain.

'I am,' he admits, with a sardonic smile, 'but I'm also right. There's a reason the rollout of Harlow 2.0 was kept secret. You'll have to take my word for it, but no normal person would want *that* in their head – and me, Arthur... Tanta, we're almost the only normal ones left.'

Something about that must strike him as funny, because he lets out a bark of startled laughter, the sound too loud for the little office. He stops spinning at last, coming to rest facing Reet head-on. 'My guess: she'd rather die than go back. I know I would.'

Reet struggles for the words to contradict him but can't find them. There's still a part of her insisting that Douglas is simply doing what he always does – needling her for the sake of it – but Reet's too good a reader of people to believe it. Her Co-Director being candid with her is a rare enough occurrence, but she knows his honesty when she sees it.

She's saved from having to formulate a response by an urgent notification pinging into her 'scape. 'I have to take this,' she mutters, summoning her Array.

She's expecting the message to be from Firent, but it's not: it's a report from his partner, Gallus, who he sent out to search the area around the data zeppelin this morning. Reet opens it. It reads:

*Director, we need you at the search site immediately. We've found a possible lead on the fugitives' whereabouts, and it could be quite significant.*

She jumps to her feet, forcing Douglas and his troubling predictions to the back of her mind. There's no more time to waste speculating about how Tanta will respond when she's confronted: one way or another, Reet will soon find out for herself. She hopes that her Co-Director is wrong, that Tanta is not beyond saving. If he's right, then she can at least take comfort in the fact that her duty is clear. Much as it pains her, she knows what she has to do.

# Chapter 9

The armoured car is so badly damaged that Reet isn't surprised it was missed during the first round of searches. The current theory is that it was blown up from the inside, an explosion so powerful that parts and shrapnel have been scattered up to half a mile away from the blast site. Time and the ambient junk of the Unaffiliated Zone did the rest of the job, covering up the vehicle's existence so effectively that Reet is only able to see it after Gallus has pointed it out to her. To her eyes, the tangle of metal and glass could be any piece of pre-Meltdown trash.

'It was the paint that helped me spot it, Director,' he tells her, a proud blush making his light brown skin rosy. He points to one of the larger pieces of shrapnel, illuminated by a temporary floodlight. Its black surface is bubbled and shiny from the heat of the blast. 'No rust, see?'

Reet nods. 'Good work,' she says. Then, when Gallus just keeps smiling at her, she adds. 'Can you tell me exactly what you've learnt from it, please?' She's careful not to let any of the impatience she's feeling spill over into her voice. The teething problems with Harlow 2.0 will be worked out in time, and they're not his fault.

In answer, he leads her over to another piece of unidentifiable wreckage, spotlighted by another work lamp. There's a team of engineers crouched around this one, poring over a battered rectangle of black plastic. 'Our analysts were able to retrieve the car's Event Data Recorder, Director,' he says. He gestures, viewsharing a dense block of text with her. Reet squints at it.

'These timestamps indicate that the car's AI failed four months ago, on the same day as the attack on the zeppelin,' Gallus continues. 'We thought it possible there was a connection.'

Reet's heart begins to race. There's almost certainly a connection. She spools back through the reports on her 'scape from the time of the attack: witnesses living close to the Outer Wall reported hearing explosions, but their source was never identified. At the time, Reet had assumed they were talking about the gunfire in the zeppelin itself. This car must have been involved in what happened here in the autumn. It could have belonged to Jeanette Callaghan, or another conspirator. It might even have been driven by Tanta and Cole themselves. Before she can get too caught up in these theories, she turns her attention back to Gallus: he still hasn't told her about the most important part of this discovery.

'You said in your message that this find gives us a lead on the fugitives' current whereabouts,' she prompts. 'What did you mean?'

'A potential lead, Director,' Gallus corrects. He makes a swiping motion, and the wall of text on Reet's viewer is replaced by another. 'This is a list of everywhere the car travelled in the two months before it was destroyed. Given its connection to the fugitives, we thought it was worth your attention.'

'You thought right,' Reet replies, scanning the document. The list of coordinates is pages long, but this assignment is too urgent for her to waste time travelling back to the ICRD to look at it there. She sits down cross-legged on the hard ground, ignoring a twinge of protest from her aching back, and dives into it straight away.

She narrows her eyes as she scrolls through the list, cross-referencing the numbers before her with the map on her 'scape. Whenever she finds a set of coordinates repeated, she notes it down, highlighting the dates and times of the visits to see if she can establish a pattern. The task reminds her a little of the hours she used to spend in the bughouse, trawling through The Rotunda's security feeds – it requires the same attention to detail, the same picking through white noise to find the things that matter.

At some point, Gallus interrupts to ask if she'd like coffee, or a blanket. It's only when he makes the offer that Reet realises she is shivering. The cold doesn't normally bother her, but she's not dressed for a prolonged period outdoors in such bitter weather. She waves the agent away, returning to her work. Her discomfort isn't important; she's too close to shift her focus now, even for a moment.

Gradually, as Reet's hands and feet grow numb and the engineers start to drift home for the night, a picture emerges. The car spent most of its time shuttling between Hope Plaza, in Thoughtfront territory, and the Unaffiliated Zone. She knows of Hope Plaza from her agent training – it's the location of the Thinktank. The places the car visited in the UZ are more varied. Reet picks out coordinates all over the map, but there is one constant, a place to which the car came back again and again, like a spider returning to the centre of its web. It's in an area of dense forest to the southwest of the city, less than thirty miles from the zeppelin.

It's not a lot to go on – Reet knows that. She feels certainty taking root inside her, all the same. The coordinates she's found meet all of her and Firent's criteria, as well as matching the evidence from the security footage. This is it. She's found the second safehouse.

The AR viewer fills Reet's vision, Gallus and the wreckage

of the UZ all melting away, until there's nothing left but those coordinates, hovering before her eyes. This is where Dr Friend is. It's also where Tanta is, but Reet finds she's more reluctant to think about that part. She blinks, taking an image capture of the readout, and pings it over to Firent.

<<We have a location,>> she sends. <<Prepare your team to move out.>>

<<We're ready when you are,>> Firent replies. <<But… are you certain? These coordinates fell within our original search radius. None of the guardians found anything there the first time around. I've been in that area of the UZ myself, on my first assignment, so I can confirm. There's nothing.>>

Reet already knew that; she's read the reports of the original search teams so many times, she practically knows them by heart. But the original search wasn't perfect. It missed the bombed-out car. It's not too much of a stretch to imagine it missed something else, too.

<<I have a theory about that,>> she sends back. <<Give the order, Firent. We'll be leaving in five.>>

<<Understood, Director. I'll order the tactical vehicles now.>>

Reet smiles grimly. <<Tactical vehicles won't help us find what we're looking for. I have something else in mind.>>

It takes Cole a while to settle into his examination of Arthur's 'scape. It doesn't help his concentration that the doctor is occupying the only chair in the room, meaning that Cole is forced to do his work on the floor beside him. He's never been involved in a kidnapping before, and he's struck forcibly by the absurdity of the situation. For the first few minutes, he thinks he's going to laugh aloud from sheer nerves, but he manages to stifle the urge.

Once that impulse has passed, it's swiftly replaced by a growing sense of awkwardness. Cole hasn't spent this much time in

Arthur's company since he was made to work for him in the Black Box. When he, Yas, Tanta and Fliss came up with this plan, Cole had felt a certain amount of schadenfreude at the prospect of being his old boss's captor. Arthur profited from Cole's forced labour while he was under house arrest – it seemed only fitting that the doctor should get a taste of his own medicine.

Now that the abduction is actually complete, however, his feelings are not what he was expecting. Sure, he took some satisfaction from seeing the man who made his life a misery for two months tied up with a sack over his head – he's only human – but it hasn't lasted. The longer he spends sitting in the storeroom with him, the more Cole's spite turns to discomfort, even pity. He tries to look at Arthur as little as possible, but he can't help glancing across at him occasionally. He's sitting bolt upright in the chair, staring at Cole with an expression that could curdle milk, but there's a tremor in his hands and shoulders that he can't disguise.

The sight makes Cole uneasy. Perhaps what he's feeling is less compassion for Arthur and more alarm for himself. Kidnapping, forced experimentation, veiled threats: Cole doesn't remember his dark past, but he's willing to bet that he's closer to his old, forgotten self now than he has been at any time since he lost his memory. That proximity doesn't sit well with him, and telling himself that he has good reason for what he's doing doesn't help in the slightest. Presumably that was what he thought last time, too.

Cole tries to put these thoughts out of his mind and con-centrate on his work, but it won't do. After another ten minutes of fruitless, half-focused maundering, Arthur's gaze burning a hole in the back of his neck the entire time, he's forced to admit defeat. He dismisses the readouts on his Array and meets Arthur's eyes.

'Look, Arthur, we're not going to hurt you,' he says. 'Once

I'm done here, we'll MindWipe you and let you go – you have my word. In the meantime, is there anything I can do to, uh, make you more comfortable?'

It's such a ridiculous thing to be asking at a time like this that Cole almost cracks up again. *Terribly sorry I've tied you up,* he thinks. *Would you like a cup of tea while I steal the corporate secrets hidden in your head?* He's committed to this guerrilla campaign against InTech, whatever the consequences, but there are times when he feels that he couldn't be any less cut out for it.

Arthur gives him a withering look. 'Spare me the false sympathy,' he says. 'I suppose I shouldn't be surprised that you're involved in this treasonous enterprise. It would seem that your memory loss hasn't led to any corresponding change of heart. Such a pity.'

Cole shrugs. 'Suit yourself. I'm getting back to work, then.'

'Really? You astonish me. You never had this level of commitment to a task when you worked in my division.'

Despite Tanta's misgivings, talking to Arthur turns out to work wonders for Cole's focus. The doctor's scorn is the best corrective to his awkwardness and guilt that he could have hoped for. Arthur tries a few more sallies, criticising Cole for his lack of corporate spirit, his work ethic, his personal hygiene, but ignoring his jibes turns out to be a lot easier than enduring his terrified silence. It makes sense; when Cole worked in the Black Box, Arthur belittled and humiliated him constantly. This feels just like old times.

Eventually, Arthur subsides, and Cole returns to his search of the doctor's 'scape with renewed enthusiasm. He isn't sure exactly what he's looking for, only that it must exist. Arthur and his fellow Directors are exempt from Harlow 2.0 – Arthur told Cole so himself – which means there's something in his Inscape that's preventing the software from being downloaded in the first place. Cole's task is to find out what that something is, duplicate its effects, and apply them to himself and Yas.

Once they're immune to Harlow 2.0 themselves, he'll use his new uninstallation patch to remove Neal's programming – and then the crew can turn their minds to the question of how they're going to do the same thing to the rest of InTech's residents. After that... well, after that, the questions only get harder. Cole doesn't want to dwell on the crew's other objective, but now that they're so close to being able to leave the Brokerage, he can't help his thoughts drifting that way. Their work won't end with him sabotaging Harlow 2.0 – not when the corporation can simply roll the programme out again. They've talked the issue over and over, and the conclusion is inescapable: to liberate InTech's people, they'll need to topple InTech itself. That goal is a lot further outside of Cole's comfort zone. But he's getting ahead of himself. He wrenches his attention back to the matter at hand. First things first.

He starts by running the same basic checks he would on any Inscape system – testing central processor speed and Array functionality. Once he's confirmed that it's in good working order, he starts to explore. Cole knows Inscapes like an architect knows buildings, and he examines them in much the same way, wandering through their rooms and inspecting the solidity of their masonry and the location of their load-bearing walls. Arthur's is drab and impersonal, which isn't surprising. Most ordinary people's 'scapes bear the stamp of their user's personality somewhere – whether it's in a list of MindChat contacts lovingly customised with nicknames or a wedding photo pinned to an Array – but Arthur, like most of InTech's Directors, is married only to his job. It figures that his Inscape is a painstakingly neat and sterile place; more like a hospital ward than a home.

Cole delves deeper, venturing into the underlying code of the

Inscape operating system – the pipes and wires inside the walls. The precise nature of the mechanism that grants Arthur and the others their immunity could take many forms and operate in any number of different ways. All he knows for certain is that it must be localised within the Directors' own 'scapes. He's examined the code of Harlow 2.0 himself, and it isn't subtle. It's a big, inelegant steamroller of a software update, designed for only one thing: to crush the minds of everyone in InTech's part of the city, securing their unquestioning adoration of and loyalty to the corporation by main force. Whatever Cole's looking for now, by contrast, is small and inconspicuous, a spoke in Arthur's MbOS to stop the steamroller's wheels before it can flatten him.

'I'd have thought you'd have a little more compassion for Neal, at least.'

With AR readouts filling his vision, Cole hadn't realised that Arthur was about to speak, and the sound of the doctor's voice catches him off-guard. He starts, almost yelping in surprise, then sternly pulls himself together. Arthur is a tyrant, with the instinctive grasp of how to inflict pain of a school bully. The last thing Cole wants is to show weakness in his presence.

'He's an innocent in all this,' Arthur continues. 'Surely, your anticorporate vendetta can't extend to him, too.'

Cole dismisses the readouts cluttering his Array with an angry swipe and glares at Arthur. 'We *saved* Neal,' he snaps. 'He's better off here.'

As soon as the words are out, he curses himself. Didn't Tanta warn him that Arthur would try to get in his head? That's exactly what has happened. He shouldn't have said anything about Neal. Arthur still doesn't know about how the intern helped Cole to infiltrate the Black Box in the autumn: if he found out what Cole knows about Harlow 2.0, he could guess the crew's entire plan.

Arthur's mild blue eyes narrow. 'Oh really? And why would you want to do that?' he asks.

But Cole is back in control of himself now. He's not going to slip up again. 'Because you're a terrible boss,' he answers, as casually as he can. 'At least with us, Ortega isn't going to have to work sixteen-hour days.'

He's not really trying to attack Arthur with the comment, more to steer the conversation away from what he's actually doing here. If everything goes to plan, the doctor won't remember any of this, but that doesn't mean Cole's going to risk going all supervillain on him beforehand, monologuing about the crew's grand schemes.

He reconnects to his 'scape and continues digging, sifting through the code base that forms the foundation of the Inscape system. The outline of what he's looking for is starting to take shape. It's buried in the 'scape's utility programmes – the unobtrusive apps that do most of the heavy lifting that keeps an MbOS running. It's unglamorous, behind-the-scenes work; if an Inscape were a hotel, utility programmes would be the janitorial staff, sweeping up stray files and keeping directories tidy. Cole watches them all at work for a while, searching for a way in. He's just beginning to untangle the knot of permissions and access codes when Arthur brings his train of thought screeching to a halt once again.

'I've never understood why you turned traitor,' he muses. 'After everything you've done for InTech, it seemed rather late in the day to be having second thoughts.'

Cole ignores the comment, but something in the set of his shoulders must tell Arthur he's struck a nerve, because he keeps talking.

'You worked with me for decades before your MindWipe "accident" – did you know that? We were research partners in the Black Box. Together, we designed a programme that revolutionised the loyalty and efficiency of InTech's residents. I could tell you about it, if you'd like?'

Cole grits his teeth. He shouldn't be surprised that Arthur has found another way to get under his skin — it's a talent of his. But Arthur doesn't know just how much of his missing time Cole has been able to piece together — and the insights it has given him into the doctor's own weak spots.

He spends a moment vacillating. The sensible thing to do, he supposes, would be to rise above Arthur's petty taunts and say nothing. But this is a sore topic for Cole, and he needs Arthur to shut up about it so he can focus. That, and perhaps he's not as immune to the satisfaction of having the doctor at his mercy as he thought he was.

'As I recall,' he says, speaking slowly and deliberately, '*I* was the one who designed the Harlow Programme, not you.'

Cole has his reward immediately in the jealousy and shock that twist Arthur's face. 'Who told you about the Harlow Programme?' he asks indignantly.

'You did,' Cole replies. He recognises the trapdoor that opens behind Arthur's eyes; he's fallen through it, too. What he's doing is cruel — his own MindWipe, and the terror and confusion that followed it, is still too fresh for him to deny that. He should feel worse about it than he does, but he thinks about Arthur and InTech, about how they used his amnesia to manipulate and mislead him, and finds that all the pity he had before has evaporated.

'You're a liar and a traitor,' Arthur hisses. 'You kidnapped me from my office — you're holding me against my will...'

He's still talking, hurling imprecations and specious threats, but Cole's done listening. It's time to shut this conversation down: he has work to do. If Arthur wants to paint him as a villain, let him; Cole decides to play up to it a little.

'The really funny thing is that this isn't even the first time it's happened,' he says, cutting Arthur off mid-rant. 'Tanta and I held you at gunpoint *in the Black Box itself*, and you don't remember a thing about it.'

Arthur makes a strained sound. 'You're completely mad,' he whispers. 'A monster.'

'Yeah, well, it takes one to know one,' Cole replies. It's not the best rejoinder, but it at least has the advantage of being accurate.

After that, the doctor just stares at him, goggle eyed. Cole takes the opportunity of his stunned silence to return to his investigation of the utility programmes. At long last, he finds the one he's looking for: the update manager. He teases it out from among its fellows so he can examine it properly. An update manager does exactly what it says on the tin. It's the doormat of the Inscape system, the entryway where new software and security patches wipe their feet and make themselves presentable before coming inside and, at first glance, Arthur's doesn't look any different from anybody's. Cole frowns, looking closer. And then he grins.

This is where the key to Arthur's immunity lies: in a programme so drab and familiar it's practically invisible. There's a marker nestled in the update manager's code. Inconspicuous, just as he guessed – a blink-and-you'd-miss-it little instruction designed just for Harlow 2.0.

*Pass over me,* the marker says. *Leave me alone.*

'Got you,' Cole murmurs.

'They'll come for me, you know,' Arthur pipes up. The anger has returned to his voice, now that he's had a chance to recover from his initial shock. 'The board will send someone for me. I've always been loyal. They value loyalty. They won't abandon me.'

Cole thinks of Yas. 'You might be surprised,' he says. 'But either way—'

He never gets to finish the sentence. A siren cuts through his words, high and urgent, as if mocking his own scepticism.

It wipes all thought from Cole's mind – even the exhilaration of his discovery. He's heard the sound many times before, and almost never without a frisson of terror. It's the Brokerage's perimeter alarm.

# Chapter 10

The sensors that make up the Brokerage's perimeter alarm system are sensitive pieces of equipment. They can be triggered by something as light as a footfall, and it's not uncommon for the crew to be woken in the night because a fox or a feral cat has strolled through the clearing above the bunker, and for one of them to have to stumble out of bed and switch the klaxon off manually. Tanta knows, though, even before she reaches the control room, that that's not what has happened this time.

She finds her suspicions writ large on the bank of monitors that connects the Brokerage to the world above ground. The screens are a riot of chaotic motion – almost more than Tanta can take in. The forest, usually still save for the birds and the movement of the trees, is humming with activity, vehicles and people. It's a sight Tanta has been dreading ever since she and the others first came to the Brokerage. On some level, it's one she's been expecting since she and Fliss returned from the city – though she had thought they would have more time than this.

Somehow, the ICRD has managed to catch up with them mere hours after their escape.

At first, the density of the foliage and the quality of the footage makes it hard for Tanta to determine exactly what kind of strike team InTech has sent after them. She was expecting bulky, camouflaged ICRD tactical vehicles, but the machines on the monitors are moving too slowly – and even through the night vision of the cameras, she can see that they're too brightly coloured. Then she manages to make sense of the scene before her, and her heart sinks.

'Damn. I was really hoping that all this was on account of a particularly large rabbit.'

What with the whooping of the alarm, Tanta didn't hear Yas come in. 'They've brought excavators,' she tells the older woman, gesturing to the monitors.

The diggers are mechanical monsters, with caterpillar treads and long, jointed necks. Their buckets, tipped with metal teeth, dip into the ground again and again, devouring it in ravenous bites and spraying crumbs of dirt in their wake. Behind them, Tanta can see other machines that she doesn't have a name for. They have claw-like appendages, and they're grabbing the trees and ripping them from the earth like weeds.

On the grainy screens, this frenzy of destruction is silent and remote, but that isn't going to last. The violence of the machines is methodical. They're disembowelling the forest bit by bit, examining each square foot of living earth for evidence of their quarry. It won't be long before the excavators' teeth tear the crew's hidden sanctuary apart.

Yas and Tanta exchange glances.

'I'll get Fliss and Ortega ready to evacuate,' Yas says. 'We can take the tunnel. Fliss left a car parked at the exit.'

'I'll check on Cole,' Tanta replies.

Yas is already heading for the door, but she throws an uneasy look over her shoulder. 'Let's hope he works well under pressure.'

They both know what will happen if Cole fails. If he can't figure out whatever is protecting Dr Friend and the other Directors from Harlow 2.0, then he and Yas won't be able to leave the Brokerage at all – at least, not without losing their minds.

Dr Friend smirks at Tanta as she walks into the storeroom. She jerks her head at Cole, ushering him outside. From the doctor's expression, it's clear he's guessed what's going on, but she won't give him the satisfaction of saying it out loud in his presence.

'They've found us, haven't they?' Cole asks, as soon as he and Tanta are out in the corridor.

'Not quite, but it won't be long,' Tanta replies. 'They're digging up the forest.'

'I've found what we need,' Cole says, speaking quickly. 'It's a kind of pass-over marker, a line of code that prevents Arthur's Inscape from downloading the software.'

To his credit, he doesn't spend any more time explaining his discovery, though Tanta can tell he's dying to expound its implications in full. 'Have you found a way to apply it to your and Yas's 'scapes?' she asks.

Cole grimaces. 'Not yet. How long do I have?'

A distant *thump* ripples through the bunker, answering Cole's question without Tanta having to open her mouth. He flinches, but then his expression sets.

'I'll get to work,' he says.

The booming noises from outside the Brokerage increase in volume and intensity as Cole resumes his investigation of the pass-over marker, until he feels like he's in the middle of a war zone. Each blow seems to strike from nearer at hand; at first, the rumbling sounds like distant thunder, then an earthquake, then as though the earth is splitting down to its core. Cole works through it all, shutting out the sounds – and, as time goes on, the ominous shaking of the walls, floor and ceiling. He has no other choice.

At first, he's hoping his task will be a simple matter of cloning Arthur's pass-over marker and applying it to his and Yas's 'scapes, but as so often happens, things turn out to be more complicated than that. As soon as Cole's had the chance to examine the marker properly, it's obvious that it isn't generic: it's unique to Arthur, with its own signature derived from his Inscape ident. In other words, copying it won't work – any other 'scape would reject the cloned marker as invalid. That makes his job many times harder, not least because it doubles his workload: he's going to have to forge markers for his 'scape and Yas's separately.

He's frantically tapping in code when the storeroom door opens and Neal, Fliss and Yas run in. Fliss is towing the intern by one arm; he's following her in a sort of daze, a bemused smile on his face. They head for the escape hatch at the back of the room and Fliss types in the code, using her body to shield the keypad from Arthur's keen glance.

Cole tries not to watch them – he needs to focus – but it gives him a queasy feeling in the pit of his stomach to see Fliss and Neal leaving. Half of his anxiety is on their behalf, the rest on his own. He wishes he could go with them; the thought of him and Yas being stuck here when the excavators crack the Brokerage's shell makes him want to vomit from pure terror.

There's a shriek, louder even than the shrill tones of the alarm, as Fliss pulls the first airlock door open.

'Yasmin, Cole. I'll see you on the other side,' she says. Her voice doesn't shake, but there's a ferocity in it that makes her feelings plain. The words are a demand as much as a farewell: *you'd better not fucking die.*

'Count on it,' Yas replies. She sounds completely at her ease, but then, she's trained for these kinds of high-stakes situations.

Cole doesn't have the words or the time to respond, but he raises a hand in farewell, and as he hears the door clang shut again, he wishes the bandit godspeed in his heart. He and Fliss are not really friends, not even now, but that doesn't matter. They've all been stuck down here in the dark and the fake daylight for four months, and the pressure of living so far underground has bonded them into something stronger.

He wonders, briefly, if this is how Tanta used to feel back when her Harlow Programming was operational. Did she see her colleagues the same way Cole sees her, Fliss and Yas now? If so, Cole can understand – finally – what the corporation might once have meant to her. He has never had comrades in arms before – people he'd die for, if it came to it. Despite the chaos around him and his own mounting fear, the thought warms him. It's nice.

He doesn't have long to cherish the revelation. Another vibration, like a mortar shell, shakes the Brokerage, and this time it brings a rain of dust and debris with it. Cole glances upward: hairline cracks score the ceiling.

He pings Yas a 'scape access request and an instant later he's in, and racing to finish the code for her pass-over marker before the roof caves in. The only thing he needs to complete it is a signature derived from her Inscape ident, but his hands are shaking so much that he can barely input the necessary haptic commands. He clenches his jaw, trying to force some steadiness into his trembling fingers. Once he's finished with Yas's marker, he'll need to make another for himself. If he's very lucky, InTech won't find him and kill him before he's done.

'This abduction of yours isn't turning out quite as you'd hoped, is it?' Arthur sneers. 'If you thought working in the Black Box was bad, wait until you experience life in a secure sleeper facility.'

Cole isn't intending to reply to this gloating monologue – he doesn't even have the attention spare to be irritated by it – but he does wish Arthur would shut up.

'Perhaps if you ask very nicely, I may intercede with Reet

and Douglas on your behalf,' Arthur continues. 'How would you like to participate in human trials for the next iteration of the Harlow Programme, instead? It does seem fitting.'

Behind him, Cole hears Yas snort. 'That's optimistic,' she mutters.

There's a pause. Cole imagines Arthur craning his neck to see who's mocking him.

'What do you mean?' Arthur asks. 'What's optimistic?'

'That you've assumed the people trying to collapse the building on your head are here to rescue you.'

Cole is impressed. He had to work hard to rattle Arthur, but Yas has achieved it with a single, throwaway comment.

'Why else would they be here?' Arthur snaps.

'Oh, I'm sure they'll try to take you back,' Yas says. 'But I don't think they'll try that hard.'

'I am the Director of Research and Development for the entire corporation.' Cole can picture Arthur drawing himself up in his chair as he speaks, face pale with rage. 'InTech can't afford to lose me.'

'Mmm. You're half right,' Yas replies. 'The way the brass tend to see things is that they can't afford to let anyone else *keep* you, which isn't the same thing at all from your perspective. But do go on telling us about how you're going to use us all as lab rats when you get back.'

In the thunderstruck silence that follows this pronouncement, Cole slides Yas's pass-over marker into place.

'Yas, you're done,' he announces. 'Get out of here.'

An impact – the loudest yet – drowns out Yas's response. Worse even than the noise, and the cracks that have deepened in the walls and ceiling, is the rush of cold air that floods in under the storeroom door in the wake of the blow. It's that, more than anything else, that let's Cole know that their time is up. The ICRD has broken through.

While Cole works, Tanta packs. There isn't time to take much, but there are certain things the crew can't afford to leave behind. She starts with water, filling two canteens for each of them and then another couple for good measure. She loads the bottles into two bags, which she leaves by the escape hatch.

Their earpieces and touchscreen devices she slings into a backpack, along with as much of their kit as will fit. They still have the weapons and body armour that Fliss was given by her old Thoughtfront employers, and they'll need every bit of it if they're to survive in the Unaffiliated Zone for long. Tanta puts her own armour on and slips a handgun into her belt, then packs the rest.

When she's finished, she heads back into the control room. There are things she needs to destroy, too. On the Brokerage's computers there are lists of informants, double agents, and the locations of safehouses — records that it would be unconscionable to allow to fall into InTech's hands. Tanta deletes them all. At first, she's able to keep track of the destruction of the forest while she works, but over the course of ten minutes, the monitors wink out one by one as the Brokerage's security cameras are crushed along with the trees or flung to the ground and trampled under the caterpillar treads of the excavators.

By the time the last security feed has gone dead, Tanta doesn't need cameras to tell her how close the search and recovery team have got. She can hear their approach herself: the buzz and whine of hydraulics, the rumble of displaced earth. The vibrations rippling through the Brokerage are so intense now that cracks are beginning to appear in the walls and ceiling.

She's in the central corridor, on her way to check up on Cole and Yas, when the first excavator breaks through. There's a crack, and what looks like a metal tooth appears in the ceiling at the other end of the hallway. It's followed by several more, easing their way into the concrete like someone taking an exploratory bite of an unripe apple. Tanta edges backwards, and then the teeth come together with a grinding *crunch*, a noise that jars every bone in her body.

When they withdraw, a chunk of the ceiling vanishes with them.

Tanta has missed moonlight, but seeing it now, spilling into the Brokerage like blood from a gaping wound, it looks incredibly wrong. Chill night air flows in with it, and the noise of the machines. And then, worse still, the grinding of hydraulics ceases, and she hears the slam of a cab door.

She backs into the storeroom before any of the ICRD's agents can spot her through the hole.

'They're here,' she announces to the room at large. No one looks surprised.

She crosses to the nearest shelving unit and pulls it towards the door. As a barricade, it won't do them much good, but it's better than nothing. Yas puts her shoulder to it from the other side and together, they heave it into place.

'You guys should go on ahead,' Cole says. He's staring into the middle distance as he speaks, his hands darting through the air and his focus locked on whatever is on his 'scape, but his whole body is shaking. 'I'm almost done.'

'I'm not going anywhere,' Tanta replies.

Yas looks similarly disinclined to budge. 'Please, Cole,' she says, 'leave the heroic self-sacrifice to the professionals.'

Cole's right, though – they needed to be out of here ten minutes ago, and the situation is only getting worse. Tanta pulls the pistol from her belt and crosses to Dr Friend's chair, where she loosens his bonds. When she's done, she gestures at him with the gun, urging him to his feet, and moves him between the others and the door. If the ICRD does make it in here before she, Cole and Yas can beat a retreat, at least they'll have some leverage.

As if on cue, the door rattles in its hinges as something slams into it from the other side.

'How close to done is "almost"?' Tanta asks, not taking her eyes from Dr Friend.

'Every time someone asks me that,' Cole replies, teeth gritted, 'they add ten seconds.'

The tempo of his frenzied hand movements is slowing, though. A minute later, he makes a swiping motion in mid-air, dismissing whatever has been occupying his attention.

'Finished,' he says.

The door bursts open, the shelving unit toppling over and sending tins and jars of preserves crashing across the floor. Framed in the doorway, a manual battering ram clenched in both hands, is Reet. There's a squad of armed agents behind her, but for all Tanta cares, she may as well be alone. The sight of Reet obliterates everything else: she's flooded with relief to see her alive and unharmed. Her ex-lover looks exactly as Tanta remembers her – same hazel eyes, same solid, wrestler's physique. They lock eyes, and for long seconds all Tanta can think of is Reet's scent of spices and flowers, the feel of her arms around her. They stand facing each other, nothing between them but the fallen shelving unit and a lifetime of shared history.

Then Reet takes a step into the room. Tanta tightens her hand on Dr Friend's arm, and on the gun she's holding to his head. She curls her finger around the trigger.

'Don't come any closer,' she says, and her voice is steadier than she feared it might be, her stance surer. Without turning, she calls over her shoulder, 'Cole, Yas, grab the bags and open the door. We're leaving.'

Behind her, she hears the beep of the keypad. Reet stops. The agents swarming in behind her stop too, eyeing Tanta warily. Tanta lets her eyes play over their faces, realising for the first time how many of them she recognises. Firent is there, staring at her with a pleading expression. They're all CorpWards, in fact. It's an indication of just how much things have changed since Tanta left the city. She thinks, for an instant, of Gallus and Berturan, the older agents she met on her first day in the ICRD. They must be dead-eyed automatons by now. Are they still agents? Or is the ICRD staffed entirely by young, Harlow-Programmed Corporate Wards? It's a strange thought. For a moment, Tanta looks at Reet and the loyal wards lined up behind her and feels like she's looking into a parallel universe, one that offers her a glimpse of the future she could have had.

That's not the most striking change that has taken place over the last four months – not to Tanta, anyway. As she stares at Reet, Tanta realises that she has no idea what her ex is think-ing. Her face, once an open book, has snapped shut – or it's written in a language Tanta can't read anymore. She thinks of Reet's pleas over the loudspeaker as she and Fliss fled the city a few hours ago. Tanta was convinced, then, that she could hear Reet's intentions in her voice as clearly as she used to. Was she deluding herself?

The moment stretches. Tanta has to say something else, to bring this fragile standoff to a conclusion, but she finds herself reluctant to speak. In the silence, it's almost like she and Reet are together again. She wants to savour that, even though she knows it's a lie.

In the end, Reet saves her the trouble. No more than five seconds can have elapsed before she says, 'Stand down, Tanta. Release Dr Friend and surrender.'

Her voice is cold and commanding and utterly devoid of feeling. Something inside Tanta crumbles at the sound of it. All this time, she has allowed hope to fool her into believing the impossible. There is no 'we can still fix this' – there is no 'we'. Reet would say anything to bring her back in, because those are her orders. Whatever her personal feelings, she was never going to choose Tanta over InTech – and she never will.

'I can't do that,' Tanta answers. The words break on their way out of her mouth, spilling across the floor like shards of cut glass. Back when she was Harlow-Programmed too, she would never have found it this difficult to keep herself together. Her feelings used to be small, tidy things – things she could pack away into a box when the situation required it. She wonders, now, how they ever fit into the space InTech left for them.

Cole appears at her elbow. 'We're ready,' he murmurs.

Tanta doesn't like him being so close to the agents and their guns. She takes a step to the side, putting herself and Dr Friend between him and Reet. 'My crew and I are leaving,' she says. 'If you try to stop us, I'll kill Dr Friend.'

'Do,' Reet says carelessly. 'It won't change anything.'

Dr Friend blanches. 'Now, Reet, you don't mean...' he stutters.

Reet ignores him. For the first time since her ex burst into the room, Tanta thinks she sees a flash of emotion cross her face – there, then gone again. 'It's over,' Reet says. 'Please, Tee. You have to surrender.'

'I can't,' Tanta says again. There's no point saying more. She does anyway. 'I have to do this, Reet,' she adds, and she wishes, wishes with everything she has, that there was a way to make her soulmate understand.

'So do I,' Reet replies. She raises her gun, pointing it at Tanta's head.

And then Cole is stepping in front of her, his hands in the air. 'Hey,' he says, reaching towards Reet. 'Don't—'

The gun's retort is a thunderclap, a sound so loud and large it pushes every other noise out of the room. It seems to push

Cole backwards, too. He staggers past Tanta, his mouth opening in an 'O' of shock and pain. If he shouts, she cannot hear him. Reet swings the gun around to face Tanta again, her face expressionless.

What Tanta does next, she does largely on instinct. She throws Dr Friend forward, pushing him onto a startled Reet. Reet topples back, winded despite her bulk. At the same time, Tanta grabs Cole's arm and tows him towards the open doorway, where Yas is standing. She still doesn't know where the bullet went, but she soon finds out, from the blood that begins to trickle down her partner's arm, slicking her hand. She can't stop and assess the extent of the damage – Reet is already recovering, shoving Dr Friend away and raising her gun once more. Tanta only knows Cole is alive because she can feel his pulse, a frantic, panicked thing like a trapped mouse.

'Stop! Reet, everyone! I order you to stop!' Dr Friend's voice is an octave higher than usual, a frightened babble like a crying child. His eyes are wide, his limbs shaking. He looks like a man who has only just realised he's in the middle of a firefight.

His frantic cries are almost incoherent, but Reet understands them. Tanta, still backing towards the door, sees the moment the order hits home. Reet freezes up, the mask of her face cracking to reveal, beneath it, a bright flicker of panic.

Tanta knows exactly what's going through her mind, because she's experienced the same thing herself. She remembers that paralysing indecision all too well, from the night she and Cole diffused the bomb at the top of the Needle, over four months ago. Dr Friend isn't Reet's superior anymore, but he was until very recently. His direct order is tugging on strings of protocol and ingrained obedience that Reet isn't used to ignoring.

Her confusion won't last for more than a couple of seconds; Tanta doesn't give her time to recover. She fires once, a deliberate near miss that sends all the agents darting for cover. Tanta uses their disarray to turn and pull herself and Cole into the airlock, assisted by Yas from the other side. Once they're all in, Tanta slams the door to, feeling the full force of its ten-inch-thick reinforced steel thudding into the frame.

Silence falls like the dropping of a veil, sudden and complete.

Yas opens the second airlock door and together, she and Tanta help Cole through. Now that they're behind cover, Tanta has the leisure to notice that he's been shot in his right shoulder.

Yas goes to swing the second door closed behind them as they enter the corridor proper, but Tanta lays a hand on her arm.

'Leave it,' she says. The first door won't open unless the second is closed. It's counterintuitive, but in this instance, reducing the barriers between them and their pursuers will make them harder to catch. Reet's manual battering ram will take a while to break open a door this heavily reinforced. She'll probably have to bring machines down here to cut through the wall itself, or find the tunnel and dig it out from above ground. That will buy the three of them some time, though not as much as Tanta would like.

Beside her, Cole has slumped to his knees. 'We have to keep moving,' she says gently. She takes hold of his arm again, intending to help him to his feet, but he lets out a moan of pain and she hastily releases her grip. His breathing is rapid, his face sheened with sweat.

'She – she shot me,' he says. And then, with a visible effort. 'Are you and Yas OK?'

'We're both fine,' Tanta replies. She finds that she's struggling not to cry. She blinks the tears away, but the scene keeps replaying behind her closed eyes. She's not sure what's worse – that Cole has taken a bullet meant for her, or that Reet was the one who pulled the trigger.

She forces herself to examine his injuries. The entry wound

is small, but there's a red crater in his back that hurts to look at. Tanta blinks an instinctual command to her datamed, but gets nothing but a flashing <<Error>> message. Her Inscape is cut off from InTech's servers – has been since she arrived in the Brokerage – and it can't help her now. As this fact is borne in upon her, a helpless terror begins to rise within her, making her thoughts slippery. She's been trained to turn to InTech's medical database when she or one of her colleagues is injured in the field – without it, she knows no more about first aid than the greenest recruit. Cole has a ragged hole in his shoulder, his blood is seeping into the packed earth of the tunnel, and there's nothing she can do about it.

From beyond the airlock door there's a dull thud. It snaps Tanta back to attention. It's clear that Cole's in no condition to be moved right now, but it's equally clear that they don't have a choice. She's unzipping her jacket, intending to use it to staunch the bleeding, when Yas reappears at her shoulder.

'I found this in the airlock,' she says, handing Tanta a medical kit. Tanta opens the clasps eagerly. There are bandages inside, and she does what she can with them, wrapping layers of gauze around his wounds and pulling them tight. Cole clenches his jaw while she does it, trying to keep quiet, but it's a futile effort. His low groans turn into broken sobs of pain. Each one sends a fresh jolt of fear through Tanta's chest.

Yas must see how her hands are trembling, because she lays one of her own on Tanta's shoulder, giving it a squeeze. 'When we catch up with Fliss, she'll be able to dress it properly,' she murmurs. 'She knows a lot about field medicine.'

That's news to Tanta, but welcome news. The thud comes again, louder this time.

'Time to go,' Yas adds. 'Cole, do you reckon you can walk?'

It's not really a question, and they all know it, but Cole manages a nod, his face screwed up against the pain. Tanta and

Yas lift him to his feet and together, they make their way deeper into the escape tunnel. Blood is already soaking through Cole's bandages.

'You're all right. You're going to be all right,' Tanta tells him. She has no idea whether it's the truth.

# Part 2

# Chapter 11

It's a long walk to the end of the tunnel. Cole's choked sobs become hoarse, then die away entirely. He's still in pain – that's clear from his gritted teeth and the way the sweat stands out on his forehead – he's simply too exhausted to give voice to it anymore. Tanta and Yas do what they can, urging him on with whispered reassurances. At intervals, they exchange a glance over his bent head, a silent acknowledgement of their own tension.

Every second, Tanta expects to hear the sounds of pursuit at their backs – the crunch of the excavators breaking through the ceiling or, worse, the click of a safety being eased off, letting her know that it's over. If Reet and the other agents do catch up to them, the tunnel would be the worst place to make a last stand. It's narrow and low-ceilinged, with no cover anywhere. All her instincts are screaming at her to run, to get clear of this death-trap as soon as possible and out into the open again, but that's not an option. They can only go as fast as Cole can manage, and he's pushing himself as hard as he's able to already.

Crowding up behind these immediate concerns, Tanta is aware of a host of other worries nagging at the edges of her attention. Chief among these is the question of where she and the crew will go next. The Brokerage may have been cramped and airless, but for four months, it was their refuge. More than that: it was their base of operations, a place full of resources and tech, of which they've managed to salvage only a tiny fraction. In their secret, absurdly one-sided war against InTech and the Harlow Programme, it was their greatest asset – and now it's lost to them forever. What will they do without it?

She can ignore this issue for the time being, but she's uncomfortably aware that it requires a solution, and sooner rather than later. For now, it's all she can do to keep Cole on his feet and moving: he's been slowing steadily since they left the Brokerage, the pain of his injury wringing him out like a sponge.

So they limp onward through the tunnel, and time passes, and Tanta tries hard not to let Cole know just how frightened she is that they'll never make it to the other end.

They do make it to the other end, though by the time the passage begins to slope upwards, Cole's bandages are red and dripping, and Yas and Tanta have made a seat of their interlocked arms and are carrying him between them. The tunnel gives out several miles to the southeast of the Brokerage, beyond the forest, its exit hidden in the remains of a pre-Meltdown office block.

When she hauls herself through the grating and into the abandoned building, Tanta is relieved to see Fliss waiting for them there. The bandit was sitting on the floor a little distance away with Neal, but leaps up at her appearance to help lift Cole through. Tanta and Fliss take his arms while Yas boosts him from below. Once he's out of the tunnel, he curls up on his side on the floor, breathing hard.

Fliss's eyes widen at the sight of his bloodied clothes. 'What the hell happened?' she demands.

Yas, the last to emerge, dumps the crew's bags on the floor and swings the grating shut. 'Run-in with the head of the ICRD,' she replies. She looks like she's about to say more, but then she catches sight of the night sky through one of the glassless windows of the office. It's a dizzy vastness of stars, and it draws her gaze like a lightbulb draws a moth. 'Oh,' she murmurs, drifting towards it. 'It has been a *while.*' An icy draught sweeps through the window and she leans into it with a shiver, equal parts cold and pleasure.

The spell only lasts a second. Then she wrenches herself away from the view and joins Tanta and Fliss at Cole's side.

'What can we do?' Tanta asks.

'You can start by giving him some room,' Fliss snaps, waving the two of them away. 'And hand me that medical pack.'

The bandit kneels next to Cole, looking him over with an experienced eye. She pulls a face at his soaked bandages, then another when she's unwrapped them.

'This wound should have been packed,' she says. 'He's lost a lot of blood.'

Tanta is too anxious to respond to this. 'Can you help him?' she asks, her voice tight.

'Get me some water,' Fliss orders her, without looking up. 'Yasmin, clean your hands and then start cutting lengths of gauze.'

While Tanta and Yas carry out these instructions, Fliss rolls up her sleeves and rubs alcohol gel over her hands and arms. She mixes the contents of one of Tanta's canteens with a sachet of powder from the first aid kit, then uses it to flush out the wound. Once she's done that, she takes the canteen's canvas strap between her hands and puts it to Cole's lips.

'Bite down on this,' she instructs him.

To Tanta's horror, what Fliss does next is to put her fingers directly into the exit wound on Cole's back, probing at the exposed tissue.

'Gauze,' Fliss barks to Yas.

151

Methodically, she begins working the strips of gauze into the hole, packing it tight. If Cole was in pain before, it's clear that this process causes him a new level of agony. He howls around the strap of the canteen, the sound no less awful for being muffled. By the time Fliss has finished, he's shaking uncontrollably – but her ministrations have stopped the bleeding more effectively than Tanta was able to. The bandit redresses the wound with bandages and tape, then raises Cole to a sitting position, propped up against a wall, and hands him another of the crew's precious canteens. As he sips it, his breathing gets a little easier.

'How are you feeling?' Tanta asks him.

'I've been better,' Cole replies weakly. Tanta is relieved to hear him speaking at all.

'You're lucky the bullet missed the artery,' Fliss says. 'Try to keep your right arm and shoulder as still as possible, or you'll make it worse. I don't like this,' she adds, to the room at large. 'That dressing should be changed and cleaned every few hours – at least for the next couple of days. We'll need more medical supplies.'

'If Cole is stable, then we can figure that out once we're underway,' Yas says. 'Right now, we need to get out of here.'

Tanta nods. The sooner they get going, the sooner they can find a new base of operations – though where they could possibly go, she still isn't sure. She tries to imagine camping out in the Unaffiliated Zone and shooting down corporate supply drones, like Fliss and her old crew used to, but can't picture it. Maybe they'll be able to find another abandoned building to squat in. It's a dispiriting thought. 'Where did you leave the car?' she asks.

'Yeah, about that.' Fliss shifts uncomfortably. 'It's gone.'

'Gone? What happened to it?' The words come out sharper

than Tanta intended. Her visions of life in the UZ were depressing, but this is a catastrophe.

Fliss bridles. '*I* don't know, do I? It was gone when I got here. Someone must've nicked it.'

'You didn't hide it?!'

'Of course I did!'

Tanta swallows the retort rising in her throat. 'I'm sorry,' she says instead. 'I shouldn't have blamed you. Is Cole in a fit state to walk?'

'He should be OK for a bit,' Fliss replies, mollified, 'but he really wants a professional looking at that shoulder.'

'Well, that's off the table,' Yas says. 'There's no way we're making it into a corporate medical centre without being red-flagged and detained.'

'Could we try one of Bayanto's company towns?' Cole asks.

Yas shakes her head. 'There are extradition agreements in place for fugitives like us, and InTech's too big to piss off: we won't be any safer in another corp's territory than we would be in the city.'

The feeling of helplessness Tanta had in the tunnel returns, stronger than before. She's used to medical care being locked behind paywalls, but in the past it has always been close at hand – no more than a credit charge and a short trip in an ambulance away. Now, they're in the middle of nowhere – and there's nowhere they can go. For a dizzying moment, she feels completely alone, as cut off from civilisation as though she's drifting through space.

'I wasn't thinking of a *corporate* medical centre.'

All eyes turn to Fliss. The bandit doesn't look as self-assured as usual. She's staring at Cole's bandages, a frown deepening on her face as she figures something out the rest of them aren't privy to. 'We have to go to Gatwick,' she says at last.

★

Fliss was expecting shock – and maybe a few protests along the lines of 'it's impossible!' or 'we'll never make it!' What she gets is three blank faces. Well, four, if you count Neal, but his face has been blank the whole time.

Yasmin raises an eyebrow. 'And Gatwick would be...?'

Fliss sighs. She's long known that the corporations take little interest in anyone who isn't themselves. It's a good thing, by and large: neglect is better than unwelcome attention, and the corps don't generally have any other kind to spare. Still, she'd thought her new crew would at least know of Gatwick's *existence*.

'Only the biggest settlement in the wasteland,' she says. 'I grew up there. You seriously haven't heard of it?'

At this, realisation dawns on the older agent's face. 'Do you mean the southern unaffiliated encampment?' she asks. 'I think I remember covering that in basic training.'

This is almost worse than ignorance. 'It's not an *encampment*,' Fliss protests. 'It's a city. There are more than ten thousand people living there.'

Yasmin lets out a snort, which she tries to turn into a cough. Fliss isn't fooled.

'What?' she asks, shooting her a poisonous look.

'Sorry. That's... not a very large city, by corporate standards.'

Tanta is frowning. 'I don't think I've heard of it.'

'They probably dropped it from the course,' Yasmin replies. 'It's not as though it' – she breaks off with an apologetic glance at Fliss – 'well, it doesn't pose much of a threat.'

'Are there really medics there?' Tanta sounds sceptical.

'My *mum's* a medic there,' Fliss retorts. 'How did you think we lived? If you were assuming we slept in caves and ate berries, you're in for a fucking surprise.'

Of course, her mum has always told her that she shouldn't touch anything to do with the corps with a ten-foot pole. How she and the Gatwick Assembly will feel about Fliss turning up with three corporate fugitives and an abductee in tow, she doesn't like to think. She tries to brush aside the unease that stirs in her at the thought. Mum will be pleased to see her – she always is. The corporate trouble Fliss is bringing with her is just something that Constance Loh will have to look past.

'Medical help won't be a problem,' she continues. 'And we can lie low there afterwards, too, if the Assembly agree to it – it'll be safe. It's getting there that's the issue. It's half-a-day's trek from here, if we're fast. With Cole in the state he's in, I'd guess it'll take us twice as long.'

'InTech will be out looking for us,' Yasmin says. 'We'll have to move cautiously in any case.'

'And there's the Red Flags to consider,' Fliss adds. 'Last I checked, this whole area is their turf.' Once, she wouldn't have thought it likely the Red Flags would risk harassing a group as well-armed as theirs, but times have changed. She thinks about the intel she had off Sonia about how Thoughtfront is arming wasteland crews again. At the time, she'd dismissed the news; suddenly, it doesn't seem so irrelevant anymore.

'Are they anything like your old crew?' Tanta asks.

Fliss snorts. 'Not much. Think bigger – and meaner.' Unlike Fliss's old crew, the Red Flags don't limit themselves to shooting down corporate supply drones; they raid the smaller wasteland settlements, too, taking from people who already have nothing to spare. 'They're nasty fuckers,' she summarises. 'We don't want to tangle with them if we can help it.'

'Especially not now that they might be carrying Thoughtfront weapons,' Yasmin chimes in.

'All in all, walking to Gatwick isn't a great option,' Fliss concedes, 'but I don't see what others we have.'

When no one disagrees with her, she starts gathering their stuff.

★

155

They arm themselves and put on the body armour that Tanta was able to salvage from the Brokerage, then set out as soon as Cole is able to walk again. It's late and everyone is tired, but given the dangerous territory they'll be crossing and the people at their heels, they all agree that it's safer to travel through the night. The darkness won't hide them completely from the eyes of InTech's surveillance drones, but it will at least make them harder to spot. They stick as far as possible to the more built-up areas of the Unaffiliated Zone, using the shadows of the pre-Meltdown buildings to help cover their flight.

They walk in a three and a two, Tanta and Yas supporting Cole between them while Fliss stays in front with Neal, carrying the bags and scouting the path ahead. The UZ, usually so barren and empty, is alive with more corporate activity than Tanta has seen since her defection. Stealthed UAVs glide through the air like bats, scouring the area for signs of the fugitives.

There are no lights to give these search drones away, but Fliss can hear them coming. She walks with her head tilted slightly to the left, angling her uninjured ear towards the sky. More than once, Tanta and the others are trudging obliviously onward when Fliss shoos them back into a doorway, only for the drone to glide by a second later, swift and deadly as an owl. Not for the first time, Tanta is heartily glad that the bandit is with them. Even now that they're no longer dependent on her for food and supplies, she's still their eyes, their ears, and their guide.

As the night wears on and they get further from the city, the drones thin out. That's just as well, because the buildings do too, the dilapidated shops, houses and office blocks giving way to open fields. Tanta doesn't like being this exposed, especially when they can't run, but they don't have a choice. Cole kept up well enough for the first hour, but his pace is slowing inexorably as his strength fades. At first, Tanta checked in with him at intervals to see how he was doing, but it's got to the stage where even talking seems to cost him more energy than he can afford.

Three hours into their trek, the silence of exhaustion has fallen over the whole crew. Tanta needs to stay alert – she should be scanning the flat landscape for threats, or listening out for the subtle whir of motors that lets Fliss know a UAV is coming so that she can learn to recognise it, too – but she's struggling to keep her mind in the present. It's partly her mounting anxiety over Cole, and partly Reet.

Tanta can't stop thinking about their last encounter. Wherever she looks, she seems to see Reet's expressionless face floating on the textured blackness that surrounds her, a trick of the dark. She knows how wide the gulf is between Reet's programmed loyalty and her own newfound freedom. While the Harlow Programme is in Reet's head, she'll never see Tanta as anything but a traitor, an enemy. Even so, she has never allowed herself to contemplate the idea that Reet might try to kill her – her mind baulked at the thought of it.

As she trudges through the UZ, trying to keep her eyes open and her senses sharp, there's a part of Tanta that's in a parallel universe. She can't drag her thoughts away from the reality where Reet didn't miss her shot – the reality in which she killed Tanta, and the rest of her crew, and presumably considered it a job well done.

Perhaps it's because Tanta feels as though a part of her *has* died: the part that used to sit talking with Reet on the Ward House roof, that slept with her in a blanket fort, the two of them against the world. Those days of closeness and camaraderie are gone, but Tanta was clinging on to the idea of them, nonetheless. In all her months of self-imposed exile, she never gave up hope that her relationship with Reet might be salvaged. Now that hope is gone.

It doesn't change anything, of course – not really. The plan remains the same: reverse the rollout of Harlow 2.0, and make sure that InTech is never in a position to inflict a programme of corporate mind control on its residents again. Tanta remains committed to that course. The city is her home: she won't stand by and see its inhabitants sacrificed to the megalomania of the corporation that claims to be protecting them.

She's prepared for failure – she's known from the start that it's likely. It's the prospect of success that has shifted for her. In her most optimistic projections of victory, she imagined herself rescuing Reet, then reconciling with her. She sees now how foolish she was being. Tanta betrayed Reet, lied to her, fled from her. Even if she manages to remove the Harlow Programme from her head, there is no switch she can flick to make Reet love her again. Her anger and hurt are something Tanta may never be able to put right.

Nothing has changed – except that for Tanta, everything has. She's starting to realise that even if she manages to get back to the city, there may well be nothing and no one waiting for her there.

Fliss is as knackered as Tanta, but in better spirits. The crew are moving at Cole's pace, which is little faster than a crawl. At this rate, it's going to take them all night to reach Gatwick, but she doesn't mind. Neal isn't a bad walking partner: ever since the doc told him he could trust the crew, he's been calm, almost serene, following them with no need for prompting. On top of that, the programming in his head means he barely seems to notice Fliss exists, which has the added benefit that he doesn't bother her with awkward questions. She walks ahead with him in silence, keeping her eyes on the wasteland and her good ear on the sky, and thinks about her hometown.

Though she's pissed off about the loss of the Brokerage – it was a good hideout, and the closest thing to a permanent home that she's had in a long while – she's not sorry to be returning to Gatwick. In fact, she's surprised to find, as she and her new crew traipse through the dark, that she's actually looking forward to it.

When Fliss left the settlement, four years and many aeons of experience ago, she was glad to see the back of it. It's a nice enough place, if you don't mind fixed mealtimes in a communal mess hall, or being woken at dawn every morning by the commotion from the poultry sheds, or having to follow a work roster that puts you on composting duty every other week. Fliss did mind all of these things, considerably, which is one of the reasons she left. The other, of course, being that she wanted to do something a bit more exciting with her life than dig for tubers in the settlement gardens or grow penicillin in her mother's medical culture lab.

Now that she has put those things firmly behind her, though, Fliss finds herself happy to be coming back – for a visit, at least. Everything that drove her to leave Gatwick has taken on a cast of nostalgia since she turned her back on it. She thinks of the mess hall with fondness, and even composting duty carries memories of camaraderie. She and Sonia were on the compost heaps more often than most people – probably because of all the trouble they got into.

She's still worried about her mum – and especially about what she's going to think of the company Fliss is keeping nowadays. Fliss and her mum get on all right for the most part, but they've always been at odds over Fliss's choice of career. On the occasions Fliss has been back, to visit or to trade, in the years since she left, her mum has operated a strict 'don't ask, don't tell' policy: Fliss never tells her what she's been up to in the wasteland, and Mum doesn't ask where her wayward daughter came by the food, tech and medicines she brings with her to sell.

*You can't win against the corps, and you can't bargain with them.* That's Mum's motto — in fact, it might as well be flown on a banner from the tallest of Gatwick's defunct air traffic control towers. The settlement relies on being too far beneath the corporations' notice to attract their wrath. And now here's Fliss, bringing InTech's most-wanted right into their midst. She's half amused at the thought, half alarmed.

Well, she'll just have to cross that bridge when she gets to it. And if she knows the Assembly, they're unlikely to send her and the crew packing without at least giving them a chance to catch their breath — it's not like Gatwick to turn away strangers.

The crew are halfway across a wide, stubbly field when Fliss's thoughts of home are interrupted by a choked-off sound behind her. She spins around; she's just in time to see Cole stumble, going down onto one knee.

'With me,' she barks to Neal. She races to Cole's side, alarm gripping her by the throat.

In the near-total darkness, he, Tanta and Yasmin are little more than solid shadows. Fliss fumbles the cracked smartphone from the backpack and turns it on. Cole looks *bad*. He's covered in sweat, and when Fliss takes his hand to check his pulse, it's hot and clammy. He looks at her as she kneels in front of him, and his eyes are unfocused, empty of recognition.

'I think I'm sick,' he mumbles.

'No talking,' Fliss commands. 'Drink this.' She takes Cole's canteen from his belt and puts it to his lips.

She's shocked by how far he's deteriorated in such a short space of time. Tanta and Yasmin crouch beside him, propping him up. Once he has swallowed a few mouthfuls of water, they lower him to the ground. Tanta takes off her jacket and folds it under his head, a makeshift pillow.

160

'You're going to be all right,' she murmurs, her voice softer than Fliss has ever heard it before. 'We're almost there. You're going to be fine.' To Fliss, she adds, 'Do you know what's wrong with him?'

Fliss knows the ex-agent well enough by now that she can hear the shadow of anxiety in her tone. 'He's running a bit of a fever,' she replies, doing her best impression of her mum – calm and businesslike. 'Let's take a look at his shoulder.'

It's hard to keep up the act once she's peeled back the bandages. To untrained eyes, the bullet wound might not look much different than it did four hours ago, but Fliss's mum taught her enough that she can see something is seriously wrong. Cole's shoulder is swollen and blotchy, and when Fliss angles the smartphone directly above the wound, she can make out several angry red traceries beneath the surface of the skin, radiating out from the bullet hole in a circle that's grown worryingly wide. Blood poisoning: she's all but sure of it. Fliss is no medic, but she knows what will happen if it's left untreated for long.

'We need to pick up the pace,' she says.

She's re-dressing the wound when she hears the guttural whine of approaching motors. More than one, by the sound of things, and already too close to outrun – especially with Cole in his current state. She looks up at Tanta and Yasmin.

'We can't move him yet,' she says, answering their unspoken question. 'Best we can do is lie low, hope they pass us by – whoever they are.'

'Neal, get down!' Yasmin hisses. The intern is still standing in the middle of the field, as prominent as a giant mushroom – and showing about as much inclination to budge.

The words are no sooner out of her mouth than two slices of yellow light cut through the darkness of the wasteland: headlights. They swing towards the crew, spotlighting Neal. They're joined by another, and then another, until the centre of the field is lit up like a stage. Fliss shields her eyes, squinting against the sudden brightness. Beyond the glaring lights, she can just make out the black shapes of vehicles, hemming them in.

They're surrounded.

# Chapter 12

The lights freeze Fliss solid, every muscle in her body going rigid. Sometimes, when she and her old crew were driving at night, their truck's headlamps would pin a deer in place, the glare seeming to root the helpless animal to the spot. Now, Fliss is the deer, paralysed by terror. She shakes it off because she has to. She knows what's happening here – has heard about it from the ragged remnants of other wasteland crews – and at the moment, she's the only one out of the five of them who does.

'It's the Red Flags,' she mutters. 'A hostile takeover.'

Tanta leans closer. 'What does that mean?'

Any answer Fliss could have given is prevented by the slam of a car door. Footsteps crunch across the frozen field, coming to a halt just beyond the circle of light.

'Evening all,' a man's voice calls. 'Now, which one of you is in charge?'

Fliss glares at Tanta and Yasmin, jerking her head fractionally to the side: *keep quiet*. It's a common tactic among Red Flag raiding crews to shoot whoever answers that question in the face, forestalling the messiness of any leadership challenges or attempts at armed resistance.

'Our boss is dead,' she replies. 'Got downed by a drone two hours ago – same one that shot my friend here.' She nods towards the prone Cole, careful not to make any sudden movements with her hands. His presence gives the lie some texture and plausibility – she hopes it's enough.

The Red Flag laughs. It's a swaggering sound, with an undertone of malice that Fliss doesn't like. 'It's your lucky day, then. We're recruiting.'

It's not an offer – it's barely even dressed up like one. Fliss is still relieved to hear it: it confirms that these raiders have taken them for just another wasteland crew to be absorbed. If they'd clocked them as corporate fugitives with a potential bounty on their heads, she's sure this conversation would have gone very differently. She tries to sound enthusiastic as she replies, 'You'd take us?'

'Like I said, you're lucky. We got some powerful backers, and they're keen for us to expand our operation. Stick with us, you'll have a cut of everything we take – and we're heading for our biggest take yet.'

'Sounds like a sweet deal,' Fliss says. 'Where do we sign?'

Her feigned acquiescence must work, because after a moment, the man and one of his crew step into the circle of light. The Red Flag leader is tall and tanned, his second pale and blond. Each of them is carrying a sleek pistol. The blond's is tucked almost out of sight, but the leader has his on display, dangling from a flashy holster on his hip. Fliss recognises the guns as Thoughtfront kit, almost identical to the ones the corp once gave her old crew. Those weapons could be switched on and off at Thoughtfront's will, which means there's a chance these pistols are locked and unusable right now, but Fliss doesn't want to bet on it. Beside her, she feels Tanta start at the sight of the two men, a motion so slight she wouldn't have noticed it if she wasn't pressed up against the ex-agent shoulder-to-shoulder.

There are too many eyes on them for Fliss to ask what has caught her attention. Instead, she uses the raiders' approach to scan the rest of the field, trying to figure out what they're up against. Now that her eyes have adjusted, she can see the shadowy outlines of a car and three motorbikes ranged around them in a rough circle. The bikes all have people on them, and there's another figure lounging beside the car. At this distance, Fliss can't make out their faces, or what they're packing.

Then the two raiders are at their side, staring down at them. The blond one kneels and frisks the group swiftly, removing their guns and tossing them into the long grass. He searches their bags, too; he shows little interest in the duffel full of weapons and gadgets, but takes the water. When he's done, the leader jerks his head back the way they came.

'Leave the rest of your kit,' he says. 'Where we're going, you won't need it.'

Fliss nods, getting to her feet. Her legs are shaking. After a moment, Tanta and Yasmin do likewise.

'What about our friend?' Tanta asks.

The Red Flag leader flicks a disdainful glance at Cole. 'You won't need him either.'

'Fine by us,' Fliss says quickly, jumping in before Tanta can respond. There's no way for her to communicate to her and Yasmin what she has in mind – she's just going to have to hope they trust her enough to follow her lead.

There's a pause, no more than a heartbeat in reality, though to Fliss it feels drawn out to the point of torture. Then Tanta dips her head. 'Lead the way,' she says.

The three of them follow the two Red Flags to the car. At the edge of the circle of light, the leader turns again, scowling. Neal is still standing in the middle of the field, looking down at Cole with an abstracted expression.

'Is your friend deaf?' he asks. And then, raising his voice, 'You: over here, now!'

His attention is on Neal, so he doesn't notice Fliss draw

165

level with him. She looks to Tanta and Yasmin, meeting their eyes – with luck, it's the only signal they'll need. Then she knees the Red Flag leader in the crotch, putting all her force into the blow.

The other raiders react quickly, but Fliss is faster. She shoves the bandit leader over, toppling with him out of the glare of the headlights and into the anonymising darkness beyond. He curls in on himself as he falls, hands wrapping around his stomach. Fliss lands on top of him and pins her left arm against his throat, fumbling with the other for the pistol in his belt. She can hear gunfire around her, but the Red Flags have been staring into the circle of light for so long that their eyes aren't adjusted to the night around it.

The bandit leader is recovering. He struggles against Fliss's hold, still groaning with pain. He rolls over, pushing Fliss against the side of the car. She can feel the rubber of the front tyre pressing into the side of her head. She braces herself against it and pushes back, but he's stronger than her. An arm whacks into the side of her head, and then he's on top of her, crushing her into the frozen ground.

Fliss does the only thing she can think of, which is to jab the man in the eye. He screams, and she hits him again, punching him in the throat. He hits her back, harder than before. Lights dance in Fliss's vision and for a moment, the world slips sideways. She scrabbles with her left hand – the Red Flag is holding her right to the ground – and feels at last the smooth outline of the pistol beneath her fingers. She wraps them around the trigger, presses the gun into his thigh, thumbs the safety off, and fires.

The crew leader's howl is louder this time. Fliss feels something warm and wet spurting onto her, and knows she's hit an artery. She pulls the gun free from the holster, readying herself to fire again. The Red Flag leader slumps down on top of her, pinning her in place.

'Where is she?' a voice yells. Running footsteps crash Fliss's way.

'Here,' the leader moans, his voice already growing faint. 'Give me a hand.'

A hand does appear, groping for Fliss's face. She opens her mouth and bites it, chomping down until she can taste blood. There's a yell, followed by a terrible snap. A moment later, someone shoves the dead leader's bulk aside. Fliss draws a deep breath, relishing the return of space and cold air.

'You OK?' Yasmin's voice floats down out of the darkness. Another hand comes into view – this one helps her to her feet.

'I'm good,' Fliss gasps. She still feels a little as though she and the ground are heading in opposite directions. She hands Yasmin the pistol she took from the bandit leader, still slick with blood.

'Thanks,' Yasmin says. 'You catch your breath. Tanta and I can take it from here.'

While Fliss leans against the side of the car and waits for everything to stop spinning, Tanta and Yasmin stalk the darkness outside the headlights, picking off the remaining Red Flags one by one. Fliss sees very little of the carnage that follows, but she hears enough to make her glad of that. The noises coming from the night around her are grisly: bursts of frantic gunfire, wild shouts cut short with awful suddenness. The main thought on Fliss's mind is similar to Tanta's of a few hours ago, though she doesn't know it: she's glad the two ex-agents are on her side.

The sounds of combat are interrupted by the revving of a motorcycle. Fliss looks up in time to see one of the cones of light reverse and turn. It speeds away. Not long after that, silence falls over the field. Fliss makes her way unsteadily back into the ring of light to check on Cole and Neal, where Tanta and Yasmin join her. They're both breathing heavily.

'You handled that well,' Tanta tells her, as Fliss crouches down to examine her patient. There's a note of respect in her voice that makes Fliss glow, though she'd never admit it.

'You weren't so bad yourself,' she replies.

Cole is alive, and no more badly injured than he was already – although that isn't saying much. Neal, who stood oblivious in the centre of the field throughout the firefight, is clutching his arm. Once Fliss has convinced him to let her take a look, she sees he has been grazed by a bullet, leaving a deep red gouge across his left forearm. He cries out in pain when she cleans and dresses it, but doesn't seem inclined to complain otherwise.

'The blond one fled,' Tanta tells Fliss. 'Should we be worried about him?'

'Nah. After what you did to the rest of his crew, I doubt he'll be coming back for round two.' Fliss pauses, remembering something from earlier. 'You looked funny when we saw him. What was that about?'

'I thought I recognised him,' Tanta says absently. She's staring at Cole, watching the shallow rise and fall of his chest.

A beep from behind them sends them both spinning around. Yasmin is leaning out of the window of the Red Flags' abandoned car. 'Hop in,' she calls. 'Next stop, Gatwick.'

The car devours the miles that would have taken them the rest of the night to traverse on foot, racing through the UZ at Fliss's signature breakneck speed. Outside the windows, fields, overgrown hedgerows and the shells of outbuildings whiz by them in a blur. Inside, Cole gets worse. He's lying across the back seat, his head in Tanta's lap, and he's fading before her eyes. At first, he grips her hand, but it's not long before his grasp goes limp, and his eyes roll back into his head. He becomes incoherent, moaning and crying out things that none of them can understand. Ten minutes after they set out, he slips into unconsciousness. As Fliss pushes the car to its limits, and Cole's breathing becomes shallow and strained, Tanta is at last forced to confront the possibility that he might not wake up.

It's a thought her mind recoils from – worse, even, than the idea of losing Reet. The last four months have seen Tanta's sense of herself shattered, then rebuilt from the jagged fragments. Cole was by her side for the entirety of that process. At a time when she had to lie to everyone about who she was, he was the one person she could be honest with about who she was becoming. She's not ready to be without him. She isn't sure she knows how.

Tanta is so distracted that when Gatwick finally comes into view, she doesn't even realise it. Her first sign that they've almost arrived is when Fliss slows the car, and she looks up to find that the buildings have returned. Many of them bear marks of damage from the Meltdown Wars, blocky edifices with jagged holes in their masonry and tall spires twisted by the heat of long-ago bombs. At first, Tanta takes them for the usual ruins – until she notices the lights twinkling in the windows.

'Oh good,' Fliss says. 'The generators are working.'

As they draw closer, the weed-rucked road they're driving on becomes smoother and more even, the fields to either side of it no longer bare but filled with neat rows of crops, or the dark shapes of animals. Ahead of them, she can just make out a wire mesh perimeter fence, topped with a looping scrawl of barbed wire, and a group of figures massed outside it. To Tanta, these signs of civilisation bring her the biggest sense of relief she's experienced since Cole was shot. For the hundredth time over the course of the short ride, she feels his pulse. It's faint, but it's there.

'Not long now,' she murmurs. 'It's going to be OK.'

But Fliss is slowing the car to an uneasy crawl.

'Gate's usually open,' she says. 'And I've never seen a security team this big out this late before. Something's wrong.'

As the fence comes into clearer view, the people standing outside it start running towards them. They're carrying a bewildering assortment of weapons – Tanta can make out machetes, handguns and even a few jerry-rigged corporate stun batons – and they don't look pleased to see them. Fliss stops the car a few yards away from the gate and the group of guards – Tanta's trying hard not to think of it as a mob – surround it, weapons out.

'I thought I told you not to come back!' a woman's voice roars. A tall figure emerges from the crowd and bangs the muzzle of a shotgun against the windscreen. 'Get out of the fucking car and throw your weapons on the ground – now!'

It's so far from the reception she was led to expect that for a moment, Tanta isn't sure how to respond. She looks to Fliss, at a loss. Fliss winds the window down and pokes her head out.

'Paige, it's me – Fliss Loh!' she calls. 'I've only popped back for a visit. What's with the lynch mob?'

That sends a ripple through the group. A torch spotlights Fliss's face, making her squint. A man walks over to the tall woman. 'It does *look* like Fliss. Shouldn't we—'

'Shut up,' the woman – Paige – snaps.

He doesn't protest again, but as he melts back into the crowd, Tanta sees him raise a radio surreptitiously to his ear. She hopes he's relaying the news to someone else within the settlement – ideally someone more reasonable. If Paige herself recognises Fliss, she gives no sign of it. She repeats her order, only this time it's backed up with a warning shot over the car's roof. Fliss ducks back inside hastily.

'Tell her we've got an injured man with us,' Tanta urges her,

her voice low. 'We need help. We can pay, if that's what they want.'

Fliss turns over her shoulder to glare at her. 'Does it look like they're hoping to trade? 'Come off it, Paige,' she shouts again. 'You *know* me – I'm Constance's daughter!'

'You're a fucking Red Flag,' Paige shoots back.

Fliss bristles. 'No, I'm not! We—'

'You're in a Red Flag car and right now, that makes you our enemy. I'm only going to ask you one more time: get out, or we shoot.'

'She hasn't said she *won't* shoot if we do what she says,' Yas points out, speaking in an undertone. 'As soon as we step foot outside, we lose the only defence we've got.'

Tanta gives her an agonised look. 'What choice do we have? Cole's *dying*, Yas.' Saying it out loud sends a weight dropping through her, cold and hard as a stone.

'I've had enough of this,' Fliss growls. She puts one hand on the door handle and raises the other in the air.

'Fliss, don't,' Yas urges.

But Fliss is already swinging the door open. 'I'm coming out, Paige,' she calls. 'I'm unarmed. Now will you please stand down and let me and my friends in? We're not raiders.'

Paige swings her shotgun onto her back and steps up to meet her, toe to toe. She's more than a head taller than Fliss, and the bandit has to crane her neck to look her in the eye.

'Turn around,' Paige barks.

Fliss frowns. 'What?'

'Turn around and put your hands on the back of your head!' When Fliss doesn't move, Paige makes a grab for her wrists.

'What the fuck are you doing?' the bandit demands, side-stepping her. 'You're not seriously going to—'

She doesn't get to finish the sentence. Paige punches her in the face, cutting her off with a yelp of pain and surprise. Her second blow knocks the slight bandit to the floor. At the same time, the circle of guards closes in around the car, blocking Yas and Tanta in. There's nothing they can do but watch in horror as Paige draws back a heavy-booted foot and kicks Fliss in the stomach – once, then again. A guard makes to smash one of the side windows with the butt of a shotgun, but Yas is ready for that. Her pistol is in her hand and trained on the window before the man has landed a blow.

'Don't try it,' she warns.

In the back seat, Tanta draws her own gun with a pang of despair. She's acutely aware of the weight of Cole's body resting against hers, the life running out of him like sand through an hourglass. They came here to save him, but they'll be lucky, now, if he's the only person they lose. Yas darts a glance at her, one hand on the steering wheel, and Tanta nods. The only thing for it is to fight. If they run down the guards in front of them, there's a chance it will distract Paige long enough for Fliss to get free.

Tanta is readying herself to fire and Yas has her finger on the ignition button when the sound of a siren cuts through the night air, making them both pause. There's an ambulance speeding down the road ahead. It screeches to a halt just inside the perimeter fence, its bonnet practically touching the wire mesh, and its driver's door flies open.

'You hold it right there, Paige Scarrow!' a voice inside shouts.

To Tanta's surprise, the voice stops Paige in her tracks, one boot still raised over Fliss's prone form. 'Somebody cuff her,' she orders. A guard moves in on Fliss, twisting her hands behind her back, while Paige strides towards the gate.

Tanta's expecting a figure to emerge from the ambulance, but for a moment, nothing happens. Then there's a mechanical sigh and a whir, and the cab of the vehicle sinks to the ground, like it's kneeling down. A ramp unfolds from within, swiftly followed by a woman in a self-propelled wheelchair. She zips down the metal slope as though she's going to ram through the gate by main force. In fact, two white-scrubbed medics emerge from the back of the ambulance and open it for her. She skids to a stop just outside the circle of guards.

Paige looms over her. 'Security is my department, Constance. Back off and let me do my job.'

'I would, if you didn't keep making your job my problem,' Constance snaps. 'My team were barely able to save the last "raider" you laid hands on tonight. I'm here to make sure you take these ones in *without* beating them to within an inch of their lives.'

Tanta listens to this exchange through the window, fascinated despite herself. It reminds her of a dispute between Directors, only it's playing out on a dark road in the barren wilderness of the Unaffiliated Zone, rather than around the olive-wood table of the Needle's Executive Conference Suite.

Constance brushes past Paige and sweeps towards the car; the crowd part for her automatically. She sucks in a shocked breath at the sight of Fliss. The guard who handcuffed her has pulled her up into a kneeling position; the others stand around her with an uncertain air. Tanta, straining to see through the throng, is immensely relieved that the bandit is conscious. Her lip is split, the skin of her face red and bloodied, but her eyes are focused – and furious.

Constance rounds on Paige. 'How dare you attack my daughter?'

'She was resisting arrest,' Paige replies, unruffled. 'I was well within my rights to restrain her.'

Constance glares daggers at her, but she doesn't remonstrate further.

'I'm all right, Mum,' Fliss says, the words coming out thick around her swollen lip. 'But my friends and I have got two hurt men with us.'

'How bad?' Constance asks, without taking her eyes from Paige's face.

'One's just a bullet graze. The other's a gunshot wound to the right shoulder. Fever set in four hours after original insult. Initial assessment is septicaemia.'

Tanta is struck by the shift in Fliss's register. The bandit doesn't usually fling around medical terms so casually.

Constance tosses her head, a gesture Tanta recognises well. 'Still think I have no business here, Paige?' She wheels her chair backward a few paces and addresses the crowd. 'Now, here's how it's going to go. You're all going to take a breather while my team and I extract our patients. Then, you can escort the others into the security building by the North Terminal – *gently* – while I see to their friends. Do I make myself clear?'

She must do, because after a second, Paige nods, and the group of guards breaks up, moving a little distance away from the car in ones and twos. Once they've dispersed, the medics move in, a small drove emerging from the back of the ambulance with a stretcher in tow. With Tanta's help, they lift the unconscious Cole onto the gurney. Neal requires some coaxing before he'll leave the car, but eventually Yas is able to induce him to follow the medics into the back of the ambulance.

When her team is finished, Constance examines Fliss, shining a light into each eye and checking her chest for broken ribs. 'How are you feeling?' she asks, 'Any dizziness? Confusion?'

'I'm fine, Mum,' Fliss repeats.

'You'll have to go with the others then. The three of you will be in Scarrow's custody until the Assembly have figured out what to do with you,' she says, nodding to Tanta and Yas.

Fliss is visibly shocked. 'Mum!' she protests. 'We haven't done anything wrong!'

'I'm sorry, Felicity. It's out of my hands.' Constance spins on the spot to face Paige again. 'But if you lay another finger on her without the Assembly's leave, you'll answer for it to me.'

'I know my duty, Constance,' Paige says, her tone brittle as glass.

'Of course you do,' Constance replies. It sounds much less like an agreement than it does a threat.

# Chapter 13

Paige Scarrow's security team are less aggressive after Constance's intervention. They seem chastened by her scolding – even if Paige herself was unmoved by it – and they escort Tanta and Yas out of the car with something approaching professionalism. They are cuffed, frisked for the second time that night, and their bags and weapons are confiscated. Two of the security team stay behind with the gear and the car, while the rest surround the crew in a tight phalanx, Paige at its head. As the guards nearest to them take hold of their arms, Tanta looks over her shoulder to see their only means of escape being driven away with all of their stuff inside. Her chest tightens at the sight. They've made it into Gatwick, but how on earth they're going to get out again, she isn't sure.

'That was my mum, by the way,' Fliss says unnecessarily, as they're marched through the gate. 'Constance.'

Tanta can't help thinking it's not a good name for her. The woman was like a whirlwind in medical scrubs.

They haven't walked far when the ambulance shoots past them, its blue lights flashing. Tanta cranes after it, trying to catch a glimpse of Cole through the bodies of the guards hemming her in on all sides, but can't see him.

Fliss catches her eye. 'Mum's good – better than me. He's in safe hands.'

Tanta nods, though she's not reassured. Cole and Neal might well be the safest of all of them right now, but that's not saying much.

The sky has clouded over, reducing the landmarks around them to a collection of shadows, but as they're taken further into the settlement, the moon re-emerges and Tanta is able to make out more details. The crew and their escorts are walking down a road lined with houses made of rammed earth and adobe, the roofs thatched like the top of The Rotunda. The structures look ancient, but Tanta suspects they're actually the newest here. Several huge, pre-Meltdown buildings loom beyond them, their silhouettes cratered by bombs; the homes, by contrast, are un-damaged – the unaffiliated must have built them when they moved into this place.

At first, Tanta can't work out what Gatwick was before the Meltdown – a resort town? An industrial park? – but then the group turn a corner and she sees the plane. It's sitting in the middle of a roundabout at the end of the street, and it looks to have been converted into a children's play area. Tyre swings dangle from its wings and a rope ladder runs up its side to an open door near its nose. The immense barrels of its engines have been gutted and transformed into fun tunnels, complete with stairs up and a slide down. Tanta has seen pictures of airplanes on the Learning App, back when she was a child herself, but she's never encountered one in real life before. It's enormous – she has trouble imagining how something so bulky could ever have managed to get airborne.

About five minutes after they pass the plane, they reach a long, red-brick building and are marched inside, into a bright space lit by ceiling-mounted strip lights. To Tanta, it looks like a budget version of InTech's windowless rooms: there's a processing desk, a couple of interview suites and offices, and a single, large holding cell.

'How long are you planning on keeping us here?' Fliss demands.

'Take their cuffs off,' Paige raps, ignoring the question.

Once the guards have done that, the three of them are made to remove their shoes and belts, and then locked in. There's a little shuffling and some conversation, muffled by the holding cell's thick metal door, but after a few minutes, muted footsteps announce the bulk of the security team's departure. In the return of silence, Tanta and Yas sweep the cell for bugs and cameras. The room contains two rows of chairs bolted to the floor, an ancient physical telecommunications device hanging from the wall, and an ominous bucket behind a glass door in the corner – but nothing else.

When they're satisfied, they join Fliss, who is sitting against the back wall – the cheap plastic chairs look too uncomfortable to bother with. Yas gives the bandit a wry look. '*We can lie low in Gatwick*,' she says. '*It'll be safe for us there.*'

Fliss returns the look with interest. 'I didn't hear you suggesting any better ideas.'

Yas concedes the point with a gesture that's halfway between a nod and a shrug.

'It's changed a bit since the last time I visited,' Fliss admits, after a pause.

'What do you think had the security team so on edge?' Tanta asks, though she suspects she knows the answer.

'We weren't the first people to turn up tonight,' Fliss replies. 'You remember what the Red Flags told us: they're expanding their operation. Time was, they wouldn't risk hitting Gatwick directly – it's too big. Now that Thoughtfront are backing them, I'm guessing that's changed.'

Tanta nods. With InTech blockading its supply lines, Thought-front can hardly afford to support its growing ranks of bandit and raider allies by itself. It must have told them to make their own arrangements – so now they're targeting Gatwick and other unaffiliated settlements like it for food and supplies.

'They might be press-ganging some of the people here into joining them, too,' Yas muses. 'They tried it with us, after all.'

The three of them ruminate on this in silence for a while. Tanta is struck by how radically the crew's circumstances have changed in such a short space of time. Less than an evening ago, they were in the Brokerage, plotting the next phase of their plan to liberate InTech's side of the city. Now, they're caught in the middle of a power struggle in the UZ, one that was nothing more to them yesterday than a piece of saleable intelligence.

She wants to stay focused on their primary goal, but the ex-InTech agent in Tanta can't help but wonder what Thoughtfront hopes to gain from this fresh partnership with the raiders of the Unaffiliated Zone. It can't be for their superior fighting skills – she and Yas made short work of the Red Flags they encountered – and as far as she's heard, the corp has been unable to target InTech's supply drones since the crew put an end to its alliance with Jeanie. What, then?

*It's not your business to find out anymore*, she tells herself. But isn't it? The crew's freedom might depend on them figuring out an answer – after all, if they don't know exactly what kind of threat Gatwick is facing, how are they going to convince the powers that be here that they're not a part of it?

The hours in the holding cell hang on Tanta like weights. Questions about Thoughtfront and the Red Flags give way by slow degrees to fresh worries about Cole. Being apart from him is awful, even knowing that he's in the hands of professionals. Now that they've been separated, Tanta finds her imagination conjuring up far worse visions than the ones she had before her own eyes when they were together. She imagines Cole dead on an operating table, Constance shaking her head as she draws a sheet over his face, and the image grows and grows until there's no room in her mind for anything else.

At some point she must fall into a shallow doze, because when their cell door opens, it wakes her up. She starts, blinking the sleep out of her eyes. There's sunlight spilling into the holding cell, though she can't tell what time it is. Constance Loh appears in the doorway. In the daylight, Tanta can see that she's east Asian, with tanned skin, a round face, and long black hair shot through with strands of grey. She's wearing a short-sleeved top despite the cold weather, and her bare arms are thick and muscular. Tanta would know who she was even if Fliss hadn't told her: the family resemblance is striking. Tanta sits up straight at the sight of her, almost too afraid to ask the question that kept her up most of the night.

Constance pre-empts her. 'Your friend will live,' she says.

For an instant, Tanta is lighter than air. Cole being all right means that everything is all right; his survival tips the scales of her mood from incipient despair to delirious relief. She opens her mouth to say thank you, but Constance is already rolling past her and over to Fliss, who rises to meet her. She gives her daughter a tight hug, then looks her up and down, frowning. 'You're covered in blood,' she tuts.

'Most of it isn't mine.'

'Why doesn't that reassure me? And what happened to your ear?'

Fliss lost the top of her left ear more than four months ago, the result of a run-in with Jeanie's fleet of drones, but she doesn't seem inclined to volunteer this information. 'You should see the other guy,' she says, instead.

Constance sighs. 'There are some spare scrubs in my bag.' She turns around, and Fliss reaches into the satchel strapped to the back of her chair. 'Are you going to introduce me to your friends?' she asks, once the bandit has finished changing.

'Yasmin, Tanta,' Fliss says, jerking her head at each of them in turn. 'They're *not* Red Flags, and neither am I.'

Constance reaches up and strokes her cheek. 'That goes without saying, Felicity. I know you better than that. Unfortunately, I'm not the one you need to convince.' She turns her chair so she's facing all three of them. 'I've managed to persuade the Assembly to hear your case early. They'll see you at their next sitting.'

'Can we see Cole first?' Tanta jumps in.

'I'm afraid not – they're waiting for us now. Come with me.'

Two guards fall into step behind the crew as Constance leads them out of the security station. She slaloms past the desk and down the ramp at the door, pushing herself forward with long, smooth motions of her arms. They emerge into bright winter sunlight and a sky like a scrubbed floor, last night's clouds all swept away. Constance hurls comments and advice over her shoulder as she hurtles down the road, going so fast that Fliss, Tanta, Yas and their security escort have to trot to keep up with her.

'A lot has changed since you last visited, Felicity,' she says, swerving around a bend so sharply that Tanta imagines sparks flying from the wheels of her chair. 'The Red Flags have started hitting us directly. They're raiding our supply stores, even kid-napping new recruits. People are scared, and they're looking for someone to blame. Lucky for you, I'm the speaker for medics this year, so I can put in a good word for you.'

'That's something,' Fliss replies. 'What about the other speakers?'

Constance reels off a list of names, most of which are lost to Tanta in a squeal of tortured rubber as the senior medic pulls up short to avoid running over another pedestrian heading towards her.

'—Ruske, of course, and that dreadful Scarrow woman.'

Fliss pulls a face. 'Oh, shit.'

'It could be worse,' Constance says bracingly. 'You'll have me on your side, and the speaker for agriculture, too – that's Gracie Smith,' she adds, to Tanta and Yas – as if that clarifies anything.

'That's a start,' Fliss says, though she sounds uneasy.

They've reached the pre-Meltdown buildings that Tanta spotted last night. Constance steers them through a thicket of concrete pillars and footbridges and over to an immense structure with a glass front. Inside, a wide lobby gives way to a maze of arterial corridors. Tanta tries to keep track of the twists and turns, but what with Constance's speed and the unfamiliarity of her surroundings, it's a struggle to keep her bearings. The list of directions in her head is getting to the point of being untenable when they screech to a stop at the end of a hallway, before a pair of frosted glass doors. Through them, Tanta can make out the blurred shapes of seated people. There's a rustling, shuffling quality to the sound beyond, as of a crowd waiting in expectant almost-silence.

Constance pauses outside the doors, looking them all over with appraising eyes. 'Yes, you'll do,' she says. 'Now, remember: eye contact, don't mumble, answer any questions put to you clearly and honestly.' She pauses, reaching out to rub something off Fliss's face. The bandit squirms away, her cheeks going pink. 'You should be all right. Scarrow will push for execution – she usually does – but I doubt the Assembly will go for it.'

'Wait, what—' Yas starts, but the medic silences her with a hand as the double doors slide open.

Cole's return to consciousness is like the tide: it comes and goes in waves.

He's in the tunnel, stumbling along between Tanta and Yas, and trying to ignore the pain he's in. His right arm jolts as he moves, sending regular spasms of agony through his upper body. He looks down: there's a red flower blooming on the bandage around his shoulder, dark petals unfurling across the white gauze in an ever-widening radius. Cole thinks this might be a problem.

Then he's on his back, looking up at a sky smeared with stars. There are far more than you'd ever be able to see in the city, but they're all running together, and someone is leaning over him and—

He's still on his back, racing down a bright corridor. He briefly wonders if the white brilliance around him means he's in heaven, then realises that it's just strip lights. He tries to shield his eyes, but someone lays a firm hand on his arm.

'Lie still,' a voice says. 'You're going to be—'

The next wave sweeps Cole back into himself. He coughs, sucks in a breath deep as a half-drowned man's, and opens his eyes. He's washed back up on the shore of the here and now, and he isn't dead. For some time, that fact alone is more than enough to occupy his mind. Then another thought comes to him, and he clutches at his trouser pocket, feeling for the outline of the data card that contains his Harlow Programme uninstallation patch. It's still there. He sags in relief.

After that, he lies still, staring at the white panelled ceiling and trying to piece together what he's missed. His right arm feels strange: half fizzy, half numb. He flexes it cautiously. It still bends at the elbow, but he finds he can't move his fingers. That's an alarming development – Cole hopes it isn't a permanent one.

He thinks he's been out for a while, though he has no way of telling how long. He has no idea where he is. The ceiling isn't giving much away, so after mentally checking himself over he decides to make the attempt to sit up. It's a qualified success: reluctant to rely on his right arm, he levers himself up using only his left, which takes longer. The effort, or the change in elevation, leaves him dizzy. For a minute or two, the room reels around him like a carousel, and he fights down a surge of nausea.

Gradually, things come back into focus. Cole is in a clinic of some sort. The walls are whitewashed, and there's a bed to his left, identical to his own, with a metal frame and thin sheets. It's occupied by a pale young man with blond hair. Cole can't see an AR profile, so he's probably unaffiliated. He's sleeping – or perhaps he's been knocked unconscious. He's been badly beaten, his face and arms a mass of bruises.

Cole glances to the right. There's an IV pole next to his own bed, and he follows the snaking tube of the drip down and across to where it vanishes into his good arm. A little beyond the drip, Neal is sitting on a cushioned chair, staring into the middle distance to Cole's left. He's the first familiar face Cole has seen since regaining consciousness. He never thought he'd be pleased to see those empty eyes, that stapled-on smile, but he is.

'Neal,' he hisses, speaking low to avoid waking the other patient.

The trainee focuses on Cole slowly.

'What happened?' Cole asks him. 'Where are we?'

'Some people brought us here,' the intern answers. 'They treated you and bandaged my arm, and then they left. I thought you were dead,' he adds, without emotion.

Cole had managed to work out that much himself, but at least Neal seems to have some idea of what's going on here. 'Where are Tanta and the others?' he asks.

'They're not here.'

'Yes, I can see that, Neal. Do you know where they've gone?'

'They went away with the other people.'

'*What other people?*'

Cole tries several variations on the same queries, but can elicit little in the way of helpful responses. Neal seems certain that Tanta, Yas and Fliss were together when he saw them last, and that they left him willingly. If he knows more than that, he's keeping it to himself. Eventually, Cole gives up his questioning with a sigh. Gingerly, he swings both legs over the side of the narrow bed. There's a twinge of protest from his shoulder as he shifts his weight, but it's nothing like the pain he was in the last time he was conscious. Either he's on the mend, or there's more in the IV drip than just antibiotics and water. Either way, Cole finds that he's able to take a few, halting steps towards the door.

'You can't leave,' Neal says, from behind him. 'They locked us in.'

That sends a spasm of sick panic through Cole. They've been arrested? Does that mean the ICRD has caught up with them? As soon as the thought occurs to him, he realises that can't be what has happened. If InTech had found them, he never would've woken up. He peers through the glass panel set into the clinic's wooden door. There's a bland corridor beyond, with white-scrubbed medics hurrying to and fro, chatting and wheeling gurneys. There are no windows in the clinic itself, but he can see a corner of one from across the corridor. Squinting, he makes out a wide area of cracked tarmac, on which is parked a row of what look, implausibly enough, to be pre-Meltdown commercial jets. It doesn't look like anywhere in the city that Cole has ever seen — on either side of the riverbed.

So, they've been detained, but not by InTech. They could be in a black site belonging to another corporation, or somewhere else entirely. After a few minutes spent watching the corridor, Cole retreats back to his bed and lies down again. He's confused, and worried for Tanta, Yas and Fliss, but it's obvious to him that there's nothing he can do for them. He has no idea where they're being kept, and even if he did, what then? Attempting escape in his current condition would be foolhardy, and he'd be no use to them even if he succeeded.

No, the only thing he can do is wait, and trust in Tanta to come back for him when – or if – she can. Well, there is *one* other thing he can do. With his left hand, he takes the data card from his pocket.

'Neal?' he asks. 'How would you feel about helping me with some research?'

The headquarters of the Gatwick Assembly contains more people in one room than Tanta has seen in the entirety of the last four months. The space Constance leads them into is an atrium with a high ceiling. It's filled with chairs, arranged in a series of concentric circles around a podium on a central dais, and every one is filled. The walls of the place look like an indoor apartment block, lined with interior windows and balconies, and Tanta can see more people craning out of these. The overall effect is vertiginous, and extremely disconcerting. She feels uncomfortably exposed as Constance shepherds her, Yas and Fliss into the middle of the hall, all the eyes turned her way pressing down on her like a physical weight.

Constance takes them to the foot of the dais, where two rows of chairs have been positioned at right angles. The line of three must be theirs – she nods towards it, then rolls around the podium and parks her chair at the end of the other row, which is filled with ten sombre-looking people.

'Those are the speakers,' Fliss murmurs, as the three of them sit down.

Tanta scans their faces, trying to glean what she can from them. Apart from Constance, there's one other she recognises: the tall, pale woman who was leading the security team that apprehended them last night – Paige Scarrow. The other eight are strangers to her.

'Do you know any of them?' she whispers to Fliss.

'Paul and Andy used to run the creche when I was a kid,' she says, nodding toward two short, elderly white men. She pauses, reflecting. 'I got kicked out for biting.'

'That's not very encouraging.'

Fliss shrugs. 'I'm sure they don't remember. The one we've got to watch out for is Paige. She—'

She breaks off as an expectant silence falls over the crowd. The doors through which they entered open again and a black man – mid-sixties, with greying hair – strides down the aisle between the seats and mounts the dais. He's wearing a pair of grimy glasses that he takes off and polishes on the hem of his shirt as he surveys the hall. It only smears the dirt around, as far as Tanta can see, but he replaces them, apparently satisfied, and clears his throat.

'The Assembly is now in session,' he announces, in a resonant voice that's at odds with his slender frame. 'Chair Theodore Ruske presiding.'

The words have the ring of ritual to them, and the crowd responds accordingly. There's a collective exhale, a shuffling of feet and chairs, as everyone focuses their attention on him. Ruske polishes his glasses again, then glances down at a sheaf of papers on the lectern in front of him.

'First order of business: the unidentified hostiles apprehended last night outside the North Gate. Do the parties involved in this matter have anything to bring to the Assembly's attention?'

In the front row of seats, a long, pale arm rises into the air. Paige follows it, getting to her feet. Ruske nods in her direction. 'Chair recognises Paige Scarrow, speaker for security,' he intones.

'My fellow speakers,' Paige begins, with a sideways nod that takes in the rest of the row she was sitting in. 'Chair.' She inclines her head towards Ruske. 'The security force were alerted to a disturbance this morning, shortly after 03:00 hours, when guards posted on the North Gate observed a black all-terrain vehicle driving towards the settlement at speed. Given the recent Red

Flag attacks, we were concerned, and set out to detain the vehicle in question. We were met immediately with resistance.'

She spits the words in Tanta, Yas and Fliss's direction.

'That's not what happened,' Tanta says – or tries to say. Constance shoots her a warning look at the same time as Fliss kicks her in the shin, and the words die out in a mumble.

Ruske coughs pointedly. 'You will be given a chance to speak in due course. Please continue, Paige.'

Tanta nods, embarrassed. Speaking up was a mistake, one she won't make again. On the surface, the Assembly seems foreign, but beneath its unfamiliar customs and terms of address is a structure she is beginning to think she recognises. She may not understand the specifics of the protocols playing out before her, but she recognises the pomp and circumstance instinctively, from a lifetime of drilling in InTech's own bureaucratic procedures. The man on the dais, Ruske, must be the one in charge: he's the one giving the orders. The speakers opposite him seem to be like InTech's Directors, pre-eminent in their individual spheres, but bowing to the Chair's ultimate authority.

Tanta isn't sure what all the other people are doing here – perhaps they've just come to watch – but they're not important. Ruske is the one they need to convince. Tanta stares at him, her mind whirring. He looks unsure of himself and seems committed to procedure. Both are things she can use. If she watches carefully, and bides her time, she's confident she can make a case to him that will win him over. For now, she returns her attention to Paige, who is still speaking.

'The hostiles were heavily armed, refused to comply with our instructions, and couldn't account for where they'd come from or what they'd been doing last night,' Paige is saying. She spreads her arms, indicating the crowd around her. 'There was another attempted Red Flag incursion at the North Gate last night, around 18:00 hours. My team were on site and repelled the threat with force. These three and their accomplices turned up at the same place mere hours later, wounded, and with no plausible explanation for what they were doing in the area. I put it to the Assembly that they'd come back to finish the job. They're Red Flags and we need to deal with them before they do any more damage to us and ours.'

Her voice rises towards the end of her speech, becoming hoarse and strident. Tanta watches her face, the darting of her grey-blue eyes and the tremor in her hands, and understands why Fliss and Constance are both so wary of this woman. Paige is confused, frightened and angry – none of which are good qualities in a leader – and her fearmongering is having an effect on the whole Assembly. There are heads nodding around her, and glances, both fearful and furious, thrown in the direction of Tanta and her fellow prisoners.

Tanta thinks back to what things were like in InTech's side of the city in the autumn when the food shortages started to bite, the protests and the not-quite-riots. A panicked crowd can be a dangerous thing, and Paige already has this one nervous. Ruske looks less convinced, though: his expression, as he removes and cleans his glasses for the hundredth time, shows focused attention, but no reflection of the suspicion in Paige's eyes.

'Attacks like this are exactly why I believe we ought to accept Thoughtfront's offer,' Paige continues.

This shift in her argument is so unexpected that Tanta almost repeats her earlier blunder. She forces down the questions rising to her lips, watching the crowd instead for some indication of what on earth Paige is talking about. Her suggestion does not meet with the same approval as the diatribe that preceded it. There's a smattering of applause, but it's limited to one section of the Assembly – probably the rest of the security force. Elsewhere, Tanta sees uneasy glances and pursed lips. Beside her, Fliss catches Ruske's eye and raises her index finger. It's a protocol he must recognise, because he nods in her direction, and Paige pauses.

'Yes?' she says, with a scowl.

'Since when does Gatwick make deals with the corps?' Fliss demands.

'That's an internal security matter,' Paige snaps.

Ruske lifts his hand. 'I see no harm in answering her. To address your question: we haven't – yet. A representative from Thoughtfront approached us two weeks ago, offering weapons to aid in our defence against the Red Flags in exchange for one thousand recruits for their peacekeeping force. The Assembly is still considering his proposal.'

'And it needs to come to a decision,' Paige jumps in. 'We can't afford further delay: the events of last night have made that abundantly clear.'

Tanta raises her own index finger. She's hoping to make the point that Thoughtfront is the one arming the Red Flags in the first place, but she's barely begun to explain before Ruske cuts her off. 'Unless you have a question, you *must* wait your turn to speak,' he says, frowning at her. 'This is your final warning. Paige, you may continue, but Thoughtfront's offer is not the matter currently under discussion. Limit your arguments to the issue at hand, please.'

For a moment, Paige's pale face grows whiter, and her jaw sets. Then she gives a single nod, the motion as stiff and stilted as if it's been forced from her. 'To return to *the issue at hand*,' she says, 'holding these prisoners would be an exercise in kicking the ball down the road, and sending them away would be even worse – there'd be nothing to stop them from coming back and attacking us again. I know some of you will find the prospect of making an example of them unpalatable, but in view of the threat we face, it is necessary.'

Tanta glances at Fliss, then at Yas. The older agent raises an eyebrow, an expression Tanta can read easily enough. If this trial, or whatever it is, doesn't go their way, they're going to have to fight their way out. She looks behind her. There are two guards on the doors, burly women armed with batons. Not much in the way of security, but that's not the real problem. Fliss said there were upwards of ten thousand people living in Gatwick, and at least two hundred of those are gathered in this hall. Tanta and Yas may have their ICRD training on their side, but Gatwick has the numbers, the weapons – and Cole, still locked up in a medical bay somewhere. Tanta's muscles tense, her heart pounding with adrenaline that doesn't have an outlet. If Ruske is convinced by Paige's argument, there's very little they'll be able to do about it.

Paige seems to be wrapping up now. She folds her arms again. 'That is why I am moving for an immediate vote on the matter,' she says, her voice rising above a surge of muttering from the rest of the Assembly, and that's when the analogy Tanta has been building in her head collapses, plunging her into freefall.

'A vote?' she hisses to Fliss.

Fliss nods. 'That's how this works.'

Tanta knows what a vote is, of course: they have them all the time on the reality shows and celebrity contests InTech's Entertainment and Media Division puts out by the bucketload. She learnt about ancient 'democracy' on the Learning App back when she was a child living in the Ward House, but she thought the practice had died out with the Meltdown Wars. Seeing it happening in front of her is like coming face to face with a dinosaur.

And the implications for her, she realises, could be just as serious. Tanta understands politics – the politics of InTech, its Directors, and its board – but this is something different altogether. She knows how to talk to the conduit, bypass difficult team leaders and manage obstreperous colleagues; she has no idea how to work a crowd.

Somehow, she needs to make the Assembly see that Paige has it backwards – that the crew are not Gatwick's enemies, and Thoughtfront is not their saviour, but what will she do when they ask her to prove it? She can't trust them with the truth about who she, Cole and Yas are – not with InTech so close on their heels – and even if she could, they have no reason to believe her. A creeping chill rises through her, bringing a single thought with it. She's in strange, dangerous waters – and she's completely out of her depth.

# Chapter 14

Cole is used to taking refuge from the unknown in his work. It's a habit he fell into in the early days after his MindWipe, when every idle minute was like a rug waiting to be pulled out from under him, plunging him into the terror of his amnesia. His thoughts fall back into the old, familiar pattern readily as he syncs his Inscape to Neal's and accesses his Array. There's really nothing else to do: either Tanta, Fliss and Yas are alive and looking for him, or...

But Cole isn't going to think about what comes after the 'or' – that's the whole point of the exercise.

He is a little sorry to be testing his prototype software patch now, with only Neal and an unconscious patient for audience. This is an important moment, one that he wishes Tanta, Fliss and Yas could be here for, though he isn't going to let that stop him. The crew's efforts to reverse Harlow 2.0 are too important to delay.

Still, Cole takes his time scanning the data card with his 'scape reader and checking the code before he introduces it to Neal's MbOS, allowing himself to feel the full weight of what he's about to do. If this works – and he's all but certain it will – then Neal will be restored to himself again, which will mean that Cole can do the same thing for the rest of InTech's residents.

In theory, at least. There are some steps in between him and that goal – find the rest of the crew, escape from wherever it is they're being held, get back into the city – but once again, Cole pushes these considerations firmly to the back of his mind. They're questions for the future. Right now, there's only one thing he needs to do.

He sets the code to compile, using the downtime to conduct a mental inventory of his injuries. When (*if*) Tanta and the others come back for him and Neal, they'll likely have to leave in a hurry. His right arm still feels strange. He tries again to move his hand, focusing all of his energy on the attempt, and manages to bend his index finger. Cole's not a doctor, but he's pretty sure he's got some kind of nerve damage. Whether it's the kind that'll heal on its own or not remains to be seen. At least he can still walk – the most important consideration right now – though he's not sure how he'd hold up on another forced march like the one from the Brokerage.

When the patch is ready, he gets Neal's attention again. This is difficult; the intern is spacier than usual, staring over at the patient in the other bed with a look of trancelike concentration, but by dint of much effort, Cole at last convinces him to turn his way.

'Neal, would you scan this data card and download the contents to your 'scape?' he asks, holding it out for him to see.

For a moment, he thinks Neal is going to refuse. His unfocused eyes narrow, as if he's thinking it over. But his programmed trust, transferred to Cole on Dr Friend's orders, must still hold, because after a few minutes of thought, he smiles again. 'Of course.'

Cole watches while the intern does as he asks, trying not to betray his tension. There's a delay of a few minutes while the software patch downloads. Neal's 'scape hums and whirrs to itself, mulling over the new code, the download timer on his

Array ticks down, and Cole waits, breath held. The timer has reached thirty seconds, and Cole is almost convinced that he's succeeded, when there's a slew of error messages, and Neal's MbOS spits the patch out like a petulant child.

{*This is not a valid addition to the Inscape system*} an automated message informs him. {*Pirated and unauthorised software edits are strictly prohibited.*}

Cole frowns. That should have worked. True, this software patch is a prototype, but it's not a complete shot in the dark. He developed it based on the copy of Harlow 2.0 that he and Neal stole from the Black Box in the autumn. He was sure – as sure as it was possible to be, pending the results of practical trials – that it would get the job done. So why has it failed?

'Should I try again?' Neal asks.

'Not yet,' Cole replies. To figure out what has gone wrong here, he's going to have to examine Neal's Harlow 2.0 software directly. He gets down to it, shaping the haptic commands awkwardly with his left hand. He's used to using both, so his progress is slow and difficult. He gets his first hint of an answer when he goes looking for the programme files and finds that he can't access them. There's a wall of security protocols blocking his way – security protocols that don't exist in the version of Harlow 2.0 he was working on.

Cole nods to himself. He understands what has happened now. He and the rest of the crew have been stuck underground for four months. A lot has changed in that time – InTech and Thoughtfront have gone to war, the ICRD has a new Director, and it looks as though Harlow 2.0 has received a few security updates. In other words, his uninstallation patch should still work as intended – but first, he'll have to find a way to sneak it past the programme's new defences.

He's a little irritated by the prospect, but not daunted. If he could solve every technical problem on his first try, he'd be something more than a genius. So InTech has beefed up Harlow 2.0's security. So what? The Inscape is by far the most secure MbOS around – Thoughtfront's MindEye can't hold a candle to it – and is widely considered, both within InTech and outside it, as unhackable. That's never stopped Cole before. He dives back into the code, searching for the loophole that he knows will be there, somewhere.

Only the more he looks, the more he begins to worry that there isn't one. The new security protocols are a lot like the plated shell of an armadillo, smooth and hard and completely free of easy access points. Over the course of the next two hours, Cole works his way around the programme's impenetrable surface in growing dismay. When he first encountered Harlow 2.0, he pictured it as a ramshackle old castle, cobbled together from scraps of other peoples' code. That's still true, as far as it goes – but inelegant though the structure may be, its walls are sound, its moat deep and filled with crocodiles. Cole can find no way to bypass its fortifications at all.

A terrible possibility dawns on him: when he removed the backdoor from Harlow 2.0 in the autumn, he may have fixed its only major security flaw. He had no choice at the time, but there's still a cruel irony in his position now. He's been waging war against his forgotten self for months, trying to right every wrong of his dark and bloody past, from his creation of the Harlow Programme to his days as a cyberterrorist. But in seeking to save InTech's residents, he may have condemned them to a lifetime of mental servitude. It feels grimly fitting that his first real attempt to make amends for his past crimes has only made things worse: it seems to be the perennial pattern of his life.

Cole rests his head on his good hand, weighed down by a sense of guilt that's almost unbearable. It's something he's usually able to keep at bay, but right now, it hits him with its full force, as bad as the night he realised he was responsible for the Harlow Programme. He comes out of it slowly and with difficulty, using the problem of the security protocols like a rope to haul himself out of the pit of self-loathing.

This is usually the point in his process where he'd rise to his feet and start pacing the room in the hopes that the motion will wear out his bleak thoughts, perhaps even shake some new ideas loose. With the drip in his arm, he doesn't think that'd be a great idea, so he settles for stretching his legs and wiggling his toes, his attention still on Neal's 'scape. That's when the impossible happens. He's staring at the blank wall of Harlow 2.0's security protocols when suddenly, that wall opens in front of him.

There's a gap, a way into the software that wasn't there before.

As quickly as it appeared, it's gone again, leaving Cole wondering if he imagined it. He's narrowing his eyes to examine the protocols more closely, all thoughts of taking a break forgotten, when a crash from beside him jerks him back into the outside world.

He disconnects from Neal's 'scape – hurriedly, but not without a pang of regret – to find the intern has leapt to his feet. The sound he heard was Neal's chair falling over. He must have pushed it back in his excitement.

And Neal *is* excited: Cole is used to him displaying about as much animation as a toaster oven, but now his eyes are fever bright, his face illuminated by a grin like a crescent moon. He strides past Cole, walking around his bed without even looking at him, and as Cole turns his head to follow the intern's progress, he sees that the young man in the bed next to his has opened his eyes, and is looking Cole's way. He has one finger raised to his temple – and suddenly, he has a profile, the AR border limning him in pale red.

Neal reaches the man's side and crouches beside him, putting one hand tenderly on his arm.

197

'Do you require assistance, Colleague?' he asks.

*Oh. Oh dear.* Cole has a feeling that things are about to get very bad indeed.

Fliss has known how the Assembly works – and the personalities involved in keeping it running – since she was a child, so while she's no happier than Tanta about Paige's pronouncement, she is at least more prepared for it. Speakers are selected to represent Gatwick's various roles and departments by a yearly ballot. Most of them come and go, never staying in place for more than a couple of years, but Paige is unaccountably popular with the security force, and has thus become something of a fixture. Fliss has never liked her; before Paige, Gatwick used to simply banish its worst criminals – there was plenty of wasteland for them to lose themselves in, after all – but since she became speaker for security, the settlement has taken to hanging them instead.

That change told Fliss all she's ever needed to know about Paige Scarrow, and she's been content to avoid her like the plague ever since. She has no choice but to interact with her now, though. Paige's move for an immediate vote is rejected, of course. Theodore Ruske shakes his head.

'Slow down, Paige,' he says. 'Before we table motions for voting, does any other involved party have anything they'd like to—'

Her mother's hand shoots up before he's finished the sentence. Ruske nods at her. 'Chair recognises Constance Loh.'

'May I remind you, Paige Scarrow, that one of these "hostiles" you're so gleefully talking about stringing up is my daughter?' Fliss's mum snaps. 'Are we executing children for coming home to see their parents now? You all know Felicity.' She gestures towards Fliss, then sweeps her arms wide, taking in the whole Assembly. 'You've known her since she was a baby.'

She's about to continue, but Paige raises a finger. Mum nods, giving her the floor.

'*Do* we?' Paige asks. 'Your daughter has been gone a long time, Constance, and who knows what kind of company she's been keeping? The raiders kidnapping our people know exactly where to find them. They know where we stable our livestock and keep our supply stores.' She fixes Fliss with an icy glare. 'Who better to give them information like that than someone who grew up here?'

It's a low blow, even from a weasel like Paige. Fliss has to clench both fists and bite her lip to keep herself from breaking a score of the Assembly's rules – and not just the ones on speaking out of turn. Mum comes to her rescue, jumping in to reply where she cannot.

'We've never made a secret of those things, Paige. It doesn't take a traitor to ferret them out. And I didn't see you so eager to throw Felicity to the wolves when you had the crown cough last February. Three days you were hacking up your own lungs on a breather bed, and the only reason you pulled through at all is because I'd just got a new shipment of Desivin in.'

'As for all of you agreeing with her' – Mum spins in her chair, raking her gaze over the crowd. – 'I'm not going to name names, because private business ought to stay that way, but I'd say more than half of you have been in my office for pills and implants this year alone.'

Paige's finger jabs the air again. 'What has that got to do with anything?' she snaps.

Mum looks at her for a long, cool moment before she replies, 'Who do you think got me the Desivin, Paige? Who do you think brought me the birth control meds? You'll notice there aren't many medics baying for my daughter's blood. That's because the drugs she obtains for us are what keep the medical centre stocked and operational. Felicity might run with bandits, but she's no Red Flag, and you know it.'

Despite the circumstances, Fliss feels a glow spread through her, warming her face. Her mum is laying it on a bit thick: she and her old crew were just one of many groups of traders who brought medical supplies to Gatwick, and it's not like they did it out of charity. They were paid, and paid well, for every shipment they ever brought Mum's way. The praise touches her, all the same. Mum has never even acknowledged Fliss's choice of career before, let alone celebrated it; Fliss had always assumed she was slightly ashamed of her. It's nice to find out she was wrong.

It could just be part of her strategy, of course – and Fliss can see the wisdom of it. Paige is trying to whip the Assembly up into a frenzy of fear about dangerous outsiders, but that's hard to do when Mum keeps reminding them that Fliss was literally born here. It's working, too: the temperature in the room is shifting, albeit fractionally. Fliss seeks out the familiar faces in the throng of seated people and sees many of them looking right back at her. Not all of the expressions she meets are friendly, though.

It's a good tactic, but it won't be enough – not on its own, and not least because it's an argument that only works on one out of the five of them. Fliss can practically see the little cogwheels turning in Paige's nasty mind. She's going to suggest killing the others and keeping Fliss in indefinite detention, or something similarly hideous. Paige is afraid of anything she doesn't understand – and in Fliss's opinion, you could fit the things she *does* understand onto the head of a pin.

'Felicity has worked hard for this community,' Mum continues. 'She's done things many of us couldn't or wouldn't dare attempt for ourselves. You can vote with Paige Scarrow if you want, but if you do, you won't just be depriving a mother of her child – you'll also be stripping Gatwick of one of its most important allies.'

That's overdoing it, even Fliss has to admit, but it gives her an idea. This debate has given her a glimpse into the Assembly's anxieties – the ones that Paige is weaponising against her, but also the ones that she can exploit.

She raises her hand tentatively. Mum catches sight of it and nods in her direction.

'I've said enough,' she finishes. 'I think it's time we let my daughter speak for herself.'

Ruske turns to her. 'Chair recognises Felicity Loh.'

'It's Fliss,' says Fliss, getting to her feet. The prospect of addressing so many people at once is intimidating. Usually, the only people she has to convince of anything are her crew, but the Assembly are no different, really – there's just a lot more of them.

*And they're thinking about hanging you,* Fliss reminds herself, but that's nothing new. Her old crew tried to shoot her and dump her body off the side of a car park. She's dealt with people trying to kill her before. She takes a deep breath, stilling the tremor in her hands.

'And what my mum said is true. I'm on Gatwick's side, and so are my crew. What's more, I bloody well *can* give a full account of our whereabouts last night: we were busy fighting Red Flags – probably the same ones who tried to get in through the North Gate.'

There's a susurrus from the crowd. Now that Fliss has their attention, she launches into an account of their run-in with the raiders with as much gusto as she can muster, laying the details on as thick as jam. By the time she's finished, many of the faces in the crowd are staring at her with the rapt attention of children at story time. The speakers are bursting with questions – Paige in particular is practically levitating out of her seat. Fliss ignores her, nodding to Gracie Smith instead. She knows Gracie in passing, and Mum said she was likely to be sympathetic.

'If all of that is true,' Gracie says, laying a slight, sceptical emphasis on the *if*, 'then your friends must be truly impressive fighters. How did they come by those skills?'

'Well, before they joined my crew, they were both corporate spies,' Fliss replies.

That draws an audible gasp. They never have truck with the corporations in Gatwick – at least they didn't before this Thoughtfront representative came along. This is probably the first time the Assembly have even seen a corporate spy. Tanta narrows her eyes, shooting Fliss a warning look which she cheerfully ignores. The ex-agent has no choice but to do this Fliss's way, and she knows it.

'That's right,' she continues. 'Both my friends used to work for one of the biggest corporations around. And then they quit and came to work for me. They're pretty hot stuff: there's not much they don't know about the goings-on in the city. They know that Thoughtfront rep is lying to you, for instance.'

Fliss is on thin ice here: belabour this point too much, and Ruske will shut her down for going off-topic. She throws the revelation in as though it's a casual aside, but she's as serious about it as anything she's had to say yet. She has no idea why Thoughtfront would want recruits from Gatwick, but she knows from bitter experience how the corporation treats its 'subcontractors' – and just how much a deal with them can cost. The fact that the Assembly are even considering an alliance with them is deeply concerning, and a sign of how serious their Red Flag problem must be. Fliss doesn't want her hometown making the same mistake she did.

'That's ridiculous,' Paige bursts out, earning herself a dis-approving look from Ruske.

'If you don't have a question, Paige, please restrain yourself until Fliss has finished.'

'Did you ever wonder how the Red Flags got so trouble-some?' Fliss asks. 'They never used to be a threat to Gatwick. My crew know the answer: you're not the only ones Thoughtfront's been courting. They made a deal with the Red Flags, and now they're playing you off against them to make another. You want to defend yourselves against raiders – I get it – but you can't do that by getting into bed with the corporation that's arming them.'

This time, Paige raises her hand as she's supposed to. Fliss nods respectfully, ceding the floor. 'Security moves that we call this charlatan's bluff,' Paige spits. 'We should put the hostiles back in holding, and then I will lead a team to assess these outrageous allegations personally. We'll search for the bodies of the raiders Felicity *claims* to have bested, and then ... then ...'

She trails off, as Fliss half suspected she would. The truth is, Paige has no answer to any of this, because it's utterly beyond the sphere of her competence. Fliss lets the silence stretch till it's the thinness of a hair before she raises her hand again.

'I have a better idea,' she says. 'Putting us back in holding won't make a lick of difference to your problems, so why not put us to work instead? You want evidence of what I'm saying? Let us prove it to you. We'll investigate Thoughtfront's pact with the Red Flags, and what they're planning next. It's what my crew are good at – what they're trained for. If anyone can get you some answers, it's us.'

'Can we talk about this?' Tanta mutters, under her breath.

'No,' Fliss replies. This is happening, whether the ex-agents like it or not. And Tanta subsides because she must know, just as well as Fliss does, that this is their best shot of getting out of here with their hides intact.

★

The young man in the bed beside Cole's is thin but wiry, with close-cropped blond hair and shrewd eyes. Neal offers him his arm as he sits up, but he doesn't need it. He gets to his feet by himself, swinging his legs over the side of the bed with an ease that belies his battered appearance.

'Neuroengineer Cole?' he asks.

Cole doesn't see any point in trying to dissemble – is not sure he'd be able to, in any case. His mind and heart are racing, his thoughts too slick with terror for him to keep hold of them. Neal called this young man 'Colleague'; that and his newly-uncloaked AR profile mean he must be from InTech, but the alert expression in his eyes and the easy way he speaks both tell Cole that he hasn't been programmed with Harlow 2.0. He's a Corporate Ward, then – probably around Tanta's age, or a little younger.

Cole manages a nod. The rest of his body feels frozen. 'Who are you?' he asks.

'My name is Arden,' the boy replies.

The generated name confirms his guess. He *is* a CorpWard, and Cole can't think of any explanation for why he'd be here, or why he'd recognise him, apart from the worst one: he's from the ICRD.

Cole's mouth is dry, his palms sweaty. He thinks of Tanta's call with the ICRD two days ago, when she sold them the intelligence about Thoughtfront working with unaffiliated bandits again, and curses his luck. Arden's probably not here for him at all, but from the way he's staring at Cole, that won't stop him from completing a side-mission.

Through his fear, Cole becomes aware that he's still clutching the data card in his left hand. It's hidden beneath the bedsheet, thank god. If the agent takes it, everything the crew has been working towards will be lost.

'May I sit up?' he asks. 'I'm not armed.'

When Arden nods, Cole props himself up on his elbows, then turns laboriously onto his side, gripping the edge of the bed as he shuffles himself upright. He uses the motion to slide the data card underneath the thin mattress, disguising the action as best he can. There's no doubt in his mind about what the ICRD's orders are concerning him. Arden may not have come here to find him, but he's not going to leave him alive. *At least now I'll leave my work behind*, Cole thinks. With luck, the crew will come looking for him and discover it – and maybe, just maybe, they'll find some way to finish what he started.

While Cole adjusts his pillows, Arden walks to the foot of the bed, putting himself in between Cole and the door. 'I have a few questions for you, Neuroengineer,' he says. His tone is polite, though he doesn't take his eyes off Cole for a second. 'If you don't mind?'

Cole forces another nod.

'Where are Tanta and the other fugitives?'

'I don't know,' Cole replies. 'When I woke up here, they were gone.' He's glad it's the truth – he hasn't got the presence of mind to concoct a lie.

Arden stares at him. 'You're not working for Thoughtfront, are you?' he says.

'No. We never have.'

The agent nods, as though this confirms something he already suspected. 'Then why did you attack our zeppelin last autumn?'

The question makes Cole realise that actually, he *does* have the presence of mind to lie. He can't betray the rest of the crew – and aside from that, he's pretty sure that explaining the existence of either of the Harlow Programmes to this CorpWard would make him die of shame. 'I don't know what you're talking about,' he says.

He braces himself for pain – and wonders, as he does so, just how much he'll be able to withstand before Arden forces the truth out of him – but the CorpWard only shrugs. *I could make you tell me,* that shrug seems to say, *but pretty soon, it's not going to matter.* 'Watch the corridor,' he instructs Neal. 'Tell me if anyone passes by.'

Cole sweeps the room with panicked eyes, searching for escape routes that just aren't there. He could scream for help. He could try appealing to Neal. He could attempt to fight back, futile as it would be. He realises, with a sense of finality like the thud of a closing trapdoor, that he isn't going to do any of those things. Arden is a Harlow-Programmed CorpWard, just like Tanta. The software and hardware in his head – the reason he's standing here now, about to kill for his corporation without so much as a moment's pause – is of Cole's making. He can't defend himself against this child, not when he's wronged him so badly already. Even through his fear, there's a part of Cole that is resigned to what is coming. It feels fitting to die at the hands of a Corporate Ward – it feels like justice.

'Wait,' he says, as Arden takes a step towards him. He's surprised by how calm he sounds. It must strike the CorpWard, too, because he stops, letting Cole speak. Cole swallows. 'I'm not trying to beg, and I know it won't make a difference, but I'm sorry. For all of it.'

Arden dips his head in a slight nod. 'I'm sorry too, Neuroengineer,' he says. 'Lie still. I'll make this as painless as I can.'

Which, at the end of the day, is more than he deserves. Cole shuts his eyes.

There's a lot more talking after Fliss finishes her speech, but it's just that – talk. In reality, the issue has already been decided. Tanta can tell by the expressions she sees in the crowd, Paige Scarrow's thwarted, furious silence, and the way the speakers' questions have changed from whos and wheres – *who do you think you are? Where were you last night?* – to hows and whats. *How is this going to work? And what are your rates?* Fliss has an answer to every enquiry, a solution to every mooted obstacle. Tanta suspects she's enjoying herself.

For her own part, her tension morphs by slow degrees into boredom as the talking drags on. Everyone seems to have something to say, and very little of it is to the purpose. The Gatwick Assembly is like an endless board meeting, only with twenty times more people. Tanta catches herself wishing that her original misconception was correct and Ruske really did have the power of the board's conduit to stop some of these windbags in their tracks.

When the Assembly finally vote on Fliss's proposal, they do it by filing out of the atrium through two doors at the back of the room, one for the *ayes* and one for the *nays*. Clerks with tally counters stand at these exits, counting up the numbers for each side. If there was any doubt in Tanta's mind before the vote, it swiftly vanishes once it begins. She doesn't need a tally counter to tell which way things are going to go – Paige, accompanied by most of her security force and about a dozen others, stalks through the *nay* door. Everyone else goes the other way.

Even with the outcome so obvious, it still takes an eternity of shuffling and counting and yet more talking before the Assembly members are all seated again and Ruske formalises the result. 'The Assembly votes in favour of Felicity Loh's motion by 187 votes to 33,' he says, at long last. 'Motion passes. The vote on Thoughtfront's proposal will be deferred pending the results of her team's inquiry.'

There's a ripple of chatter, and some scattered applause. Ruske turns to Tanta, Yas and Fliss. 'Thank you for your patience. You may go now, and begin your investigation. You can retrieve your gear from the security office, and I'm sure Constance would be happy to take you to the medical centre, where you'll find your three companions.'

'Three?' Tanta asks.

Ruske peers at the papers on his lectern. 'Yes – the two men you came here with, and the one who arrived just before you.' He glances up at her, his expression chagrined. 'I think I must apologise for our security team's treatment of him. They were not … gentle. Constance has assured me that his condition is not serious, however.'

'There are only five of us,' Yas says. 'Whoever this guy is, he's not part of our crew.'

A horrible sense of foreboding slithers through Tanta. She thinks of the Red Flag who escaped last night, the one who looked familiar, and wants to kick herself for letting him get away. She's lived in the city her whole life; there's really only one place she could have recognised him from. 'The man who arrived before us: was he pale-skinned? Blond?' she demands, directing the questions at Paige.

After a second's thought, Paige nods. 'So you do know him, then?' she sneers.

'He was one of the raiders we fought off last night, idiot!' Fliss shouts. 'You left him alone with Cole?'

'We – we thought he was with you,' Ruske says weakly. 'Paige told us—'

Tanta doesn't wait to hear more. She turns and runs for the door, Fliss and Yas on her heels.

# Chapter 15

The sprint through Gatwick to the medical centre is one of the longest journeys of Tanta's life. She has to force herself to let Fliss pull ahead of her. She has no idea where she's going and the bandit does, but her instincts and her dread are goading her into a dead run that would leave Fliss behind if she gave into them.

They're most of the way down the corridor when Tanta glances over her shoulder to see Constance following them, the muscles on her arms standing out as she pushes herself forward. She has two guards in tow. In other circumstances, Tanta would think this a sensible precaution. Right now, she couldn't care less. If this Red Flag, or corporate agent, or whoever the man is, has hurt Cole, then Tanta won't need help to subdue him – and she's not planning on leaving enough of him intact to make a security escort necessary.

The medical centre turns out to be on the other side of the same, enormous building that houses the Assembly's meeting place. They race back across the lobby through which they entered, down another maze of winding corridors and ante-rooms, and then into a clean, white space, filled with hurrying medics. Through the floor-length windows that line this part of the building, more airplanes are visible, along with outbuildings of rammed earth and clay that have been bolted on to the main, pre–Meltdown structure.

Tanta lets it all sweep past her as she dashes by; there's room for only one thought in her mind. The long corridor they're in is lined with numbered doors; through their windowpanes, Tanta catches glimpses of clinics and consulting rooms. She narrows her eyes, zooming in on the panels and scanning the rooms beyond as she passes.

'They're in sixty-seven!' Constance barks, from behind her.

Tanta sees it. The door must be locked, but it's not reinforced and looks hollow. She kicks it, aiming for the handle, and it bursts open. There's a yell from the other side, and Neal goes sprawling – he must have been standing right behind the door. Tanta doesn't have any more attention to spare for him: Cole is lying on a hospital bed inside. The blond boy from last night is leaning over him, haloed in pale red, his hands around Cole's throat.

The tableau has a hyperreal quality. Every detail seems to leap out at Tanta at once, as if the people and objects in the room are illuminated from within. She throws herself towards the blond boy and punches him in the side of the head. There's an audible crack as her fist makes contact – she's not sure if it's from her hand or the boy's skull, and in her state of heightened consciousness, she doesn't care. She grabs the boy by the arm and the back of his shirt and wrenches him away from Cole. He crashes into the room's other bed over and tumbles to the floor, dazed. He must have four inches and almost thirty pounds on Tanta, but she barely felt the strain of throwing him. A distant, disconnected part of her mind wonders where this strength is coming from, but it's not important right now.

Cole is lying horribly still, his eyes closed, but as Tanta stares at him, she sees a slight breathing motion in his chest. It's all she needs. She turns back to the boy, who is beginning to sit up. She closes with him. Faintly, as if it's coming from a great distance away, she can hear Neal screaming. That doesn't matter either. She punches the boy again, and then wraps one arm around his neck.

His eyes have rolled back into his head when Tanta becomes aware of another noise, cutting through Neal's yells. It's quieter, but it arrests her attention in a way nothing else has been able to since she realised Cole was in danger.

'Tanta! Stop! You need to stop!' Cole's voice is hoarse to the point of inaudibility, his eyes bloodshot, but at least he's talking.

Tanta doesn't slacken her hold.

'You can't kill him! We need him!' There's something so desperate in Cole's tone that it shakes Tanta back into reality. The room around her begins to look normal again, its unbearable, illuminated clarity fading.

'Why?' she asks.

'Because he's the key to undoing Harlow 2.0.'

Cole's intervention comes not a moment too soon. By the time Tanta releases the boy, his face is almost purple, and he's lost consciousness, but he's alive. The two security guards cuff him anyway, before hauling him out of the room.

'Put him on the other side of the medical centre, in room 212,' Constance instructs them. 'And this time, secure him to his bed.'

Tanta's not fully reassured by these precautions. The boy must be an ICRD agent, and the thought of him locked up in a hospital room in the same building as Cole makes her nervous. If Cole is right about him, though, then it's a necessary risk. She can't ask him why the boy is so important straight away – there are more important things to take care of first, not least Cole himself. Constance sweeps in and takes charge of this, leaving Tanta, Yas and Fliss to calm down a frantic Neal.

The senior medic bombards him with questions about what happened and how he's feeling. She asks him to move his right arm, and shines a light into his bloodshot eyes. Once her examination is complete, she adds some drugs to his IV drip and makes up a cold compress for his neck.

'You should be fine. Just try not to incur any more serious trauma,' she tells him sternly, as though his two brushes with death were his fault.

'How soon before he's back on his feet?' Tanta asks. The fingers of her left hand – the one she broke last summer – throb as she speaks, and she flexes them cautiously. Her burst of super-human strength over, she's starting to feel the consequences.

'Oh, he can walk already,' Constance replies. She turns back to Cole. 'The sepsis is clearing up, and your gunshot wound should heal nicely so long as you don't over-exert yourself. The bullet hit your brachial plexus – that's why your arm feels numb and you're having trouble moving your fingers. From tomorrow, I want you to start gentle physio five times daily. I'll give you some exercises. I'd like to keep you in for the rest of the week, but I suppose that's out of the question?'

Cole glances at Tanta. 'I'm afraid so,' she replies. They're still on the run from InTech, and now that everyone in the Assembly knows that she and Yas are ex-corporate spies, staying put for so long would pose too great a risk.

Constance nods briskly. 'Give me two days, then. For observation – and to make sure you don't get into any more fights.'

'It was an assassination attempt, not a fight,' Cole protests.

Constance gives him a very Fliss-like look. 'Same difference, medically speaking. You need to rest up. I have a feeling that will be easier here than on the road with my daughter and her friends.'

'I think we can manage that,' Tanta says, with some reluctance. 'Thank you for everything you've done for us, Constance.'

After the senior medic has gone – leaving a sheet of physio-therapy exercises, some antibiotics, and a set of detailed instructions on how to change Cole's dressing – and Neal has been restored to a semblance of calm, the crew settle into chairs around Cole's bedside.

'So, what did I miss? And where are we?' Cole asks. His voice is hoarse and scratchy, and he's massaging his injured throat. There are bruises blooming there, black against his dark brown skin. Tanta looks away.

'We're in Gatwick and, strange as it sounds, we've just been hired as freelance investigators,' Yas says.

She recaps the day's events succinctly, with an agent's eye for the pertinent details. When she is finished, Fliss flashes them all a wolf-like grin.

'I guess you three should start calling me "boss" now,' she says.

'That was just a story you spun to get the Assembly on-side,' Tanta snaps. 'Don't forget it.'

She's annoyed, though she suspects she doesn't have any right to be. Fliss's story may have revealed Tanta and Yas's identities, but it also saved their lives, and it wasn't as though there was time for her to clear her plan with the rest of the crew in advance. Still, Tanta chafes under the feeling of having been signed up for something she never volunteered to do. The crew already have an assignment: to reverse the rollout of Harlow 2.0 and overthrow InTech's leadership. This investigation into Thoughtfront and the Red Flags is a distraction – one they don't have time for.

Fliss glares at her. 'Oh, I'm sorry. Next time someone's trying to string you up, I'll just keep my big mouth shut, shall I?'

Tanta doesn't answer. Fliss isn't really the target of her anger. She's angry about ... everything: Reet, the derailment of the crew's plans, the bruises on Cole's neck, which could have been so much worse than bruises. She turns to Cole, deciding to change the subject.

'The boy who attacked you—'

'Arden,' Cole cuts in. 'He's a CorpWard.'

'Arden. What's so important about him?'

Cole takes a deep breath. Speaking is painful for him, but Tanta can tell from the gleam in his eyes that this is something he's eager to share. 'While you were speaking to the Assembly, I tested my software patch on Neal. It didn't take – InTech has updated Harlow 2.0's security protocols. They're practically airtight, now. I was examining them, searching for a way in, when an ... opening appeared – a temporary weakness in the software. It happened just as Arden uncloaked his Inscape. I don't think that was a coincidence.'

'What has Arden's 'scape got to do with hacking Harlow 2.0?' Yas asks.

'Neal recognised Arden the moment he turned his profile back on,' Cole replies, his voice animated. 'He called him "Colleague" before either of them had exchanged a word.'

Tanta is not so distracted by her own emotions that she can't connect the dots here. 'The programmed residents who attacked me in the city knew I wasn't with InTech anymore just by looking at me,' she says slowly. 'It's like there was something in their software that ...'

'That marked out other InTech employees as friends, and everyone else as hostiles,' Cole finishes. 'I was thinking of that, too. My theory is that whenever two people programmed with either version of the Harlow Programme come into contact, their Inscapes exchange something – information on their roles, or an authorisation code, I'm guessing – that lets each of them know the corporate affiliation of the other. It allows them to function as a sort of network – they all know they can trust each other, and they all know, instantly, who should be excluded from that trust. I never spotted it before, because up till now, I've only ever investigated the software in isolation. This was the first time I'd seen it respond to the presence of another person's 'scape.'

The end of his speech dies away into a gravelly wheeze. Fliss pours him a glass of water. 'Is that why they don't notice people like me? Because we don't have any headware for them to scan?'

Cole gives a half nod, wiggling one hand in a gesture Tanta takes to mean *probably*.

'And you think this exchange will give your uninstallation patch a way to bypass Harlow 2.0's new security protocols?' she asks, keen to keep things on topic.

'It's the only way past them I've found so far,' Cole replies, once he's drained the glass. 'It's got to be worth a shot. To be certain, though, I'll have to spend more time with Arden and Neal, watching their Inscapes interact.'

'Arden is probably our best lead on what Thoughtfront and the Red Flags are up to as well,' Yas muses. 'I'm betting the ICRD sent him undercover to investigate them.'

'Finding out what Thoughtfront and the Red Flags are up to isn't our main objective,' Tanta says. Her voice sounds petulant, even to her own ears.

Fliss bristles. 'Speak for yourself. Thoughtfront hung my old crew out to dry. I'm not letting them do the same to everyone here. I don't see how helping Gatwick is any less important than freeing InTech's people.'

'They're both important,' Yas jumps in, heading off a potential argument at the pass. 'As of right now, though, gathering evidence for Gatwick is the only objective we're being paid for. I'm not saying saving InTech isn't worthwhile, but it *is* pro bono.'

Fliss nods vigorously. 'We don't have a way back into the city yet, and by the sounds of it, Cole has some tuning up to do on his patch as well. Might as well make some chit while we're figuring those things out.'

Tanta realises, with a sinking feeling, that this isn't an argument she's going to win. And after all, Fliss and Yas do have a point. Until Cole manages to adapt his software patch to Harlow 2.0's new security measures, their plan has stalled. 'We're agreed, then,' she says. 'Our next step – for both our missions – is to talk to Arden. We should have a break first, though. I think we all need it. Shall we meet back here in a couple of hours?'

'Sounds good to me,' Yas replies, rising to her feet. 'Fliss, any idea where we can get something to eat around here? And I'd love a shower.'

Fliss joins her at the door. 'I can sort you out. Come with me. You too, Neal.'

Tanta waves the three of them off. Once they've left, she turns back to Cole. 'I need to talk to you,' she says.

Cole's expecting that Tanta wants to check how he's feeling, or quiz him some more on what he's learnt about Harlow 2.0's new security protocols, but as soon as they have the clinic to themselves, she starts shoving the chairs and the other bed up against the walls, clearing a space in the centre of the room.

'Um … what are you doing?' he asks her.

'Can you stand?' Tanta's back is to him, her shoulders set.

'…Yes.' When she doesn't reply, Cole realises that she means for him to do it now. He gets out of bed, careful not to get his IV line tangled.

As soon as he's on his feet, Tanta crosses to his bed and shunts it up against the far wall. Only then does she turn to face him at last.

'Attack me,' she says.

'What?'

She walks back into the middle of the room and assumes a

fighter's stance – legs apart, knees bent. 'Attack me. Throw a punch.'

Cole is mystified. 'Constance told me that's exactly the kind of thing I should be avoiding. Besides, I thought hitting things was more your department.'

Tanta sighs, a short, sharp exhalation. 'I'll attack you, then, and you defend yourself.'

She's on him in an instant, closing with Cole before he can blink. He yelps, throwing up his left hand in a pitiable imitation of her own stance. For a second, he thinks she's actually going to hit him, but she just ducks under his guard and taps him in the middle of the chest.

'You're dead,' she says.

'Wait, but I—'

She springs backward, dancing on the balls of her feet, then comes at him again. This time, Cole makes a lame attempt to swipe at her as she leaps towards him. She spins away from his arm, comes up behind him and taps the back of his head. 'You're dead. Again.'

'Tanta, why are we doing this?'

'Next time, keep your arm closer to your chest – it'll be harder for me to get under your guard that way. And pivot to follow my movements. Don't let me get behind you. OK, let's try again.'

'No!' Cole goes to fold his arms, then realises he can't. He puts his left hand on his hip, instead. 'I'm not fighting you. Not until you tell me what the hell this is about, anyway.'

Tanta stares at the floor, her fists clenched. Cole's bracing himself for her to rush him again when she speaks. 'You said it yourself. I've always done the fighting. That's left you vulnerable. You need to learn how to defend yourself.'

For the first time, Cole notices the tremor in her hands. She isn't meeting his eyes. 'Is … this about what happened with Arden?' he asks.

'I won't always be able to protect you!' The words come out of her in a wail. 'This isn't the city, or Sodis. We're on our own out here – there's no InTech backing us up.' She's shaking all over, now. 'If I'd arrived just a minute later than I did, you'd be dead!'

'But that's not what happened,' Cole reminds her, startled into gentleness. 'I'm OK. It's OK.'

'It's *not* OK!' Tanta looks up at him at last and Cole sees, to his shock, that her eyes are filled with tears. 'You're the only person with the skills to reverse the rollout of Harlow 2.0. If something happened to Yas, or Fliss, or me, the others could keep going. Without you, we've got nothing. I have to keep you safe. We *need* you, Cole.'

Guilt twists in Cole's gut. He thinks back on his encounter with Arden. At the time, the thought of dying at the hands of someone he had wronged so terribly had a certain rightness to it. Now, that self-destructive fatalism feels foolish and irresponsible. *You wanted to make amends, remember?* he scolds himself. *You can't fix anything if you're dead.* He forces himself to meet Tanta's gaze. She is also someone he has wronged, and he doesn't need to hear her say it aloud to know that she'd much prefer it if he stayed alive. They're almost all either of them has right now.

'I'm sorry,' he says. He takes a few steps towards her, suddenly embarrassed. He could lose half his fingers and still be able to count on one hand the number of times he's seen Tanta upset. He's almost never heard her cry before. Despite being older than her, he's more used to her comforting him than the other way around. He puts his good arm around her, though the gesture feels awkward. Part of him is expecting her to grab it and use it to flip him onto his back. Instead, she leans into the hug, wrapping both arms around him tight enough to hurt.

'You can't die,' she says, the words muffled by his shirt.

'I don't intend to,' Cole tells her, and means it. 'Look, you can teach me self-defence if you think it'll help, but is there something gentler we could start off with? I *have* just been shot, you know.'

She lets out a laugh that's half a sob. 'Sorry. You should be resting.'

'Don't apologise.' Cole feels another pang of remorse; Tanta doesn't know it, but this was a wake-up call he needed. He'd gladly die to right the wrongs of his past, but no one is asking him to. What is required of him is harder but, ultimately, of more use. He can't hold his life so cheaply – not when the stakes are this high. There are too many people counting on him.

# Chapter 16

For the next two hours, Tanta drills Cole in escaping holds, dodging blows, and how to distract or incapacitate an attacker long enough to make a quick getaway. It's rudimentary stuff – things she covered before she was out of basic training – but it's a start. They have to go carefully: Cole only has the full use of one of his arms, which makes intensive training difficult. They do more talking than sparring. When Tanta does demonstrate a manoeuvre, she does so slowly, avoiding anything that might hurt Cole's neck or shoulder.

Cole makes heavy work of it, asking a thousand questions and mimicking Tanta's movements with obvious difficulty. He doesn't complain, though, and by the time they decide to call it quits, Tanta thinks he's a little better able to look after himself than he was before.

She's feeling a little better, too. Cole's not much of a sparring partner but training him has helped to work some of the fear and fury out of her system, nonetheless.

'If all else fails, go for the face,' she says, while Cole catches his breath beside her. 'Or the groin, if you're fighting a man. Both are areas where you can cause a lot of pain without the need for much physical strength.'

'Thanks for the vote of confidence,' Cole replies, rolling his eyes. 'Won't the others be back soon?'

'You're just trying to get out of more exercises,' Tanta teases him, but he's right. Yas, Fliss and Neal turn up a few minutes later, bearing sandwiches, greenhouse apples, and flasks of hot tea from Gatwick's mess hall. They eat and drink in silence; it's their first meal since they fled the Brokerage, and they're all too famished to talk.

Fliss is the first to speak again. 'So, this Arden,' she begins, brushing crumbs off her jacket. 'Aren't we worried he's going to tell InTech where we are?'

'He can't,' Yas replies. 'Not yet, anyway. With the data zeppelin still docked outside the city, latency in the UZ is too high. He can't use his 'scape to send messages back home,' she clarifies, noticing Fliss's baffled expression.

When everyone is finished, they set off for room 212, Fliss leading the way.

'How are we going to play this?' Yas asks, as they approach.

Tanta has been wondering that herself. Arden's a trained ICRD agent: they won't be able to force him to talk. 'I think we need to tell him the truth,' she says. 'Or a version of it: we're not with Thoughtfront, we're investigating the same thing as he is, but on Gatwick's behalf. He won't talk to us if he thinks we're a threat to InTech, but if we can convince him our interests are aligned, we might have a chance.' She turns to Cole. 'Will you be able to access the MbOs information you need from outside? I'd rather not have you in the same room as him if it can be avoided.'

'Oh, same here,' Cole says vehemently. 'I can work in the corridor.'

'All right, then.' Tanta glances at Yas. 'Want to tag team this?'

Yas gives an exaggerated sigh. 'Well, InTech already know I'm back in the mix by now. Might as well make it official.'

★

Cole has little interest in the intelligence being traded inside Arden's sickroom; all of his attention is reserved for a different kind of exchange entirely: the wordless communion between MbOSes. As soon as Tanta, Yas and Fliss have entered the clinic, he makes himself as comfortable as he can sitting against the wall outside, accesses Neal's 'scape, and gets to work.

The first thing he does is to go looking for some record of the communication between Arden and Neal's Inscapes that he saw earlier. A search of Neal's MbOS event logs reveals nothing, however. Cole is not entirely surprised: the Inscape system keeps records of mundane interactions between 'scapes – MindChat ident exchanges, verification queries, and the like – but both the Harlow Programme and its successor are highly classified. It's likely that any activity pertaining to either of them is inaccessible to the average Inscape user. Cole was lucky to see... well, whatever it was he saw, in real time.

Next, he retraces his steps from earlier in the day, looking for evidence of the transmission where he saw its effects – in the security protocols that surround Neal's Harlow 2.0 software. He circles the perimeter of the programme like a scout outside an enemy compound, eyeing its barbed wire and turret guns with a calculating eye. Now that Cole has seen the opening in the software once, it's easier to spot again. There's a single interface protocol woven into the security arrangements protecting Harlow 2.0 – a door set within the reinforced wall. It's closed and barred now, but designed to open when another Harlow-Programmed 'scape comes knocking.

Cole spends some time seeing if he can get it to open up for him, too, but to no avail. He suspects this isn't a problem that will yield to time, inventiveness, or skill – he simply doesn't have the required shibboleth. It doesn't matter, though, because he *does* have the next best thing: Arden.

'Neal, I need your help again,' he says.

A little experimentation informs Cole that the interaction is triggered by proximity – a distance of ten metres or less – and repeated every seven minutes while the two subjects are within range. In the interests of speed, he has Neal walk up and down the corridor, allowing his 'scape to forget and then re-encounter Arden's several times in quick succession, rather than waiting out the full seven minutes each time. Using Neal in this way makes him uncomfortable – the whole exercise feels a little like playing peek-a-boo with a grown man – but Cole reminds himself that ultimately, he's doing this for the intern's benefit. For his part, Neal doesn't seem to mind the indignity, following Cole's instructions with dreamy indifference.

Cole watches the door in Neal's Harlow 2.0 software swing open and shut, open and shut, observing each blink-and-you'd-miss-it opening as closely as he can. As he gets his eye in, details start to leap out at him – things he missed the first time around. Each time Neal gets within range of Arden, it's like their MbOSes shake hands, trading stories on how they've been and who they've been talking to. The greeting takes the form of two packets of data, exchanged in a fraction of a second.

It takes Cole another few minutes – and Neal a few more trips up and down the hallway – before he's confident enough of what he's seeing to act on it. The next time Neal reaches the clinic and the door in his software opens, Cole is ready for it. He pounces on the data packet from Neal's MbOS with the speed and rapacity of a cat and copies it over to his own 'scape, where he can disembowel it at his leisure.

'You can stop now, Neal,' he says. 'I've got what I need.'

Neal gives him another one of his disconcerting smiles. 'OK.'

'Why don't we go back to room sixty-seven and wait for the others there?' Cole suggests. He's eager to find out exactly what he has on his hands here, but he'd rather not do it sitting on the hard floor of the corridor.

As soon as he and Neal are back in their own quarters, Cole begins taking the data packet apart. He was right that it's a handshake, of sorts – a way for two Harlow-Programmed 'scapes to verify each other's identity, but as he digs through its entrails, Cole realises that it's more than that. It's also a surveillance tool, for one thing. The packet contains records of every other MbOS Neal has come into contact with over the last month, complete with timestamps and locations.

More interestingly, Cole finds a space reserved for secure transmissions. This makes him grin – it's a cleverer innovation than he would have expected from Arthur Friend. It means that in an emergency, InTech can use the handshake as a decentral-ized communications network, spreading messages, warnings or orders from one Harlow-Programmed resident to the next. It might take a little longer than an all-residents alert, but it's far more secure and—

Cole pauses in his dissection, struck by an idea so fizzing with potential that it almost gives him an electrical burn. The solution to Harlow 2.0 is staring him in the face, and if he can pull it off, it won't take months to achieve, or even weeks. He could put an end to the programme right now. If he could sneak his software patch into Neal's handshake protocol, it would transform it into a self-propagating virus; it would spread from 'scape to 'scape, uninstalling the Harlow Programming of everyone Neal met, and everyone they met, and on and on, until the entire city was free.

This revelation is followed an instant later by another. To make this wonderful idea work, Cole would need to do the impossible: to force the door in Neal's Harlow 2.0 security measures – the door that he's already established is locked to anyone without Harlow Programming of their own – to open for him.

Cole dismisses his Array and shuts his eyes, massaging his forehead. He's not sure whether he's feeling elation or despair. He has found the perfect mechanism to reverse the rollout of Harlow 2.0, and it's right in front of him – but it's like he's watching it operate through six inches of reinforced glass. He's on the outside of the system, looking in, and he has no idea how to pass through.

Arden is lying in bed when Yas, Tanta and Fliss enter the room, his arms cuffed to the side rails and his legs restrained with straps. Tanta looks the set-up over with a professional eye. Credit where it's due, Gatwick's security force have done their jobs well this time around; the CorpWard won't be going anywhere in a hurry.

He looks up as the three of them walk in, watching them with an alert expression. He is sizing them up, just as they are him, looking for their strengths, their blind spots. It's clear, from the way his eyes widen, that he recognises them. Tanta recognises him, too, now that she's had a chance to place him. Back in the Ward House, he was a face in the crowd, part of the throng of Tanta's juniors. Thanks to the Harlow Programme, she loved them all, though she did not know them. An echo of that feeling flickers in her now, though it's swamped by the much larger consciousness that this is the man who almost killed her partner. She doesn't share Cole's sentimentality about the Harlow-Programmed CorpWards. Wronged and manipulated Arden may be, but that doesn't mean he's not dangerous. She doesn't want to kill him, but she will if she has to.

Fliss takes a seat at the side of the room. She's got them this far, but this is Tanta and Yas's area of expertise, and she knows it. The two ex-agents take up their stations at the foot of Arden's bed. By unspoken consent, they wait for him to begin the conversation.

'I was told you were dead, Agent Das,' he says at length.

'Yeah, well, I got better,' Yas replies. 'Getting out of Thoughtfront territory did wonders for my constitution.'

It's a good start. If Arden was told Yas died, he was probably also informed that it was at the hands of a Thoughtfront interrogation squad. There's no way she'd have defected to the side of the corp that tortured her – her presence here is the closest thing Tanta can get to proof that the crew aren't working for InTech's inveterate enemy. Arden hasn't mentioned anything about Dr Friend's abduction, either – to them or to Cole – which means he was likely sent out on this assignment before it happened. All in all, their chances of convincing him to talk to them are about as high as they can be – though that's not saying much.

'We know who you are, Arden, and we know why you're out here,' Tanta says, before he has another chance to speak. 'We're interested in making a trade.'

The young CorpWard waits a beat or two before he replies. Tanta can guess at the cogs turning in his mind, because she knows her own. She thinks back on her conversation with Jeanie on the Brokerage smartphone last summer, a time so distant it feels like another reality entirely. She remembers what it's like to confront an unknown on the corp's behalf, the delicate balance of how much to give away in order to gain something of value. Now she's the unknown, and Arden is her – caught without backup, walking a tightrope in the dark. The reversal of roles is strange, but Tanta brushes the feeling aside.

'You seem to know a lot of things,' Arden replies. 'Care to tell me where you're getting your intelligence?'

As an opening salvo, it's not bad. Arden is cool under pressure: countering with a question of his own is a good way to stall for time, or to trick his interrogators into revealing more than they intended. Tanta gives herself a mental shake, derailing this train of thought. Her natural sympathies are all on Arden's side here. Not a minute ago, she was thinking that she had none of Cole's sentimentality towards this young CorpWard. It's true: what she has is empathy for him, which is even worse. She needs to stop identifying with him. He's not her colleague anymore – he's a hostile subject.

'The Brokerage has its ways,' she says, her own voice as cool as his. 'Though I'm not at liberty to discuss them.'

She's taking a risk with this, but it's a calculated one. Right now, Arden may believe any number of things about Tanta and her fellow defectors. By dropping the Brokerage's name, Tanta is giving his formless suspicions a shape – and one that won't be so unpalatable to him as the prospect that she's gone to work for a rival corporation. A loyal CorpWard like Arden would never help an enemy agent – he'd literally rather die – but he might be persuaded to share intelligence with a neutral third party, if Tanta can convince him that that's what the crew are.

Arden's brow creases fractionally before he smooths his expression again. 'The Brokerage. That's an odd choice of employer. I imagine our health plan is better.'

'There are other benefits,' Tanta says.

'Such as?'

'Are you thinking of joining?' Yas asks, which shuts him up.

After a reflective pause, he continues. 'The Brokerage sells classified intelligence. I've never heard of them committing sabotage before. If you're with them, why did you attack our data zeppelin four months ago?'

'It was a woman called Jeanette Callaghan who attacked the zeppelin, not us,' Tanta shoots back. 'We stopped her.'

'Same question, then: why help us?'

'We're not allowed to be sentimental about our old corp?' Yas replies. 'Jeanie's actions would have killed thousands of people. We might be defectors, but we still have consciences.'

Arden's frown returns. 'I thought you were working with Jeanette.'

Yas quirks an eyebrow. 'Were we? We both survived, yet left the zeppelin undamaged. If we'd been on her side, why not finish what she started?'

'You're saying you swept in and saved the day. So why did you run?' Arden counters.

Tanta holds out both hands, palms up. 'Come on, Arden: you've already answered that question for us. Everyone at InTech thinks we're traitors. We were hardly going to stick around.'

It's a plausible story – close enough to the truth that it might just pass for it, in the right light. Arden inspects it, and Tanta inspects him, waiting to see if he'll go for it.

'What kind of trade did you have in mind?' he asks.

Tanta feels a familiar sense of triumph – one she hasn't experienced since her days as an ICRD agent. It's been too long since she's had a chance to use this particular skillset: passing a lie like a counterfeit note, to buy information and bypass obstacles. She's missed it.

'An intelligence swap,' Yas replies. 'This settlement has purchased our services to investigate the same thing that brought you to the Unaffiliated Zone – Thoughtfront's alliance with the local raiding crews. Tell us what you've learnt, and we'll do the same.'

Arden eyes the two of them shrewdly. 'Intelligence isn't much use to me as long as I'm a prisoner. Clearly, you have more influence with the people who run things here than I do. Get me out. Then, I'll tell you everything I know.'

'That's out of the question,' Tanta says. 'We'll give you intel, but that's all we'll give you. You'll have to find a way out of here on your own.'

It's a long time before Arden replies. He stares at them both, his face a careful mask. 'The bandits I was with when I met you last night are part of a much larger group – the Red Flags,' he says at last, speaking slowly. 'From what I've been able to gather, they've been raiding unaffiliated settlements for months, taking food, supplies, and conscripts. They're massing to the northwest – a force at least five thousand strong.'

That's a much larger figure than Tanta was expecting, though she doesn't let her surprise show. She'd already gathered from Ruske's account that Thoughtfront is building an unaffiliated army, but how the corporation has manged to assemble so many people, so quietly, is a mystery to her.

But Arden isn't finished. 'The word is that Thoughtfront has a way of getting them past our defences and into our territory.'

Tanta stiffens. She understands, now, why Arden is so willing to work with her and the crew. When he was captured outside Gatwick, he was probably trying to get back home – or to find a broadcasting device that would let him circumvent the signal blackout in the Unaffiliated Zone. As of now, he's the only person in InTech who knows about the threat growing beyond the corporation's walls. He must be desperate to warn them. For Tanta's own part, Arden's revelation changes this discussion from a secondary concern to a matter of potentially vital importance.

'That's very helpful,' Yas says. 'Now—'

'I wasn't done,' Arden interrupts. 'Before we came across you, my raiding group met up with Red Flag leadership to receive orders, and I managed to place a tracker on their vehicle. I know where their stronghold is. Get me out of here, and I'll lead you right to it.'

In true agent style, Arden has saved the most enticing part of his offer till last. This is exactly what the crew need – not just for their hired assignment for Gatwick, but for their plans to liberate InTech, too. If Arden's intel is accurate, he's offering them a way back into the city. Still, Tanta is torn. 'I meant what I said before,' she says. 'You just tried to kill my partner. We can't let you go.'

'I'm not asking you to.' Arden gives an open-palmed shrug, though the cuffs make the gesture difficult. 'Convince the people in charge here to release me into your custody. I'll take you to the stronghold, you'll help me break in and find out what Thoughtfront is planning – we're both happy.'

Tanta is almost offended by the brazenness of this ploy. Arden's odds of making it out of Gatwick without anyone seeing him are slim, and if he's spotted, it will spark a pile-on that could all too easily end in a lynching. Making a run for it while outside and on the move, however – even with a couple of ex-ICRD agents as his captors – is an easier proposition. Arden gains nothing from this bargain except a better chance to escape, and he and Tanta both know it. He's inviting her to measure her own skills against his, to take his wager that he'll outsmart her once they're out in the field, and barely even trying to hide it.

Tanta admires his confidence – for a rookie agent, he seems to have an awful lot of it – but looking into his cunning blue eyes, she realises it's a bet she's willing to make. Arden's smart – there's no doubt about that – but she and the crew are smarter. She'll take this nascent escape attempt of his and turn it to her advantage. She flicks a glance at Yas, then Fliss.

'We might be able to work with that,' she says.

# Chapter 17

'It's a trick,' Fliss says.

Tanta nods. 'Of course it's a trick. The question is, can we get what we want and get clear before Arden pulls it? I think we can.'

The crew are back in room sixty-seven, their temporary base of operations, filling Cole in on what Arden told them – and what he's offering.

'You've changed your tune,' the bandit replies. 'You weren't so keen on investigating the Red Flags *before* you found out they might be our ticket back into the city.'

'Does it matter what my motives are? This brings us closer to both our objectives.'

Fliss shrugs. 'I'm not saying I'm not game. And I can't see the Assembly minding if we take him – they'll be glad to be rid of him. But what are we going to do when he tries to murder Cole again?'

Cole's face heats as the rest of the crew look his way. He clears his throat. 'I could uninstall his Harlow Programming. It would loosen InTech's hold on him – make him easier to reason with. Arthur may have beefed up security in the new version, but that doesn't mean he's altered the original.' In fact, Cole would be surprised if he had. The first Harlow Programme is several orders of magnitude more complex than its successor, the backdoor within its software carefully hidden. Arthur has probably tried to tinker with it, but privately, Cole suspects the task would have been too much for him.

But Tanta is shaking her head. 'That wouldn't be enough to get Arden on our side. You remember what I was like when I lost my programming: it took me months to reach the point I'm at now. Removing his would only make him unpredictable – at least at the moment, we know where we stand with him.'

'Not to mention the fact that if he escapes, he could tip our hand,' Yas points out. 'If he makes it back to the ICRD, you can bet they'll give his 'scape a thorough check-up – especially after what happened with you, Tanta. We don't want InTech finding out we have the ability to deprogramme its residents.'

There's a pause as the crew contemplate this.

'We'll just have to be careful,' Cole says, at length. 'As careful as we can, anyway. If Arden can really show us a way back into InTech territory, working with him is worth the risk.'

'What about you?' Tanta asks him. 'Did you manage to find out any more about the weakness in Harlow 2.0's new security measures?'

Cole tells them about the handshake protocol – the good news and the bad. 'I'm not sure what's next,' he admits, when he's finished. 'I need more time to think about it.'

'Will you want Neal for that?' Fliss asks.

He sees what she's driving at. He doesn't like the thought of bringing the intern to a Thoughtfront military base any more than she does. Thankfully, it's not necessary. Cole has already established that there's no way through the door in Neal's software. Whatever the solution to undoing the rollout is, he won't find it in the intern's 'scape. 'We should leave him behind, if the Assembly will let us,' he replies. 'He'll be safer in Gatwick, and if we do make it into the city, it's not like I'll have any shortage of Harlow 2.0-programmed residents to pull data from.'

The bandit nods. 'Mum will make sure no one quibbles about that.'

'If we're all agreed, then shall we tell the CorpWard we're taking him up on his offer?' Yas suggests, getting to her feet.

'One more thing.' Tanta looks around the circle, meeting everyone's gaze in turn. 'Fliss is right: Arden is a threat to us all – especially Cole – and we can't lose sight of that. We're agreeing to his terms so we can find out what Thoughtfront and the Red Flags are planning, and find a way into the city, but that's as far as it goes. As soon as we've accomplished those goals, we should all consider our alliance with him terminated.'

With Cole still under observation in the medical centre, the crew have almost a day and a half to rest up, prepare, or otherwise amuse themselves before their departure. As often happens to Fliss when she visits Gatwick, she spends the first afternoon in a kind of nostalgic whirl, visiting childhood haunts and catching up with old friends, but by the time evening rolls around, she's already itching to be on the road again.

Since they can't leave yet, she decides to go for a walk to work some of the restlessness out of her system. She takes a route she's familiar with, looping around the reservoirs and solar generators on the edge of town, then up past the security station and back to the medical centre. She figures she might as well drop in on Paige while she's out, to retrieve the crew's car and weapons. Fliss is looking forward to seeing the look on the head of security's face when she's forced to hand their stuff back.

It's dusk when she sets out, the sun no more than a band of yellow on the horizon. The air is cold but fresh, the settlement quiet. Many of the larger buildings – the Assembly hall, the school complex in the South Terminal – are going dark as people finish work for the day, but the windows of the houses are lighting up one by one, warm beacons in the night.

Walking along the peaceful streets, past communal gardens and henhouses, sadness steals over Fliss. It always goes the same way when she comes back: she'll arrive full of enthusiasm and excitement, but it never lasts. Gatwick will always be home, but it's not *hers*. It belongs to people like Mum and Theodore Ruske – people with the will and the inclination to do all the thankless work that keeps a society running, year after grinding year. That's not Fliss. She wonders, in a vague way, if it's Tanta. Certainly, if she succeeds in her goal of setting InTech's half of the city free from its corporate rulers, she'll need to find *someone* to figure out what to replace them with.

It feels surreal to be at the stage where InTech's collapse is anything more than a pipe dream, but if Cole can really turn his software patch into a virus, and Thoughtfront really have a way to sneak into InTech territory unnoticed, then two of the crew's biggest obstacles may just have been removed.

Fliss makes a mental note to talk to Tanta about this, when there's time. Running a city is far from her area of expertise, but she knows enough about what's involved, from watching her mum and growing up around the other Assembly members, that she has a sense of how vital it is. A bunch of free people is a great start, but unless Tanta and Cole have some idea of how to bind them together, they'll just trickle away into the wasteland. You need people – because what good is anything without them? – but you need ideas, too, structures that give the people a shape to move and mean within.

That's why it's so important to Fliss that she succeeds in convincing the Assembly not to strike a bargain with Thoughtfront. The corp will gut the settlement without a second thought, just as it gutted her old crew. Fliss has never wanted to live in Gatwick, but the thought of coming back one day to find that her home has leached away into the dirt – all of the people who should have been holding it together gone off to fight in a war they can't win, for people who think they're disposable – makes her nauseous. She's not going to let it happen.

There are two guards on duty outside the security building when Fliss arrives; they give her hostile looks but let her in without comment. Paige is in her office, talking on a handheld radio. When Fliss walks in, she shoves the walkie talkie into her belt and strides out to meet her.

'I've come for our stuff,' Fliss says.

She can see the crew's backpack and other bags from where she's standing – they're sitting on Paige's desk – but the head of security makes no move to get them. She stares at Fliss, face impassive.

'Are you and your associates leaving?' she asks.

'Not yet,' Fliss replies.

'Then what's the hurry? You can come and get your things on your way out.'

There's no bitterness in Paige's tone. She sounds calm – polite, even. Fliss feels a stirring of unease; she isn't used to the speaker for security being friendly, and she doesn't like it.

She's about to reply when the door opens behind her, and she turns to see Mum coming in. She comes to a stop by Fliss's side. 'Paige. Felicity,' she says. 'I hope I'm not interrupting anything?' She, too, sounds like she's making an effort to be civil – a rare enough occurrence when she's speaking to Paige Scarrow, Fliss knows.

'I was just getting our gear,' Fliss says.

Her mum gives her and Paige a bland smile. 'That's good timing, then. I'll help you carry it back to the medical centre.'

Fliss's stomach clenches. She's heard many a shouting match between her mum and Paige, but this careful courtesy is worse. Everything about this situation is putting her on edge. She's glad to see Mum, but what is she doing here? And why are she and Paige acting so weird?

For a moment, Paige looks as though she's weighing something up. Then she walks back into her office. She emerges with the bags, handing them over without further delay. Having the crew's weapons and tech back loosens the knot of tension in Fliss's stomach, but doesn't do away with it completely.

'I need the car, too,' she says.

'Of course.' Paige half turns, then raises a hand to her forehead. 'Oh, I completely forgot: it has a burst tyre.'

'Where is it?' Fliss presses.

'You needn't worry about replacing it yourself,' Paige continues, as if she hasn't heard her. 'I'll make sure my team have it repaired before you leave.'

Mum narrows her eyes. 'The car looked fine when I saw it last night. How did it get damaged?'

'Do you know, I really couldn't say,' Paige replies. 'It must have happened when we were impounding it. There was a lot of chaos last night, and accidents do happen sometimes.'

There's a pause as the two women stare each other down. After what feels like a long time, Mum tosses her head, breaking eye contact. 'Typical security force,' she snaps, sounding more like her normal self. 'It's a wonder your ham-fisted lot don't break everything they touch. Well, Felicity, I suppose I'd better get back. Walk with me?'

Fliss knows her mum well enough to understand that this invitation only sounds like it's optional. She turns and follows her without argument. Outside, night has fallen, and the wind is picking up.

'What the hell was that about?' she demands, as they emerge.

Mum gives her a sideways look and shakes her head. She doesn't speak until they've left the security building far behind them, and even then, it's only to pose a question of her own.

'Exactly how bad would it be if the Assembly accepted Thoughtfront's proposal?' she asks, her voice quiet.

'Bad,' Fliss replies. 'I've tangled with them before. They might say they're recruiting for a peacekeeping force, but they're lying – they're at war with InTech. Any people you send them won't come home.'

Mum sighs. 'That's what I thought. Scarrow doesn't agree, however. I was there when the Thoughtfront representative addressed the Assembly, and I saw her reaction: she's convinced an alliance with them is the answer to all our problems.'

Fliss thinks back to when she struck her own pact with Thoughtfront. At the time, she was so taken in by the corp's fancy weapons and advanced technology that she hadn't paid attention to the strings attached to them until it was too late. Reluctant as she is to admit it, she can understand how Paige has made the same mistake.

'You think what happened to the car wasn't an accident?' she asks. 'That she's trying to keep us here?'

Mum considers the question carefully before she answers. 'As things stand, I'd say the majority of the Assembly is inclined to reject Thoughtfront's offer – you know how people here feel about the corporations – but the balance is shifting with each new Red Flag attack. Scarrow doesn't know how your investigation might affect that balance, but if she can delay you and your friends for long enough, public opinion might swing her way on its own. Then she could argue that you're not producing results, force another vote on the issue.'

'But we already *had* a vote!' Fliss bursts out. She doesn't like Paige Scarrow, but the woman is an undeniable believer in law and order. 'She wouldn't just ignore the Assembly's decision. Would she?'

'Scarrow feels that Gatwick is facing an existential threat,'

Mum replies. 'I think there's not much she wouldn't do to protect it.'

Fliss grits her teeth. Paige isn't entirely wrong, but her vaunted solution is far worse than the problem she's trying to fix. Not that there's any point in trying to convince her of that. Paige is the kind of person who only grows more determined in the face of opposition and besides, she already thinks Fliss is a liar.

All of which leaves the crew in a very difficult position. Paige controls Gatwick's security, which means she also controls the gates in and out of the settlement. If she's committed to keeping them here, there isn't a hell of a lot they can do about it. Fliss tugs at the collar of her jacket; despite the cold air and the open sky, she can feel the walls of the settlement pressing in on her, stifling and oppressive. She's more desperate to be gone than ever, but leaving is no longer the easy prospect it was an hour ago.

'Fuck this,' she says. 'My crew and I need to get out of here.'

'I agree,' Mum replies. 'That's why I'm going to seek an extraordinary meeting of the Assembly, try to force Scarrow out into the open. She'll find these delaying tactics harder if Ruske and the other speakers get wind of what she's doing.'

She sounds as brisk and confident as usual, but Fliss isn't convinced. If Mum's right, then Paige has already flouted the Assembly once. Who's to say she won't do it again?

# Chapter 18

It's ironic, Tanta thinks. In the Brokerage, the crew felt almost unbearably cramped, observing each other's little squares of personal space with a respect that approached the religious. Yet now that they're out in the big, wide world, far from taking the opportunity to spread out, they've drawn together even more closely than they were during their confinement, clinging to one another instinctively. Their second night in Gatwick sees them all sleeping together in clinic room sixty-seven, Cole and Neal taking the beds while, Tanta, Fliss and Yas take turns napping on the floor. Fliss has filled them in on her conversation with Paige Scarrow, and Constance's fears, and they've all agreed that it's safer to sleep in shifts. They may have the Assembly's confidence, but that doesn't mean they're safe here.

Yas takes first watch, for which Tanta is grateful – she's bone-tired from the crew's flight from the Brokerage the night before. Despite the hard floor and her own unease, she falls immediately into a deep sleep, untroubled by dreams.

She is woken some hours later – she's not sure when exactly – by a persistent tapping on her shoulder. She opens her eyes, blinking in the gloom. She's expecting to see Yas, come to wake her for her shift, but it's Constance who is leaning over her.

'The situation is worse than I thought,' she says, as soon as she sees that Tanta is awake. 'We have to go – right now.'

Tanta sits up, instantly alert. Beside her, Yas is rousing Fliss. The older agent already has the crew's backpack slung over one shoulder.

'What's going on?' the bandit asks, her voice still muzzy with sleep.

'Apparently, there's a security team on its way over here to take me and Tanta back into custody,' Yas replies. 'Can't say this stay hasn't been interesting.'

That sends Tanta straight to her feet. She shakes Cole awake, careful to avoid his injured shoulder.

'It seems that once Paige learnt you and your friend are corporate runaways, she came up with a new way to get her hands on Thoughtfront's weapons,' Constance explains, as Tanta helps Cole on with his body armour. 'She's hoping to circumvent the Assembly completely – offer the two of you to the corp instead of the troops they've asked for. My friend on the security force gave me the heads-up.'

Tanta thinks of the man from last night – the one who radioed Constance when the crew were detained outside the North Gate – and offers a silent prayer of gratitude for Fliss's mum and her connections.

'But I never said which corp they were from!' Fliss protests, a tad defensively.

Constance gives her an old-fashioned look. 'We may keep to ourselves in Gatwick, but we're not fools. There are only two major players in the city, and I'd imagine Thoughtfront would love to get its hands on defectors from either one of them.'

After that, the bandit looks at her feet, uncharacteristically chastened. Tanta resists the urge to comment. Fliss's speech to the Assembly may have landed them in danger now, but at the time, it saved all their lives.

They leave Neal asleep and hurry across the medical centre to get Arden. The corridors are brightly lit, but mostly empty. They see a few medics, who nod to them cordially as they pass, but no one else.

'Do you know how long we've got till security gets here?' Tanta asks Constance.

'Not long,' she replies. 'I've got some of my team ready to run interference at the front entrance, so we'll at least know when they arrive.'

They're all on edge as they approach the CorpWard's room. A part of Tanta is expecting to find it empty, and Arden fled, but he's still exactly where she and Yas left him. He's asleep, but wakes when he hears the creak of the door and sits up in bed.

He regards Tanta curiously as she steps into the room. 'I thought we weren't leaving till tomorrow.'

'Change of plans,' she mutters, undoing his restraints. She leaves his hands cuffed.

Tanta thinks Constance is going to take the crew out the same way they came in yesterday, but the senior medic leads them in the opposite direction, deeper into the medical centre's maze of corridors. Eventually, they reach a pair of double doors that lead out onto a rain-washed square of tarmac. There are three ambulances backed up to the exit – bulky, rectangular vans painted in pale yellow-green, with red and yellow hazard markers striped across the foldout doors at the back.

Constance points to the nearest one. 'Everyone in, and keep quiet.'

The five of them need no further instruction; even Arden seems to have gathered how serious the situation is. They climb inside with the bags, crouching near the foldout doors so they're not visible through the narrow windows. Shut in the darkened compartment, Tanta can only measure their progress through sounds – the whir of Constance's ramp, the thud of the cab door slamming closed. She strains her senses for warnings of pursuit, but can hear nothing over the sound of the engine.

The ambulance speeds along for what feels like a long time – long enough that Tanta begins to wonder if they have passed through the gates already and are on the open road. She's disabused of this hopeful notion when they slow to a crawl, and the siren comes on. Constance lets it play for three seconds – three drawn-out whoops – and then silences it.

A minute after that, they come to a complete stop, and Tanta hears the whir of one of the front windows sliding down.

'Open up,' Constance snaps, her voice drifting muffled through the divider.

'No one's allowed out,' a man's voice says. 'Paige's orders.'

'We've just had an urgent call from Crawley. There's been a Red Flag incursion – three people were stabbed.'

'I'm sorry. I'm under strict orders to—'

'I'll let you radio them to explain that there's no help coming, then,' Constance interrupts, her voice level. 'You know Crawley doesn't have an emergency room of its own.'

Most of Tanta's attention is focused on trying not to breathe too loudly, but she has room to be impressed by the senior medic's ability to bluff under pressure. She'd make a good agent.

The man is stumbling over another excuse.

'Those people will bleed out if you don't let me through,' Constance tells him. 'I'm sure you don't want that on your conscience. I'll only be twenty minutes.'

There's a strained pause. Tanta and Yas look at one another, hands going to their guns. They're tensing to burst from the back of the ambulance when they hear the metallic shriek of the gate swinging open.

Once they're through, the crew are free to watch as Gatwick recedes through the ambulance's narrow back windows. No one is following them – not yet, anyway – but all the same,

Constance waits until they've put a few twists and turns between them and the settlement before she slows the ambulance
to a stop once more.

'This is where I leave you,' she announces, sliding open the
divider between the cab and the back.

Fliss looks appalled. 'Mum! You can't go back to Gatwick!
What if Paige arrests you?'

Constance lets out a belly laugh. 'I'd like to see her try!'

'You'd be all by yourself,' Fliss protests, 'and there might be
Red Flags around.'

That earns her a wry look. 'It's twenty minutes down the
road. I'm not a child, Felicity. I'll be fine.' Catching sight of
her daughter's expression, Constance continues more seriously.
'Besides, I'll be safer going home than tagging along for your
investigation. You and your friends are racing headfirst into
trouble – don't deny it, you always do. I'll take my chances on
my own, thanks.'

There's not much Fliss can say to that, though it's clear from
her expression that she doesn't like it. She and her mum share a
hug on the side of the road, and then Constance wheels herself
swiftly back the way they came. There's no time to watch her
out of sight. Yas and Arden get into the cab – she to drive and
he to guide her – and the crew set off again.

Gatwick is visible behind them for a long while, the lights
from the houses and the pre-Meltdown buildings twinkling in
the darkness. Then they turn to the west, into the great forest
that swamps the Unaffiliated Zone on that side of the city, and
it's lost to sight.

The mood in the ambulance is gloomy and pensive. Cole dozes,
head leaning against a gurney. Fliss bites her nails, her thoughts
clearly still on her mum and her hometown. For a long while,
they travel in silence, nothing to hear except the low hum of

243

the electric engine and the sighing of the wind through the trees outside. Tanta thinks their path is taking them around the city to the north, following the curve of the Outer Wall, though with the location tracker in her 'scape disabled, she can't confirm this. Having no certain sense of where she is makes her uneasy, as does the fact that it's Arden who's directing them.

'My understanding was that Thoughtfront's corporate army is one of the strongest around. Why would it be building a militia of unaffiliated raiders?' Cole asks, after they've been driving for almost an hour. He pitches his voice low, to keep Arden from overhearing, but it's already sounding stronger than it was yesterday.

Tanta has an idea, but Fliss answers before she can. 'Isn't it obvious? Harlow 2.0 types can barely even see people without headware. The Red Flags could march in through InTech's front gate and they'd still have the element of surprise.'

'It's the only explanation that makes sense,' Tanta agrees. 'If Thoughtfront strikes before InTech has a chance to patch out the problem, the raiders could wipe out a significant proportion of InTech's troops before they even realise who they're supposed to be fighting.'

It's only as she says this aloud that its implications begin to sink in. All the intelligence the crew have had from their Brokerage contacts indicates that Thoughtfront is losing this war, but if she and Fliss are right about this new strategy, it could shift the balance of power between the two corporations decisively. It's a desperate plan, but what other choice does Thoughtfront have? Its leaders have always been jealous and fearful of the Harlow Programme, and now they have seen that programme used to shackle and subvert the minds of all of InTech's residents at once. They must be wondering how long it will be before their old enemy decides to do the same thing to them.

The corporation north of the riverbed is facing annihilation, and its only recourse is to respond in kind. The thought makes the hairs on Tanta's arms and neck stand on end. The struggle between InTech and Thoughtfront is not her fight, not anymore, but she can't shake the queasy feeling that the crew might get back to the city only to find that there is no InTech to liberate anymore.

After an hour, the ambulance begins to slow. Arden slides open the divider between the two sections and pokes his head through.

'According to my tracker, the stronghold is half a mile further on,' he says. 'I suggest we walk from here.'

*Of course that's your suggestion,* the cynic in Tanta pipes up. *Once we're out in the open, it'll be that much easier for you to make a run for it.* A much larger part of her acknowledges the good sense of the idea: they can't risk the ambulance being spotted by anyone inside the Thoughtfront compound.

Yas manoeuvres the ambulance into a dense stand of trees, nosing the cab into a thicket of vines and brambles for good measure. The vehicle is still more conspicuous than Tanta would like, but its bright bodywork has been grimed by what must have been years of active service. With any luck, anyone who comes across it will think it has been abandoned. The crew climb out and cluster together. Usually, this would be the point at which Tanta would brief them all on the plan, but tonight, she looks to Yas instead. When it comes to Thoughtfront security protocols, she's the expert.

'The good news,' Yas says, 'Is that whatever this facility is, it's likely to be relatively lightly staffed – by Thoughtfront operatives, at least. This far outside the Outer Wall, there's not much the corp can do to protect itself from an all-out assault, so my guess is it'll be relying on this place not being found at all. Expect a small force of well-armed guards, to minimise digital signatures, and more of a focus on surveillance and secrecy than defence. That said, the guards who *are* stationed here won't be looking to take prisoners. So guns, not stun batons.'

'How do you suggest we proceed?' Arden asks.

'Get closer, scope the place out, and find out what security we're dealing with. Then we'll have a better idea of how to bypass it.' Yas holds up a pair of Brokerage earbuds. 'I'm going to stay in the ambulance with Cole and direct you remotely, in case we need to get out of here in a hurry. Any questions before you move out?'

When no one answers, she presses one of the earbuds into her ear, hands the other to Tanta, and swings back into the cab. 'Good luck, then.' And, with a sideways glance at Arden, 'Try not to kill each other.'

The rest of them walk on into the forest, Arden leading the way. After half a mile, the trees ahead begin to thin, the wood's rapid expansion checked by the remains of a pre-Meltdown town. It's in even worse repair than the ones closer to the city, the houses and shops sunken in on themselves or rotted away to almost nothing. Many of the old buildings have young trees pushing up through their roofs or leaning crookedly from their empty windows. The woodland is devouring this place by inches, pulling all things built and made back into the hungry dirt.

About a hundred yards ahead, the trees peter out completely at what must be the centre of the old town. Tanta can see a few taller buildings and the cracked remains of asphalt roads, eaten away by weeds. There's no sign of a Thoughtfront base.

'There's nothing here!' Fliss hisses, glaring at Arden.

'The car I'm tracking keeps returning to this location,' the CorpWard insists.

Tanta, too, is wondering how five thousand Red Flag troops could be concealed in this abandoned settlement. But Arden has no reason to lie to them – not before he's got what he came here for, anyway. 'We'll stay within the trees and circle around,' she whispers.

She waves the other two on ahead of her, pointing round to the east. Fliss moves off immediately. Arden hangs back, watching her. Tanta could swear that there's the hint of a smirk playing around his lips, though it vanishes as she meets his eyes.

'After you,' she says, pointedly. Arden may be cuffed, but she's not going to let the CorpWard get behind her if she can help it. At a certain point this evening, he'll attempt to double-cross them – it's inevitable. Tanta suspects he'll simply try and escape – the odds of anything more drastic are not in his favour – but there's no doubt in her mind that he'd kill her if he could. If it comes to it, she's willing to do the same.

The buildings past the end of the treeline are in better condition than the ones claimed by the forest. Their reconnaissance reveals shops, bars and restaurants, their roofs sagging and ivy climbing in through their windows, but still recognisable and largely intact. There's a high street running past to the north, terminating in a humped roundabout. The only traffic on it now is a couple of squirrels. They see no people – no signs of any human activity at all. Aside from the wind, which moans through the empty buildings and makes ghostly shadows dance on their walls, the place is still and silent.

'I don't understand,' Arden says. 'The car keeps coming back here. There *has* to be something.' The confusion in his voice sounds so real that it's either genuine, or he's an even better actor than Tanta.

'Like fuck there does!' Fliss rounds on him. 'I don't know what you're trying to pull, but—'

Tanta shushes them both, holding up a hand to reinforce the command. There *is* another sound: carried on the wind, and almost drowned out by it, she can hear voices – and they're getting closer. She waves Fliss and Arden deeper into the forest.

247

After a tense minute, two black-uniformed guards pass by, walking with the leisurely, swinging pace of a patrol.

Tanta narrows her eyes, bringing their faces closer. They leap into focus, and a little flash of satisfaction thrills through her. She can't do as much with her 'scape now as she used to. A lot of its functionality – MindChat, location tracking, her datamed – relies on connecting to the InTech network, which is impossible with latency in the UZ so high, and not an option for a defector in any case. She feels like she's running this field mission without her full complement of senses, but these limitations make her relish the 'scape functions remaining to her all the more fiercely.

She's too far away to hear what the guards are saying to one another, but she catches a scrap of conversation on their lips as they move out of sight.

*...last crew come in, and then we can wrap things up here. I'll be glad to see the back of this place.*

Tanta can't make out any more than that, but the presence of guards suggests there's *something* here worth guarding. 'It looks like we arrived just in time,' she murmurs. 'They're talking about closing this base down.'

'Are you going to take them out?' Arden asks.

Tanta shakes her head. Arden isn't armed, and she and Fliss only have the cartridges their pistols are loaded with – the rest of their ammo and weapons are back in the ambulance with Yas and Cole. They need to avoid getting into a firefight at least until they've finished this scouting trip.

'Come on,' she says, waving them all forward.

They move slowly, following the same path the guards took, but sticking to the trees. The ground ahead slopes upward into a steep, wooded bank, at the top of which is a barbed wire fence.

'This could be something,' Tanta murmurs.

'It's pre-Meltdown,' Fliss says dismissively.

'Actually, Thoughtfront aren't averse to using pre-Meltdown installations when it suits them,' Yas says into Tanta's ear. 'I wouldn't put it past them to make use of existing security structures, especially since they're trying to keep a low profile.'

Tanta was thinking the same thing. She relays Yas's message to the others, then climbs the bank and starts making her way along the fence, searching for a hole or weak spot she can exploit. The wire mesh is sagging in places, and covered with a thick layer of rust, but the barbed wire has weathered the ages well – almost too well, in Tanta's opinion.

'Look at this.'

Arden's voice comes from further away than she was expecting – Tanta glances up sharply to see that he's managed to get almost two hundred yards further along the fence. She gives herself a mental shake. He's slippery; she needs to keep a closer eye on him.

He's pointing at a section of fencing. As Tanta draws level with him, she can see what's caught his attention: it's new. Someone has taken pains to sandpaper the shine off its surface, but it's free of the rust that marks its neighbours. A subtle enough difference, but it's all the clue Tanta needs to confirm Yas's theory. Someone is using this pre-Meltdown fence for something – why else would they be repairing it? She peers through it. There's nothing on the other side but a high, grassy ridge, edged with weeds and bracken and, about five metres further on, a second length of fencing. The space in between the two fences is long and narrow. Tanta cranes her neck left and right, but can't see its endpoint.

It doesn't look like any kind of compound she's seen before, but it bears investigating, all the same. Tanta walks back over to an older section of fencing and strips off her jacket, which she throws over the metal spikes like she's smothering a fire. It won't provide perfect protection against the barbed wire, but its thick, waterproof fabric is stronger and more durable than civilian clothing. She scales the fence and vaults over to the far side. Her feet hit the ground with a hollow thud.

She crouches, immediately on the lookout for any guards who might have been alerted by the sound, but after a tense minute, she concludes that they are still alone. Peering at the grass beneath her feet, she tears at it with a cautious hand. It doesn't take long before her fingers touch something harder and colder than earth. Just visible through the layers of dirt are the corrugated grooves of a metal roof.

'Hey, come and look at this!' she hisses.

Fliss takes a running leap at the fence, swinging herself up and over the barbed wire with the air of someone who has done it many times before. She crouches at Tanta's side, inspecting the metal.

'It looks like a shipping container or something,' she says.

'Little help?'

Tanta and Fliss look up. On the far side of the fence, Arden raises his handcuffs and gives them a meaningful clink.

It takes longer to get the CorpWard over the fence, but they manage it eventually, by dint of much pulling and swearing under their breaths. Once all made it to the other side, Tanta shows them what she's found, and passes it on to Cole and Yas, too.

'Maybe the compound is underground,' Arden suggests.

Tanta considers it. 'The fences go on a long way: I'd guess this is a tunnel to the base, rather than the base itself.'

Fliss kicks at the grass. 'But there's no way *in*. What are we going to do about that?'

'Let's—' but Tanta's suggestion is drowned out by a sudden wall of sound, a drawn-out, rattling whoosh, like the exhalation of a consumptive giant. The noise sets the ground beneath their feet thrumming, and sends Fliss and Arden diving for cover, but to Tanta, it's the answer the crew has been searching for.

Her earpiece crackles into life. 'Tanta, was that what I think it was?' Cole asks.

Tanta grins. 'It was.'

Like Cole, she's heard that sound before.

# Chapter 19

'Trains,' Arden repeats, his face blank.

Tanta feels a sneaking sense of satisfaction at knowing something the cocky young CorpWard doesn't. 'Trains,' she says. 'Thoughtfront uses a converted, pre-Meltdown underground network to hold and transport prisoners within its own territory – Cole and I discovered it during a covert assignment last summer. I just never knew it extended outside the city before.'

There was a time when Tanta would have found the revelation alarming – that Thoughtfront has managed to construct a secret tunnel into the UZ without InTech learning anything about it suggests that the ICRD's world-beating intelligence network is developing a few blind spots. Now she's no longer with the ICRD, she's free to be excited by it. She thinks back to when she and Cole first discovered the train system, half a year ago. It's bigger than she ever could have anticipated, but the core of her thought then is still true now: there are ways under and around the structures the corporations have built, ways that existed long before the corps were even founded. Ways that Tanta and the crew can use.

'If there are guards here, the train terminal must be above ground,' she says. 'If we stick close to the edge of the fence and keep to the shadows, we may be able to sneak into the compound by following the line of the tracks.'

She's done it before – though back then she had to walk along the tracks themselves, trying to avoid falling onto the live rail. She's devoutly glad she won't have to do that this time around.

They move off, walking in single file and hugging the fence. Tanta makes Arden go first. She's reasonably satisfied that he was telling the truth about this place, but if he's left anything out, he'll be the first one to have to deal with it. After a few minutes, he stops.

'This looks like it,' he says.

Tanta draws alongside him and cautiously, the three of them climb to the top of the rise. From their position on the raised ground atop the train tunnel, they have a good vantage point over much of the abandoned settlement. Almost immediately below them are a pair of platforms. A red-and-white passenger bridge spans the space between them, accessed by an enclosed staircase on the left-hand side. The platforms look like the ones Tanta and Cole encountered beneath Thoughtfront's side of the city: two lips of concrete, jutting out over each side of a lowered section of ground.

Right now, that lowered space partially is filled by the train Tanta heard passing beneath them a few minutes before. It's not white, like the one from which they rescued Yas. Instead, its metal carapace has been painted with camouflage in mind: a muddy mix of greens and browns, the colours merging in patterns designed to baffle the eye. The rails are only exposed for a section of fifty metres or so before they pass into the tunnel on top of which Tanta, Fliss and Arden are now stood, but it seems Thoughtfront is not taking any chances with this operation being discovered.

On the left-hand platform, behind the staircase, there's a long, low structure with a pitched roof – probably the old station building. Tanta would guess that it now serves as a break room for off-duty guards: there's a single, dim light coming from one of the windows. Zooming in, she can see a woman sitting at a foldout table. There's a radio beside her: the forces stationed here must be using it to communicate with Thoughtfront HQ in a way that won't be picked up by InTech's scanners. The rest of the guards are out patrolling the platforms, two on each side. Their attention is focused on the train; no one has noticed Tanta and the crew, and given the darkness and the distance, they're not likely to.

'If this place is anything like the enhanced interrogation facility that Cole and I broke into last summer, then it's a staging post,' Tanta says. 'They must be bringing the Red Flags here and then transporting them into the city on the trains.'

'Are you saying this network runs all the way into InTech territory?' Arden asks, appalled.

Tanta is counting on it, but she's not about to tell Arden that. 'Get inside, and we may be able to find out,' she replies. 'I count five guards. If we assume that the two we saw outside the station are still on perimeter duty, that makes at least seven.'

'That's the standard size of a Thoughtfront peacekeeper squadron,' Yas chips in.

Tanta nods. There were seven guards in the torture facility, as well, which was a similar size. Back then, she was able to kill or neutralise all of them by herself – but back then, she'd had access to her Inscape's full range of functions, including a MindChat connection to plan her attack with Cole in silence.

*But this time, it's not just the two of you,* a voice inside her says. It's true: she has a crew now – though Fliss might differ with her on whose crew it is exactly – and that has to tilt the odds in their favour.

'We can manage seven,' she says.

She's thinking out the plan of attack as she speaks. She and Fliss can probably shoot at least two guards from their current position. While the other three are confused and panicking, scrambling to locate the snipers and get behind cover, she'll slip down and take them out, too. If the crew are lucky, they'll have time to hide the bodies before the last two get back to base. With the peacekeepers dead, they'll be able to go through whatever records or maps this place has to offer at their leisure.

Before all that, though, they need to head back to the ambulance to gear up – and to secure Arden. Now that they've found the base, their alliance of convenience with the CorpWard has almost run its course. He's probably already plotting how to sabotage or double-cross them, and Tanta doesn't want to have to keep track of him and his machinations during a shootout.

'We've completed our reconnaissance, Yas,' she continues, touching her earpiece. 'We'll meet you and Cole back at the ambulance.'

Beside her, Arden coughs. 'Ah,' he says. 'We might not want to leave just yet.'

'Why not?' Tanta asks.

The CorpWard's eyes flick to the left, past the station and up the potholed road.

'That car I'm tracking? It's coming back.'

They hear the low hum of the car's engine a bare second after Arden gives the warning. It pulls up outside the station building a moment later, a bulky all-terrain vehicle almost identical to the one the crew encountered on their way to Gatwick.

'Get down,' Tanta murmurs, lying flat on the rise. 'They might have torches.'

She positions Arden next to her, keeping a grip on his arm

for good measure. He must have seen the car coming on his tracker from miles off, yet chose to mention it only at the eleventh hour – which is all the confirmation Tanta needs that their interests are no longer aligned. He seems content to stay put for now, at least; like Tanta and Fliss, he's keen to find out more about what's going on here.

The car's doors open, and five raiders pile out. Tanta thinks back to the snippet of conversation she caught from the patrolling guards. They talked about a 'last crew' coming into the station: this must be it. If these are the last Red Flags to pass this way, the rest must already be in the city, either holed up in some underground Thoughtfront base, or somewhere beneath InTech. It's a disconcerting thought – one that makes Tanta glad, for the first time, that Arden is with them. She's content to let him escape, so long as whatever double-cross he has in mind doesn't put the crew at risk. If he's smart, he'll run back to InTech and warn it of the danger it's in. Tanta certainly hopes he does. She may have turned her back on her parent corp, but even after all this time, it's still the place she thinks of as home. The prospect of armed raiders lurking in its basements and sewers, emerging to massacre its residents in their sleep, is one she'd like to avoid.

The Red Flags open the boot of the car, from which two more figures emerge, a man and a woman. Beside her, Tanta feels Fliss stiffen: the last two people are unarmed, and the raiders are urging them forward with the butts of their pistols. Conscripts. Fliss looks angry enough to attack right then and there.

'Not yet,' Tanta hisses. 'What are they saying?'

The Red Flags aren't as discreet as the Thoughtfront guards, and snatches of their conversation are drifting up on the breeze. It's in cant, a different variety to the city version that Tanta learnt in basic training. After listening for a moment, Fliss gives a contemptuous snort.

'Fuckers are talking about how they're going to divide up InTech's turf,' she whispers. 'Saying they'll set up shop at the top of the Needle, start selling headware to the wastelanders.'

Tanta can see why this would make the bandit laugh. If the Red Flags think Thoughtfront is going to give them InTech's territory in exchange for their help, they're fools — whatever the corporation has promised them.

The silent facility is springing to life, now. The door at the front of the station building swings open, and the guard from the break room emerges, gun in hand. That's strange; aren't the raiders Thoughtfront's allies?

'Keep your voices down,' she urges.

A Red Flag laughs. 'Why? InTech'll know about us soon enough.'

He pushes the male conscript over to the guard and grabs hold of the man's arm, rolling up the sleeve to the shoulder. Then, to Tanta's consternation, the guard jabs her gun into the exposed flesh and pulls the trigger. The man winces, but there's no sound. Tanta narrows her eyes, magnifying the baffling sight, and that's when she realises that the device the guard is holding is not a firearm at all, but a bulky, metallic thing a bit like a piercing gun. As she watches, the other conscript is pushed forward, and the guard repeats the process.

'They're *chipping* them,' Arden murmurs, the word twisted with distaste. 'Like they're animals.'

Tanta thinks about the chips and wires and trackers that InTech has put inside Arden himself and considers pointing out the obvious, but elects to bite her tongue. With his Harlow Programming active, the CorpWard is incapable of understanding her.

'With what, though?' she asks instead. 'A location tracker?'

'We can ask them when we get back,' Fliss growls. 'Let's go get Yas and take these bastards out.'

She half rises from her position, but Tanta touches her arm, forestalling her. 'We need to think carefully before we make our move,' she cautions. The arrival of the Red Flags has almost doubled the number of their adversaries at a stroke. A fight now, even with Yas's help, is not one they'd be likely to survive.

Fliss squirms uncomfortably. 'Well, we can't wait until they leave. Those are Gatwick's people they're forcing onto that train!'

Tanta is turned towards Fliss, so she doesn't notice Arden move until he pulls free of her grasp. She does notice, though, when the night's quiet is shattered by an ear-splitting yell.

'INTRUDERS!'

Her head whips around. While she was trying to convince Fliss to move slowly, Arden has taken matters into his own hands. He's standing on the rise, jumping and shouting.

As one, every guard and raider in the facility turns towards him. A heartbeat later, the shooting starts.

As the night erupts into chaos, Tanta starts counting. There are eight rounds in her magazine – the same amount in Fliss's – and eleven hostiles. That makes sixteen shots between them, and only five chances to miss before they're out of ammo and the Red Flags and the guards kill them both.

She wastes one of those precious shots on Arden: as she fires, the CorpWard dives off the rise, into the tall weeds and bracken at the bottom of the slope. *Ten hostiles*, Tanta amends. She may have missed, but Arden is using the turmoil he's created to make good on his escape – she can hear his footfalls crashing through the foliage.

She follows him down, not to give chase, but to get into cover. At the bottom of the ridge, concealed from the guards on the platform by the sloping sides of the train tunnel, she touches her earpiece.

'Arden has given away our position,' she barks to Yas. 'I'm going in.'

Then she sprints along the inside of the fence, making for the train station.

The guards on the left-hand platform still have their guns trained on the top of the tunnel, so when Tanta bursts onto the scene, it takes them a second to refocus their weapons on her. That second is all she needs. She shoots the first man in the head and runs into him as he collapses, using his body to protect herself against his colleague's bullets. *Nine.* From behind him, she fires another shot at the second guard. She hears a dull thud as the woman drops to the ground – *eight* – and lets her human shield fall so she can reassess the situation.

The Red Flags and the guard who greeted them must still be outside the station, though Tanta estimates she has seconds before they arrive. Before then, she needs to find some more cover. She races for the enclosed staircase, pounding up the steps and onto the footbridge.

From her new vantage point, she can see beyond the platform again. The Red Flags and the peacekeeper have disappeared, presumably into the station house; the conscripts have fled. The two guards on the right-hand platform are still shooting up towards the rise, where Fliss is lying. She's completely motionless – she looks dead – but then her hand twitches, and the third guard falls. *Seven.* Tanta just has time to admire Fliss's marksmanship when there's a yell, and the fourth goes down, too. He's not dead, but wounded. A second shot takes him in the chest, and he lies still.

That brings them to six – one more guard and the five raiders – but they've already wasted at least two shots between them. A volley of bullets pings off the footbridge's panelling, forcing

Tanta to duck. When she risks another glance over the side, she sees that the Red Flags have burst onto the platform – and that they've been joined by the two peacekeepers who were on patrol. She grits her teeth as she updates her mental tally card. *Eight. Again.* They're sheltering behind a pair of domed Thoughtfront shields – the ones that are the shape and thickness of an umbrella but can somehow withstand armour-piercing rounds. Tanta curses. She knows from bitter experience that whatever material Thoughtfront uses for its shields is almost impossible to penetrate. She could have considerably more firepower than she does and still never get through it.

On the platform, one of the Red Flags is taking careful aim at Fliss through something long-barrelled and nasty-looking.

'Take cover!' Tanta shouts to her.

Fliss hops down from the rise a second before the gun goes off, the bullet hitting the top of the tunnel in an explosion of grass and turf. She lands on the roof of the train and slides down it onto the right-hand platform, putting its metallic bulk between her and the Thoughtfront troops.

'Get the doors open!' someone yells.

A peacekeeper breaks from behind one of the barriers and sprints towards the train, presumably to do just that. Tanta misses the first time, gets him in the chest on the second shot. The remaining troops back up hastily against the wall of the station house. *Seven again.*

'Don't come any closer!' she yells.

Unfortunately, she's pinned down, and the troops know it. She and Fliss have a minute's grace while the people behind the two shields confer. Then one of the groups starts advancing towards the staircase.

'Yas?' Tanta mutters into her earpiece. 'We could really use some backup.'

There's no reply. Tanta assesses her options and finds that

none of them are good. She has – she checks the window in her magazine – three rounds left, and seven people she needs to kill with them. She aced all her marksmanship simulations in basic training, but even she can't make those numbers work. Fliss, meanwhile, is stuck behind the train, unable to help her out.

She darts a glance over the side of the bridge. A bullet ricochets off the panelling, inches from her face. One group of fighters is moving towards her in lockstep, while the other – the one still sheltering under the awning of the station – provides covering fire. The advancing group are manoeuvring their shield carefully: Tanta can't get a clear shot at them, even from above. They've almost reached the stairs. She braces herself.

And then there's a roar from the road outside, followed by a crash like a building falling down. Tanta's ears ring. When she can collect herself, she looks again to see that a building *has* fallen down. The train station is in ruins, a gaping hole in its brickwork. Protruding from that hole is the red and yellow striped back of the ambulance. The group beneath the awning have been scattered, their shield flung away. The ambulance moves forward a fraction, and then Yas reverses again, running over three of the Thoughtfront fighters with a crunch that Tanta can hear all the way from the bridge.

'Sorry I couldn't answer before,' Yas's voice buzzes in her earpiece. 'I was driving.'

Her intervention couldn't have been timelier, but Tanta doesn't have the breathing space to thank her for it. She scans the platform, raising her gun to her eyeline. The three raiders hit by the ambulance are unmoving, their bodies bent at angles that are hard to look at. The survivor left the safety of the shield in her haste to leap clear. Tanta takes her out as she dives back towards it, a clean shot through the temple.

'I'm on the bridge,' she tells Yas, her voice ragged with adrenaline. 'There's a second group coming up the stairs.'

She bites her lip, tasting blood. They're so close to getting out of this. To fail now, with just three fighters left, would be a frustrating way to die. A staccato burst of gunfire peppers the footbridge with bullets, announcing the group's arrival. Tanta crouches, huddled against the panelling. She's still pinned down – and all her hopes are pinned on Fliss and Yas.

'Hey!' comes Fliss's voice. 'Over here!'

Tanta leaps up. She's in time to see Fliss emerge from the mouth of the tunnel – she must have run round behind the train. She skids to a halt at the foot of the stairs and opens fire. The Thoughtfront fighters try to swing their shield around, but they're the ones who are trapped now, stuck between Tanta and Fliss on the narrow staircase.

It's over in seconds. When silence falls at last, Tanta picks her way over the bodies and joins Fliss at the bottom of the stairs.

'Thanks for the assist,' she pants.

Fliss gives her a weak smile. 'Where would you be without me?'

Yas steps through the hole in the station house, then, joining them on the platform. 'Well, looks like you were both right,' she says. 'It *was* a trick, and you *did* manage to get clear.'

'Just about,' Tanta replies. It was a close enough thing that she's hardly inclined to say *I told you so*.

'Oh, I found this outside.' Yas waves the strange chip gun the guard from the break room was carrying. 'Thought our in-house engineer might want to take a look at it.'

'Good thinking,' Fliss says. 'Where is Cole, anyway?'

'I dropped him off outside the station before I drove into it. He's already been strangled – I didn't want to give him whiplash, too. Cole,' Yas calls. 'You can come out now: it's over.'

'Actually, it's not quite.'

The sound of Arden's voice makes Tanta start. She had thought he'd be halfway back to the city by now. She turns to

262

the source of the sound. The CorpWard is at the other end of the platform, coming out of the station's break room, and that smirk Tanta thought she saw on the edges of his expression before has come fully into the spotlight now. He's holding a gun to Cole's head.

# Chapter 20

'We're going to take this nice and easy,' Arden says, advancing along the platform. 'Drop your weapons and go and stand against the wall.'

Tanta holsters her gun immediately and raises her hands, but does not throw the pistol aside. It's empty – but Arden doesn't know that. 'And what's your plan then?' she asks. It seems improbable to her that Arden could have one – at least, one that makes sense. She's confused by his play here: it's not what she would have done. Cole is a valuable asset, and the ICRD probably wants her, Fliss and Yas dealt with as well, but there's no way Arden can dispatch them all – or get them back to the city by himself. Look at how the four of them fared in their attempts to keep him under guard. With the numbers reversed, his task becomes an impossible one.

Arden doesn't reply, but his eyes flick to the station at his back, and then Tanta understands. The radio. When she saw Arden, he was emerging from the break room. He's been deep in the Unaffiliated Zone for days, with no MindChat signal; he must have a frequency he can tune into to receive further instructions from the ICRD – and he's just used it to report in. His task isn't completely impossible, then: if he can keep the four of them here, with Cole as leverage, for an hour or two, then he'll have all the backup he needs.

That's still a big if, though. As Yas and Fliss comply with Arden's instructions, walking over to stand beside Tanta against the station wall, Tanta watches the CorpWard carefully. Anger thumps in her head and her heart, sharpening her senses. He must have taken the pistol he's holding from one of the dead Thoughtfront fighters, which means it can't have that many rounds left. It may not even be loaded. There are lines of concentration creasing the young man's forehead, and a tremor, barely perceptible, in his hand where he grips the gun. He's feeling the strain of this impromptu hostage situation, though he's good at hiding it. Arden is a young agent, fresh out of training, taking on a bigger fish than he's likely encountered in his life before. He has overplayed his hand, and at least part of him knows it.

'You should have run,' Tanta tells him. 'It's going to take an ICRD strike team, what, two hours to get here? By the time they show up, we'll be gone, and you'll be dead.'

It's a promise as much as a threat, though Tanta doesn't yet know how she's going to make good on it. Right now, it's enough to make Arden flinch, an instant of weakness.

'If I die, I'm taking your partner with me,' he replies, and Tanta is satisfied to hear that the tremor has spread to his voice now, too.

It's a good sign. She only needs him to drop his guard for a second – the smallest distraction will be enough to allow her to strike and this time, she won't hold back. This CorpWard has threatened Cole for the last time; he's going to regret it – though if she does her job right, he won't regret it for very long. She catches Cole's eye, trying to convey her intentions through her glance alone. *Don't worry*, she thinks at him. *I'm going to get us out of this.*

He stares back at her with a stricken expression. When she makes eye contact with him, he shakes his head, just a fraction. Tanta knows Cole well enough by now that she can interpret the gesture. He's not pleading for himself, but for Arden. She can hear all his arguments in the CorpWard's defence as surely as if he's sending them to her via MindChat. *He's only doing this because of his Harlow Programming! A few months ago, you weren't so different from him!*

*What do you expect me to do?* she catches herself thinking back at him. Arden has a gun to Cole's head – and it's not even the first time he's tried to kill him. How does Cole want her to respond?

For an instant, Tanta allows herself to see things from Cole's perspective – the one from which Arden's youth and inexperience are not weaknesses she can make use of, but reasons to stay her hand. She sighs. 'My partner can handle himself,' she says to Arden, though the words are meant for Cole alone. If he's so keen for her to change her plan of attack, she's going to need his help with it.

Arden has recovered himself sufficiently by now to start towing Cole back towards the break room. Presumably, he intends to lock them all inside. 'Follow me,' he raps. 'Slowly.'

While they move, Tanta locks eyes with Cole, praying that he remembers the self-defence lessons they went over in Gatwick that morning. When they get to the break room door, Arden reaches out to kick it open with one foot.

'RED FLAG!' Tanta screams, pointing at the mouth of the tunnel.

'You can't honestly think I'd fall for that,' Arden replies, turning to sneer at her – and that's when Cole rams his elbow into the boy's nose. There's a spurt of blood, shockingly red against the CorpWard's pale skin, and for an instant, he relaxes his grip on Cole's arm. Cole struggles from his grasp, and then does exactly what Tanta taught him, which is to run like hell.

'Get on the train!' Tanta shouts. She, meanwhile, is sprinting towards Arden. She reaches him while his gaze is still unfocused, his senses dulled by pain. He points the gun unsteadily in her direction, but she weaves in under his guard and punches him with her right hand, one short jab to the throat. While he's choking on the blow, she brings her left arm up beneath his elbow and leans on his upper arm with her full weight, bearing down until she feels a pop. Arden's right arm goes limp, the gun in his hand firing once at the floor before it falls from his nerveless fingers. The bullet ricochets off the ground, blowing out one of the train's windows in a shower of glass.

Tanta sweeps out with one leg to kick the gun away, but as it clatters across the platform, Arden's good fist slams into the back of her head, so hard that sparks of light seem to burst like fireworks in her vision. He hits with more force than her, but it was a desperate blow, too clumsy to break Tanta's neck and not quite hard enough to knock her out. There's a high singing in her ears and she feels as though she's moving through water, but she manages to keep a tenuous hold on consciousness. Before Arden can draw back his arm for a follow up, she hooks her left leg behind his right heel and throws herself forward, knocking them both to the ground.

It's no more elegant a move than Arden's was, but it does the job. The CorpWard's head slams into the concrete platform with an audible crack, and he lies still. Tanta disentangles herself and gets to her feet. Fliss and Cole are on the train, staring at her anxiously from the open doors. Yas is still standing against the wall of the station house, watching proceedings with interest.

'You looked like you had it covered,' she says, when Tanta shoots her an old-fashioned look.

'Help me restrain him, at least.'

Arden isn't dead: Tanta can see the motion of his chest, and his eyes are already stirring uneasily beneath their closed lids. He'll come round in a minute or two, and she has no idea where his handcuffs have got to. Yas lopes across to her and takes hold of the CorpWard's legs.

'We'll take the radio out and shut him in the break room,' Tanta says. 'Let his strike team break him out when they get here.'

There's a manual lock on the break room door; it doesn't take them long to discover the key, hanging on a hook just inside. Together, they haul the unconscious Arden in and prop him up against the table. He's stirring by the time they lock the door, his face scrunched up against the pain in his head. Tanta uses the butt of her pistol to break the key off in the lock for good measure. As she turns back to the train, she finds Cole at her elbow, a worried look on his face.

'He'll be all right,' she says, which is probably true. 'Is your shoulder OK?'

'Fine,' Cole gasps. He's still out of breath from his frantic run along the platform, but he looks unhurt. 'Look: I didn't even reopen the wound.'

Tanta nods. 'Glad to hear it. You did well, by the way.'

'I had a good teacher,' he replies. 'What now?'

'Now we get out of here before the ICRD brings the wrath of god down on our heads,' Yas says.

The crew pile into the train. Despite its camouflaged exterior, on the inside it looks identical to the one on which Tanta and Cole found Yas, back in the Thoughtfront torture facility. There are three long bands of motor cortex immobilisers embedded in the ceiling – thankfully switched off, for the moment – and a pair of control consoles at the front and the back. Yas walks over to the one at the front and begins inputting commands.

'Looks like it uses the same autosteering system as the train they held me on,' she announces to the carriage at large.

Tanta joins her at the console. 'Any idea where it'll take us?' If they're lucky, the train will go straight through into InTech's territory, though there's always the possibility that it might pass through other Thoughtfront bases along the way.

They pore over the console's logs together. There's no map in the admin files, but there is a 'history' section that catalogues the train's previous journeys. Yas feeds the list of coordinates into her 'scape.

'It's spent all its time over the last four months shuttling between the same two stops,' she says. 'There's a spot to the northwest of the UZ – that's where we are now, I'd imagine – and then ...' She trails off, staring at her Array.

'Soo ...' Fliss says, after Yas's silence has stretched on just a little longer than is comfortable, 'does it go to InTech?'

Yas shakes her head. Her voice, when she replies, is hoarse. 'It goes to the Thinktank. Thoughtfront's ICRD.'

# Chapter 21

Tanta has broken into secure locations before, in both corps' territories – Thoughtfront's enhanced interrogation facility, the Black Box, the archives beneath Sodis. At the time, those operations felt difficult, dangerous and critical, put together with precious little time for preparation or planning. They all pale in comparison to the task ahead of her now. The Thinktank is the most heavily guarded building in the whole of Thoughtfront, and soon, the crew will be hurtling towards it in a metal box at about fifty miles an hour.

'Should we turn around?' Cole asks. 'Regroup at Gatwick?'

Tanta shakes her head. 'We can't. In a few hours, this station will be swarming with ICRD agents. They'll put guards on the tunnel – they might even destroy it. And at the other end, it won't be long before Thoughtfront figures out what happened here and locks its underground network down. This is the best route into the city we've found, and this could be our only chance to take it. If sneaking through the Thinktank is the toll we have to pay to get back into InTech, then so be it.'

'How bad is this Thinktank?' Fliss asks.

'Well, it's huge, for starters,' Tanta replies. 'There'll be hundreds of staff on the premises. That could work out in our favour, though: I doubt most of them will know everyone who works there. We'll have the advantage that we're coming in on a scheduled train, too – they'll be expecting us.'

'Cole,' she says, turning to him, 'would you be able to cloak our Inscapes – disguise them as Thoughtfront MindEyes?'

Cole frowns. 'I can, but not as thoroughly as those ICRD neurotechs did when we went undercover last summer. I can tweak our profiles and digital signatures no problem – they'll stand up under a visual inspection – but the internal functions will be a challenge. If anyone asks us to viewshare a document, or speak to them through Thoughtcast, we won't be able to.'

'That should be enough,' Tanta says. 'We'll be posing as guards from this facility: they would have been on a short-range, private network while they were out here. If anyone asks, we can say we haven't been reconnected to Thoughtfront's systems yet.'

'Please don't tell me we have to wear their uniforms,' Cole protests. 'I mean, they *died* in them!'

Tanta raises her eyebrows; now is hardly the time to be getting squeamish.

'What about me?' Fliss asks.

'You'll have to be a Red Flag,' Tanta tells her.

The bandit pulls a face. 'Yuck.'

'At least you're not playing dress-up in dead men's clothes,' Cole says, giving her a dark look.

Yas clears her throat, cutting through this squabble. She hasn't spoken since she discovered the train's destination, and Tanta has a good idea why. 'Tanta's right,' she says. 'This is your best shot at getting into the city, and you should take it, but ... I can't come with you.'

Cole nods – like Tanta, he must have had an inkling that this was coming – but Fliss looks aghast. 'You can't bail on us mid-job!' she protests. 'We need you!'

'On this one, you'll be better off without me – and I'm not just saying that. I've been in the Thinktank before,' Yas explains.

'High-up people in Thoughtfront know what I look like. I'd blow your cover.'

That seems to mollify Fliss, though she still doesn't look happy. 'Where will you go?' she asks.

'Back to Gatwick, to claim our payment. We've figured out what the Red Flags are up to, as promised – and something tells me that once the Assembly learn Thoughtfront intends to use their people as shock troops, they won't be so keen on striking a deal with it.' Yas flashes them all a grin. 'Don't worry: I'll look after your cuts till you get back.'

There's a defiance in her expression – and in her faith that this won't be a one-way trip. Tanta returns her smile. She's sorry to be parting from Yas, especially given how unlikely it is that they'll see each other again, but considering the way their relationship started, she knows she's lucky to have worked alongside her at all. Yas has been her idol, her adversary, her uneasy ally. Whatever happens next, Tanta is proud to have been able to count her as her friend.

'Thank you for everything, Agent Das,' she says. 'It's been an honour.'

They gather what they need from the dead guards and the back of the ambulance, then bid goodbye to Yasmin on the platform. Fliss puts the bravest face on this parting that she can, but inside, she's troubled. Of all her new crew, Yasmin was the one Fliss liked most – possibly because she's been ex-corporate for longest and has had a chance to get some of those smooth city edges roughened up a bit. Leaving her behind is hard, and what's worse is that Fliss can't shake the feeling that Yasmin is just the start. The plan is reaching its final stages – soon, there'll be nothing holding her, Tanta and Cole together anymore. Her new crew is falling apart, just like the old one did.

Perhaps the ex-agent can read some of these worries in Fliss's expression, because she offers to help her carry the crew's kit over from the ambulance to the train, giving the two of them some time alone before she leaves.

'I'd come with you if I could, you know,' Yasmin says softly, as they're gathering the bags.

'I know,' Fliss replies. 'Be careful out there, yeah?'

She nods. 'You, too.'

A thought occurs to Fliss. 'When you get back to Gatwick, will you check in on Mum? I want to make sure she made it home OK.'

'First thing,' Yasmin promises. 'In fact, I'll do you one better.'

The ex-agent digs around in one of the bags and hands Fliss a white plastic pendant on a length of string. Fliss turns it over in her palm. There's a silver button in the centre of the pendant and a small switch on the side.

'You toggle that to turn location tracking on and off,' Yasmin says, indicating the switch. 'And you press the button to talk.'

'All right,' Fliss says, nonplussed, 'but what's it for?'

'For getting in touch with me, of course! I'll fill you in on how things are going in your hometown if you catch me up with what's happening in mine.'

That makes Fliss feel a little better, but the mood on the train is still subdued as the remnants of the crew watch Yasmin reverse the battered ambulance out through the gap in the station wall and drive away. Once they've waved her out of sight, Tanta inputs the necessary commands into the train's control console, and they rattle off into the darkness.

The train is long and empty, the tunnels pitch-black and filled with nothing but the rumbling noise of their passage, but Fliss knows that the feeling of isolation hanging over them all is not one that they can trust, or that will last. They're headed straight for the Thinktank, and while she doesn't know exactly what they'll find there, she's pretty sure it'll be bristling with weapons and not inclined to take kindly to strangers.

Even so, the crew all take a minute to recover themselves after the separation from Yasmin, and the gruelling battle on the platform that preceded it. Tanta slumps down against a wall, her head leaning on the control console and her eyes closed. Cole, in characteristic fashion, takes the chip gun from where it's resting on top of the crew's kit bag and begins inspecting it, unscrewing the cylindrical chamber from the back and tipping out the contents into the palm of his hand. Fliss comes over to watch him as he works, looking over his shoulder. To her, the thing resting on Cole's palm looks like a rack of tiny metal beads, each no bigger than a grain of rice.

'Any idea what those are?' she asks him.

Cole doesn't reply immediately, instead pinching one of the beads between his finger and thumb. He lifts it carefully from the rack and examines it, turning it this way and that. Fliss squints at it. Up close, she can see that it's not a single piece of metal, but two interlocking parts, held apart by a minuscule hinge and several filament-thin wires.

Cole's eyes widen. 'I've seen this before.'

Tanta looks up at that. 'You have?'

'Remember those EMP charges you retrieved from the Thoughtfront operative last summer?' he asks her. 'I took one apart to examine it at the time. There was a mechanism very like this inside.'

'So Thoughtfront is chipping the Red Flags with *subdermal* EMP devices?' Tanta says. 'I didn't know it was possible to make them that small.'

Cole shakes the rack of beads. 'It probably *wasn't* possible till Thoughtfront's engineers cooked these up. They've always been ahead of InTech when it comes to weapons innovations.'

'There's ahead, and then there's being in another race entirely!

There's no way InTech will be able to defend against these — especially not in such large numbers.'

'What do they do?' asks Fliss, who isn't entirely following this conversation.

'When they're activated, they'll take out any electronics nearby,' Cole explains. 'Inscapes, radios—'

'Gate scanners, cameras, automated defence turrets,' Tanta interjects. She looks appalled. 'If Thoughtfront deploys the chipped Red Flags tactically, it could wipe out InTech's security infrastructure in a single stroke. It wouldn't be down for long, but even so ...'

Fliss is confused. 'Isn't that good for us? The more distracted InTech are when we come up through the tunnels, the less likely they are to catch us, right? It'll just make our job easier.'

'That's assuming this is an attack InTech can survive,' Tanta replies. 'Our objective is to free the corporation's Harlow-Programmed residents. If Thoughtfront's plan succeeds, then by the time we get there, there may not be any left.'

The closer the crew get to the Thinktank, the tenser the mood in the train becomes. Once Cole has disguised his and Tanta's 'scapes, they do the same to their appearances, changing into the black uniforms they took from the station in strained silence. Fliss hands out three Thoughtfront-issue handguns, the chip gun, and a pair of stun batons for Tanta and Cole. There's not much more they can bring with them that won't arouse suspicion, but Tanta takes a pair of earpieces and the Brokerage smartphones, too, concealing them in her uniform's inner pockets. They'll need ways to stay in touch once they get through to InTech's side of the city — assuming they make it that far.

As soon as she's dressed, Tanta turns to Fliss and Cole. She's not their leader, but as the only ex-agent among them, it falls to her to brief them on what to expect here. 'The Thinktank is Thoughtfront's most secure facility,' she tells them, 'but, if we play this right, we'll be in and out before our presence is even noticed. Once we've arrived, we'll blend in with the other raiders and guards while we search for the route Thoughtfront is using to send the Red Flags into InTech. That's our only objective: as soon as we find it, we leave. Any questions?'

Cole rubs a hand over his mouth. 'There was meant to be a whole crew of raiders on this train. What if someone asks us where they are?'

'I'll do all the talking,' Tanta reassures him.

He gives her a hunted look. 'What do we do if they figure out we're imposters?' he asks, the words a croak.

The answer to that, of course, is that there's nothing they *can* do. Being caught out in the heart of Thoughtfront territory won't mean a chase and a daring escape – it's game over. Tanta doesn't say this aloud. 'They won't,' she replies, instead. 'Just follow my lead. We'll be fine.'

Her confidence isn't feigned, because she knows exactly what she has to do. What happens next is all about appearances, and Tanta knows the importance of appearances. No one will question their presence in the Thinktank if everyone assumes that the Thinktank is exactly where they're supposed to be.

Tanta honed the skills she'll need to call on now in the ICRD, but deep down, she suspects that they're something she would have learnt to perfect even if InTech had never taken her in. The Harlow Programme made her loyal, but it didn't give her the ability she has to shapeshift while staying the same, to trade her personality like a false coin that everyone accepts as valid currency.

There's an irony in the fact that this talent – one of the only things Tanta knows to be truly hers – is all about deception, but she doesn't care. It's something she was born to, just as Cole was born to his genius. At this moment, Tanta's mood couldn't be more different to that of her two companions. Time, numbers and probability are against them. They have nothing but the barest scraps of a plan. And yet she feels ready; she even feels excited. Ahead, the tunnel brightens, and Tanta shrugs on a new persona like a second skin.

The train squeals to a halt in a grimy, grey-walled hall. This station is nothing like the one they left in the Unaffiliated Zone, and nor does it bear much resemblance to the enhanced interrogation facility Tanta and Cole broke into last summer. Thoughtfront seems to have left this part of the pre-Meltdown underground network largely as it found it. It's windowless and dimly lit, though a double staircase in the centre seems to hint at more open spaces above.

As the train's doors slide open, Tanta scans the space they're about to enter, rapidly assimilating all the information it has to offer her. Her gaze softens, her attention spreading like a net in seawater, open to every detail she can use. There's a second platform visible across the hallway, and two people standing guard at the foot of the stairs. She, Cole and Fliss step out of the train, and the guards come towards them. One is a tall, thickset white man, wearing a jacket and trousers very similar to Tanta's own stolen uniform. His colleague is a slender, brown-skinned woman in plainclothes – an agent, perhaps.

'You're late,' the woman says. 'And where's the rest of the crew you were meant to be escorting?'

'Why do you think we were delayed?' Tanta snaps. 'They never showed. This one' – she hooks a thumb at Fliss – 'was the only one who came. Said the others were rounding up a few last volunteers and then they'd be there. We waited, but we had a schedule to keep to, and ...' She trails off into a *more than my job's worth* shrug.

The woman is watching Tanta carefully. 'And the rest of your squadron?'

'They're still at the station, waiting to see if the others show up,' Tanta replies.

'We didn't hear about any of this from the forward base,' the woman says. She's still watching Tanta with that guarded, alert expression. 'Why didn't they radio ahead?'

'They didn't?' Tanta asks, without missing a beat. 'Oh, great. Fucking fantastic. Don't ask me: they told me you'd know we were coming.'

The agent is asking too many questions. Tanta examines her from the corner of her eye. She doesn't think the woman suspects her – not yet, at least – but if she keeps on tugging at loose ends like this, it's only a matter of time until she unravels the whole flimsy fabrication. Tanta needs to find a way to neutralise her before that happens. She's still thinking this problem over when the woman puts her thumb to the base of her chin, calling something up on her MindEye. Her lips don't move, but Tanta can guess that she's communicating what Tanta has just told her to someone higher up the food chain.

'Peacekeeper,' she says. 'Would you check in with the forward base, please?'

The peacekeeper pulls a handheld radio from his belt and presses a button on the side. 'Forward base, come in,' he barks.

Tanta tenses. This is bad. The woman's vague sense of unease is about to get a whole lot more distinct – and when that happens, Tanta will lose control of this situation.

The guard frowns. 'Come in, forward base,' he repeats.

This time, the look the agent throws Tanta's way has a measure of suspicion in it.

'If you're having trouble getting through to them, it might be because of the chips.'

Cole's interjection is so unexpected that Tanta almost jumps at the sound of it. Didn't she just tell him that she'd do all the talking? She flicks a glance his way – *what are you doing?* – but he ignores it.

The woman turns her sharp gaze on him.

'The chips we have to put in the raiders' arms on arrival at the forward base,' Cole pursues. 'I know they're fragile, but sometimes people handle them carelessly – drop them, that kind of thing – and they mess with our radio equipment.'

Tanta's heart judders like a glitchy AR overlay. This is a dangerous play for so many reasons. Have Thoughtfront's peace-keepers even been briefed on the nature of the EMP chips? If not, this reference to their signal disrupting abilities could give them away. But the woman relaxes, just fractionally, and nods.

'Wouldn't be the first time *that's* happened,' her colleague says, rolling his eyes. 'Your squadron should be more careful with company resources.'

For an instant, Tanta is lightheaded with relief. 'Yeah, well, accidents happen. We're on a tight schedule,' she replies, keen to turn the conversation. She indicates Fliss again. 'Speaking of which, could you show us where to take her?'

The agent nods. 'Follow me.'

Tanta lets the woman draw ahead as she leads the three of them along the platform. 'That was a good save,' she murmurs to Cole.

Her partner is still shaking with nervous energy. 'Well, I learnt from the best,' he mutters.

The agent takes them past the staircase and over to an old service lift. She doesn't look back to check if they're following her. Tanta puts one hand on the stun baton in her belt; if she's going to take the woman out, now would be the time. She weighs it up but decides against it. Far from giving the game away, Cole's ruse seems to have finally convinced the agent that they are who they say they are. If they keep quiet and play along, she'll take them exactly where they need to go.

An incredulous part of Tanta wonders if sneaking through the Thinktank is really going to be this easy. They're almost at the lift when the sound of rapid footsteps behind her makes her realise, with a sinking feeling, that it isn't. She turns. The burly peacekeeper is jogging towards them.

'Hey! You! Stop!'

Tanta's chest tightens with alarm. She readies herself for a fight, but the peacekeeper hasn't drawn his gun, and there's no backup sprinting along the platform behind him. When he reaches the group, he's out of breath.

'You,' he says again, pointing to Tanta. 'You need to come with me right now. Wheeler wants to talk to you.'

# Chapter 22

The peacekeeper heads up the double staircase at a run, and Tanta hurries in his wake. What choice does she have? She casts a quick glance over her shoulder as she leaves; Cole and Fliss stare back at her, eyes wide. There's a lot she'd like to give them both: instructions, advice, warnings. Cole may have saved all their skins with his quick thinking a minute ago, but Tanta doesn't think either of them is ready to be undercover without her just yet. *Well, they'd better be*, a grim voice inside her says. Until she can extract herself from this unexpected summons, it's not like they have another option.

She turns her focus with an effort, forcing herself to concentrate on the task ahead of her. Passing as a Thoughtfront guard was hard enough when she only had to fool other peacekeepers. Now, it looks like she's going to have to keep up the act for a member of Thoughtfront's management.

At the top of the stairs is a circular hall with a low ceiling – still underground, judging by the artificial lights. The white-washed, windowless walls remind Tanta of the compound of holding cells hidden beneath InTech. Several corridors branch off the hall like the spokes of a wheel; the peacekeeper makes for the one straight ahead. While they rush through the maze-like passageways that thread beneath the Thinktank, Tanta tries to figure out how she's going to get out of this situation with her cover intact.

She starts with the most basic question: *who the hell is Wheeler?* She racks her brains, trying to remember whether the name ever came up in one of her ICRD briefings. She can't recall it – that could mean that Wheeler is too low-ranking to have come to InTech's notice, or that they're someone who's been promoted since Tanta left. She could ask the man guiding her, but if Wheeler's some kind of senior peacekeeper then the question would betray a suspicious level of ignorance.

'Do you know why Wheeler wants to see me?' she essays.

'He didn't say,' the guard replies.

*OK, so Wheeler's a man.* That doesn't give Tanta a lot to go on, but it's a start. 'Did he seem … annoyed?'

The peacekeeper grunts. 'Wheeler's always annoyed.'

They're just coming up to the foot of an escalator when the light panels on the ceiling flicker and go out, plunging the corridor into darkness. The peacekeeper curses.

'That's the fourth time this week,' he says.

Thoughtfront's internal affairs are none of Tanta's business anymore, but her interest is caught, nonetheless. 'We don't get many updates out at the forward base,' she says slowly. 'Has it been … bad at home?'

'Bad? Like you wouldn't believe.' The man turns to face Tanta, dropping his voice to a conspiratorial whisper. 'The chiefs are saying the blackouts are because of winter storms, but the rumour is that our friends across the riverbed have bombed half our generation facilities into the ground.'

Tanta lets her face fall. 'Damn.' It's further evidence of just how badly Thoughtfront is faring – and of InTech's determination to end this decades-long conflict once and for all.

The escalator has frozen in its tracks, forcing Tanta and her escort to walk up it. The lights come back on as they reach the top, revealing a space as vast and open as a cathedral. There are windows in the ceiling and wide arches set around the edges of the hall. Tanta looks around, trying not to stare. She recognises this place, with its curious mixture of indoor and outdoor, though she's only ever seen it from the outside before. Standing unnoticed within the main lobby of the Thinktank itself is a surreal experience – the kind of thing a young ICRD agent might dream of as the pinnacle of their career. Even Tanta can't help but feel a flicker of excitement. She's in the nerve centre of one of the most powerful corporations in the world, and Thoughtfront doesn't even know it.

Of course, it lessens her triumph somewhat that Thoughtfront is clearly in chaos. It's not just the blackouts. Late as it is, the lobby is swarming with people, the throngs of peacekeepers, agents and other staff making the vast space seem cramped. A thousand rigid shoulders, darting eyes and hurried strides testify to a workforce who are stressed almost beyond endurance. AR banners flicker and dance on the walls. Tanta doesn't have time to read them all as her guide hustles her through the crowds, but she catches sight of a few slogans.

*Save Power, Save Food, Save Your City!*

*The War Begins at Home: Join The Peacekeepers Today!*

*Watch Your Tongue – Infiltrators Are Among Us!*

They're all similarly fervid. Tanta thinks of InTech's Communications Division. Their propaganda is subtler than this, but during the food shortages in the autumn, a lot of the messaging was essentially the same. She already knew that InTech had Thoughtfront on the ropes, but it's different seeing it for herself.

There's a sweeping glass staircase in the centre of the lobby, leading up to a mezzanine floor of smart glass offices that look out over the hustle and bustle below. As she and the peacekeeper climb it, Tanta gets a queasy feeling in the pit of her stomach.

Added height usually translates into more seniority – there's a reason Reet and Kenway's offices are all the way up on the fourteenth floor of the ICRD – and she's still no closer to working out who she's supposed to be meeting.

'Um, you might have noticed that I'm fairly fresh from basic training,' she says. Her nervousness is barely an act. 'How should I address Wheeler? I don't want to piss him off any worse than he is already.'

That gets her a strange look from the peacekeeper. 'Call him Minister, of course. Don't they teach you new recruits anything?'

'Right. Of course,' Tanta mutters. Her mouth is suddenly dry. She doesn't have the expertise on Thoughtfront that Yas has accumulated, but she understands enough of the corporation's jargon to know what a Minister is – every agent does. She's about to walk into a briefing with the Director of the Thinktank.

The agent doesn't say much as she shows Fliss and Cole into the lift. That's just as well, because it's taking all Cole's energy to keep from passing out. He's never been in an enemy base without Tanta before, and the sense of vulnerability, of exposure, is dizzying. He's in a lift with a woman who would kill him – or worse – if she knew who he really was, and his only defence is a cover he wasn't responsible for creating, and doesn't know how to maintain. He concentrates on staying upright and keeping his breathing regular and even, and for a while, that's all he can do.

A sharp pain in his foot snaps him back to the present. Fliss is glaring at him.

'—all right, Officer?' the agent is saying. She looks annoyed – it's clear she's been trying to get Cole's attention for some time.

'Sorry,' he says, meeting her gaze. It's an effort to get the words out. 'I'm fine. Long night, that's all.'

'I was asking if your orders were to return to the forward base or to accompany the subcontractors to the drop zones,' she says, testily.

'Oh! The – the second one,' Cole replies.

They're still descending, going deep enough that Cole's ears pop. He thinks of the layers of earth and subterranean rooms between him and Tanta and fights down a bubble of panic. Eventually, the lift doors slide apart with a shriek of ancient metal. They open onto a dark corridor, lit fitfully by the kind of temporary lamps one finds in caves and archaeological digs. Pre-Meltdown posters still line the walls.

The agent leads them to the end of the passage, where a flight of steps descends into deeper darkness. Cole's legs start shaking as he follows her down the stairs, and nothing he can do will steady them.

'Hey.' Fliss's voice is little louder than a breath. She gives Cole's arm a brief squeeze. 'Calm down. Tanta will catch up to us.'

Cole takes a deep, shuddering breath. Fliss is right: this is Tanta's job, and she's good at it. All the two of them need to do is stay together until she finds them again.

The stairs give out onto a double platform, separated by two archways. At the end of each one, a tunnel mouth yawns, a circle of blackness in the gloom. There are a couple dozen Red Flags sitting or strolling between the platforms, bristling with Thoughtfront-issue weapons. Cole sees handguns, assault rifles and several other, nastier-looking things that he can't name – but they're not what arrests his attention. Arden told the crew that Thoughtfront had recruited five thousand raiders – he was expecting this space to be packed.

'Where are the rest?' he blurts out.

The agent frowns at him. 'Of the subcontractors? They're

already on their way to the drop zones. We're T-minus four hours.'

''Course we are,' Fliss says. 'You know that, *Officer*.' She turns to the agent. 'So, we're hitting InTech at dawn, then?'

'That's correct,' the woman replies. 'Now, if you'll excuse me, I have to return to my post. I'll leave my colleague to complete your briefing.' She darts Cole one last, curious glance, and departs.

'Four hours,' Fliss mutters, once the woman has left. 'Plenty of time.'

It doesn't feel like it to Cole. Up till this point, the crew's plan for getting into InTech territory has been somewhat fluid, an objective the exact shape and timeframe of which remained uncertain. Not anymore. In just four hours, they'll be back in the corporation they fled from four months ago. Cole could cope fine with that prospect on its own; he's more concerned by the fact that he, Fliss and Tanta won't be making the journey by themselves, but with thousands of Thoughtfront troops in tow. They're going home – but by the time they get there, home will be the middle of a war zone.

Wheeler is a tall, thin man with close-cropped grey hair, who doesn't look like he has ever smiled in his life. When Tanta enters his office, he has his back to the chaos of the floor below and is massaging his temples with tired fingers. He turns as the door clicks shut behind her, pinning her in place with a frown. There's nothing tired about his eyes, which are green as her own, and sharp as cut glass.

He touches a finger to his chin.

'I'm not on the Thinktank's channels yet, Minister,' Tanta says hurriedly. Of course, if Wheeler tries to add her to those channels, the game will be up immediately. She'll have to fight him, then attempt to flee through a building full of Thoughtfront agents. She wouldn't give much for her chances.

Wheeler waves a hand. 'There's no time to sort out the authentication process now,' he says. 'Just keep your voice down, will you? I don't want anyone else hearing this. Now, tell me exactly what happened before you left the forward base.'

The next part is easy – relatively speaking. Tanta falls into the attitude she always used to adopt when reporting to her managers at InTech – shoulders straight, head up – and spins Wheeler a lie from whole cloth. She embroiders her account with enough details from the forward base and the train to make it appear believable, and with no one to dispute her version of events, she's reasonably confident he'll buy it. The real challenge lies in figuring out what Wheeler wants to hear – and why he's summoned her in the first place. He's hard to read in that regard: he keeps his face studiously blank while Tanta talks, his sharp eyes the only sign that he has any opinions about her story at all.

'That's it?' he asks her, when she's finished. 'Nothing untoward took place? You didn't notice anything amiss?'

Tanta shakes her head. She's not sure where Wheeler's going with this. 'Minister?' she hazards.

Wheeler sighs, running a hand through the stubble on the top of his head. There's a long pause before he speaks again. He eyes Tanta narrowly, for long enough that she becomes uncomfortable. Eventually, he shrugs, as though he has lost some internal battle with himself.

'I think you have a right to know that all of your co-workers at the forward base are dead,' he says. 'They were ... attacked – probably very shortly after you and your surviving colleague left. You were the last people to make it out.'

Tanta doesn't need to feign her shock. There was no one, peacekeeper or Red Flag, alive at that base to report back to

Thoughtfront – she made sure of it – and yet Wheeler has already heard the news. There's no way he could have learnt of what happened so quickly. Unless…

There was *one* person alive at the Thoughtfront base when they left, of course. Arden would never share corporate secrets with InTech's enemy, but someone in the strike team he radioed for backup just might have. Tanta doesn't want any surprises when she, Cole and Fliss cross over into InTech's side of the city; if Thoughtfront has managed to recruit another high-level mole within the corporation, the crew need to know about it. She scans the office: there's a box of tissues on Wheeler's desk that should work perfectly for what she has in mind.

She adopts a veneer of grief, letting her shoulders slump and her eyes fill. 'All of them?' she asks, putting a tremble into her voice.

'All of them. I'm sorry.'

Crying on cue is not something Tanta is called on to do often in her line of work, but it's well within her skillset. Crocodile tears roll down her cheeks, and she turns away from Wheeler, patting down her uniform in apparent embarrassment. As she does so, she slips one hand into the inner pocket of her jacket and palms one of the Brokerage earpieces, flicking its receiver to the 'on' position.

'I do apologise, Minister,' she chokes out. 'It's just, I only spoke to them an hour ago, and – and…'

'That's quite all right, Officer,' Wheeler replies, with a softening glance. He pushes the box of tissues across the desk towards her. 'Please.'

Tanta takes one, dropping the earpiece into the box in the same smooth motion. She gives a loud sniff. 'Thank you,' she mumbles, dabbing furiously at her eyes.

She's blowing her nose when the door opens, and another man walks in.

'Minister Kumar,' Wheeler greets him. He nods to Tanta. 'You're dismissed, Officer. Operative Cartwright informs me that your colleague is waiting for you in the lower tunnels.'

'Yes, Minister,' Tanta sniffs, backing out of the door.

As soon as she's outside, she puts the other earpiece in and hurries away. It's time to rejoin Cole and Fliss and get out of here. The Ministers' conversation plays in her ear while she strides down the staircase and back across the lobby — somewhat muffled by the tissue box, but still audible.

'Well?' Kumar asks.

'She left before it happened,' Wheeler sighs. 'She didn't have anything to add to what our contact already told us.'

There's a tense pause. 'Do we still move forward with the attack?'

'I don't see that we have a choice. You've read the reports on the new Harlow Protocol — the instant InTech finds a way to get it past our defences, we're finished. Our own people will tear us apart. The window of opportunity is only narrowing. I'm going to instruct...'

The rest of Wheeler's words trail off into inaudibility; he must be walking away from the receiver. There's the sound of a drawer opening, followed by the clunk of something bulky being placed on the desk. Tanta reaches the escalator down to the tunnels and pauses at the top, waiting to hear the rest.

'Are you there?' Wheeler snaps. It's clear that he's not talking to Kumar anymore. Tanta imagines a radio on the desk like the one at the forward base, Wheeler leaning over the transmitter.

'I'm here,' a crackly voice replies.

The sound of it makes Tanta freeze. She *knows* that voice. All of her fears about Thoughtfront's attack return, in greater force than before. If she's right about who's on the other end of the radio, then InTech is in deeper trouble than she thought.

'We're going ahead with the plan,' Wheeler says.

'Acknowledged.'

'We're relying on you to handle any interference from the ICRD.'

'Leave it to me, Minister,' the voice says smoothly, and Tanta can practically hear the smirk in it as it continues. 'By tomorrow morning, there won't be an ICRD anymore.'

# Chapter 23

'Take me through it again,' Reet says. 'From the top.'

Arden looks like death – he's purple with bruises and his nose is broken – but he does as his Director asks with patience and politeness, answering all of her questions in minute detail. Reet has a lot of them. When her strike team found the young agent, covered in blood, fifty miles from his drop point and locked in a pre-Meltdown station house, he had already missed a scheduled check-in and she was beginning to assume the worst. His account of his meeting with Tanta and Cole's 'crew' and what they discovered at the secret Thoughtfront base has shown her that her idea of the worst didn't even come close to how bad things really are.

The two of them are sitting in her office on the fourteenth floor of the ICRD, surrounded by the sounds of construction. The section lieutenants of Douglas's Auxiliary Defence Force have been reinforcing the building's security and defence systems all day, an operation that seems to involve a lot of banging and drilling. The noise is giving Reet a killer headache, but given what Arden has to report, it's worth it. Thoughtfront's invasion attempt – long feared, planned for, and anticipated – is upon them at last.

'The Thoughtfront guards were implanting the raiders with some sort of chip,' Arden is saying.

Reet nods mechanically. 'A subdermal EMP charge,' she says. Her engineers have already examined the chips they recovered from the site and determined them to be yet another terrifyingly advanced Thoughtfront weapon.

'Tanta, Cole and their associates overpowered me and escaped the base. They took the train into Thoughtfront territory.'

'But you don't think they were working for Thoughtfront?'

Arden shakes his head. 'There's no way. They killed the guards to a man. They'd never take an act so far. And...' He pauses, as if half-unwilling to continue. 'They could have killed me, too, if they'd wanted to. They knew I'd report everything to you, and still chose to spare me. No Thoughtfront operative would have done that.'

He's right – and despite the seriousness of the situation, Reet feels a treacherous flicker of relief. She strives to suppress it. *It doesn't change anything*, she tells herself. And yet the knowledge that Tanta hasn't betrayed InTech so completely as to be working with the corp's worst enemy is still comforting.

It's far from the most significant part of Arden's report, though. Thoughtfront has amassed an army of thousands of unaffiliated foot soldiers, found a means of moving them into InTech's territory unnoticed, and armed them all with devices that could wipe out the corporation's entire communications and security network. Set beside a threat of such magnitude, whatever Tanta and her crew are planning no longer matters.

Reet has only been without access to her 'scape once in her life, in the aftermath of the Ward House fire. She still remembers the feeling with a queasy sensation of horror – it was like a dulled sense, or losing the ability to see in full colour. She knows from her briefings on Harlow 2.0 that the sense of dislocation and strangeness she felt will be one hundred times worse for everyone else. The programme is more inflexible than its predecessor, its users less able to adapt to sudden changes. With their programming down, InTech's residents will be as helpless as children.

'There was no evidence of the planned entry points for the invasion?' she asks, already knowing Arden's answer. Her team has been over every inch of the forward base and found nothing.

He shakes his head. 'My supposition is that they'll be coming from underground, but I don't know where.'

Reet fights the urge to bang her head on the desk. A survey team with radar scanners would be able to figure it out, but with the whole city to check, it's an effort that would take weeks. They don't have that kind of time: according to Arden's report, the bulk of Thoughtfront's forces are already in place. And even if she managed to find the entry points, what then? Most of InTech's guardians are barely even able to *see* the unaffiliated, let alone fight them.

In a year or two, the corporation's Harlow 2.0-enhanced residents will have fully adjusted to their new programming. Dr Friend has assured the board that their initiative will improve, along with their ability to recognise and respond to the 'scapeless. In the short term, though, those assurances are meaningless. In the short term, Thoughtfront has found the programme's most significant blind spot and is poised to enact a plan that will exploit it to the full.

Reet can feel herself spiralling again, her grip on the situation slipping. She does what she always does in such situations: grits her teeth and clenches her fists, regrounding herself in reality through sheer force of will. She *will* keep it together. She has to – InTech is counting on her.

She focuses on the problem before her, trying to break it down into its component parts. She can't stop the raiders from getting through into the corp's territory or prevent them from setting off their EMP charges when they arrive. As far as she can reason it out, there are only two steps that are within her immediate power: she can shield InTech's infrastructure from the effects of the devices as best she can, and she can assemble a force who will be able to both target the unaffiliated and withstand the shock of losing their 'scapes and keep fighting. There's really only one group of people in the city right now who fit that bill.

'I'm putting together a defence team, and I want you on it,' she tells Arden. 'Are you still in contact with the rest of your cohort?'

The CorpWard nods briskly.

'Send them a message: wherever they're working, whatever they're doing, they're to report to the ICRD on my orders now. All of them.'

As Arden walks out of her office, Reet is already sending an expedited request to the new Ward Houses, requisitioning all wards who have completed basic marksmanship training. She pings Douglas, too, to update him on the situation, but he doesn't reply. Reet lets out a huff of annoyance. Her Co-Director's work performance has been erratic for some time now, but she was hoping he'd take an invasion a bit more seriously.

<<This is urgent,>> she sends again. <<Thoughtfront is making its move. You need to assemble the Auxiliary Defence Force and then get back to the ICRD *right now*.>>

When this still elicits no response, she growls in frustration and turns her attention to what else she can do. A coordinated EMP attack will obliterate InTech's UAV fleet, but only if the drones are in range when it happens. If she could shield them from the blasts, somehow...

Reet is so engrossed in her thoughts that it takes her a while to realise she can hear something beeping. It's faint, and almost drowned out by the drilling and hammering around it: a familiar sound, but one she hasn't heard in a while, so it's a few seconds before she's able to place it. When she does, she dives out of her office and races across the open-plan space beyond. It's the Brokerage phone, the one in Douglas's room.

She wrenches open the door to his office; it's empty, as it so often is at the moment. The phone is in the concealed cupboard at the back of the room. It's been ringing for so long that Reet thinks she's missed the call, but as her fingers fumble with the invisible catch of the cupboard door, clicking it open, the sound becomes louder. She grabs the phone, jabs the button on the interface, and presses it to her ear.

'What do you want?' she asks.

For a moment, there's nothing but soft breathing on the line. Reet almost drops the phone, her palms suddenly slippery with sweat. Even distorted as the sound is by static, she knows who is on the other end. She's heard that breathing enough times before, close beside her in the bottom bunk in dormitory five, a susurrus that has lulled her to sleep more nights than she can count.

'Reet,' Tanta says. 'It's me. We need to talk.'

# Part 3

# Chapter 24

It's almost dawn by the time Reet has everything in place. There's a thin, smouldering band of red on the horizon, the fuse of a powder keg. She's reviewing the progress of the evacuation of the city centre when she gets a call on MindChat. It's from Douglas – at long last. This is the first Reet has heard from him all night.

<<Where are you?>> he asks.

<<I'm in the ICRD. Douglas, I've been trying to get hold of you for hours! Why didn't you answer any of my hails?>>

<<I've been a little busy coordinating our response to an imminent invasion, in case you hadn't noticed,>> her Co-Director snaps.

Reet, who has been doing the same thing, doesn't bother to point out how much more efficient they would have been if they'd worked on this together. She dislikes the way Douglas treats her as an inconvenience and an afterthought rather than an equal partner, but she knows by now that there's no altering his mindset. <<What do you need?>> she asks, instead.

<<Nothing. When I saw your location tracker was off, I got concerned. That's all.>>

<<I turned it off to avoid Thoughtfront hackers figuring out

where I am,>> Reet replies, tartly. <<If I were you, I'd do the same.>>

<<That's ... a sensible precaution. Thank you for the suggestion.>>

It's probably the nicest thing Douglas has ever said to her. Reet softens. <<I appreciate you checking up on me,>> she sends.

<<I'm still Co-Director of Residents' Affairs. It's my job to manage the security of InTech's upper management,>> he replies, stiffly. <<Besides, the board would have my head if I let anything happen to their newest protégé.>>

<<Well, I'm secure. And so is your job. Now, will you join me so we can discuss troop deployment? I have some ideas I'd like you to look over.>>

<<I'm on my way,>> Douglas sends, before disconnecting the call. Reet glances at the clock on her Array. It is 6:02 a.m.

At 6:03, Tanta, Cole and Fliss are making their way through the tunnels beneath the city. They set off a few hours after Tanta caught up to the rest of the crew, following the Red Flags into the darkness. The raiders in front of them seem to know where they're going, even if the three of them don't. The crew follow along behind the two dozen or so others sharing the journey with them, close enough not to lose their guides, but far enough back that they're free to talk unobserved.

'I still can't believe you told the ICRD we were coming,' Fliss mutters.

'I told them the raiders were coming, not us.'

The bandit snorts. 'And how would you know that unless you were with them? I'm sure InTech can put two and two together.'

'If I hadn't said anything, there wouldn't have been an InTech to get back to,' Tanta snaps. 'This invasion might have given us a way into the city, but if it succeeds, our plan is sunk. You've seen how people with Harlow 2.0 in their heads fight. They'll keep going until someone in charge tells them to stop — and with the corporation's headquarters at stake, no one's going to. They'll be slaughtered: if the Red Flags don't kill them, Thoughtfront's peacekeepers certainly will.'

It's half of the truth. The other half being, of course, that Tanta couldn't knowingly leave Reet in danger. She had to warn her of the threat to her life — from the invasion and from Thoughtfront's new mole both. She's not about to share that part of her reasoning with Fliss, though. Her history with Reet is something she carries by herself; she doesn't even talk about it with Cole.

'She's got a point,' Cole says. 'Can't free the city if everyone in it is dead.'

Fliss subsides with a grumble, and they continue walking in silence. Tanta's glad of it; she's too worried to sustain a conversation. The fact is, she's still not sure if she succeeded in her aim. Reet listened to her warning, but did not acknowledge it, hanging up on Tanta mid-sentence without saying a word in reply. She doesn't know whether Reet took anything she had to say seriously — and she has to admit that her ex has every reason to be sceptical. Tanta's a traitor, after all, and she has let Reet down before. The suspense is torturous, but she has no way of alleviating it. All she can do is keep going, and hope that she has been believed.

They've been walking for another minute when a vibration passes through the tunnel, low and ominous as a foreshock. Tanta, Cole and Fliss exchange glances.

It's beginning.

★

At 6:05, a basso rumble like a peal of thunder shakes the city, and the ICRD vanishes. It doesn't happen all at once. The noise comes first, along with a series of lights, flashing across the building like the cameras of a scrum of eager journalists. For a fraction of an instant, the ICRD looks the same as always: big and angular and solid, its walls of mirrored glass reflecting the burning line of the horizon.

Then it buckles in the middle, almost gracefully, as though it's a ballerina taking a bow, a frothy skirt of smoke billowing around it. And then it's gone, all fourteen stories folding in on themselves, sinking to the ground, and the smoke rolls outwards, a huge, boiling wave of clouds erupting from the blast site. It roils through the surrounding streets, enveloping the Needle like the sea foam around the base of a lighthouse.

Reet watches this cataclysm from the narrow windows of the Black Box. It's an unreal sight, one her mind rebels against, as it would seeing her limbs severed from her body, or a gaping hole in her chest. The ocean of smoke, the missing building in the skyline, is a violation of her city's integrity that's almost as hard to take in. It looks like the end of the world.

Well, Reet has spent all night putting plans in place to ensure that it won't be.

She turns away from the awful sight and faces the crowd of CorpWards behind her. They're in the biggest room in the Black Box, an open-plan office on the first floor, but they still fill the space, with several dozen people spilling out into the corridor beyond. At the front of the throng, her own agents – Firent and Arden among them – stand to attention, watching her with pin-sharp focus. Behind them are other familiar faces; some Reet knows from The Rotunda or her old block of flats, others she hasn't seen since the night of the Ward House fire. Many of the youngest CorpWards she's never met before.

This room is the place where the Harlow Programme was

born, though the wards gathered here don't know it. Their origins are a secret that Reet keeps for them, bearing the dangerous truth so they don't have to. Today, though, there's nothing she can do to keep them from danger – in fact, she's sending them into it. She surveys the people before her, a confused and confusing mixture of trainees, neuroengineers, senior guardians and managers. Only a dozen of the assembled wards are ICRD agents. Only half of them have any kind of weapons training. All of them are shocked and frightened by what they've just witnessed.

Reet coughs, clearing away the little detritus of nervousness gathered in her throat. 'You've all heard the rumours,' she begins, speaking over the gasps and murmurs, the scattered tears. 'I'm here to confirm that they're true: Thoughtfront is invading. You are the first line of defence against that invasion.'

A silence – part respectful, part terrified – falls over the crowd. 'I know many of you aren't trained for this kind of work,' Reet continues. 'You're probably wondering why I've requested you for this assignment. The truth is, you're the only ones I could count on.'

She can't tell them why, of course – not without giving away details of Harlow 2.0 and these wards' own programming that she isn't authorised to breathe a word of to anyone but Douglas, Arthur, and the board themselves. She opts for a less highly classified explanation, though one that's no less true. 'We are all Corporate Wards. InTech is our family, and I know that no one will fight to defend it like you.'

Nods, now, from the assembled wards. It's a theme Reet knew they'd warm to. 'I can't promise you we'll win,' she concludes, 'but I can say this: there's no one I'd rather face this with than all of you.'

This, too, is true, though as she speaks, Reet feels the absence of the one person she always thought she'd have by her side – a dull ache like a phantom limb.

She gives the wards their orders, breaking them up into units of five and assigning each one to a skyscraper or office block in the city centre. Where she can, she includes an agent or guardian with groups of civilians, so they'll have someone they can ask questions and look to for leadership once the fighting starts. Arden and Firent hand out weapons – old-fashioned, non-MbOS-synced sniper rifles that they had to dig out of the darkest recesses of the ICRD's kit department – and red and white flares.

'You won't be able to use MindChat once the EMPs go off,' Reet tells them all, when they're ready to move out. 'If you need backup, use your red flare and Agent Firent will send out another unit. And remember, you take orders from no one but me or my agents. Not the community guardians, not the Auxiliary Defence Force, *no one*. Is that clear?'

There's a chorus of assent, and then the wards disperse, heading to their stations. Within ten minutes, the only people left in the room are Reet, Firent, and a handful of reserve troops. Firent is staying in the Black Box to coordinate these backup forces, and for another assignment that's his alone.

'You know what you have to do?' Reet asks him.

He nods.

'Not until you see the white flares go up, OK?'

'I know,' Firent says. 'Where will you be stationed, Director?'

For a moment, Reet considers answering him honestly. It's tempting. It would be a relief to share the task ahead of her with someone else, but it would hurt Firent's morale and she can't do that to him – not when the battle before him is so important. 'I'll join you back here,' she says. 'But not yet. There's something I have to take care of first.'

With no glimpse of the outside world by which to measure the passage of time, the walk beneath the city seems endless. As they draw closer to their destination, the tunnel Tanta, Cole and Fliss are in grows ever more crowded. They catch up with other groups of raiders ahead of them, and more join from platforms along the way. Soon, they're marching at the back of a column that's thousands strong. It's no great challenge for the three of them to hide in the mass of people. Tanta and Cole simply disable their AR profiles, and they merge with the 'scapeless fighters around them.

The Red Flags are carrying a huge variety of weapons. Everywhere she looks, Tanta can see the full extent of Thoughtfront's expertise in military tech, from shoulder-mounted rocket-launchers to suit-embedded plasma weapons. One group of raiders are all outfitted with strange, bulky devices with long black nozzles and fuel tanks that look like flame-throwers; another carry battering rams and incendiary grenades. None of these weapons are MbOS-synced – the EMPs would render them inoperable, and the raiders don't have the MindEyes to use them, in any case – but that only makes the firepower on display more intimidating. Smart guns are Thoughtfront's stock in trade and even without them, it's still managed to put together an arsenal that looks like it could topple an empire.

There turn out to be several drop zones. The tracks they're walking along branch at intervals, and at each one there's a squad of peacekeepers in hi-vis jackets, carving off a portion of the column and directing it up one of the diverging paths. This process seems to go on forever, until it doesn't anymore. The three of them are footsore and exhausted by the time they see a faint light ahead of them. The tunnel gives out onto another dim platform, and then they're all running through a deserted station and up a bank of motionless escalators.

Tanta, Fliss and Cole are still at the back of the crowd, and they hear the sounds of the invasion long before they see it. Shouts and gunfire rise over the drum of thousands of running feet. Then there's a brighter light ahead of them – a ragged hole in the low ceiling – and they're climbing through it.

They emerge in a department store; it must have been built over the defunct station so long ago that the station itself was forgotten. Raiders are sprinting through the shop and up the steps that lead to the exit, weapons at the ready. As they pass through the doors, they all make the same gesture, smacking themselves in the upper left arm with the palm of their right hand to activate their subdermal EMPs. Tanta feels the effects an instant later, like a shockwave passing through her brain. The world dims and flattens, losing the clarity lent to it by her 'scape and its array of audio-visual enhancements. She's experienced the sensation before, so she's ready for it, but it's still unpleasant.

Tanta races for the exit. She drags Cole with her as she runs, and one glance through the packed crowd tells her that Fliss is close on their heels. They push their way through the automatic doors, emerging into a cold dawn. It's a particularly beautiful one, the sky alight with oranges, pinks and reds, like a slow, silent bonfire.

Beneath it, the city is burning, too. Tanta stares, feeling as though the wind has been knocked out of her; she can hardly believe that this is the same place she left only four months ago. The air is shimmering with heat. As she watches, a squad of raiders smash in the door of a building opposite the shopping centre. Ropes of flame leap from the black nozzles in their hands, licking hungrily at the walls. A rocket-propelled grenade shrieks past overhead, blowing out the windows of an office block across the road in a fireball that sends the raiders nearby running for cover.

The Red Flag soldiers are not disciplined, but they don't need to be. In the face of their EMPs and their overwhelming firepower, InTech's defence seems to have collapsed. Residents are screaming, but louder than their cries is the thunder of the raiders' plasma weapons, which splits the air again and again. It's a sound that transports Tanta back to last summer, when she was fighting the Thoughtfront operative, and she has to suppress a surge of remembered fear. She stumbles, almost falling, and looks down to see a dead man at her feet, a charred hole in his chest. By his uniform, he was an InTech street cleaner.

There are other bodies around her – both community guardians, and ordinary people in the wrong place at the wrong time. The usual aromas of the city are dulled by smoke and the bitter, chemical tang of gunfire. The bulk of the Red Flag column is still marching down the road – a line of flamethrowers at the front burning the path ahead clear of obstacles and people alike – but splinter groups have broken off down side-streets, where Tanta catches glimpses of smoke and broken glass. She is hardened to violence and death, but there's something uniquely awful about the sight of her home under attack like this. She had always planned to return to InTech as a liberator, not as part of an invading army.

There's no time to reflect on this irony. Even as the shock and dismay wash through her, another part of Tanta's mind is piecing together the scene, trying to make sense of it. She scans the Red Flags around her. The ones with guns and plasma weapons are firing upwards as they move, the dawn light glinting off the muzzles of their assault rifles. A woman in front of her falls, the shot coming from nowhere Tanta can see.

InTech's defence hasn't collapsed completely, then; Reet must have positioned snipers on the rooftops. It's a smart move, especially for dealing with a mercenary force like the Red

307

Flags. The city is a forest of glass and chrome high-rises. The snipers could be anywhere, or everywhere, and though they're not making much of a dent in the invading army, they *are* hard to defend against. They're picking the raiders off one by one – a demoralising prospect. A few of the soldiers – conscripts, Tanta's guessing – are breaking away from the column and running.

Of course, the Red Flags aren't the only ones who could be picked off. As if to reinforce the point, the man beside Tanta drops like a stone, felled by a bullet through his right eye. Another falls to the ground with a howl, blood spurting from his arm. Tanta hunches her shoulders, trying to make herself as small a target as possible. She has to get Cole and Fliss away from the fighting and find somewhere for them all to shelter until it's over.

She spins on the spot – ignoring the self-preservation instinct that's screaming at her to duck and cover – and tries to get her bearings. Embarrassing as it is, she has no idea where in the city they are right now. Time and turmoil have made the street she's standing in hard to recognise, its once-familiar contours blurred by gunfire and blood.

There's a *whoosh* above her, like a firework, and a white flare arcs into the sky. A signal – but for what? Tanta doesn't have long to wonder. She's still searching for a landmark she recognises – and feeling panic start to close its fingers around her throat – when she makes out dark spots on the horizon to the south. She squints at them, zooming in: they're drones – drones that are somehow still flying despite the EMP blasts that have just rocked the city.

*Oh,* very *clever,* Tanta thinks, and despite the dire implications for her and her crew, she feels a flicker of pride. She understands what the flare was for now: it signalled that there were no more raiders emerging from the tunnels. Reet must have found a way to protect some of InTech's smart weapons from the Red Flags' EMPs – an ace up her sleeve that she's held back till she was certain the raiders had exhausted their charges. The snipers would never have been enough on their own, but InTech's UAVs are coming in to bolster their efforts.

The drones are upon them almost before she finishes the thought. A rush of displaced air to Tanta's left makes her dive reflexively to the side, pulling Cole and Fliss with her. The shell explodes an instant later, the sound hitting her like a solid object and knocking her to the ground. She goes into a roll and rises to her feet, then helps the other two up. The air is thick with the sound of shellfire, now, mingling with the thunder of the plasma weapons and making the ground shake. The Red Flag column falters, thrown into disarray by this unforeseen threat.

Tanta is still not sure where they are, but there's no more time to figure that out – they need to get out of here before they're blown to pieces. She takes Cole and Fliss by the hands and tows them across the road, against the movement of the raiders, making for an alleyway. Another shell goes off behind them as they reach it, throwing them forward. They collapse on the paving stones in a crumpled heap. Tanta's ears ring, and for a moment, she can taste thoughts.

*Where'd Reet hide the drones, anyway?* she thinks muzzily. The question is large and baggy, but she knows the answer. It must have been in the Black Box. It's the biggest Faraday cage in InTech's territory – the only one large enough to conceal the entire fleet. And with that thought, Tanta feels herself click back into place in the city like the last piece in a puzzle. If the Black Box is to the south of her, then that means she's in the north of InTech's territory, close to the riverbed. She glances up to confirm it, and there's the tip of the Needle – just visible at the end of the alleyway they've landed in – peeking out from between an office block and an old bridge.

She's home. She knows exactly where she is. And she also knows where the crew can go to get to safety.

The Rotunda has changed a lot since Tanta saw it last. Its half-timbered, white stucco walls are grimy from months of neglect, and the domed roof of pink glass that sits atop the thatch that capped the original building has been smashed in the middle by one of Thoughtfront's bombs. It used to remind Tanta of an egg in a nest – now, it is as if whatever giant bird was growing inside it has hatched and flown away. An AR sign on the front of the building reads, simply, *Condemned*. The wrought-iron gate out front is locked, with a heavy chain to reinforce the point, but that's no difficulty for Tanta or Fliss. They scale it, then help Cole up after them.

The boom and crash of the battle is still loud enough to make them all nervous, but The Rotunda is in one of InTech's entertainment districts – hardly a priority for Thoughtfront. Tanta would guess that the Red Flag columns are all making for the Needle and other strategic locations, if the shells haven't scattered them. There's no one on the street to see her force the door, and the eye of the security scanner beside it is dark and sightless.

The inside of the building is in the same state of disuse. Rain has been falling in through the hole in the ceiling, damaging the once immaculate flooring. The Rotunda of Tanta's memory was suffused with a rosy glow; now, there's a shaft of harsh, unfiltered winter sunlight piercing the circular hall, spotlighting the weeds that are beginning to force their way up between the cracked and weather-damaged tiles.

Everything else is almost as Tanta remembers it – the bar, the spiral staircase behind it, the tables and VR booths. The bar is even still stocked, as though the enhanced hospitality venue was simply abandoned one morning at the end of the night shift.

'We should be safe here for a while,' she says.

Cole nods. 'I doubt redeveloping this place is top of InTech's to-do list.'

In other words, The Rotunda is as good a base of operations as any they're likely to find. They can lie low here, wait for the chaos that has seized the city to die down, and figure out what on earth they're going to do next.

Tanta starts stacking tables and chairs up against the broken door to deter any stray raiders that might come this way – or at least give the crew advance warning of their arrival. Fliss comes to help, which she appreciates; the fatigue of their frantic run through the city is catching up with her, and it's an effort to keep herself moving. It's not just tiredness. With every step, she feels as though she's wading through memories, thick as treacle. The whole building is crowded with them, scenes from the past overlaid on the dust and detritus of the present like a series of AR slides. She remembers meeting Reet here at the end of countless shifts, hiding out in the executive suites and talking about how their days had gone. The time they walked in on a patron and had to flee the room, stifling scandalised laughter. The day she made agent, and Reet held her while she cried.

Tanta was expecting being here to be painful, but whatever she's feeling is nothing so straightforward. She doesn't yet know whether Reet has survived the day's fighting, and in her anxiety, there's something comforting about being in a place so suffused with her ex's memory. Since the Ward House burnt down, The Rotunda has become one of the only places that bears witness to a past where Tanta and Reet were happy, and together. In a complicated way, she's glad to be back.

The makeshift barricade complete, the exhaustion Tanta

has only just been keeping at bay threatens to overwhelm her completely. In former days, you wouldn't have been able to pay her to sleep in one of The Rotunda's pleasure rooms – not before their weekly deep clean, anyway – but right now, she can't imagine anything more lovely than resting in a real bed, whatever its history.

Before they sleep, though, there are some things the crew need to discuss. She forces herself to walk over to Cole, who is slumped at one of the remaining tables. She and Fliss take seats beside him. Tanta stares at the exhausted, demoralised faces in front of her and feels her own spirits flag. The three of them make a sorry war council. They're bedraggled and drained, hiding out in a condemned brothel – and they still have a corporation to topple. The mismatch between them and their opponent has never been more obvious, but it makes no sense to dwell on it. They've always been outgunned, but they've made it this far. That has to count for something.

'What now?' Fliss asks, dully.

Tanta sits up straighter, summoning all her powers of optimism. 'Now, we rest,' she replies, as brightly as she can. 'After that, we only have two objectives left.'

Which is a huge oversimplification, and Cole and Fliss both know it. Their first objective is to disseminate Cole's uninstallation patch, and last time Tanta checked, his investigation into how to do that had hit a dead end. She glosses over that for now. Rehashing the difficulties they face will only dishearten them all further – especially given that reversing the rollout of Harlow 2.0 is likely to be the easy part.

Just as Jeanie pointed out last autumn, undoing the update is half a solution at best. In order to make it stick, they'll need to take more drastic measures. They all understand the necessity of what they have to do next. It's something they've discussed and agreed on. It doesn't make the task any less daunting now they're face to face with it at last. They can't liberate InTech's residents while the city is still being governed by the same people who wanted to enslave those residents in the first place.

Their second objective is to assassinate InTech's board.

# Chapter 25

Reet's destination is the Needle, though she doesn't tell anyone else that. Here, at least, Thoughtfront's coordinated EMP attack works in her favour. Comms are down across the city. The raiders must have sent out advance teams to the data zeppelin and InTech's other backup servers, because they're offline, too. Her digital signature is gone; she can't so much as send out an emergency MindChat signal. Aside from the Corporate Wards she was with in the Black Box, there's no one in InTech right now who knows that Reet is alive.

That's just as well, because she knows for a fact that one of the most powerful men in the city wants her dead.

'Kenway is working for Thoughtfront.'

When Tanta gave her the warning, Reet almost dismissed it out of hand as the bitter ramblings of a disgraced former agent. Tee never liked Douglas, not even when she worked for him. Now that she's a defector herself, why would Reet take her word for anything? She had heard her ex-girlfriend out just long enough to establish that there was no way of tracing her call, and then hung up in anger and disgust.

It was only after she'd rejected Tanta's claims outright that Reet was forced to consider their plausibility. Mulling the matter over in her office, doubts, dressed up as memories, wormed their way into her thoughts. Douglas had never made any secret of his dissatisfaction with their power-sharing arrangement; whether or not he had actually defected, Reet had to acknowledge that he had a motive to do so. Once she'd accepted that, other details began to leap out at her: Douglas's insistence on procuring exemptions from Harlow 2.0 for his section lieutenants. The way he'd discouraged Reet from investigating Thoughtfront's relationship with the unaffiliated raiders – the loose end that led to her unravelling the entire invasion plan.

Before long, there were enough of these warning signs to constitute a possibility that Reet couldn't ignore. Even as she took steps to protect herself, she'd hoped, desperately, that they were unnecessary. She and Douglas may have had their differences, but he was still the man who got Reet her first job as an agent, her mentor: the thought of him being a traitor was almost too painful to contemplate.

Well, the destruction of the ICRD has turned horrible possibility into undeniable fact. The building wasn't bombed – Reet watched it happen, and she's certain of that. It was demolished, torn apart from the inside by a series of planned explosions. And while there are a number of people who could have done such a thing in theory, only one of them spent the bulk of yesterday overseeing the 'reinforcement' of the entire structure.

Tee was telling the truth – though why she'd bother to warn Reet about the danger she was in, Reet still isn't sure.

She pushes that question from her head, as she has several dozen times over the jog from Inspire Labs. It doesn't matter now: all that matters is stopping Douglas.

Reet may have turned off her location tracker, but her Co-Director didn't. Before the EMP blasts took out InTech's comms, he was in a saferoom below the Needle, along with the rest of the corporation's Directors. That's where Reet is headed now. It takes her much longer to get there than it would normally. The pace grates on her – with every step, she's worrying about the safety of her fellow Directors, and of the board – but with InTech's traffic management mainframe out of commission, she doesn't have another choice. She sticks to the back streets, following a circuitous route that should keep her out of the worst of the fighting.

She can't avoid it entirely, of course. The sounds are all around her: shouting, sniper fire, the shriek and thunder of shells. More direct evidence of the running battle being fought in InTech's streets comes to her in snatches – she'll skirt a main road lined with corpses, or pass a fleeing resident, trying to escape the carnage. Reet hates being unable to monitor how her troops are doing personally, but she does the best she can, watching the sky for the white signal flares that will let Firent know when to send out the UAVs, and the red ones that indicate a unit is in trouble.

The red flares are few and far between. For a long time, it's the only sign Reet gets that things are going well. The second sign comes when she gets in sight of the Needle, at long last, to find that none of the fighting columns have reached it yet. The sounds of warfare are louder here, but the streets immediately surrounding InTech's headquarters remain empty for now.

Which is not to say the building itself is safe. Reet would love to believe that the guardians standing to attention around the square columns at its base are her allies, but she knows better. Her suspicions are confirmed when, creeping closer, she spots the bodies in the shadows: the original unit assigned to protect the Needle. By the looks of things, most of them were shot in the back.

The pile of bodies seems to grow and grow in Reet's vision, until she can't see anything else. Her jaw tightens, her hands clenching into painful fists. She granted Douglas twenty-five exemptions from Harlow 2.0 for his section lieutenants – the same section lieutenants who were working on the ICRD yesterday. He has turned them into a private army, and she gave him the means to do it.

Reet's guilt and rage are great enough that she almost rushes the line of guards there and then. She resists the urge with an effort of will, holding herself still and seething till it has passed. Then she circles the building at a distance, her movements as cautious as she can force them to be.

The Needle is ablaze with the rising sun – a stark contrast to the dusty wreckage of the ICRD beside it. There are ten lieutenants guarding its main doors, but only three apiece on its other faces, including the staff entrance. A patrol of four circles the building at intervals. Reet takes her time, picking her spot and her moment carefully. She creeps into the shadow of the remains of the ICRD, letting its ruins conceal her from sight, and swings the sniper rifle from her back. When she judges the patrol is on the other side of the Needle, she takes a deep breath and lines up her first shot.

She gets the first guard cleanly through the forehead – a better fate than he deserves, in Reet's opinion. His two colleagues scatter to left and right, running for help, but the other lieutenants are some distance away and there's no decent cover in sight. She picks them both off before they've even reached the corners of the building. As the third guard falls, she sprints from her hiding place and over to the staff entrance. It's locked, but opens to her directorial authorisation code. Reet feels a grim sense of satisfaction: there's nothing Douglas can do to keep her out.

She swings the sniper rifle back over her shoulder as she steps through the door, drawing a pistol from her belt. The inside of the Needle is dark and quiet, its staff evacuated and the gun and shellfire muffled by its glass walls. The Directors' saferoom is on basement level four, but the lifts are still out, so she takes the emergency stairs.

The first thing Reet sees when she emerges from the stairwell is the body of the board's conduit, slumped against a wall and looking about as glassy-eyed and vacant as he did when he was alive. She skirts around him, advancing up the hallway towards the saferoom. When she reaches the steel-reinforced door, she pauses, taking stock. Two of Douglas's section lieutenants are still unaccounted for. If they're with him inside, it'll be three against one — assuming her Co-Director hasn't recruited any more traitors to his cause.

By rights, Reet should be daunted by these odds, which are steeper than any she faced in her brief time as a field agent. Rather than allowing herself to get nervous, she summons her rage again, letting it fill her to the brim. She thinks of her murdered colleagues, killed by the very people who should have had their backs. She thinks of trust and loyalty repaid with betrayal. When she feels as though she could rip the door from its hinges, she taps in her code and swings it wide.

She takes in the room beyond at a glance. The rest of InTech's thirteen Directors are sitting around a table, Douglas Kenway at their head. His two remaining lieutenants are standing to either side of him. The guards raise their guns as the door opens, but Reet's already ducking back behind it. She fires from behind its steel bulk, aiming high to avoid the seated Directors and spreading the shots as wide as she can.

When she looks again, the back wall is pockmarked with bullets and the guards are dead. That's the good news. The bad is that Douglas has managed to retrieve one of his fallen lieutenant's weapons and is holding the rest of the Directors at gunpoint.

'Take a seat, Director,' he orders Reet, waving the gun at his hostages. 'We'll wait for Thoughtfront high command together.'

Dr Friend's face is white; Harpreet Toor, the Director of Trade, stares at Reet with wide and beseeching eyes. At the sight of them, Reet's angry certitude falters. There's a pause, so taut a thought would snap it. And then she steps into the room.

'Good.' Douglas gives her a nasty smile as she walks towards him.

When she doesn't stop, his expression turns to one of alarm. 'Drop your weapons!' he shouts.

Reet shoots him in the foot. He howls, crashing to the ground. She has to swallow a bark of laughter. Douglas has been management track all his career – Reet knows that from his file. He's never undergone firearms training, never had to so much as throw a punch. His safety wasn't even off. This treasonous plan of his only ever had a hope of succeeding because Reet was supposed to be dead by the time he carried it out. If it hadn't been for Tanta's call, she'd be buried under fourteen stories of rubble by now, and InTech's headquarters would be under Thoughtfront control.

Reet strides towards Douglas where he's lying, curled in on himself on the floor, and kicks the gun from his hand. She kicks him again for good measure; it's unprofessional, but she can't help herself. She's tired of people turning on her corporation, and on her. She's tired of the people who are supposed to be her friends and allies letting her down.

'Is anyone injured?' she asks.

The rest of the Directors are huddled against the opposite wall of the saferoom, staring at her in a mixture of shock and blank terror. A part of Reet is disgusted by their passivity. They outnumbered their captors four to one, and yet none of them lifted a finger to prevent the coup playing out before their eyes. She would have thought that InTech's continued existence would be more important to them.

'Would one of you shut the door?' she adds, when none of them move or speak. 'There are more traitors outside, and they'll be here soon.'

That gets them moving. While Dr Friend makes the safe-room secure again, Reet retrieves the dead guards' weapons and unloads them. Douglas, meanwhile, has managed to sit up.

'You should let them in, Arthur,' he gasps, addressing Dr Friend. His voice is ragged with pain. 'Your exemption won't last forever. Do you really think the board would leave a mind like yours to its own devices? What do you think will happen to you when you've outlived your usefulness?' He looks around, staring at each Director in turn. 'To all of you? You should be – helping me.'

Reet has heard just about enough of this. 'Shut up,' she snaps. 'You've betrayed everyone in this room. You should be ashamed.'

Douglas lets out a choked laugh. 'Oh, spare me. The writing was on the wall for all of us, and Thoughtfront offered me protection. I acted in self-defence.'

'And I'm sure Thoughtfront extended that offer to all your colleagues. It would be so unlike you to stab everyone else in the back to save your own skin.'

'You're delaying the inevitable,' Douglas shoots back. 'There are troops advancing through the city as we speak. They'll be here soon, and when they take the Needle—'

'I've dealt with your troops,' Reet says coldly. 'Nobody's coming for you.'

That takes the wind out of Douglas. He slumps, and silence falls over the room at last. Reet's glad; she's suddenly bone-weary.

She sits beside her former Co-Director, her gun trained on his head, enjoying the quiet. After half an hour or so, the low hum of her transformer tells her that her 'scape is coming back online. Ten minutes after that, there's a series of beeps from outside, and the saferoom door opens.

Reet's instantly on the alert, but the stern, grey-haired woman who walks into the room is unarmed. By the large router on her head and her vacant expression, she must be the board's new conduit.

'Representative,' Reet murmurs, nodding respectfully.

'Report, Director Reet,' the woman says.

Reet gives the best account she can of the invasion attempt, Douglas's treachery, and its aftermath. 'I'm not sure yet how my forces have fared, Representative,' she concludes, 'But now that my Inscape is back online, I should have their reports soon. The Needle appears to be secure for now.'

'Have you anything to add, Douglas Kenway?' the conduit says, the syllables clipped and precise.

Douglas's only response is to attempt a lunge in the conduit's direction. Reet yanks him backwards, twisting one arm behind his back and driving him to his knees.

'I'm sorry, Representative,' she stammers. 'I'll take him to one of the holding cells.'

'That will not be necessary,' the conduit replies. She touches a finger to her temple.

Reet has never seen a conduit use their Inscape while on duty before. Their job is to be a mouthpiece for the collective consciousness of the board, and nothing more. The woman shapes a few haptic commands, the gestures jerky and graceless. At her feet, Douglas's struggles intensify.

'Don't you dare,' he hisses. 'Don't you *dare!*'

'Your exemption from Harlow 2.0 was always conditional upon your position, Douglas Kenway,' the conduit says, raising her voice above his protestations. 'You may now consider that position terminated.'

Douglas makes a last, desperate attempt to wrench himself free of Reet's grip – as though trying to outrun what is coming. For an instant, he is far stronger than she could ever have anticipated, and he manages to struggle to his feet. Then his whole body goes slack, and he topples over where he stands.

'You may release him now, Director Reet,' the conduit says. 'He poses no danger to us.'

Cautiously, Reet relaxes her hold on Douglas and peers at him. There's a lost look in his eyes. When he sees Reet leaning over him, his lips stretch into a wide smile. The expression has none of his usual malice: it's an infant's grin, trusting and guileless. His mouth opens and shuts, but he does not speak.

Reet stares at him, awed by the board's mercy and kindness. They could have ordered Douglas killed, or imprisoned for life in a secure sleeper facility. They could have subjected him to enhanced interrogation to find out exactly what he told Thoughtfront. Instead, they have opted to let him live – and live as a free man, at that. It's more than he deserves – and yet, at the same time, Reet can't help but remember what Douglas said to her once, in an unguarded moment: that he'd rather die than get the update. Reet can't wrap her head around that stance, but she doesn't think he was lying.

*Well, if he felt that way before, he won't soon,* she reassures herself. She's seen what Harlow 2.0 can do – it smooths away worries, doubts and fears. It makes people happy.

'We are in your debt, Director Reet,' Harpreet says, recovering something of her poise. 'And yours, too, Representative. Without your intervention—'

The conduit holds up a hand, silencing her. 'First Jennifer Ash, and now Douglas Kenway,' she says. 'The internal threats we face are beyond tolerable limits. Drastic action is required to protect the integrity of the corporation.'

There's a long pause before the woman speaks again. At last, she continues. 'It is the judgement of the board that exemptions from the Harlow Programme can no longer be justified. They allow too dangerous a degree of liberty.'

The colour drains from Dr Friend's face. 'Now, wait just a moment, Representative. Kenway's private army was a mistake we cannot allow to be repeated, but—'

'I am glad you agree, Doctor Friend.'

'Representative, surely we can discuss this,' Harpreet chokes out, but the conduit is already shaping the haptic commands.

There's a clamour, rising to an uproar. Several Directors run for the door, as though that would make a difference. Others try to rush the conduit, but Reet puts herself in between them, gun drawn. 'I *invented* this programme!' Dr Friend is roaring. 'It's mine, and I will not allow you to—' And then he stops in his tracks, and there's silence again.

Reet stares around a room of vacant faces, her whole body going hot, then cold. She understands the board's reasoning completely: people who haven't been optimised with one of the Harlow Programmes can't be trusted – what happened with Douglas proves it. The implications for her, though, are harder to accept. She's the only Director left.

'May I ask a question, Representative?' she says.

The woman's head jerks down, then up again.

'InTech *needs* Directors. I mean, we can't survive without them! Who will take their place?'

'Replacements must be recruited from among the Corporate Wards,' the conduit says placidly. 'See that the process is completed as quickly as possible, Director Reet.'

'B – by myself?'

'The former Directors will be on hand to offer assistance, once they have recovered from their transition.'

Reet forces herself to nod. She has never felt more exposed. 'Yes, Representative,' she says. 'I'll do my best.'

# Chapter 26

Cole is as tired as Tanta when he collapses onto one of The Rotunda's highly suspect beds, but unlike her, he can't seem to make sleep stick. Perhaps it's the fact that it's broad daylight outside, the glow of the sun creeping in around the edges of the door and through the scratches in the blackout material covering his room's tiny window. Perhaps it's the pins and needles tingling up and down his injured arm. Or perhaps it's the technical conundrum that has been gnawing at his thoughts ever since he left Gatwick.

He has found the perfect way to reverse the rollout of Harlow 2.0 and its predecessor. Embedding his uninstallation patch in the two Harlow Programmes' handshake protocols would allow it to jump from 'scape to 'scape at an exponential rate, spreading it across the city in a matter of hours. As a mechanism, it's simple, elegant, efficient – and impossible to access. And the worst part is that it's still the only solution he's been able to come up with.

Cole has been trying to destroy the Harlow Programme for over a decade. Creating it may have been the neuroengineering breakthrough of the century, but undoing it is the work of his life. To be so close to his goal, yet unable to achieve it, is beyond infuriating.

He tosses and turns for a few hours, trying unsuccessfully to disconnect from the churn of his thoughts. After a while, he sits up and tries out one of the physio exercises Constance gave him, slowly opening and closing his right hand. It's exhausting, but doesn't bring him any closer to sleep. Eventually, he takes the mildewed duvet from the bed and walks back through into The Rotunda's central hall. It's freezing in there, but beautiful, the dome suffusing the whole room with the pink light of perpetual sunset. He sits down at one of the little tables, wraps himself up as warmly as he can, and gets to work.

He still has the data packet he copied over from Neal's 'scape – the one that's exchanged between Harlow-Programmed MbOSes whenever their handshake protocol is activated. Slipping his uninstallation patch in among its contents, along with a transmission instruction to ensure that it's passed on, is the work of a few hours. Cole gets to it, though he's not sure yet what good it will do. It doesn't solve his biggest problem, which is that he still doesn't have a way to activate the hand-shake protocol himself. With no Harlow Programming – of either variety – of his own, it's impossible for him to introduce the doctored data packet to another person's 'scape. InTech's Harlow-Programmed residents exist within a closed system. Cole can observe that system to his heart's content, but affecting it – that's another matter entirely.

Once he has finished working on the data packet, he turns his mind to this more difficult challenge. He's as stumped as he was back in Gatwick, though, and another day of banging his head against the brick wall of the problem brings him no closer to an answer. The light falling through the hole in The Rotunda's domed roof is turning golden by the time he gives the effort up as futile and dismisses the notes cluttering his Array.

His eyes, bleary from long focus and lack of sleep, make out a figure standing in the doorway of the room opposite him, and his pulse spikes for an instant before he realises it's just Fliss. Her black hair is sticking up around her head in tufts, and as she approaches, Cole sees that her eyes are red. He imagines he looks similar; the days of living on the run have taken their toll on all three of them. She sits down beside him, scrubbing at her face like she's trying to clean the exhaustion out of her head.

'Sleep well?' he asks her.

She shrugs. 'Better than you, by the looks of things.'

'I've been trying to crack that handshake protocol I told you about,' Cole says, 'but I'm not having much luck.'

Fliss assumes a listening posture, plonking her elbows on the table and resting her chin against the heels of her hands. Cole wasn't expecting her to be interested in the technical details of this obstacle, but he's not sorry to have someone to explain it to. He outlines the issue to her in layman's terms, and she hears him out attentively.

'So you need to get into the system, but you can't, because you're not in the system,' she summarises, when he's finished. 'Sounds like a dead end to me.'

'Succinctly put.' Cole pauses. 'There is *one* thing I've thought of trying,' he admits. The idea has been lurking at the edge of his mind for some time now, a wolf circling the fringes of a campfire.

'What?'

'I could revoke my own immunity. If I removed my pass-over marker, my 'scape would install Harlow 2.0 automatically. I'd be inside the system, with the uninstallation patch already hidden in my MbOS. *I* could be patient zero, as it were.'

Fliss is already shaking her head. 'It's too risky. First of all, you've never tested this patch of yours, so we don't know how well it's going to work. What if it doesn't? You'll be gaga, and we'll be stuck. Second, if you get Harlowed, who's going to help us take out InTech's big boss?'

'You mean the board?'

'Whatever. Point still stands. We'll need you for that.'

A few days ago, Cole might have been inclined to take the gamble. Now, he thinks of Tanta's admonishment back in Gatwick – *you can't die* – and realises that Fliss is right. Sacrificing himself to Harlow 2.0 is exactly the kind of grand gesture that the crew can't afford for him to make right now.

They sit in silence for a while after that. Fliss chews her lip. 'I think you're on the right track, though – for what it's worth,' she says, at length. 'You need a way to be in the system, but also not in the system, right?'

'Right. But that's – Oh. *Oh!*'

Cole was about to say *that's impossible*, but the revelation stops him in his tracks. For a moment, he can't talk at all. His mouth opens and shuts, but no words come. The epiphany is sudden and all-consuming – a shaft of pure insight that breaks the problem before him open like an egg.

'Fliss, you're a genius,' he says, when the power of speech returns to him.

The bandit grins. 'You got that right. Why, what did I do?'

A door to the left opens, and Tanta emerges, yawning. 'What *did* she do?' she asks.

'She solved it! Well, *I* solved it, but you helped,' he says, treating Fliss to a smile even wider than her own. 'I know how we're going to reverse the rollout of Harlow 2.0.'

Tanta's smile is more restrained, but no less warm. 'I knew you would, Cole,' she says. She joins them at the table. 'Tell us what we need to do. And after that, I think it's time we discussed our second objective.'

★

After Cole has explained his solution, the crew spend the best part of an hour asking questions, raising objections, and putting forward ideas. There are doubts, misgivings, and not a few muted arguments, but when the talking is done and the words have all been weighed and measured, they find that they can fit them together into something approaching a plan. Not an easy one, or one that's certain to work, but a plan, nonetheless.

They lapse into silence with the arrival of the sunset, watching it paint the walls of The Rotunda in pink, red and gold. The colours put Tanta in mind of another evening, sitting with Reet on the Ward House roof.

'It'll be dangerous,' she says, after a while. 'There's a lot that could go wrong. And even if we succeed, there's no guarantee we'll survive.'

'We know,' Fliss replies.

'Still, it bears repeating.' She turns to Fliss. 'If you wanted to back out—'

Fliss punches her in the arm. 'Shut up, Tanta. We're crew. I'm not going anywhere.'

That makes Tanta smile. What's coming next will be difficult; she's glad she doesn't have to face it alone. She falls silent again, savouring these last few moments of peace with her friends as night comes on and the dome of The Rotunda darkens above them.

By tomorrow, one way or another, this will be over.

# Chapter 27

While Tanta and Fliss are sleeping, and Cole is racking his brains over the handshake protocol, Reet spends her day in a state of suspended disbelief. That things have turned out as they have for her is, quite obviously, impossible. She'd barely been in the ICRD a week before she was promoted to Co-Director and now, less than four months after that, she's the most senior person in the corporation besides the board themselves. It can't be real – but that doesn't change the fact that in this fantasy of hers, or whatever it is, the city is still at war, and she is the sole general left on the battlefield. She's managed to resist Thoughtfront's attempted coup so far, but that doesn't mean today's fight is over.

After a minute of terrified paralysis, Reet decides that she has no choice but to go along with the delusion for now. She has to press the advantage she's gained, however slender it may be, or soon enough her corporation will be back on the defensive again. She staggers out of the Needle, already almost dead on her feet, and sets to work.

Now that peoples' 'scapes are coming back online, it's not long before reports from Reet's CorpWard troops start flooding in. She sifts through the messages, alerts and image captures as she walks back to the Black Box – the streets are still too chaotic to make ordering a car feasible. The notifications she receives all tell the same story: Thoughtfront's raiders are in disarray, fleeing back into the tunnels or dead in the street. Thanks to the orderly evacuation of the city centre, InTech's own losses are minimal by comparison.

The first thing Reet does is to order her forces back down to ground level so they can help rout the remaining raiders and treat the wounded. Next, she lifts her evacuation order and re-assigns every non-essential employee to the clean-up and repair effort. They'll have their work cut out for them. Everywhere she looks, Reet sees evidence of the destructive battle that has played out here: buildings damaged by the UAV fleet's shellfire, burning cars, craters and bodies in the streets. The sun is up, but its light is weak even for winter, dimmed by an ominous miasma of smoke and dust. Her city is not in ruins, but it's clear how close it came to it.

Within an hour of her giving the order, the streets are starting to fill again. The returning residents move slowly, flinching at slammed doors and shadows. Reet smiles at everyone who looks her way, doing her best to project an aura of confidence. No one smiles back, or even speaks. Everyone she meets is going about their work in utter silence – fitting, for a day when so much blood has been spilled. The residents know Reet's rank from her MbOS profile, and she finds the crowds parting before her as she walks. It's still strange to be treated with so much deference; she hopes she can live up to the trust she sees in every eye that meets hers.

Firent greets her at the door of the Black Box, his face radiant. 'They're retreating!' he says. 'We did it!'

'Excellent work, Firent,' Reet replies. 'Now, I want you to gather the ADF and send them into the tunnels. Appoint ten agents to lead them. We're going to use Thoughtfront's strategy against it.'

The hole Thoughtfront has punched through the fortifications between the two corps goes both ways, after all. Considering the day's losses, an all-out assault will leave InTech's defences short-staffed, but it's worth the risk. Reet's willing to bet that the corporation across the riverbed is not prepared for a counterstrike.

Firent nods, already sending out the order on MindChat. 'Some of the raiders have surrendered, Director. What should we do with them?'

Reet thinks about this, but only for a moment. 'Take them into custody. Use minimal force. Offer them a home and an Inscape if they enlist with the ADF. Fewer troops for Thoughtfront just means more for us.'

It's a good sign: people surrender when they can't get back to their own side, or when there's nothing worth returning to. In this case, Reet suspects it's the latter. This was Thoughtfront's last-ditch attempt to seize control of InTech's side of the city. The corp threw everything it had into the effort, and it failed. If its own troops are flying the white flag, they must know that, too. If InTech's forces move quickly, they could rout the other corporation completely before nightfall.

Of course, nightfall is a long way off yet, and in the meantime, Reet is busier than she's ever been in her life. She has orders to issue, operations to oversee, and terms of surrender to discuss. Dozens of people all need to speak to her urgently – Firent, the board, Thoughtfront's embattled Ministers – and it seems she's late for a hundred classified briefings at once. She hasn't slept in a day, but she pushes her own exhaustion aside with a firm hand. She can rest when the war is won; right now, InTech needs her. She gives herself up to the torrent of demands on her time, letting it pull her under.

She doesn't surface again for almost fourteen hours. It's close to 10 p.m. before she washes up back in her flat, with a mug of tepid coffee and another long night of reports in front of her. At least the briefing documents she has to get through make for hopeful reading. The conflict is going well. When the Auxiliary Defence Force made it through the tunnels, they found panic waiting for them. Thoughtfront's defences, weakened by the corp's desperate play for InTech's side of the city, were crumbling even before they arrived. The advance has been swift and decisive. Runners from the moving front have been checking in with Reet all day, and each report has been more promising than the last. The situation is better than she or the board had dared to hope – so favourable, in fact, that the first document in the folder sent to her by the ICRD's team of analysts, drawn up hastily over the course of the last few hours, is entitled: *The Route to Reunification.*

Reunification. It's a word Reet has heard a lot recently. She's seen it presented as both an optimistic projection and a hopeless pipe dream, but never before as a likely prospect. And now here it is, laid out in black and white on her 'scape's reader. InTech and Thoughtfront are going to be one family again – and Reet is at the head of that family.

She shivers, the skin of her arms breaking out in gooseflesh. It must be because her flat is freezing – she hasn't been home in hours. She cranks up the heating, then throws herself into her reports. She works through them mechanically, the task taking her outside of herself, so that it's only when she stops at midnight for a toilet break that she notices her sore eyes and aching back. She walks through to the bathroom and splashes her face with cold water at the sink. It shocks some of the fatigue out of her, but her body still feels heavy and dull.

As for the rest of her... Reet puts the question to herself and realises she can't answer it. She should be happy – elated, even – but she can't summon the energy. It's as if her emotions, exhausted as the rest of her, have fallen asleep.

She doesn't understand it. Thoughtfront is falling, and she's on the up and up. She has always wanted to be one of InTech's protectors – it's the reason she joined the ICRD – and now, the entire city is under her care. She's at the board's right hand, more necessary to InTech's success than anyone else in the corporation. She should be pleased and proud. If she was nervous, she'd at least understand why, but this ... numbness makes no sense at all! Standing in her bathroom, Reet searches for her feelings about the day's events in the shining porcelain of the sink, the polished tap and the black marble countertop, and finds nothing but her own distorted reflection.

'This is what you wanted,' she says, her voice husky. The words mingle with the water gurgling from the tap and wash uselessly down the drain.

Saying it aloud makes everything worse, because it's true. Reet wanted to be of service to her corp, wanted it with everything in her, and now she is, and it isn't enough. Her throat tightens, warm tears welling in her eyes. She bites down on her lip to hold them at bay. How can she be crying at a time like this? It's ungrateful. It's uncorporate.

*You're just tired*, she tells herself, swiping a hand across her damp face as if to drive the point home. *You're tired and – and stressed. You need to sleep.*

She puts her reports aside for the night and tries to do just that, but the words she washed down the sink follow her into her bedroom and float behind her closed eyes. *This is what you wanted. This is what you wanted.*

When they're replaced by the red flash of an urgent notification pinging into her 'scape, Reet is relieved to be able to sit up again and throw herself back into her work. She summons her Array and checks out the message. It's from Firent: there's no text, just a video file. Reet plays it, letting her eyes flick over the footage. Having something to concentrate on is like a balm, washing away the quiet emptiness of her flat, and the restless emptiness in her mind.

The file is a security feed from a housing complex in the centre of the city. Reet recognises the street with its strange elephant statue – it's close to the old Ward House, and she used to walk down it on her way to work. She remembers it as a busy road, but in the aftermath of the fighting, it's quiet, empty of pedestrians and traffic alike. One car cruises slowly past, its headlights making the scene brilliant for an instant before it rounds a corner and disappears. Reet lets her focus soften, opening her gaze for whatever detail it is Firent wants to show her. The street is still again, except for...

She narrows her eyes, zooming in on the grainy footage. There's a figure on the far side of the road, moving quickly. They're slight, and walk with their head down, avoiding the camera's eye. That in itself is suspicious: there's no reason for a resident to hide their face. The figure reaches the corner, their steps light and rapid. On the edge of the camera's coverage, they turn, and for an instant, their face is raised to the light of the streetlamps.

At this point, Firent has added a facial recognition tag, but Reet doesn't need it. She had a feeling as soon as she saw the figure's outline and gait; she's certain now.

She freezes the footage and hails Firent on MindChat. <<When was this recorded?>> she asks.

She's exquisitely aware of the night air prickling her skin, the heave of her own breathing, while she waits for him to reply.

<<Half an hour ago,>> comes the answer, twenty seconds – or twenty years – later. <<We have eyes on her now. I have a team heading out to bring her in.>>

<<Send me a location.>> Reet is already pulling on her boots. <<I'm on my way.>>

Firent doesn't suggest that she's got better things to do, though

Reet knows she has. She ought to go back to bed or, if she can't do that, to return to her reports; her agents can handle this. It's useless to remind herself of these facts. Her feelings started up from their sleep the moment she saw Tanta on that security footage, and they're wide awake now. She's not proud, or happy, or elated, but at least she knows why. It's because her work isn't done yet. It won't be until she's brought Tanta back in.

They leave nothing to chance. By the time Reet arrives on scene, Firent has the entire neighbourhood where Tanta was spotted surrounded. Plainclothes guardians are watching the entrance to every street and the mouth of every alley. Those not patrolling the roads are stationed on the roofs of nearby buildings, surveying the area through the viewfinders of sniper rifles loaned from the ICRD for the occasion.

Firent himself has set up a temporary base of operations in a café at the edge of this invisible cordon. When Reet joins him, he's racing around the confined space, issuing orders via MindChat and monitoring security footage on his 'scape with sweeping hand gestures, like he's conducting an orchestra. He pauses to viewshare his Array with her. He's got simultaneous 'scape feeds from what looks like half the guardians still in the city spread out across the café, all trained on the same square mile of shops and streets. Each feed, playing on a separate AR screen, is labelled with the unit designation and number of the guardian recording it.

<<I deployed ten units. They're keeping a low profile so as not to spook her, but they have her under a close watch.>> He eyes Reet anxiously. <<Is it too much?>>

Reet thinks of her last run-in with Tanta, when her ex managed to escape from under the eyes of a dozen armed agents. She thinks of Tanta's bandit accomplice, and her gravity-defying flight across rooftops and over bridges.

<<In this case, I think it's justified,>> she replies.

<<We have every escape route covered. We're ready to move in as soon as you give the word.>>

Reet nods. <<Where is she now?>>

Firent gestures a haptic command, enlarging one of the screens from the bank in front of him. It's labelled Delta Seven, and it shows an alleyway a few streets away from the old Ward House. At first, Reet can't see anything, but a motion in the shadows draws her eye and she makes out Tanta crouching in the recessed doorway of a block of flats.

<<What is she doing?>> she asks, addressing the guardian in question.

<<Eating, Director,>> Delta Seven replies. The image enlarges as the guardian zooms in, and Reet catches a glimpse of a plastic wrapper.

<<She broke into a supermarket and stole some provisions,>> Firent explains. <<We were hoping she'd take them back to her accomplices, but no luck so far. We're not sure why she's stopped here.>>

Reet is, though. Or at least, something deeper than instinct tells her she is. 'She knows we're onto her,' she says aloud. Even half smothered in the shadows, she recognises the set of Tee's shoulders, the tilt of her head. *She's waiting for me*, Reet thinks, and then looks askance at the thought, because it's ridiculous.

Firent looks doubtful, too. 'If that's the case, why isn't she running? With respect, Director, I think she's just wary. I'd suggest giving her another half hour.'

Reet submits to this assessment. This is Firent's assignment, and she knows how important it is to trust the agents under your command. But although Tanta finishes her scanty meal and leaves the alley, it's not to lead them to her co-conspirators. She walks a strange arabesque through the streets, weaving through side roads and alleys, and Reet watches her do it. She never gets close enough to the ground forces for anyone in the command centre to see her up close. They monitor her through the security feeds of Delta unit, who are stationed on every roof she passes. It makes Reet feel strange, as though Tanta is an ant in a vivarium – trapped, but in a cage that's so much bigger than her, she can't even see it.

She's a tiny figure, moving with industry and purpose – though just where she is going, and what she is doing, Reet can't tell. Her choice of route is clearly carefully considered: it avoids all the mounted security cameras, or at least, all the ones that covered this part of the city the last time Tanta was here. But she doesn't seem to be heading to any destination that Reet can see, and several times she actually doubles back on herself, as though she's trying to shake a tail.

<<Maybe she's waiting to meet a contact,>> Firent suggests, but he doesn't sound convinced by his own idea.

After forty minutes have passed without any change in Tanta's restless movements, Reet decides to call it. Tanta must have realised she's being watched – there's no other explanation for why she's behaving this way. She's not going to lead them back to the rest of her 'crew', and the longer they wait, the more likely she is to slip out of their grasp for good, finding some means of escape they haven't thought to cover.

<<Take her now,>> she sends, with a certainty she doesn't feel.

Firent nods, touching a finger to his temple. <<Ground units move in.>>

The views from all of the 'scape cameras change and shift at once as their owners start walking. Through the rooftop feeds, Reet can see the ground officers advancing through the streets in unison, their cordon closing like the mouth of a drawstring bag. It's a meticulously planned operation. She has to hand it to Firent – he's thought everything through. The guardians keep time with one another, coordinated by his instructions. There's nothing for Reet to do except watch as the net tightens around her old girlfriend.

For the first three minutes, Tanta remains apparently unconscious of what is happening. She's still nothing more than an ant on the rooftop feeds of Delta unit, walking briskly along a street of cafés and restaurants, but that's not going to last. On the myriad screens in front of her, Reet sees Tanta's pursuers converging on her, sees the moment when they meet. Tanta flashes into view on the feed of Bravo Three and, for the first time this evening, Reet gets a clear view of her face.

She looks startled – afraid – and Reet's certainty falters. Tee certainly doesn't look like she was expecting this to happen. She darts away from Bravo Three, whose own hands appear in his feed as he draws his disabler on her and orders her to stop. Tanta ignores him, weaving back the way she came. Back in the command centre, Firent barks, 'Alpha unit, cut her off!' and ten guardians break into a sprint.

<<Alpha unit moving to intercept,>> a guardian replies.

Firent enlarges Alpha unit's feeds so he and Reet can track their progress. They converge on the street from two sides, racing to block the mouth of a crossroads halfway down its length. For a moment, Tanta is visible only from the eagle's perspective of the sniper units, a dark figure running down the broad road. Then—

<<Alpha Eight in position! I have visual!>>

—she leaps into close-up again, starting back in shock from the man lunging towards her.

She sidesteps him, and Reet tenses as she sees Tanta's knee swing up towards the man's face. For an instant, the feed is darkened with blood, before a hand shoots up to swipe it away. The feed blurs as the man spins around. Tanta is sprinting past him, making for the end of the street. Reet's fists clench of their own accord, her heart keeping time with Tanta's footsteps as she flees.

'Damn it!' Firent mutters. <<Echo unit, she's coming your way!>>

He reels off a location and the AR feeds rearrange themselves as the guardians of Echo unit shift their positions. The new road Tanta has entered does not branch or turn at all; her only way out is straight through.

Even on the overhead footage of Delta unit, Reet sees the realisation hit Tanta – sees her shoulders tense and her head shoot up. She's looking for an alternative – an open window, perhaps, or a wall she can scale. For an instant she freezes in place, and Reet knows that the buildings hemming her in on either side are an unforgiving blank. Thanks to the attempted coup, the entire city has been on high alert for most of the day. The doors are all locked, the windows barred.

Once again, Reet sees the danger Tanta is in before Tanta is even aware of it. While she hesitates, she's growing larger and larger in the feed of Echo Three. He's almost upon her before she notices him and dives out of his way. She aims a punch at his nose, her fist looming in his vision for a moment before he reels backward from the blow. As he struggles to his feet, she's nothing more than a blur in the corner of his feed.

<<She's doubling back,>> Firent warns. <<Alpha unit, get ready!>>

The hunt can't last forever, however impressive Tanta's skills. It's amazing she's managed to spin it out for as long as she has – Reet wouldn't have thought it was possible in anyone else. She feints left, dashes right, seeks out side-streets and wriggles her way out of blind alleys, but she's fighting a losing battle. Her movements slow, her punches and dodges getting more and more sluggish. They bring her to bay at last outside the ruins of the old Ward House. She's on one feed, then five, then ten.

Eventually, every screen on Reet's Array is filled with Tanta's sagging shoulders, her defiant face, and Reet knows it's over. Tee's surrounded.

She doesn't want to watch, but she has to. She has to be sure. She does lower the volume, though, as Tee finally raises her hands in surrender. As the handcuffs are tightened around her wrists. As she's pushed into a waiting van and driven away.

Reet's been rigid with stress ever since she saw Tanta on the security feed. She feels as though she's been holding something sharp, something that will shatter if she's not careful, and cut her to ribbons in the process. Now, at last, that tension drains away, leaving her slack and hollow.

'You did good, Firent,' she says. 'I'm very impressed.' She means it, but it still feels like she's forcing the words out through hardening cement.

Firent darts a sidelong glance at her, then looks at his feet. 'Thank you, Director.'

There's a long pause. Then: 'Permission to ask a question?'

'Go ahead.'

'What's going to happen to her?'

'Well, she'll be detained,' Reet replies. 'Some of the holding cells underneath the ICRD were damaged in the collapse, but there are plenty still operational.'

It wasn't what Firent was really asking, and Reet knows it. The question was heavy with the weight of things unspoken, because they are unspeakable. They both know that Tanta was once Firent's friend and Reet's girlfriend, and it's comforting, sometimes, to sit together in that knowledge, but neither of them will ever discuss it out loud. Tanta's a defector now: anything they still feel towards her besides hatred must remain a shameful secret.

Reet considers how to answer him more fully. She can't speak of the past, but she can acknowledge the sharp, fragile thing she's been holding within her ever since she learnt that Tanta was in the city. It's hope: a hope so painful that she's tender of even thinking about it. Tanta may be a traitor now, but thanks to the Harlow Programme, she doesn't have to stay that way. With time and careful neuroengineering work, InTech can restore her to the person she was before.

She's wary of saying so much to Firent. The Harlow Programme is too highly classified to discuss it with him and besides, she doesn't want to get his hopes up to the fever pitch of her own — but his concerned eyes tell her that he needs an answer. Like her, he cares too much about this to simply put it out of his mind.

'What happens after that is partly up to her, Firent,' she says. 'But it's not too late for her, if that's what you're asking. I hope … I really hope that we'll be able to give her a second chance.'

# Chapter 28

Reet goes straight to Tanta's cell, not even stopping to inform the board of what has happened. They'll hardly care about Tanta's capture – she's small fry to them. To Reet, she's ... well, Reet isn't entirely sure what she and Tanta are to one another now, but that's one reason for her haste.

The destruction of the ICRD means that her normal entrance to InTech's basement complex of holding cells is currently buried under a building's worth of rubble, so Reet goes in via the Needle. She hasn't been back to InTech's headquarters since her confrontation with Douglas that morning, and it's surreal to see how ordinary everything looks less than a day later. The lobby is emptier than usual, but the door guards and receptionists are back on duty, filling the space with quiet, purposeful bustle.

The holding cells are a different story. Over a third of the complex has been closed, darkened corridors cordoned off with lines of virtual tape. The ICRD's basement levels are heavily fortified and haven't taken as much damage from the collapse of the building above them as might be expected, but even so, it will take weeks to clear away the debris. Those areas of the windowless rooms that are still functional are staffed by a skeleton crew – most of the community guardians are still on the other side of the riverbed, cementing InTech's control of Thoughtfront's territory. The guards who are left are doing their best to hold down the fort in challenging circumstances; Reet pings a *well done!* sticker to each one she passes. It's a childish reward, something she hasn't received herself since she lived in the Ward House, but perhaps some childishness is what they need right now.

Tanta is being held on sub-basement level three, block A, an area reserved for prisoners who pose the highest security risk. There are gate scanners on the doors in and out, and the cells and hallways are equipped with motor cortex immobilisers. Reet strides through the labyrinthine corridors, following the pastel-pink ribbon that borders the ceiling.

Tanta's cell is in the middle of the block; Reet has stationed two guards outside it on permanent watch. She's about to step in, but pauses in front of the room. She can see Tanta through the one-way mirror of the door, manacled to the wall and held motionless by the immobiliser in the ceiling. She doesn't look like a security risk; she looks small and helpless, afraid. Reet's skin tingles, memories she thought she'd put aside forever rising in her mind. For an instant, the cell, the chains, all melt away. She and Tanta are children in dormitory five again, hiding inside Reet's blanket fort, and Tanta is crying for her, reaching for her.

*Reet, I'm scared.*

*It's all right, Tee. I've got you.*

Reet's too conscious of the watching guards to allow herself to cry, but she feels the threat of tears blocking her throat, rising with the heat in her face. She coughs and turns away.

*You're here to interrogate her, not give her a cuddle,* she scolds herself. Tanta has made her choices. She's not worthy of Reet's protection anymore. Reet knows that, and yet the memory of their old bond is so strong that it's an effort to keep that knowledge in mind. The urge to comfort Tee, to help her, is etched into her bones. It's what she's always done.

*You're* going *to help her. Just not in the way she wants.*

And that, Reet supposes, will have to be enough. She steels herself, squaring her shoulders and smoothing her face free of expression. Then she gestures the door open and steps inside. In the corner, Tanta's eyes flick upwards, seeking hers. Reet fights the urge to look away. She stares at her old friend and lover, towering over her in the cramped space.

Her instinct is to turn off the immobiliser immediately, to give Tanta the freedom to stretch that her cramped limbs so clearly crave, but she forces herself to wait for a slow count of sixty before gesturing the haptic command that will release her. Tanta will get no special treatment from her because of their shared past, and Reet needs to make that clear from the outset.

As soon as her motor control is returned to her, Tanta sags, not trying to hide her discomfort. She shifts her weight, wincing as she eases the pressure of her cuffs, and assumes a more comfortable position, sitting cross-legged on the floor.

'Thank you,' she says. She drops her eyes and begins to massage the chafed skin of her wrists and ankles.

After about a minute, Reet realises that she doesn't intend to speak again. *Is that it?!* she wants to shout. This is her first real chance to talk with Tanta in over four months. She's not sure what she was expecting from this encounter, but it wasn't the silent treatment.

Tanta left *her*. She betrayed Reet, lied to her, and then abandoned her. Even though all of Reet's protective instincts are baring their teeth at the sight of her ex-girlfriend in chains, Tanta isn't the victim here. She has no right to sit there in resigned silence, nursing her wounds, as though *she's* the one who has been mistreated. And there's no reason for Reet to feel – she shouldn't feel... she dismisses the thought, unwilling

345

to find out where it leads. But the hot, hurt sensation in her chest when she sees Tanta reduced to this is a lot like guilt.

'I did this so you could talk, understand?' she snaps. 'Which means if you *don't* talk, I'm turning the immobiliser right back on again.'

Tanta looks up at that, though only for a moment. 'I understand.'

When it becomes clear that this is all that she's going to volunteer independently, Reet starts firing off questions.

'How did you get into the city?'

'You know how.'

'Through the tunnels, with the raiders. You're working for Thoughtfront, then?'

'You already know I'm not.'

'Where are your accomplices?'

'I can't tell you that.'

Tanta won't meet Reet's gaze. She squats down, trying to force eye contact, but Tanta only turns away. 'Are they in the city?' Reet asks.

'I can't tell you that,' Tanta says again, enunciating every syllable.

Reet decides to change tack. 'I've missed you, you know,' she says, allowing her tone to soften.

At last, Tanta raises her head. 'I've missed you too,' she replies, and Reet sees the truth of it in her green eyes, the almost imperceptible tremor in her lips.

'Do you remember when we used to sneak up to the Ward House roof together?'

Tanta nods. Encouraged by this small sign of acquiescence, Reet continues. 'I think about those days all the time. We always had each other's backs, then.' She takes one of Tanta's hands, letting the memories light up her eyes and animate her face as she speaks. 'What happened, Tee?'

346

For an instant, Tanta's face is as open as Reet's own, her eyes eloquent with unshed tears. Then she jerks away from Reet's touch, hard enough to rattle the restraints holding her to the wall. 'Don't,' she spits.

'Don't what?'

'Don't use the past as – as bait, Reet. It isn't fair.'

Sensing her advantage, Reet presses on. 'I'm not trying to trap you. I want to help you. You've always been able to read me better than anyone: look at my face and tell me if I'm lying. I just want things to be the way they were before. When we were happy. Don't you want that, too?'

'Of course I do,' Tanta says. Her voice is thick.

'Then work with me. Give me something. Where is Cole?'

'I can't tell you that,' she repeats, and a shutter drops over her expression, sealing all of her emotions where Reet can't get at them.

'But why not?' Reet asks, frustrated. 'You let Arden warn me about the invasion. *You* warned me about Douglas. You were looking out for the corp before. Now suddenly it's your enemy? I don't understand.'

'I did those things for you, Reet! Not for InTech. For you. And now that I know you're safe, there's nothing else you can offer me that I want.' Tanta's head droops again, as though this brief speech has exhausted her.

Reet recognises a dead end when she sees one. Tanta's answer is like a concrete wall; no amount of bribery or threats is going to change it. She could knock it down by force, but she's not going to place Tanta into the hands of the enhanced interrogators with their waterboards and pliers. She has the power to spare her that, at least.

Reet was angry a moment ago, but now she feels the calm of conviction settle over her. There's no point questioning Tanta further in her current state. She's confused, incoherent, unable to distinguish between friends and enemies, or right and wrong. She isn't the Tee Reet knows and loves.

Well, Reet knows how to fix that.

She summons her Array. <<Firent, where are you right now?>>

<<Still at the café,>> comes the prompt reply. <<I'm just debriefing guardian units Alpha through Echo.>>

<<When you're done, have one of the units transport Tanta to the Black Box. Ask Dr Friend to meet her there,>> she sends. The doctor should have recovered from his transition to Harlow 2.0 by now; he'll be more than capable of doing what needs to be done.

<<Yes, Director. Is she … OK?>>

Reet smiles. <<She will be.>>

'Get yourself comfortable,' she says aloud, to Tanta. 'I'll be turning your immobiliser back on in sixty seconds.'

When Tanta is secure again, Reet kneels down and kisses her gently on the forehead. 'You'll see things differently soon, Tee,' she promises her. Soon, she'll have to.

# Chapter 29

Getting through Reet's interrogation was one of the hardest things Tanta has ever done. There's no one who can read her better than Reet – no one who has a surer sense of when she's lying, or a surer ability to seek those lies out and get at the truth behind them. For Tanta's own part, Reet is almost the only person she has ever been truly open with, and that's a hard habit to break. She spent every second they were together in dread that she might tell her ex-lover more than she intended, or worse, give Cole and Fliss away without saying anything at all, through some unguarded glance or too-legible expression. She's never had to keep such a close watch on what she said and how she acted before, not even in her most dangerous covert missions.

Sitting locked inside her own mind beneath the motor cortex immobiliser in her cell is almost relaxing by comparison. She's cold, and her limbs are stiff, but the inherent terror of paralysis peaked after the first hour, leaving her relatively calm. She passes the time after Reet leaves in examining her reflection in the one-way mirror of the cell's door, and rehearsing the details of the crew's plan.

So far, and despite appearances, that plan is on track. Tanta is exactly where she needs to be – or directly beneath it, at least.

Breaking into the Needle would have been a challenge for even the most seasoned agent, and with her current resources, Tanta's not at all sure she could have managed it. Thanks to Reet, she doesn't have to: she's already inside.

All she needs to do now is escape the windowless rooms.

Reet told her she'd see things differently soon, and to her credit, she doesn't keep Tanta waiting long. The clock on her Array reads 2 a.m. when the door to her cell opens for the second time that night, and her two guards walk in. They turn off Tanta's immobiliser, unlock her neck and ankle restraints, and cuff her hands behind her back. That done, they haul her to her feet and march her into the corridor.

Tanta looks around as the guardians escort her down the hallway, relishing having her muscles back under her own control. The passageways in this section of the complex are bordered at the top with a discreet, pale-pink ribbon. That means she's on – Tanta racks her brains, dredging up knowledge she hasn't had to think about since basic training – sub-basement level three, cell block A, one of the compound's maximum security zones.

That's good, in that cell block A is the one closest to the stairs leading up to the Needle – but bad, in that 'maximum security' means there are immobilisers in the ceilings, gate scanners on all the doors, and cameras on every corner. What *that* means is that there's no margin for error here at all; Tanta is going to have to time what she does next down to the second.

She walks between her captors, doing her best impression of a meek and obedient inmate, until they turn onto the stretch that leads to the stairwell door. The cells here all stand open and empty, their interiors dark. The door is a solid steel monster of a thing, with a nineteen-point locking mechanism and an MbOS scanner for good measure. It's watched by a security camera at the other end of the corridor. Tanta glances up as they pass beneath its lidless eye – it looks like it covers the whole hallway.

When they reach the door, the guardian on her left takes a step away from her, drawing a key from a ring on his belt and inserting it in the lock.

Tanta waits until he's pulled the door all the way open before she starts to sway. 'I feel dizzy,' she says.

She staggers, falling to the left, but the guardian to her right is too quick for her, grabbing her and dragging her roughly back to her feet. As his hand makes contact with her upper arm, Tanta feels more than hears a distinct click, like she's cracked a joint. It's followed by a shock that seems to pass directly from her arm to the man's face. His mouth drops open, assuming an expression of horrified confusion.

Tanta feels the jolt, too, a sensation she's become familiar with, but one that never gets any less disconcerting. The corridor goes dim and silent as the EMP hidden beneath her skin snatches the ambient hum of the lights, sensors and cameras around them right out of the air.

The guardians are the ones staggering now, cut loose from their programmed moorings. The one by the door raises a trembling finger to his temple, trying in vain to summon his Array. Tanta pities the two men and their disorientation – she understands their panic only too well – but she's not about to let that stop her. The windowless rooms have multiple redundancies to deal with attacks like this; she has about a minute, she estimates, before the security measures surrounding her come back online. At that point, the whole block will go into precautionary lockdown, activating the immobilisers automatically, and she can't still be here when that happens.

She yanks herself free of the other guardian's slackening grasp, spins to face him, and headbutts him in the chest. He goes over heavily, crashing back through the doorway of the open cell behind him. Tanta turns her attention to his colleague, who has had the presence of mind to draw his stun baton. He advances on her, but his focus is wavering, the fetters holding his Harlow 2.0-programmed mind in check weakened by the EMP blast. With her hands cuffed behind her back, Tanta's at a disadvantage, too, but she's by no means defenceless. She aims a high kick at the man, knocking the baton from his hands. As it clatters away, she kicks him again, circling around between him and the door.

Emergency lights in the ceiling blink back on, lighting the corridor in intermittent, sickly green. She doesn't have long. Tanta puts her shoulder against the door, which is sliding slowly shut. Then she kicks the guardian a third time, knocking him off-balance. She's trying to drive him towards the open cell where his colleague has fallen, but he lunges at her instead, his face a snarl of bafflement and rage. She sidesteps him, then sweeps his legs from under him, sending him tumbling into the cell on the other side of the passage. A boot to the head – one that makes Tanta wince in sympathetic pain – and he lies still.

This next part is awkward – and not a little undignified. Tanta puts her back to the unconscious man and crouches down beside him, scrabbling at his belt with her bound hands. When she has his keyring, she rises to her feet and surveys the scene. The first guardian is lying in the open cell on the right, out of sight of the camera. The second is in the cell on the left, but he fell awkwardly, and one of his legs is still visible from the corridor. Tanta checks the clock on her Array. Fifteen seconds. She puts one foot against the second guardian's shin and shoves it into the cell. Then she turns and dives through the closing door.

Bright light in her peripheral vision and the low buzz of the backup systems coming online tell her that she made it out just in time. Behind her, the immobilisers will have slammed back on, paralysing the two guards where they lie. Tanta hits the concrete floor of the stairwell with a jarring thud, unable to break her fall. She's never been more grateful for bruises and scraped skin.

She gets up gingerly, checking herself over. The next patrol to pass this way will discover her escape – and her incapacitated captors – but by then, she'll be long gone. She hurries up the stairs, letting the coloured threads on the walls guide her. The cell blocks on sub-basement levels one and two are all low and medium security, making them easier to navigate unseen. From this point on, stealth and subterfuge are the orders of the day. Tanta doesn't want to hurt any more of InTech's residents if she can possibly avoid it. There's only one group of people she's here to kill tonight, and they're at the other end of the building.

She's expecting to encounter many more guards than she does, but the complex is strangely deserted. She ducks into an empty cell to let one patrol go past, and avoids another two by darting down darkened, closed-off corridors, but doesn't meet anyone else.

Even so, when Tanta emerges at last on the ground floor of the Needle, she's wrung-out with tension. She's in the dark belly of InTech's stronghold, and soon she'll be striking at its heart. Talent has helped to get her here, but luck played a large part, too – you can't infiltrate a place as secure as the Needle without it. She's been fortunate to avoid recapture so far, but it's only a matter of time till her luck runs out.

Cole and Fliss are waiting for her close to the building's staff entrance. It has started to snow while Tanta was underground, fat white flakes drifting down from the dark sky, and they're both shivering. Fliss has brought the guns and stun batons they were able to sneak through the tunnels from Thoughtfront, but Tanta shakes her head at the sight of them.

'You'll have to leave them out here. They'll set off the alarm.' She points at the scanner embedded in the lintel of the door.

The Needle's security arrangements are airtight; they have to be – this is the residence of the board, after all.

Fliss dumps the weapons, then hurries inside. 'What kept you?' she grumbles, as she picks the lock on Tanta's cuffs. 'I can barely feel my fingers!'

Tanta shoots her a look. 'We can swap next time, if you like, and you can be the one to pull off a solo jailbreak. Can you take care of the cameras?' She asks, turning to Cole.

'I already have,' he replies, with a touch of pride. 'I used the same trick I did in the Black Box last autumn. It's actually a really simple workaround—'

'Cole.'

'Right, yes. Another time.'

The crew creep through the deserted staff corridor and pause outside the entrance to the main lobby. Tanta knows from experience that there'll be at least five people on duty inside, even at this late hour: a receptionist and four night porters. That's five people between them and the lifts to the top of the building – and the penthouse apartments of InTech's board.

'Cole, you're up,' she whispers. When they were discussing this particular obstacle earlier in the evening, he said he had a way to take care of it.

Cole nods, his brow furrowing as he accesses his Array. There's a wait, which stretches out longer than Tanta would like. 'We don't have much time before someone realises I've escaped,' she hisses, after she's left him to work in silence for as long as she can bear. 'Whatever you're doing, you need to do it faster.'

'Give me … one minute,' Cole mutters, shaping haptic commands on the air with feverish intensity.

Thirty seconds later, he rocks back on his heels. 'Done. Check the lobby now.'

Tanta opens the door a crack, leaning around the corner. She's just in time to see all five staff members filing out of the front entrance in a neat line. The automatic doors slide shut behind them. Tanta turns back to Cole. He's grinning.

'All right,' she says to him, as they run across the silent foyer to the lifts. 'I'll bite. How did you *do* that?'

'I spoofed an emergency evacuation order, just for the five of them,' Cole replies. 'Beamed it directly into their 'scapes. They'll be halfway to the suburbs before anyone realises what's happened.'

Tanta nods, impressed. Given this morning's unrest, a second evacuation of the city centre would hardly come as a surprise. Even without their programmed obedience, Cole's fake order is not one any of the Needle's staff will think to question.

She jabs the call button; a minute later, the doors of the nearest lift glide open. Tanta feels a rush of relief as the three of them are sealed inside and the lift car begins to rise. A couple of dozen floors and a few inches of steel sheeting aren't much to put between her and the guardians of the windowless rooms, but they're better than nothing. The crew are underway now, gathering momentum as surely as an avalanche. InTech's forces may catch up with them – may even kill them – but she's determined that won't happen before they've done what they came here for.

There's silence for a moment. The three of them watch the floor counter tick upward, or gaze at their own reflections in the mirrored walls.

'So, this lift will take us straight to the board?' Cole asks. He sounds almost awed at the prospect.

'Not exactly,' Tanta admits.

He quirks an eyebrow. 'Why do I not like the sound of that?'

*Because you know me, and you know this life,* Tanta thinks, with an inward smile. *Our assignments have never been easy.* Cole is the one who got them here unseen, but they're in her territory now. Beneath her tension, and the lingering, Harlow-Programmed guilt at breaking into her own corporation's headquarters, she's not entirely surprised to find that she's enjoying herself. She missed being out in the field with Cole during the long, cramped months in the Brokerage. She may not be an agent anymore – not officially, anyway – but the last few days have reminded her of everything she loves about the job.

'This lift shaft goes all the way to the top of the building,' she explains, 'but no one can access the board's apartments without authorisation from the board themselves. Look—' She indicates the AR panel beside her: there's a button for the penthouse, but it's greyed out. 'This will only take us as far as the restaurant and event hall. The board are one floor above that.'

'So, what do we do from there?' Fliss asks.

Tanta pauses before she answers her, watching the numbers flash up on the floor counter. *Sixty-eight, sixty-nine.* She has to time this just right.

'Brace yourself,' she says, an instant before the right time comes. She slams the emergency stop button, and the lift shakes and judders to a halt. Then she turns to her two companions and grins. It's funny: she's come here to commit a brazen and appalling act of treason, something she would have been literally incapable of less than a year ago, yet she's never felt more in her element.

'From here, we climb.'

Tanta and Fliss prise the lift's inner doors open together, and then Tanta trips the latch that holds the outer ones closed. She opens them a crack and peers out into the concourse beyond. It's empty, and she's timed it correctly: the lift is poised halfway between this floor and the one below. Climbing up and into the room beyond is easily done. Tanta and Fliss hop up, then help Cole after them.

Once they're in the concourse, they can see the exposed lift shaft through the open doors, and below that, the roof of the lift car they were just inside. Tanta climbs onto it and takes hold of one of the four cables in its centre.

Cole gives her a terrified look. 'There's no way I can climb those.'

'You won't have to,' she assures him. 'If you wait on the roof of the lift car, Fliss and I will climb up and summon it once we reach the penthouse floor.'

'Can't I wait in the lift itself?'

Tanta considers the idea, but shakes her head. 'Now that the emergency stop's been triggered, The Needle's maintenance team might recall it to the basement for testing. We can't risk you being discovered. You'll be quite safe,' she adds. 'All you'll need to do is step off as soon as you see me.'

'And before I'm crushed against the roof of the lift shaft?'

'And before you're crushed against the roof of the lift shaft, yes.'

'I'd like to register my disagreement with this plan.'

'Duly noted.'

'Enough chitchat,' Fliss cuts in. 'Let's get going before we lose our chance.'

Tanta nods, taking a cable in each hand and hauling herself up into the shaft. It's draughty, and the closely-spaced cables are slick with oil. She braces herself carefully, wedging her legs between them to help keep her grip. It's not an easy journey, and for a while, it takes all of Tanta's concentration to avoid falling. She feels the cables pass between her hands and ankles as she shins up them, and she hears the rhythmic sounds of Fliss doing the same thing behind her, and there's no room in her mind for anything else.

After they've been climbing long enough that the light from the concourse beneath them has disappeared completely, Fliss's voice floats up to her through the darkness.

'What are the board like, then?'

'I don't know,' Tanta replies. 'I've never seen them before – not even photos. Come to think of it, I don't know anyone who has.'

Even the Directors only ever speak to the board through the conduit. As far as Tanta knows, they don't interact in person with anyone in the corporation.

'What, no one?' Fliss asks. 'So they just… live up here all alone, never seeing anyone? That's a bit creepy.'

Tanta has never really thought about it before, but the more she reflects on it, the more she sees that Fliss is right. It *is* creepy. The board are the true leaders of InTech – the minds that guide it, the hands that shape it. They've been running the corporation since before Tanta was born, and yet what does she actually know about them? Besides the location of their residences, and the fact of their power, almost nothing.

Tanta feels her confidence falter. She's doing exactly what an agent ought never to do – walking into a situation without knowing what she's likely to find. And yet what choice does she have?

'Tanta?' Fliss says. 'If no one's ever seen the board, how do we know what we're up against?'

Tanta shivers. But it's too late to turn back now. 'There's only one way to find out,' she replies.

Reet is woken – she isn't sure when – by a persistent beeping from her 'scape. She props herself up in bed, rubbing the sleep from her eyes. The readout on her Array says it's 3:07 a.m. She swears – she's overslept. After she returned from interrogating Tanta, she was barely able to keep her eyes open, but she had only meant to nap for half an hour.

There's a notification sitting at the top of her Array from one of the Needle's maintenance officers. Reet calls the woman back as she struggles out of her bedsheets and into some warm clothes.

<<What is it?>> she sends.

<<I am sorry to disturb you so late, Director,>> the Maintenance Officer replies, <<It is probably nothing, but we are under orders to report anything out of the ordinary. Half an hour ago, the emergency stop button was activated in lift car seven on floor sixty-nine.>>

<<That's something the night porters should be dealing with, not me,>> Reet replies, somewhat snappishly.

<<I tried to alert the porters, Director, but they did not respond to my hails. And when my maintenance team recalled the lift to basement level one for a check-up, they found it empty.>>

Reet freezes halfway through putting on her jacket. It could very well be nothing – a trivial malfunction of some sort, easily fixed – but on the other hand...

<<I attempted to escalate the matter to a less senior agent,>> the Maintenance Officer continues, <<but—>>

<<You were right to bring this to me,>> Reet cuts her off. <<Good work.>>

She disconnects from the call and walks through to her living room, where a picture window looks out on the city centre. The Needle is dark, the streets around it empty. It looks quiet – peaceful, even – but there's an uncomfortable feeling in the pit of her stomach. What she's thinking of shouldn't be possible. But what if it is? Reet wants to dismiss the worry gnawing at her thoughts, but can't quite manage it.

She summons her Array. <<Firent. What's Tanta's status? Has she arrived at the Black Box?>>

When he doesn't reply, her unease deepens. She hails him again, pushing the notification through at the highest priority level. <<Firent: acknowledge.>>

359

Nothing.

Reet makes up her mind there and then. <<I need a unit of guardians to sweep the Needle for possible intruders,>> she snaps, sending the message out on the CommGuard's emergency channel. <<All available units, please respond.>>

The delay before anyone replies is long enough that the seeds of real alarm begin to take root in Reet's chest. Her first thought is that there's been a second EMP attack, but all the reports she's had from the front indicate that Thoughtfront is in no position to attempt one. When she gets an answer at last, it's from a group of units on the other side of the riverbed. Reet orders them all back to InTech's territory immediately, but they're more than an hour away.

<<Where *is* everyone?>> she demands.

There's nothing in reply but dead silence.

Reet curses again. Then she puts on her shoes and heads for the door. Until the guardians arrive, she's going to have to deal with whatever is going on in the Needle the same way she's been dealing with everything, lately: by herself.

# Chapter 30

Tanta's mood sobers as she and Fliss draw closer to their goal. By the time they reach the top of the lift shaft, her whole body is taut, both from the exacting climb and the thought of what awaits her at the top. She shins up to just above the lip of concrete that marks the entrance to the penthouse floor, then drops down onto it. It's narrow, but still a lot easier to cling to than the lift cables.

After another minute, Fliss joins her. 'We'd better hope the board aren't too handy in a fight,' she whispers. 'My arms and legs are jelly.'

'Shh.' Tanta reaches up to trip the latch of the lift doors. She cracks them open, then peers through the gap. She can't see any guardians in the space beyond, but they aren't the only defences the board might have waiting for them.

After a minute more of observation, Tanta nods to Fliss, and they pull the doors open and step through. They emerge in an elegant lobby – thick, velvety blue carpet and arabesque designs etched in gold on the walls. There's none of the clean, corporate aesthetic that dominates the rest of the building here. It's clear immediately that this is a private residence, designed with comfort and luxury in mind.

Opposite the lift is a single dark wooden door, its surface

carved with the same delicate traceries that line the walls. *That's weird*, Tanta thinks. She was expecting a long line of entrances. Surely the board, with all their status and power, don't cohabit a single flat. She has an image of sober men and women in expensive suits crammed cheek by jowl in a Ward House-style dormitory and has to swallow a laugh.

She turns back to the lift, pressing the call button to summon Cole. It rises swiftly, but she and Fliss are ready for him as he appears. They take an arm each and drag him into the lobby, where he lands in an undignified bundle in Tanta's arms.

'Can you run a scan for digital signatures?' Tanta murmurs, when he's recovered himself. If they're walking into an ambush, she'd like to know in advance.

Cole nods, putting a finger to his temple. Then he frowns.

'What is it?'

'I'm not picking up any guardians, but . . . I'm not picking up anyone else, either.'

For the first time that evening, Tanta feels a stab of alarm. If the board have gone into hiding, or been relocated elsewhere, then everything the crew have done has been for nothing. But Cole isn't finished.

'Wait. There *is* something, but it's . . . strange. It's not like any digital signature I've encountered before.'

That makes sense to Tanta; the results of Cole's scan are not the only thing that's strange about this situation. She stares again at the lone wooden door, as dark and intricately carved as the entrance to some ancient place of worship. Its whirling patterns seem to draw her gaze – and everything else in the hallway – towards it, leaching the lobby of warmth and brightness. She gestures the other two forward. They creep across the foyer, breaths held and shoulders hunched. At the door, they pause. Tanta tries the heavy handle – it isn't locked. It swings inward without a sound.

Tanta's first impression is that there's no one in the room beyond. It's huge – almost as large as the event hall below it, with glass walls on three sides that offer astonishing views of the city – and it's almost completely empty. There's nothing in it save for a large collection of machinery at its centre: a server rack stands beside a thicket of wires, tubes and monitors that are tangled around a row of eight metal-and-glass tanks. More cables radiate out from this odd jumble in a wide circle, running to power outlets at the edges of the space.

Tanta is trying to make sense of this scene when Fliss makes a small, shocked sound, her eyes going wide – and that's when she sees the bodies. They are supported – or perhaps consumed – by the mass of wires and pipes in the middle of the room, so enmeshed with the equipment surrounding them that they are almost invisible. Eight bodies: emaciated and pale, their limbs not much thicker than the tubes attached to their mouths and noses.

Drawing closer, Tanta becomes aware of a soft swishing noise, regular as a heartbeat. It's coming from the tanks that enclose the torso of each figure. She peers at one. A pump beside it pushes air in and out, making the gaunt chest within rise and fall, rise and fall. She walks along the row, inspecting each body in turn. Aside from the slight, artificially-induced movement of their chests, they are motionless. Routers on their heads connect them to the server rack beside them, and wires connect them to each other. Their eyes flicker beneath their closed lids, as though they are in a fitful sleep, troubled by digital dreams.

Fliss prods one of the cables with her toe. 'Well, fuck,' she says.

'*This* is the board?' Cole whispers.

Tanta hears her own disquiet and surprise in their tones. Insofar as she'd ever thought about the board before, she had imagined them strong and wise, the embodiment of InTech's power. The wizened men and women before her look anything but. They're animated corpses, their bodies held back from death by the thinnest of scientific margins.

She wonders how they got this way. It must have been a gradual process – a software upgrade here, a neurological enhancement there, the transition from human to machine so slow that they barely even recognised it was happening to them. Whatever else the board are, Tanta realises, they're not hypocrites. The programmed obedience they've inflicted on InTech's residents cannot be any worse than the torturous technological immortality they've accepted for themselves.

'I suppose this makes our job easier,' Fliss says. 'I mean, they're this close to snuffing it anyway.' She speaks as softly as if she's in the presence of the dead already, and her face is drawn.

'My job,' Tanta corrects her. 'I'll do it.' These deaths belong on her conscience, not Fliss's. It was *her* the board manipulated and used, and it's her city they've got in their stranglehold. Somehow, she thinks she'll bear the guilt just fine.

She's stepping towards the tangle of bodies and equipment to do what she came here for when a click behind her makes her spin around. There's a second door in the wall through which they entered – a small, plain one that looks like it leads to a storage room of some sort. As the crew turn, this door opens, and a white woman in her mid-sixties steps out and walks towards them. She comes to a dead stop in the centre of the room, as inert as the machines around her. Fliss tenses, readying herself for a fight, but Tanta holds up a hand. The woman is unarmed, and though Tanta has never seen her before, the grey router on her head is instantly familiar.

'Representative,' she greets her.

'Tanta. Leave our presence at once. This is a restricted area. We are extremely disappointed in you.' The new conduit's voice is higher than the old one's, but it has the same flat, expressionless quality.

'Those command phrases no longer work on me, Representative,' Tanta replies. And then, 'I suppose you know why I'm here.'

She shouldn't be engaging with the conduit like this – it only gives the board more time to work out some way of protecting themselves – but the woman is the board's eyes and ears, and a part of Tanta is relieved to be able to confront them with what she's doing. It would feel underhanded, somehow, to simply kill them where they lie, without allowing them to speak so much as a word in their own defence.

The conduit pauses before she speaks again, processing a stream of information from the motionless bodies beside her. 'Leave without harming us,' she says, 'and your treachery will be forgiven. You may resume your position within the ICRD. Your agent privileges and accommodation in the city will be restored to you. All will be as it was.'

The board are not very good liars, despite the conduit's perfect poker face. Tanta knows herself well enough to admit that the offer would have tempted her, once, but the price has never been one she was willing to pay. Returning to InTech means returning to the Harlow Programme; the board would never let her rejoin the corporation as a free woman. 'I'm afraid I can't do that,' she says.

'Then you and your co-conspirators will die,' the conduit responds, her voice devoid of emotion. 'Several units of guardians are already en route to this location. They will have the building surrounded within the next ten minutes. If you harm us, they will terminate you before you are able to exit the Needle.'

Tanta can see the truth of this threat for herself. Much of InTech's side of the city is still suffering blackouts from the morning's EMP attacks, making the few lights that are visible stand out in sharp relief against the darkness. There's an armada

365

of emergency vehicles speeding through the streets towards the Needle. From this distance, they're no more than moving pinpricks of flashing red light, but they're already close enough that Tanta doesn't think she and the crew will be able to evade them all. The board may be unable to prevent her from killing them, but they'll make sure she doesn't live to celebrate it. A part of her feels sad at the realisation, but it's more for her friends than for herself. She wouldn't have come here if she hadn't accepted death as a potential outcome. 'I know,' she says. 'It doesn't change anything.'

The conduit's head twitches, her eyes flicking rapidly to and fro. 'If you consider your own termination an acceptable loss, then what is it you hope to achieve?' she asks.

Tanta figures the board deserve an answer, at least. She considers how to phrase it in terms they'll understand, then realises she doesn't know how to. The board were human once, but not anymore. For all the sense they and Tanta can make of each other's motivations and drives, they might as well belong to different species. 'You need to be stopped,' is what she settles on, in the end. 'Your actions aren't in the best interests of InTech's residents. All you do is dream up ways to get more power and control, but you're not using it for anything.'

After that, the conduit is silent for so long that Tanta decides that's the end of the conversation. She's rolling up her sleeves and steeling herself for the unpleasant task ahead when the woman says, 'Wait.'

Tanta pauses.

'If you destroy us, chaos will fill our place. That is no more in the interests of InTech's residents than the status quo. But there may be … another way.'

'Explain. You have sixty seconds.'

In response, the woman walks stiffly over to the nearest board member and takes the router from his head. It comes free with

366

a gentle sucking sound, leaving a puckered crater behind. She holds it out to Tanta. Her speech is even more staccato and disjointed than usual as she continues, as though the board are working out this desperate play as they go. 'You could... join us. Take your place within our conclave... You would be in a position, then, to enact the changes in InTech's governance that you wish to see. An... orderly transition. Without violence.'

Tanta didn't think there was anything the conduit could say that would alter her course, but this offer strikes her with more force than she was expecting. She can't deny that a power vacuum at the top of InTech will be a dangerous thing. Thoughtfront – and other corporations, too – will seek to capitalise on it, and if their attempts to seize control of territory and resources result in another war, it will be InTech's residents who get caught in the crossfire. More bloodshed is not unlikely, and any that does result will be on her hands. Tanta had accepted this risk as both necessary and inevitable, but what the conduit is proposing would circumvent it entirely.

When her own silence has stretched on just a little too long, Cole boggles at her. 'You can't seriously be considering this,' he says.

'Cole...'

'You *are* considering it?! Tanta, you can't!' He gestures at the line of gaunt bodies. 'Look at how you'd have to live!'

But that argument carries no weight with Tanta at all. She came here prepared to die.

'Our current condition is due more to our age than to other factors,' the conduit points out impassively. For a moment, her eyes lose focus, staring into the middle distance. 'There was a time when greater freedom was possible for us.'

'For this proposal of yours to work,' Tanta says, 'my vote in the conclave would have to count for more than the rest of yours combined. Otherwise, you'd just overrule me.'

The conduit hesitates, unwilling to make this last concession. It's not until Tanta moves threateningly towards the board's life support machines that she relents. 'The algorithm that governs our interactions may be edited,' she says in a rush. 'Your colleague has . . . the necessary skills to arrange it.'

'I won't do it.' Cole's lips are set in a stubborn line.

Tanta takes his hand. 'Cole, this might be our best way forward. We could achieve everything we came here for, without putting anyone at risk.'

'You'd be putting *yourself* at risk!' he snaps.

'Better me than the rest of the city. They didn't ask to be put in danger. This could protect them.' Tanta passes a hand over her forehead. Time is short, and there's a lot riding on her decision. 'I – I need a minute to think about this.'

She can't give herself much longer than that: the lights of the guardians' cars are already too close for comfort. She turns away from Cole and Fliss and walks to the far side of the room.

In the end, she takes two minutes, timing them down to the second on her Array – one for the pros, and one for the cons. She stands by the window while she thinks, gazing at the fitful lights of the patrol cars and weighing her future in her hands.

She has to admit that the board's offer holds a certain attraction for her. It would allow her to come home to the corporation that has raised her since birth, and to change it for the better. Before she became an agent, she used to dream of being one of InTech's defenders, its champions. She couldn't serve that role from within the ICRD; perhaps as part of the board, it would finally be possible.

Tanta keeps the board's representative in sight while she's considering their offer, in case they use her to try anything. As she watches her, she catches herself wondering how much of her life the woman has spent in the little closet at the top of the Needle, serving as the hands and the voice of the eight dead things in this room. She wonders when she last saw a sunset with her own eyes, and what pittance of credits the board give her as recompense for the sale of her consciousness.

A sick shiver runs through her at the thought. The board may represent order, but that order comes at the expense of InTech's people far more often than it does on their behalf. And Tanta might be able to fight against the alien logic of their hive mind for a time, but eventually, she would be consumed by it. She only needs to look at the board themselves to see that. They were human, once, but time and unbridled power have eroded that humanity. The system they represent has rotted from the inside out – Tanta becoming part of it would be a temporary fix at best.

At this point, Tanta's mind is made up, but then a final thought occurs to her – one that makes all her other considerations fade into the background. Joining the board's conclave wouldn't just avert violence in the city – it would also allow her to save Cole and Fliss. If Tanta were in control of the conduit, she could order the units of guardians on their way to apprehend them to stand down. They'd be able to walk out of the Needle free and clear, even if she could not.

There's a chime from her Array; her time is up. She hears footsteps, and looks around to see that her friends have come to stand beside her.

'I – I think I have to do it,' she tells them. 'It wouldn't be forever. Once I'm part of the board, I can take you both off the ICRD's wanted list. Yas, too. I can force them to work with you, to share power, and then we could phase them out, and I could—'

'Tanta.' Cole puts a hand on her arm. 'There's no way to know in advance what joining *that* would do to you. You're making promises you may not be able to keep.'

Fliss nods. 'It's also not what we came here for. I never signed up for putting you in charge of a city.'

They're both right, of course. InTech's residents are not children, to be coddled and controlled. The crew came here to set them free, not subject them to a more benign form of tyranny. Tanta knows this, and yet the thought of being able to keep Cole and Fliss safe is not one she can easily set aside.

'It's the only way out of this that you both survive,' she says, her voice small.

At that, Cole gives her a sad smile. 'If that's your reasoning, then shouldn't we get a say?'

Tanta looks from one to the other, reading her own resolve in their faces. They came here knowing the likely outcome, just as she did – this decision is as much theirs as it is hers. And abandoning their mission now, at the last hurdle, would be a poor way to honour their selflessness.

Slowly, the three of them walk back to stand before the conduit. Tanta looks the woman in the eye. 'No deal,' she says. 'Cole, whenever you're ready.'

Cole reaches into his pocket, producing the one weapon the crew were able to smuggle through the Needle's scanners: the rest of the EMP chips. He scatters them on the floor, a line of gunpowder. And Fliss stamps on them.

The invisible shockwave is more powerful this time. It tears through the machines in the room, obliterating Inscapes and air pumps alike. The swishing sound drops out of the air, and the conduit staggers, hit by the return of her own personality like a physical blow. Tanta knows it's only a matter of seconds until the Needle's backup systems pick up the slack. She grabs a sheaf of tubes, pipes and wires and wrenches them from their moorings, like she's ripping up a snarl of brambles. Beside her, Cole and Fliss do the same.

When they're finished, there's nothing left in the room but

themselves, the woman who was the conduit, and the wreckage of the machines that once powered the entire corporation. For a time, silence, whole and absolute, reigns over everything.

That is, until the door slams open.


Reet was halfway to the Needle when she received the conduit's distress call. She's been sprinting since then, gripped by a fear too terrible to examine or acknowledge. When she bursts into the board's residence, she takes in the whole scene at a glance – Tanta and her co-conspirators, the strange tangle of tech in the centre of the room – but she only has eyes for one thing.

'Representative!' she gasps, ecstatic with relief. The conduit looks unharmed.

Then the woman raises a hand to the router on her head, and Reet realises that something is terribly wrong. Her movements are too fluid, her face too expressive. She opens her mouth, and the voice that comes out of it is not flat and affectless, but trembling with fear.

'Wh – where am I?' the woman says. 'Can any of you tell me what's going on? The guardians had me, and then...'

Reet's heart drops. This woman is no longer the board's conduit. She's awake. A moment after that, she notices the bodies among the equipment in the middle of the room – and their terrible stillness.

'What have you done?' she asks. 'Tanta, WHAT HAVE YOU DONE?'

'I've killed the board,' Tanta replies. She sounds as if she hardly believes herself. She's holding a bundle of cables and tubes in both hands, but she lets it fall as she speaks, and her arms drop to her sides. 'It's over.'

'No,' Reet says. The word seems to leak out of her of its own accord. 'No no no nonono you didn't.' She rakes her gaze across the scene – the bodies, the wires – trying to make some kind of sense of it. She can see that the board are in trouble: their skin is sallow, and they're lying too still (*too still!*), but she doesn't know how to help them. Tanta has unplugged them from the machines that were keeping them alive – that much is clear. Maybe she can plug them back in again? She dives forward, dropping to her knees amid the uprooted equipment, but the wires are an incoherent tangle. She pulls at them uselessly, help-lessly. She has no idea what goes where.

'You didn't,' she whispers. 'Tee, you *didn't.*'

But she did. Reet knows it, just as she knows that she has arrived too late to do anything for the eight stiff figures lying before her.

She gets back to her feet. She turns to face Tanta. Her ex is just... standing there, staring at her. She looks totally calm. Reet's vision blurs, and Tanta doubles in front of her. She's her Tee, her love. She's also the traitor who has just destroyed the corporation. All of Reet's anger and hurt rises up in her throat, threatening to choke her.

Tanta takes a step towards her, reaching for her. 'I had to do it, Reet. It was—'

Reet's backhand catches her off-guard, snapping her head to the side with an audible crack. Tanta staggers, blinking away tears. Her expression of pain makes Reet simultaneously want to comfort her, and to hit her again. The woman who was the board's conduit flashes them both a look of alarm and backs out of the room. Tanta's two accomplices dart forward, looking as though they're going to intervene, but Tanta shakes her head at them, waving them away.

'Don't,' she tells them. She turns back to Reet. 'I don't want to fight you.' There's a little blood dribbling from the corner of her mouth where Reet's knuckles split her lip.

'Yeah? Well, that's too bad, *Tee.*'

Reet swings at her again, but Tanta is ready for her this time.

She sidesteps the blow, though she doesn't retaliate with one of her own. Reet growls low in her throat and spins to face her once more. A raft of memories flash through her mind as she does so: the two of them sparring in the Ward House basement, Tee helping her to train for the ICRD. She brushes them aside. A lot has changed since those days. Tanta used to be able to spot her moves coming a mile away, but Reet's harder to read now, her old tells smoothed away through months of intensive practice. Tanta dodges and weaves and backs, but she can't avoid Reet forever, and when Reet feints left, she falls for it: Reet's right hook catches her square on the jaw, and for a moment, her eyes lose focus.

Reet uses the opportunity to close with her, trying to grapple her to the ground. Tanta twists away, but she's moving more slowly than she was before. Her cheek where Reet struck her is starting to redden, and her lip is swelling up. Still, she doesn't try to resist, merely dancing back on the balls of her feet. Somehow, this only makes Reet angrier.

'Attack me,' she growls.

'No,' Tanta replies, the word slurring from her swollen lips.

Reet aims a kick at her mid-section – one Tanta is too sluggish to avoid. It winds her, and Reet rushes in again, getting one arm around her neck and raining blows on her face and the sides of her head. Tanta struggles out of her hold, but she's dazed, and there's blood sheeting down one side of her face. For all her agility, Reet is wearing her down, besting her. Even through her rage, the realisation brings a thrill of excitement. She's never beaten Tanta before, not in all their training sessions.

They're not training now, though. This time, when Tanta finally falls under her onslaught, Reet doesn't help her back to her feet. And when she pins Tanta to the floor, one arm against her throat, there's no tapping out.

At first, Tanta struggles and kicks, fighting for air. Reet hears running footsteps behind her, so she's ready for Tanta's co-conspirators when they try to come to her rescue. She knocks the bandit away with her free hand as she comes up on the left, delivering a stinging blow to her face that sends her reeling. Cole attempts to pull her off Tanta, but he can't get a good hold, and Reet's stronger than he is. She simply grounds herself and ignores him.

She will make Tanta pay with her life for the murders she's committed. Tears spill down Reet's face as she increases the pressure on Tanta's windpipe, but she doesn't have any other option. It's what the board would have wanted.

Tanta's eyes have rolled back into her head and her hands, which were scrabbling at Reet's arm, have fallen still, when Reet begins to feel dizzy. It overtakes her all at once, a wave of vertigo and nausea that almost washes her off her feet. She pauses in her work, her hold on Tanta relaxing – and then Cole and the bandit are upon her again, one on the left and one on the right. They grab her arms, and this time Reet finds, to her alarm, that she is unable to hold them off. Her muscles have gone slack as cut strings. They drag her backwards and throw her to the floor, where she lies like a rag doll, utterly unable to defend herself.

'Don't hurt her!' Tanta rasps. 'I think it's starting to kick in.'

A moment later, her broken, bloodied face appears in Reet's line of sight, inspecting her. *What's starting to kick in?*

'What the fuck did you do to me?' Reet mutters. The dizzy spell is passing as quickly as it came, the strength returning to her limbs. She tries to struggle to her feet, but Cole and the bandit tighten their hold on her arms.

'I removed your Harlow Programming,' Tanta replies. 'It started uninstalling itself more than two hours ago, when you interrogated me beneath the Needle, but the programme InTech gave us and the other CorpWards is more complicated than

Harlow 2.0, so it took a while. It will have been quicker for everyone else.'

Horror wraps its hand around Reet's heart, and squeezes. She thinks back to Tanta's arrest: she'd thought at the time that her ex was waiting for her, and then dismissed her own instincts. She'd been right. But worse – far worse – than the trap she has walked into is the terrible suggestion that she's not the only one to have fallen prey to it.

'Everyone else?' she asks, her voice a whisper.

'The rest of the city,' Tanta clarifies. 'In a few hours, there won't be a Harlow Programme anymore.'

Half a mile away and more than ten hours ago, striding back and forth beneath the cracked dome of The Rotunda, Cole explained it like this:

'You're the key, Tanta – because you're within the Harlow Programme's closed system, but outside of it at the same time.'

'How d'you figure?' Fliss asked.

'Thanks to the dummy system I set up in Tanta's Inscape last summer, InTech's servers think she already has a version of the Harlow Programme installed,' Cole replied. 'That's why she's immune to Harlow 2.0. The thing is, she *doesn't* have any Harlow Programming installed – and that's my way in. Tanta's 'scape doesn't have any of the new security measures that InTech's programmed residents are subject to. I can add a version of the handshake protocol directly into her dummy system, and it'll provide me with a backdoor into the whole Harlow network. You'll spread the uninstallation patch to everyone you come into contact with,' he summarised, turning to Tanta. '*You'll* be our patient zero.'

Tanta grinned. 'Then I'd better come into contact with as many people as possible.'

★

Back in the here and now, Reet wrenches her arm free of Fliss's grasp and jabs her finger to her temple. 'All units,' she gasps, 'Do not approach the Needle. I repeat, do *not* approach the Needle. Th – there's a virus. You need to quarantine immediately!'

Tanta doesn't try to stop her. 'It's too late,' she says, gently. 'By the time you and Firent caught up with me, I'd been walking around the city centre for hours. I must have passed thousands of people – clean-up crews, medics, engineers. And then you brought most of the guardians on this side of the riverbed to apprehend me, and I made sure I came into contact with all of them, too.

'They'll all have lost their programming several hours ago, but not before passing the uninstallation patch on to everyone they know, who will have passed it on to everyone *they* know. Most of the city will be back to normal by morning. It'll take a bit longer for the after-effects to wear off for you and the other CorpWards – but it won't hurt, and you won't be in any danger.'

There's no triumph in this speech. Tanta is satisfied, as any professional would be, by a job well done, but she can't glory in her victory when it has brought Reet this much pain.

At that, Reet stops struggling against Cole and Fliss and begins to sob. 'You're a monster,' she says. 'A murderer. I'll never forgive you!'

A part of Tanta thinks she will never get over the hatred and fury she sees in her ex-lover's eyes. For an instant, she almost regrets not taking the board up on their offer: it would be better to be merged in an inhuman hive mind right now, or even dead on the floor of the Needle, than trapped within the swamp of her own hurt feelings. She's completed her mission, at long last, but the price she paid was high. How can she be glad at having freed the city when it has cost her her soulmate?

She knows how, of course – though the knowledge doesn't bring her much comfort. She loves Reet, and part of loving someone is respecting them enough to let them make their own decisions. That's something Reet has never been able to do before: her path in life was mapped out for her by the Harlow Programme before she was even born. Having the ability to step off that path is a gift, of sorts – one that Cole gave to Tanta, and one that she has now passed on. It may well be the last gift she ever gives Reet, but that doesn't matter. Reet might never forgive Tanta. She might never see or speak to her again. At least now, she has the freedom to choose.

# Chapter 31

Cole is not prepared for success – mostly because he didn't expect he'd live to see it. Since embarking on this desperate scheme, he's been shot at, strangled, held hostage, shot at some more, and almost crushed against the roof of a lift shaft. Anyone could see that the odds weren't in his favour.

Surviving was never part of his plan, and as nice as it is to have managed it, he can see immediately that it's going to be hugely inconvenient. Winning the day and living to tell the tale means you also have to stick around for whatever comes next – and just thinking about what comes next makes Cole bone-tired. Toppling a power system is easy compared to figuring out what to replace it with. Cole's mind throngs with questions: how will the city be governed? What will happen to the Directors? Who's going to deal with the other corporations when the inevitable attempts to muscle in on InTech's resources begin?

He doesn't have answers to any of them, but he's going to have to come up with some. That's the downside to surviving – the future becomes your responsibility. It's a daunting prospect; Cole briefly considers throwing himself off the roof of the Needle, but decides against it. It's not just that he promised Tanta he wouldn't. InTech has fallen by his hand: he feels an obligation to help build *something* to stand in its place. And besides that... Cole searches his feelings, and realises that he has a certain sense of personal investment in the effort. That's new; he can barely remember the last time there was any cause on his horizon that he cared about beyond ending the Harlow Programme. Whatever else it might be, the future is going to be interesting – that alone makes it worth showing up for. And it's not as though he's going to have to face it by himself.

For the first hour after the liberation of the city, nothing much happens. Cole and Fliss cautiously release their hold on Reet, once they're sure she's not going to attack Tanta again. The Director of the ICRD curls up into a ball, her back to the crew. Tanta moves to the other end of the room, putting as much distance between the two of them as possible, while Fliss hunts up a first aid kit to clean and dress the cuts on her face. After a few minutes, Cole joins them.

'You won,' he says to Tanta.

'*We* won,' she amends, with a tired smile.

She doesn't look too happy about it. Cole doesn't know the ins and outs of her relationship with Reet, but he remembers her from the night of the Ward House fire – the way she and Tanta clung to each other – and can take enough of a guess that he doesn't pry. After Fliss has treated her wounds, he sits down beside Tanta and puts his arm around her, and she leans her head on his shoulder and cries a little. He stays with her, the same way she stayed with him when he was reeling from Jeanie's betrayal. It doesn't feel like enough, but Cole has had enough experience of loss to know that it's the only thing he can do.

Gradually, as the sun rises and the city below them becomes visible again, the people start to arrive. Cole watches them through the glass of the Needle's south wall, making their way through the streets in a steady stream. Sleepers, wagers, CorpWards. It wouldn't be accurate to call them a march – not exactly. They're all moving with the slow, halting steps of the confused and adrift, but they're all moving in the same direction: towards the Needle.

The winding column of people swells, splits, and joins again, the streams running together to become a sea. Beside Cole, Tanta gets to her feet.

'Reet,' she calls softly. 'Would you come and look at this?'

'Fuck off,' Reet snarls. She's still sitting hunched on the other side of the room, her shoulders slumped and her eyes on the ground.

Tanta doesn't say anything else, but little by little, Reet raises her head. She glances out of the window, then stares. She gets up. Finally, she comes to stand by Tanta's side.

'I destroyed the board, but I didn't destroy InTech,' Tanta says to her. 'In fact, I came here to help it.' She gestures to the growing crowd. 'InTech is down there. It needs answers, and leaders. I'm not asking you to forgive me, but will you work with me?'

The look Reet flicks Tanta's way is still full of revulsion, but there's something else in there, too – something Cole finds harder to read. She doesn't say anything for a long, long time. But she doesn't say no.

After that, the talking starts. It doesn't stop for hours and hours. At first, it's just Reet and Tanta. Then Reet makes some calls on MindChat, and Firent and Arden turn up, along with a dozen other Corporate Wards. The initial disorientation that would have accompanied the loss of their Harlow Programming has mostly passed, but they're still confused. Then, when they see the board, and learn what has happened to them, they are horrified. There is shouting – a *lot* of shouting. That doesn't stop until Reet stamps her foot and shouts louder than everyone else put together:

'InTech needs us! And if we don't pull together *right now*,

Thoughtfront will rally and take us over. Do any of you want that?'

Nobody wants that. The shouting subsides into muttering – and then, at last, it becomes talking.

At a certain point, everyone moves down to the Executive Conference Suite a few floors below, and takes seats around the round, olive-wood table.

Some time later, a bewildered guardian turns up to tell the impromptu forum that Arthur Friend and Douglas Kenway are outside the Needle and demanding entrance. Neither Tanta nor Reet are at all inclined to grant it to them, and whenever Tanta and Reet are in agreement on something, everyone else seems to be, too. The two ex-Directors are escorted unceremoniously away shortly thereafter.

Cole finds himself falling into the role of unofficial chair of the evolving discussion. It's an easy job. Once their initial shock and panic have passed, the CorpWards are the most well-behaved of debaters. No one interrupts or talks over one another. Each speaker is given a fair hearing and allowed to finish their point before the next begins.

Runners are dispatched, and communiqués sent out to re-assure the crowd below. The conversation turns from dealing with the threat Thoughtfront still poses, to figuring out what comes after: uniting the city, demilitarising the riverbed, repairing the damage each corporation has inflicted upon the other. Ideas and offers of assistance pop up from all quarters. No one says, 'That'll never work!' or 'What's in this for *me*?'

When the forum ends at last, it's dark outside, and Cole is feeling more hopeful than he has in years. As he steps out of the Needle, his shoes crunching on the newly-fallen snow, he is thinking about his past – and the ways that it might shape the future. The Harlow Programme was an evil thing, but if it had one shred of good in it, it was in the dedication and cooperation that it encouraged in the wards themselves. It's the only good to have come out of Cole's work – the one glimmer of hope at the bottom of a dark history of mental manipulation.

Cole has known this for a long time, of course, because he knows Tanta. It's strange: in creating the Harlow Programme, he helped to make her the person she is now, but she's been no less formative in shaping him. They've each been the author of aspects of the other's personality, though he's inclined to give Tanta more of the credit. Cole lost so much of himself in the MindWipe – and so much of it was bad. He has spent a lot of time wondering why the man he was before shocks and appals him now. What changed? It was a lot of things, he supposes, but the most important one was meeting her. Tanta gave him a human connection to the CorpWards he was so willing to use for his political agenda before. And she forgave him when he couldn't forgive himself, helping him to come to terms with the mistakes of his past without reverting to the person he was when he made them. She's a great leader, an even better friend. And Cole saw her compassion and drive in all the faces around the conference table.

He hears a light footstep, and Tanta appears beside him. She leans against his shoulder and he puts his arm around her, each glad of the other's company, neither of them speaking. The free Corporate Wards are ingenuous and inventive, selfless and civic-minded. Now that the shackles holding their minds in thrall to InTech have been broken, what can't they accomplish? Cole smiles as he and Tanta look out over the dark city, tilting his head up to catch the night breeze. He can't think of a better group of people to inherit the earth.

Sometime in the middle of the big debate, Fliss slips out into the hallway. She doesn't want to rain on anyone's parade, but she's bored stiff. She takes a little sightseeing tour of the Needle

– mostly in an effort to find the exit, and then steps outside into an overcast winter afternoon.

At first, she isn't heading anywhere in particular. She wanders the streets she's trodden so many times before on supply runs for the crew, gazing around at the familiar landmarks of the city made strange by the aftershocks of war. The roads are full of residents, all wearing the muzzy, confused expressions of people who have just woken up from an unscheduled nap. Their programming has unravelled overnight, loosening its grip on all their minds at once. Fliss is pleased to see recognition again in the eyes that meet hers – she was getting sick of being invisible.

Inevitably, she finds her feet turning towards the safehouse where Sonia has been living since she joined the Brokerage. Cole and Tanta may have been doing all this to save the city, but there's only one person living within these walls who Fliss really cares about. She finds her old friend seriously frightened, but alive and unharmed.

'Told you I knew what I was doing,' she says, as she ducks through the door.

'Fliss!' Sonia wraps her in a hug.

They spend the next few hours catching up and reminiscing about old times – far more interesting topics of conversation than whatever is being discussed in the Needle, Fliss would guess. When the streets darken again, she stretches and gets to her feet.

'I'd better get back,' she says. Tanta's wounds will need re-dressing, and someone needs to nag Cole to do his physio.

'What're you gonna do now?' Sonia asks her.

'I think I'll head to Gatwick for a bit – spend some time with Mum. After that...' Fliss takes a white plastic pendant on a length of string from her jacket pocket, twirling it thoughtfully between thumb and forefinger. 'Oh, I have a couple of ideas.'

★

Yas knows the fighting's over when the sounds of bombs and gunfire drifting into Gatwick on the northerly wind slacken and cease, but she doesn't find out who's won for almost a week. Then, a visitor from the city turns up at the North Gate, asking to speak to the Assembly.

The arrival throws the settlement into a brief panic. If Paige Scarrow were still speaker for security, Yas is sure she'd be all for 'repelling the corporate spy with the full might of the security force', or something similarly unhelpful. But Paige has been stewing in her own holding cell since her ill-advised attempt to go behind the Assembly's back, and in her absence, Yas has been helping Gatwick with security matters in an advisory capacity. Her report on Thoughtfront and her efforts to strengthen the settlement's defences have gained her the Assembly's respect, if not their full trust, and she counsels a more reasonable course of action. She heads out to talk to the new arrival herself. And she brings Neal with her, because, well, she has a feeling.

When Neal comes in sight of the young man at the gate, the reaction is instantaneous.

'Colleague!' he cries, running forward. 'Do you require assistance?'

'Um, no, that's OK,' the gangly blond man says, awkwardly.

'Arden,' Yas greets him. 'I'd say it's good to see you again, but we both know that would be a lie.'

Arden has recovered well from the multiple beatings he suffered the last time Yas saw him, though his nose is still squashed out of shape. He holds his hands up. 'I'm not here to fight. I, um, actually came to try and establish diplomatic relations.'

'On whose behalf?'

He puffs himself up. 'The Free City of London.'

It's only then that Yas knows who won for sure, though she'd had her suspicions as soon as Arden turned up. 'Nice name,' she says. 'I'm sure the Assembly will be interested in hearing what you have to say. Why don't you come in?'

Over the hours following Arden's arrival, Neal changes. It's slow at first. He walks back into the settlement with a more faraway expression on his face than usual, lifting his index finger to summon his Array at intervals, as if to check it's still there. By the time Arden has been reintroduced to the Assembly and shown to his temporary quarters, Neal has gone silent and still, staring at something Yas can't see. She takes him to her own digs and stays with him – it seems the responsible thing to do, and Cole would give her hell if she let anything happen to him.

After two hours of near-catatonia, the invisible fever breaks. Neal blinks once, then again, and Yas is relieved to see that the lights are back on behind his eyes.

'Where ... am I?' he asks, and it's the first time his voice has sounded normal and human in all the time Yas has known him.

'You're in the unaffiliated settlement at Gatwick,' she tells him. 'Welcome back, Neal.'

A spasm of alarm crosses Neal's face. 'Harlow 2.0 – the roll-out! I have to warn—'

'All happened already, all turned out fine. You've been out for some time, my friend.' Yas pats the chair beside her. 'Sit down. I'll fill you in. And after that, there's a neuroengineer back in the "Free City of London" who's going to be very keen to see you.'

After Neal leaves for the city, Yas wanders around Gatwick for another hour or two, at a loose end. She could have left with him, gone back to what was formerly InTech territory – and arrived to a hero's welcome, no doubt – but she doesn't really feel like doing that. She's sure that whatever's going on in the Free City is a very worthy endeavour, and that it could probably

385

use someone with her skillset to help it get off the ground, but her heart wouldn't be in it.

Yas enjoyed the work she did when she was with the ICRD, but she doesn't want to return to it. After everything that happened with Jeanie, and Jennifer Ash before her, she's a little tired of serving other peoples' agendas — even if those agendas are entirely above board. She's had her fill of being somebody else's agent. She's ready to build something of her own. And something tells her that if she bides her time a little longer, she might end up with some company.

When the communicator in her pocket starts to beep, Yas is expecting it. She pulls it out, pressing the button in the centre.

'Yasmin?' a crackly voice says.

'This is she.'

'What have I missed?' Fliss asks.

Yas fills her in, starting with her promised visit to Constance Loh and lingering with particular enjoyment on the details of Paige Scarrow's arrest. Once she's finished, Fliss returns the favour. A companionable silence falls between them when they've both traded stories, but Yas has a feeling that the conversation isn't over.

'Guess where I am,' Fliss says, at length.

'Where?'

'The Brokerage.'

Yas grins. 'Oh, really? How does it look?'

'Terrible,' Fliss replies, with relish. 'Roof caved in, half flooded, dead leaves everywhere.'

Yas thinks of the architects she's met in Gatwick, and the things they can do with wooden frames and rammed earth. 'I know a few people who could fix that.'

'So do I. I reckon we can get the generator working again, too. And after that...'

'Well, after that, there's nothing to stop us moving back in,' Yas says.

'My thoughts exactly. The New Brokerage,' Fliss says, with satisfaction. 'Trading secrets and cracking skulls.'

Yas laughs. 'If you like. It's as good a motto as any to put on the sign.'

## END OF BOOK III

# Acknowledgements

Another plague year, another novel. Writing the conclusion to the Inscape trilogy through national lockdowns and travel restrictions was not easy, but thanks to the support of my family and friends, it was at least possible.

My deep thanks and gratitude are due, as always, to all of the usual suspects: Meg Davis, my incredible agent; Brendan Durkin and Áine Feeney, my talented and supportive editors; Abigail Nathan, my brilliant copyeditor; and the whole Gollancz team.

I'd also like to thank Laura Taylor and Dave Brignull of the Hertfordshire Wellbeing Service, who helped me through a period of low mood and anxiety while I was writing this novel, in 2021. There were days when I thought I might not finish it, but I did, and that was in no small part thanks to you both. Thank you for helping me find healthier ways to work, and to exist.

Finally, I want to thank my family. My Discord writing sessions with David Carey continued to motivate me through hard times, as did the chats I had with Ben Carey, Camden Ford, and my father, Mike. This book is dedicated to my mum, Linda Carey. Her insights at the planning stage helped shape the novel into what it eventually became, and I am hugely grateful for her love, her support, and her generosity. Thank you for believing in me, Mum.

# Credits

Louise Carey and Gollancz would like to thank everyone at Orion who worked on the publication of *Downfall*.

**Editor**
Brendan Durkin
Áine Feeney

**Copy-editor**
Abigail Nathan

**Proofreader**
Bruno Vincent

**Editorial Management**
Jane Hughes
Charlie Panayiotou
Tamara Morriss

**Audio**
Paul Stark
Jake Alderson
Georgina Cutler

**Contracts**
Anne Goddard
Ellie Bowker
Humayra Ahmed

**Design**
Nick Shah
Tómas Almeida
Joanna Ridley
Helen Ewing
Rachael Lancaster

**Finance**
Nick Gibson
Jasdip Nandra
Elizabeth Beaumont
Sue Baker
Tom Costello

**Inventory**
Jo Jacobs
Dan Stevens

**Production**
Paul Hussey

**Rights**
Susan Howe
Krystyna Kujawinska
Jessica Purdue
Ayesha Kinley
Louise Henderson

**Operations**
Sharon Willis
Jo Jacobs

**Sales**
Jen Wilson
Victoria Laws
Esther Waters
Frances Doyle
Ben Goddard
Jack Hallam
Anna Egelstaff